12-01

D0463594

F
G.

12-01

Gray, Shelley
A Texan's Promise

A Texan's Promise

Other books by Shelley Gray

Hidden
Wanted
Forgiven
Grace
Winter's Awakening
Spring's Renewal
Autumn's Promise
The Caretaker
The Protector
The Survivor

A Texan's

Promise

Book 1 of the Heart of a Hero series

Shelley Gray

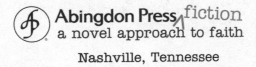

Abingdon Press fiction
a novel approach to faith

Nashville, Tennessee

A Texan's Promise

Copyright © 2011 by Shelley Sabga

ISBN-13: 978-1-61793-524-4

Published by Abingdon Press, P.O. Box 801, Nashville, TN 37202

All rights reserved.

The persons and events portrayed in this work of fiction
are the creations of the author, and any resemblance
to persons living or dead is purely coincidental.

Published in association with The Seymour Literary Agency

Cover design by Anderson Design Group, Nashville, TN

Scripture quotations appear from the King James or Authorized
Version of the Bible.

Printed in the United States of America

In loving memory of my father

Acknowledgments

I owe so much to my agent, Mary Sue Seymour, for the publication of this book.

Thank you, Mary Sue, for never giving up on me or my books. You really do make me believe in miracles!

Hear my cry, God;
Listen to my prayer.
From the end of the earth I call to you,
When my heart is faint.
Psalm 61:1-2

1
West Texas

September 1873

"*V*anessa, honey, why you crying?"

Clayton! He stood in the doorway to the stables, his presence both a soothing balm and a source of panic.

Vanessa gingerly leaned back against the wood behind her, willed herself to relax, but it was no good. It was going to be some time before she could calm down again. "I'm sorry I woke you."

"You didn't." His eyes narrowed as he stepped closer. "It's midnight. Isn't it awfully late for you to be out of bed?"

Yes. Yes, it was. It was too late for a lot of things now. Wiping her eyes with the side of her fist, she shook her head. "I'll go in soon."

Clayton crouched beside her, his knees brushing her skirts. A puff of dust flew up, mixing with his scent, all bay rum and horses. "Care to tell me what happened?"

She was thankful for the darkness. "No."

He rocked back on his heels. "It might make you feel better." Just his presence made her feel better, but that was how it always had been. Though only twenty-nine, Clayton Proffitt was the foreman of her family's ranch, had been soon after her pa had hired him six years ago. When Pa had died, Clayton kept the place going for her mother.

Now that Ma remarried, Clayton had proved to be the most upstanding man she'd ever met. The differences between him and her stepfather were like night and day.

He'd always been patient and kind to her. Had always had time for her when no one else had. Even more importantly, he knew the Bible well, and often referred to it whenever she sought his advice. Consequently, his opinion mattered more to her than anyone else's.

Which was exactly why she couldn't tell him what happened. Desperately, she breathed deep. Inhaled his scent, his goodness, before tucking her chin to her chest. "It's nothing. I'm . . . fine, Clay. I'll be out of your way in a minute. Sorry I disturbed you."

She moved to get up, but his hand stilled her. "I didn't say you disturbed me. I don't think you ever could." Peering closer, his expression softened as one calloused finger touched her cheek. "Now. There's got to be a reason you're out here crying after midnight. What happened?"

She wanted to tell him. But if she did, he'd just shoulder all her hurt and responsibility, making her wish that she was less of a burden.

She hated being nineteen and unmarried. Too old to ask for help; too innocent to be self-sufficient.

"Well, if you're not going to get up, I guess I'm just going to have to join you, hmm?" Clay sat beside her, stretched his legs out next to hers, making her feel petite and insignificant. With no small amount of humor in his eyes, he sighed dramatically. Just like he had when Delaney Brewster had teased her about having arms and legs like sticks. Back when she'd taken to praying every night for God to stop taking His time to make her a woman.

"Looks like you're going to make me guess," he teased. "Let's see . . . George Law forgot to call on you today."

Oh, Clay was so sweet to her. She hated to disappoint him. "It's not that."

"Ben Forte didn't say how pretty you looked in that periwinkle gown you like so much."

Periwinkle. Vanessa hiccupped. The only reason Clay knew such a word was that she'd corrected him when he said her purple dress was fetching. "I'm not crying about a boy."

"Well then?" He folded an arm around her shoulder and was about to squeeze her tight when she winced.

He turned, one knee facing her hip. "Vanessa?" he murmured. His voice turned concerned. There was no trace of humor lingering in his voice. "What happened?"

How could she tell him? "It's nothing." *It was everything.*

His eyes narrowed. "I don't think so." With one finger, he tilted her chin up, tilted her head so it moved into the lone ray of glimmering moonlight shimmering down from the loft's window.

She knew the moment he saw the bruise on her cheek. "I'll be fine."

Tender fingers, so gentle, brushed her hair back from her face. But his gaze had hardened. "You're bleeding."

"My cheek is, too?"

"Too?" Shifting again, he propped himself on one knee. Looking her over a little more closely. "Vanessa, what happened?"

"I . . . I didn't realize . . . " Shame—and the lethal glare in his eyes—cut off her words. What would she do if he thought she was unworthy? Ever since her pa had died, she'd felt alone except for Clay. If he turned away from her, she'd have no one left.

"Realize what?" His voice was hoarse. Urgent. Still he touched her, petting her hair, tracing the swelling on her cheek.

Against her will, the tears flowed again. Frustrated, she mopped them with her sleeve, then winced as the action brushed fabric across her back. "I . . . I can't do this, Clay. I can't say it."

Clayton changed to a near crouch. Gone were all the traces of brotherly affection. In its place was everything that had made him a brilliant soldier. Determination. Fortitude. Strength. "Let me see you. Let me see your back."

Clay's voice was firm. It was the voice he used when ordering cowhands around. The tone he used when Lovey, Vanessa's shepherd, forgot she was supposed to be working and there were still twenty head of cattle to bring in.

It was the tone Clay used with her brother Miles when Clay's patience was at its wit's end. He'd never spoken that way to her before. Ever.

"Now, Vanessa."

Obediently, she turned her shoulders, closing her eyes at his sharp intake of breath. As he very gently touched her torn gown, she stiffened, then exhaled in relief when his touch didn't hurt, it was so butterfly-quick.

"Who did this to you? Price? Was it Price?"

She turned back to face him, stunned to find him shaking. Stunned to see mist in his brown eyes. Almost roughly, he cradled her jaw with one of his hands. "Answer me, sweetheart."

Sweetheart. He'd done that for years. Called her a whole host of endearments whenever they were alone. She supposed it was because a couple of months after they'd buried her daddy, she'd confided to Clayton how she missed the words. Her pa had been openly affectionate, her mother far less so.

Clayton now called her "baby," "darlin'," "sweetheart," and "honey." Anything to make her smile. Anything to make her feel wanted.

Never had the words seemed anything but teasing.

Never had they sounded as heartfelt as they did this minute.

"Vanessa, did your stepfather do this?"

She couldn't lie. The truth hurt, almost as much as the belt had. Yet, lying to Clay would hurt worse. She nodded.

Clayton looked at her for a good long moment, then, as if he made a decision, he stood up and carefully helped her to her feet. "Come here, honey." Taking her hand, he led her to his room.

She'd seen it before. When Pa had gotten so sick, he'd asked Clay to build himself a nice suite of rooms in the back of the barn so their foreman could be within shouting distance of the house. Made up of two rooms, it had a bedroom and a small sitting area, complete with a stove. Her pa had insisted on that, since everyone knew Clayton Proffitt liked both his coffee and his privacy.

Her brother Miles said Clayton was uncannily self-sufficient. He often chose to eat by himself instead of eating with the ranch hands or joining the family in the dining room.

She'd knocked on his door a time or two. Or fifty. He'd always come out to help her with her horse or to listen when she had a problem. More than once he'd made her tea as he listened to her prattle on about anything and everything.

But now, as they entered his bedroom, Vanessa hardly had time to do more than inhale the scent of tobacco and mint before he motioned for her to sit. She perched atop his quilt, a crazy quilt she'd made for him four Christmases ago.

After checking to see that his curtains were drawn, Clay lit a kerosene lamp. Then he crouched in front of her again. When he spied her cheek in the better light a look of such concern crossed his face that Vanessa felt a fresh surge of tears struggle to come forth. She bit her lip and hoped for strength.

"Van, honey . . . what happened? You've got to tell me the truth. At the moment, I'm thinking the worst."

If she said the words out loud, it would mean it had really happened.

And that was too hard to come to grips with. "I . . . I can't."

"It would be best if you did."

Those eyes of his, so gentle and soft brown, ended her struggle. Tears fell again. "Please, Clay. Not yet." When she saw her hands were trembling, she pushed them under a fold in her skirt.

After a moment, he sat next to her, edging closer when he saw what she needed. "Come here, honey."

With a sigh, Vanessa rested her head on his shoulder. She closed her eyes and breathed deep, taking in his scent, his warmth. Finding comfort in his powerful strength. Maybe he wouldn't leave her when he found out the truth. Maybe, just maybe, everything was going to be okay.

Clay didn't know where to put his hands. Vanessa's back was marred by two thick bloody welts, each one a good six inches long. The tender skin was bruised and mottled. Fabric from her dress looked to be embedded in each one.

And that was what he could see.

He was afraid she had other injuries, areas that hadn't drawn blood, hurts he couldn't see. Finally settling on her upper arms, he gently rubbed her, said all those nonsense words his mama had said to him a hundred times, back when he was small.

Said those words Vanessa had always craved, loving words that showed she wasn't alone, that someone cared.

"Hush now, sweetheart. It'll be okay, Van."

Her crying continued, making his shoulder wet and his heart break. Figuring she needed to shed the tears and he needed time to control his anger, he held himself stiff and fought for patience.

After another few minutes, she pulled back. "Oh, my! Clayton, I'm so sorry—I've made a mess of you. I'll just go and—"

"You're not going anywhere." Tilting her chin up, he prayed she'd trust him. "Vanessa, please. Tell me. Now."

She seemed to weigh her choices, then just as quickly, gave them up. "Price . . . hit me."

Clayton swallowed hard.

Oh, Price had done more than that. In the dim light he saw the swelling under the bruise on her cheek, the cut on her lip, the awareness in her eyes that a man's strength could hurt her badly.

Clayton was also well aware of the damage a leather strap could do. "Why did he hit you?"

"Because he . . . because I wouldn't . . . " She halted, swallowed hard. Met his gaze, looked back down.

Oh, Lord, no. "Because you wouldn't . . . what?" Examining her closer, he spied a rip in her gingham near the collar. Caught sight of a fingertip bruise.

"Because I wouldn't . . . because he wanted . . . me. Me?" She looked at Clayton, wonder in her eyes. "He said horrible things. I couldn't. I couldn't, Clayton." Her eyes turned wild.

He sought to calm the memories. Rubbing her arms, still afraid to touch her anywhere else, he looked at her directly. "I know, honey."

"Price grabbed me. Grabbed the collar of my dress. I screamed."

"Then what happened?"

"He blocked the door, and I . . . I ran to the window."

She was shaking now, reliving the memory. Clayton linked his fingers through hers. When she gazed at their joined hands and drew a fortifying breath, he pushed her some more, just like he used to do with the young boys in his unit during the war. Sometimes, even the worst truths needed to be admitted. "And then?"

"He went mad. He hit me. I tried to hit him back. And then . . . then he pulled off his belt." She shuddered. "I was so afraid."

"I know." Clay had seen Price display acts of violence more and more throughout the past year.

Her pretty green eyes, so luminous and desperate, stared at him in wonder. "I . . . I didn't understand, Clay. Why? Why now?"

Because she was beautiful. Because she was untouched. "I don't know," he lied.

"He struck me. I screamed and cried and tried to get away— but there was nowhere to go."

"And then?"

She paused. "And then Momma rushed in and pulled him away." With a ragged breath, she looked down at his quilt. "Thank goodness she came."

She'd come far too late, by his estimate. Carefully, Clay turned to look at her back again. "He struck you more than once."

Back down went her chin. "I know."

"Did he . . . Vanessa, tell me the truth. Did he . . . do more than that?"

Alarmed, she shook her head.

He was frightening her. Praying to the Lord for the right words, Clayton carefully spoke again. "Honey, you can tell me. You can tell me anything, remember?" he coaxed. "Did he . . . undress?" He gazed at her legs, curled tightly underneath her. "Did he force you to—" He couldn't say it. "Tell me the truth, sweetheart. I won't think—"

She stopped him by putting two fingers across his lips. "When Momma came, he left. All Price did was hit me. I promise."

Clayton glanced at her back again. The blood was drying, right in sync with how the skin had swelled. Most likely, she'd have scars across her upper back for the rest of her life.

The thought of anyone hurting her so brought forth another wave of anger. "Where was your brother? Where was Miles?"

"I don't know. Maybe in the hall? After Momma and Price left, I locked my door and turned off my lantern. But I got so scared, Clay. The room smelled like him. When things were quiet, I came out here." She looked at him, begged him with her eyes to understand. "I couldn't stay in the house any longer."

"I understand."

Wearily, she brushed a lock of hair away from her forehead. "I . . . I don't know what I'm going to do in the morning."

He did. "I'm taking you away from here. You can't stay another night."

"But—"

"There's been rumors that Price has a disease," he said slowly, wondering how much to tell her about what the women in Camp Hope were saying about Price, "that it's affecting his mind. You're not safe." No way was he going to let Price get within ten feet of Vanessa again.

"I can't leave. Then I'll have no one."

"You'll have me." Once again, Clayton wished her family had done more than gone to church when time allowed it. Vanessa never seemed to realize that the Lord could be on her side—if she'd open her heart to Him.

"But—"

"If we don't leave, a locked door will never be enough to keep your stepfather away." He gripped her shoulders. "Do you understand, honey?"

"I do." She winced as she shifted.

Her pain brought him back to his responsibilities. He needed to take care of her. Taking care of her had always been his most important duty.

"But before we do anything, we're going to have to fix you up, sugar." Grateful for the small stove he'd insisted on having, he stirred up the dying fire then poured a small amount of water into the kettle he kept nearby. As it heated up, he poured more water in a basin, then sorted through his trunk and found his softest broadcloth. The fabric was old and worn, too soft to wear on the range—but perfect for Vanessa's tender skin.

Finally, he searched and found an old handkerchief, faded but clean. After pouring a liberal amount of hot water in the basin, he crouched in front of Vanessa again. Placing his hands on either side of her knees, he said, "We need to doctor your back. Will you trust me?"

After a long moment, she nodded.

Oh, he hated this! Swallowing hard, he said, "Your shirt— it needs to come off." Obediently, she fumbled with her top button. Clay watched her attempt loosen it but her hands shook so; tears of frustration pooled in her eyes again. "Let me," he whispered, moving her hands to one side.

Still kneeling in front of her, he unbuttoned the next two, taking care not to brush her skin with his fingers. Finally, the top of her blouse was open, a white camisole peeking out underneath. A pair of dark bruises mottled the fair skin near her collarbone.

He wanted to beat Price Venture.

After moving to sit by her side, Clayton gently guided her arms out of the sleeves, then did his best to lift the fabric from her back.

Vanessa winced as it stuck. "Oh, Clay."

"Lie . . . lie down on your stomach, sugar," he said, giving her his pillow to cradle. After smoothing her long brown hair to one side, he dipped his bandanna in the warm water. "I'm going to dampen the fabric, see if I can remove the cloth easier. I'll try not to hurt you."

"I'll be fine, Clay."

Gingerly, he dabbed the top cut, heard her sharp intake of breath, but continued when Vanessa said nothing.

After moistening it again, he loosened the fabric, gently pulled it away from her skin. Clay's hand shook as he made progress. Finally one welt was revealed, then a second. Under the second was evidence that Price had stuck her a third time, her skin was bruised and swollen.

How could this have happened? What's more, how had he allowed it? How had he not heard her cries?

"Clay? Are you done?"

Her damaged shirt was wadded in his hands. Before him lay Vanessa's back, covered by a plain white cotton camisole. Swallowing hard, he gently traced the line of the top cut. To his eye, it was obvious cotton fibers were still embedded. Though he hated the thought of hurting her further, he knew he had no choice. If he didn't clean it well, infection would set in. "I'm going to have to wash out these cuts."

"I . . . all right."

She squeezed her eyes shut. He didn't blame her. During the war, men had whimpered over less. Gently squeezing the curve of her shoulder, he murmured, "It's okay if you cry."

"I think I'm all cried out, Clay."

Knowing nothing would get done if he didn't do it, Clay steeled himself to her pain. Systematically, he cleaned her injuries, doing his best to concentrate only on his duty, not her sounds of discomfort. Finally, he poured a liberal amount of hot water onto his bandana and dabbed.

Vanessa's back arched in pain.

"It's over, sugar." With shaking hands, he helped her sit up. Next, he handed her one of his old shirts then turned away so she could cover herself again in at least the illusion of privacy.

"I'm dressed now."

He tried to smile at the picture she made. She was indeed covered; his too-large shirt was wrapped around her securely, like a robe. But it was her face that held his attention. Her eyes were filled with tears, but she was valiantly doing her best to keep them at bay.

"Some ointment would be a good idea, but it's in the back of the barn," he said, hardly recognizing the rasp in his voice, thick from worry over her. "I'll get it when I go inside to get your things."

She moved to stand up. "I'll go with you, Clay."

"No you won't. I won't let you go near Price again. Tell me what you need."

"Dresses. Boots. Undergarments." After a brief pause, she said, "Clay, maybe we should talk about this, talk about your plans. I can't ask you to leave the Circle Z."

"You didn't ask me."

"This—what happened—it isn't your concern."

How could she imagine it wasn't? He'd promised her father he'd take care of her. Had promised it with a hand on his Bible. The vow was irrevocable. "It is. You are my concern."

"Maybe Miles—"

Clayton cut her off. "Miles didn't look after you tonight. He won't protect you tomorrow. Neither will your mother. And this—" Able to look at her again now that she was covered, he added, "This will happen again."

"Maybe—"

"Honey, you know I'm right."

After a long moment, she nodded. "What can I do?"

On a peg was his mother's old carpetbag. "Put some coffee, beans, and bread in here." Remembering her tender skin, he pointed to a soft wool blanket. "Roll that up, it's cold out." He opened the door, whistled for Lovey. The pretty shepherd came running. "Stay," he ordered the dog. "Guard Vanessa."

Unable to help himself, he turned to stare at Vanessa again. She was standing by his lone chair, doing her best to look brave but failing miserably. Lines of exhaustion rimmed her eyes. The knowledge that it would be some time before she could rest made his tone harsher than he meant it to be. "Lock this door behind me. Don't open it until I come back. Do you hear me?"

Her eyes darted to the lock as if she wondered if it could really keep her safe. "I do."

Her voice sounded unsure. Would she try to bolt? "Vanessa, promise me."

His knot of fear dissipated as trust filled her gaze, gifting him with a present he could hardly bear to accept. "I promise. I won't open this door for anyone but you."

"I'll be back within fifteen minutes."

"I'll be waiting."

Clay knew where her room was. After letting himself in through the back door, he climbed the stairs, then strode toward her room. He hadn't bothered to remove his boots; he supposed half of him was itching for a fight.

When he heard nothing, he searched Vanessa's room, pulling out sturdy boots, undergarments, and calicos with the ease of a lady's maid. He silently thanked his sister Corrine for being such a ninny. From the time she'd been eight, he'd had the misfortune and experience of serving as her dresser, thanks to their mother passing soon after their little brother Scout had been born.

The silly chit had been blessed with a penchant for numerous buttons and the sore inability to fasten them easily.

The memories of Corrine's vanity reminded him to grab Vanessa's silver-backed brush and combs. He was just gazing at the pale ivory wool shawl she wore on Sundays, remembering how pretty she looked with it wrapped around her shoulders on her way to church, when Miles stepped in.

"Clayton? What are you doing in here?"

Miles was one year older than Vanessa. At twenty, he was more than old enough to be a man. Unfortunately, no one had seen him that way.

His father had ignored Miles's assertions that he was ready to manage the ranch, leaving it firmly in Clayton's hands.

When Price had come along, he too had kept a firm grip on the boy, ignoring his ideas, tamping down his efforts to accept responsibility. Now, few on the ranch thought much of Miles. The twenty year old seemed destined to falter forever on the brink of manhood—old enough to be responsible but too green to be of use.

His somewhat tentative, almost lazy disposition had driven Clayton to distraction more than a time or two.

And now the boy had the audacity to ask why he was gathering Vanessa's things in the middle of the night. "I think you have a fair idea why I'm here. It's obvious your sister can't stay near Price a moment longer."

Miles's eyes bugged. "You can't just take her."

Clay felt like he was speaking to a child. "I can, and I will."

Twin spots of color splashed across his face. "You've got to keep her here. You don't know what Price will do if she's gone missing."

A sharp image of Vanessa's back, damaged and hurting, struck him hard. "I believe I do."

"Clayton, you need to stop and listen. Price . . . he didn't mean to get out of hand."

"Out of hand?" His patience snapped. Gripping Miles by the shoulders, Clay pinned him in place. "He hit your sister with a leather strap. He tried to do far worse."

"I know." Miles's skin turned a pasty white. "But—"

Disgusted, Clayton dropped his hands, shoved Miles to one side. "If you intend to talk some more, do it outside. Your sister's waiting." Clay scooped up Vanessa's clothes and brushes, stuffed them into a pillowcase. At the last minute, he added her shawl, her diary, and her ivory fountain pen. There'd hardly been a day go by that he hadn't seen her writing.

He strode out the room, pausing as Marilyn peeked out from the master suite. A cheek was bruised and swollen, accentuating the lack of color in her face.

Gesturing to the stuffed pillowcase, she whispered, "You taking Vanessa, Clay?"

"I am."

Overwhelming relief flooded her features. "Good. Price drank almost a bottle of whiskey. He won't wake for some time. I'll do my best to keep her disappearance quiet for as long as possible."

Clay struggled for control. "Yes, ma'am."

She stepped forward and gripped his arm with a shaking hand. "Tell Van I love her. I did my best—"

Clay couldn't bear to hear anymore. To his way of thinking, Marilyn's best had been a poor effort. "I will," he said, cutting her off.

He felt sorry for Marilyn, but not enough to give her comfort. The woman should have known better. They'd all known Price had only courted and married Marilyn for the Circle Z. The man had never been anything but a drunkard and a schemer.

Marilyn should have cared about that. She should have done more for her daughter. Didn't she remember what the Bible said about taking care of God's children?

With a start, Clayton realized Miles was still by his side. "I need to go," he said to the boy before quickly sprinting down the stairs as Marilyn disappeared back into her room.

Miles padded after him. "Where will you take her?" he asked as they walked through the kitchen and out the back door. "What will you do with Vanessa?"

The night was still dark but already a mockingbird cried in the distance. He needed to saddle up Lee and get going. "You don't need to know."

"How will I find her?"

"She'll find you—if she ever cares to."

Miles's soft face went slack. "There was nothing I could do, Clay," he whined. "Price was going crazy. You should've heard him."

"*I should have heard him?*" All the anger Clayton had held at bay from the moment he'd seen Vanessa's back burgeoned forth. Violently, he grabbed Miles by the neck and slammed him against the barn door. "You make me sick, huddling in the hallway while your stepfather did his best with your sister. Listening to her screams. Allowing him to lay a hand on her. To *touch* her."

"But Clay—"

"Don't."

"Clay! Price is gonna be so angry when he finds out. He's going to send for the sheriff. Form a posse."

Clay knew that to be true. What he was doing was a hanging offense, and no one would say different no matter how many scars decorated Vanessa's back or face.

He was about to thrust Miles away from him when he spied something new in his expression. Determination? Bravery?

Clay dropped his hand. Gave him one last chance. "You're at a crossroads, Miles. You can tell Price what I did and help him get your sister back or you can be a man and protect her. I will keep her safe, you have my word."

Miles straightened his thin shoulders. "I know you will. I'll . . . do my best to help you."

Clay shook his head. His best wasn't good enough.

Miles darted out a hand, stilling him. "Clay—stop. I will protect her. The posse will be called, but I'll send them north. Clay. You . . . you have my word. My vow."

His vow.

Clay looked at the horizon. Dawn would be breaking in three hours and they had a long way to go.

But perhaps tonight Miles had finally decided to become a man. "Don't disappointment me."

Miles reached in his vest and pulled out a wad of cash. "You'll need this. Vanessa's got some money at the bank in her name, but this should tide you over."

Clay took the money. He, too, had some funds, but not enough for an extended length of time. "Thank you."

As he slipped it into his pocket, Miles called out, "Should I pray? You said Jesus answers prayers."

Clayton paused, memories of leading boys to battle flashing before his eyes. "Jesus does," he said quietly.

"Then how come this happened? How come Price came into our lives?"

"We let him."

"But his being here, it's not right. Now Van's got no one."

A sense of calm rushed over Clayton, thankful to Miles for reminding him of who was in charge of all of them—who always was, who always had been. "You're forgetting that God brought me here to the Circle Z. I'm here to take care of her. Maybe I've been here all along for that reason. Good-bye, Miles."

When Miles slipped back into his house, Clayton stepped quickly back into the barn. When he reached the locked door, Clayton did his best to make his voice tender once more. "I'm back, Vanessa."

She opened the door immediately. "Clay."

He couldn't help but stare. She'd pulled back her hair and had tied his shirt in a knot at her waist. She looked young and beautiful. She looked like Vanessa.

Then the shadows shifted and the bruise on her cheek came to life. Unable to help himself, he brushed her cheek with one finger. "You okay, honey?"

She closed her eyes at his touch. "I will be. Now."

Clayton closed his eyes for a brief moment as well. How in the world was he going to last being her savior when all he wanted to do was hold her close and never let her go?

2

After examining the contents of the pillowcase, Vanessa held up her diary. "Thank you for remembering this," she said softly, fingering the worn red leather with her name embossed in the lower left-hand corner. "I would have missed it."

"You're welcome." Clay stood at the door. "I need to get some things from the barn. Will you be okay?"

Vanessa nodded. "I'll be out in a few minutes."

When she was alone again, Vanessa released a ragged breath. The past fifteen minutes had been hard, knowing Clay was packing her things, seeing both his shadow and Miles's slighter one in her window.

Now that her back didn't sting quite so badly, visions of Price's actions flew back in a rush, frightening her all over again. The look in his eyes had scared her terribly, like nothing ever had before. She'd felt completely helpless under his grip. Shocked at his violence.

Mortified at the way he'd grabbed at her.

Embarrassed about having to tell Clayton about it. Devastated that Clayton Proffitt was willing to leave the first home he known in years to keep her safe.

How could she live with that? Yet, what else could she do? If her mother hadn't entered the room the moment that she had, Vanessa feared far worse things would have happened at the hands of her stepfather. If she stayed, it would happen again. She knew that.

And well, Clayton had always been everything to her. She wanted to depend on him. She needed him in her life—had always dreamed something special and wonderful would happen between them.

Though he'd always tried to make their relationship brotherly, Vanessa was enough of a woman to know that she'd never felt toward him the way she'd felt toward Miles.

Clayton was good and solid—and dare she admit it?—so very handsome. His neatly trimmed hair was the exact shade of the pecans that grew in the north pasture. His posture was as erect as any soldier's stance she'd ever seen.

But it was his calm way that drew her so close. Clayton was mature and dependable and never ruffled. And once, when she'd been all dressed up for her very first dance, she'd spied true appreciation in his eyes.

It wasn't like Price's oily gaze. No, Clay's was respectful but admiring. She'd spent many a night dreaming about being held close in his arms—not for comfort, but for love.

Clayton Proffitt was the reason she'd let many boys court her but few do more than quietly tell her good night.

She'd been waiting for him. Waiting for him to realize that she'd grown up. Waiting for Clayton to realize that she—Vanessa Grant—would be the perfect partner for him, the perfect woman to give him comfort and love. His ideal wife.

But she'd never wanted their relationship to be like this. Now Clayton saw her as a burden, something to be taken care of. A needy, frightened girl.

And now, well, all those dreams of hugs and sweet kisses had faded to black. Now whenever she thought of being close to a man, she could only imagine pain.

And the images made her feel more alone than ever before.

Clay's boots scuffed the floor when he entered again. "Did you pack some food?"

She looked to the neat pile she made on the table. "Yes. I packed a blanket and some clothes for you, too. Will these work?"

Clayton picked up the pair of denims and three shirts, then looked her way and smiled. "Thank you. They'll do just fine." As if from nowhere, Clayton pulled out a satchel and packed it with other supplies.

Lastly, Vanessa watched him holster his six-shooter, then pull out a Winchester. Bullets for both were stowed in the satchel as well. Finally, he crossed to his bed and picked up the worn Bible she'd seen him read time and again.

Almost reverently, he tucked it into his satchel.

After glancing out the window with a frown, he said, "Dawn's on its way. We need to go. See to your needs then meet me outside. I'm going to saddle the horses."

Quickly, she made a trip to the outhouse, then went to the back of the barn. Lee and Coco were already saddled. Lovey pranced around the horses' hooves, silently asking for attention. Vanessa leaned down and petted the dog, sad to be leaving her. Her pa had gifted her with Lovey just a few years ago. Vanessa had carried the shepherd pup around like a doll, then had gotten quite used to her company. Later, Clayton had trained the shepherd to help with the cattle. Her place was at the Circle Z.

With a worried frown, Clayton looked out toward the horizon. "Daybreak's coming. It's time we left, Van."

"I know."

His gaze ran over her, making her pulse jump and her expectations rise. Oh, how she'd adored Clayton from the moment he'd appeared at the Circle Z, looking so upright and proper. Looking so hungry for a kind word and a good meal.

Her father had given him both, and in return had received Clayton's high moral standards and unflagging work ethic.

Yes, for the past six years he'd been her benchmark, raising her expectations so high she feared no other man could come close in estimation.

Cupping her elbow, he looked at her in concern. "Sweetheart, you going to be able to ride?"

She nodded. "I'll be fine."

He easily lifted her into the saddle like he had so many times before. "If you need help—"

"I won't. I'll be fine, Clayton." And even if she wasn't, she'd never tell him. Not when he was leaving so much for her.

With ease, he mounted Lee. "Stay, Lovey," he ordered before guiding his horse toward the south pasture. As usual, the wind was blowing, kicking up red dust, making the tall grass rustle underneath.

Vanessa followed easily, giving Coco free rein to follow Lee at her own pace.

Within minutes, the stable and homestead faded into the distance. Now, only the far-reaching West Texas plains surrounded them, the horizon bare except for thickets of short, squat mesquite trees.

Vanessa didn't dare look back. It would do no good to wave to Lovey or scan the windows for Miles's shadow.

She didn't dare search for her daddy's grave with the gray stone cross above it when they rode past the cemetery. It did no good to remember the swimming hole or her mother's hugs or the wide stone fireplace she used to sit near in the winter and play with her dolls.

It wasn't the time to think about what could have been or what used to be. Time and circumstances had marked her life and had ultimately changed her future.

Their future.

Clayton picked up speed. After an hour they were off Circle Z's land and in the outskirts of Camp Hope, the old Confederate outpost during the war. Now only renegades and outcasts visited there to congregate and drink.

Vanessa had never been allowed to visit after the age of seven. But Miles had spoken fondly of the saloon there, and, of course, of the women who plied their trades.

To her knowledge, Clayton had never shown the slightest interest in such a place, though she doubted he would ever say a word to her about it even if he frequented it weekly.

He'd always taken care to shield her from men's darker ways, never speaking of such things or cursing in front of her. He continually reprimanded hands who forgot themselves when she was nearby.

Once she'd heard Clayton giving a new ranch worker a thorough dressing down because he hadn't tipped his hat and stood up when she entered the room. He chewed on another ranch hand when he'd dared to call her "Vanessa" instead of "Miss Grant."

After another hour, the pounding sense of panic she'd felt from the moment Price had entered her bedroom eased. A terrible feeling of loneliness took its place as she realized that everything she'd known before was now gone.

It was unlikely she'd ever see her friends or her mother or Lovey again. Her future was completely in Clayton's hands, and though she would have done the same for him, she ached for reassurance—anything to fend off the feeling of complete and utter loss.

"Clay, we going to town?"

Clayton looked surprised. "To Camp Hope? No. You know that's no place for a lady."

"Well, where are we going then? You haven't said."

"There's a trail coming up that cuts into an old ravine. We'll take it and then head west toward the river."

River? "Where do you have in mind, Clay?"

"I've been thinking about my sister, Corrine. I thought we'd go to her spread. You'll be safe there."

Clay had spoken his sister's name often with extreme fondness. Years ago, Vanessa had been plenty jealous of the elusive sister, sure that Clay missed her more than he'd ever miss herself. Now Vanessa also recalled that Corrine lived far away. "Isn't Corrine out in Colorado Territory?"

"She is." With a twitch of his lips, Clayton said, "She has a spread two or three days ride from Denver. I fought with her husband Merritt in the war. He's a good man."

"You'll be safe there," he said again.

Colorado! She'd never been farther than Camp Hope. Never dreamed she'd ever leave Texas. Questions about the trip, about their travels, popped up like fresh hot corn. She ached to pepper him with them, but didn't dare. Clayton never had cared much for being questioned. Already he was changing his entire life for her. No way was she going to have him deal with her worries and inexperience, too.

She was going to keep her mouth shut and follow his lead.

Sure enough, the trail he'd mentioned appeared and he guided her through a steep incline before veering northwest once more. Vanessa was glad she'd had so much experience in the saddle. A less experienced rider would surely find the steep trail something of a challenge.

Around them, the September sky was awakening. Blue jays cried sharp greetings from the pines as she and Clayton passed underneath. Dawn had come, bringing with it morning and all its heavenly glory—and the fresh batch of heat.

He circled back to her side. "You all right?"

"Yes. Of course, Clayton."

He looked doubtful but continued. "I'm hoping to make it thirty miles or so by nightfall, then with luck, we'll make it to Lubbock the following evening. It's a hard ride, but then we'll be far enough to set up camp and sleep."

She'd innocently assumed they'd rest in a hotel. Sleeping out in the elements sounded new and unfamiliar, and terribly uncomfortable. But she wouldn't complain. No way did she want to have him see her as young or inexperienced. Again. Things had changed that night. She was different now. Stronger. "That sounds fine."

"When we cross the border, into Arizona Territory, we can stay somewhere near other people," he promised, his voice holding an unfamiliar tentativeness. "Do you think you'll be all right?"

"Of course."

He glanced over his shoulder, the brim of his hat shading his brown eyes. "Promise me you'll tell me to stop if we're traveling too fast."

She knew he would, too. Even if they were in Indian territory. Even if he was anxious to water the horses. He would always put her needs before his own.

That knowledge gave her comfort, and a heavy band of responsibility—more than anything, she wanted Clayton to see her as a partner, not a child. "Clayton, I'm beholden to you. I promise I'll do my best not to complain." She smiled. "Just point Coco in the right direction and I'll go."

His lips didn't curve in response. "Don't say that. You aren't beholden."

"I know better. I'm grateful. You saved me, Clayton."

For an instant, one hand reached for her, as if he was about to caress her cheek. "How . . . how are you feeling?"

"I'll be all right."

"Vanessa, the truth, please. Is your back too painful? Do you need to stop?"

"No." Her back was sweaty. The sores stung and swelled and burned like fire. She would've given just about anything to take her shirt off and ride without any fabric touching her back. "Don't worry so."

Clayton pushed back the brim of his hat. Once again, coffee-colored eyes skimmed over her face, caressing her with unspoken concern. "Sweetheart—"

"I promise I'll let you know if I'm not okay," she whispered.

"Fine," he mumbled before reluctantly turning away, taking the lead again.

They rode for four more hours.

Finally, he stopped next to an embankment near a good-sized river. "Let's stop here for a time."

Ever the gentleman, he helped her dismount, held her elbows firmly as her knees threatened to give way.

With a faint nicker, Coco followed Lee to the river and drank deeply.

When Vanessa's legs found their bearing, she made her way to the river as well, finally bending down to splash cool water across her face and drink her share. When she saw Clayton do the same, she sat down on the grassy slope. "This feels good."

He pulled out a knapsack and handed her some bread and cheese. "It does. Eat something."

The sharp cheddar awoke her senses, just as the soft bread soothed her hunger. Glad for the bonnet that shaded her eyes, she examined him more closely.

Clayton was rubbing down the horses, stopping only to eat a few bites of bread and to fill their canteens up river. Throughout it all, he barely spoke, hardly looked at her at all. A little more distant.

What was happening to the two of them?

"We best get going."

"All right," she said, letting him help her into the saddle once more. She was just about to straighten her skirts when she realized he was still there, standing close. Comforting. "Clay?" she asked, bending down to catch his eye.

Slowly he traced a finger along her cheek, frowning at the bruise marring her skin. "Your cheek is swollen. This heat and wind isn't doing that cut any favors. You sure you're all right?"

"Yes." And she was. Her back hurt, more than she dared to admit. She was exhausted and sore from riding for hours. She was worried and still numb about everything that had happened the night before. But she could make do.

"Do you need a bandanna? This red dust is merciless."

She pulled a fresh cloth from her skirt pocket. "Don't fuss, Clayton."

After a measured look, he swung onto his saddle, then motioned Lee onward.

Both Lee and Coco were a little frisky; the break had done them good. Vanessa gripped the horn on her saddle as Coco clipped along the trail, eagerly trailing Lee.

Vanessa couldn't help but notice just how well Clayton rode. It was as if he and Lee were one. She knew there were many reasons for that. Clayton had served in the cavalry at the end of the war. Once she heard a couple of hands discussing how he'd lied about his age so he could both fight for the Confederacy and ride his palomino.

The rumors weren't surprising. After all, his natural leadership skills had earned him the position at the Circle Z. After four weeks, her father had appointed him foreman when Absalom Graves had decided to head down south and spend his last years with his only surviving son.

Though the appointment had bothered Miles mightily, Clayton had shouldered the responsibility with ease. If anything, it had seemed like he'd relished the position, obviously finding it easier to lead than to be led. In a remarkably short while, everyone started looking to him for directives, sometimes even her father.

Price's appearance had changed little. Even her stepfather knew he was no match for Clayton's abilities. So instead of working, he'd concentrated on spending the ranch's money as quickly as possible.

Now, as she left her family and placed every ounce of her trust in Clayton, Vanessa knew she'd follow him to the ends of the earth.

After all, she had nowhere else to go.

By sundown, Clayton estimated that they'd reached his goal of covering forty miles. He recalled the trail they were taking. More than once he'd followed Major Merritt along this way in last-ditch efforts to outwit the Yankees. Merritt's ingenuity had served Clayton well. Merritt was married to his sister, and he was still alive—far better off than the majority of the men who'd fought next to them.

Clayton breathed a blessed sigh of relief when they came to the ravine he'd recalled, this one with an abandoned cabin on its banks. Maybe they could finally stop for the day. He knew Vanessa desperately needed some rest. Though she hadn't said a word, he was sure the stress of the past twenty-four hours was taking its toll.

"Vanessa, hold up. I'm going to take a closer look."

Obediently, she reined in Coco and waited patiently, though she looked to be holding herself upright out of sheer willpower.

After dismounting, he pulled out his Colt and scanned the area, looking closely for any signs that it had been occupied recently. Nothing was evident.

The door, hanging precariously on its hinges, creaked an awkward greeting, but all that lay inside was a dirt floor littered with debris and the dank smell of mildew. Most likely the ravine had flooded recently.

As Lee nosed the ground for stubs of grass, Clayton eyed the tangle of woods surrounding them. All was still, only whippoorwill cried out in the distance.

Finally satisfied, he approached Vanessa. "This will serve for tonight." Curving his hands around her waist, he swung her out of the saddle, inhaling her scent against his will, as she leaned closer than usual, practically sliding herself against him until she reached the ground. He held her steady until she got her bearings. Worried she might collapse, he didn't release his grip. "Vanessa?"

She shook her head as if to clear it. "I'm sorry, Clay." With a faint blush, she said, "I think my backside must have fallen asleep. How may I help you?"

"Only one thing. Sit down before you fall down."

"I can't let you do everything. I'll help with the saddles."

He stilled her. "Darlin', don't take this the wrong way, but I can do this faster and easier without you. Once more, I'd feel better knowing you were resting."

"But—"

"Another time you can help me all you want. I promise."

Whether she was too tired to argue, or because she knew he was right, she sat. "Yes, Clayton."

⸎

They were close enough to other homesteads to make a fire without causing undue notice. By nightfall, the temperature would drop. The last thing Clayton wanted was for Vanessa to take a chill.

After settling the horses, he built a small fire a few feet from the abandoned cabin. The cabin would help shield them from the wind and help Vanessa warm up. Next he set to boiling coffee.

Against his advice, Vanessa pulled out two mugs from their saddlebags and placed the apples, cheese, and bread out on a clean bandanna. Clayton knew they both were too tired to cook beans or fish, even if he had been of the mind to catch something.

Finally, after washing up with some of the water he'd gotten from a creek they'd passed hours ago, Clayton murmured a brief prayer of thanksgiving and then they ate. As their stomachs filled, a strained silence rose between them. As well as he knew Vanessa, he'd never been alone with her for such a length of time.

His experience on the trail had been solely in the company of men, with himself in charge. He was used to giving orders, assigning watch. He had no supply of easy conversation or amusing stories suitable for feminine ears.

But as he saw her hugging her knees close, and a pained expression visiting her eyes, he knew something had to be said. As his reality sank in, Clayton found himself wondering just how to calm Vanessa, what to say.

Unfortunately, no sweet promises came to mind. Everything he used to tease her about—her vast number of pretty dresses, the curls of her hair, the endless boys who tried so hard to receive a smile from her—all that was gone now.

As if she, too, felt the tension, she unfolded her legs. "I think I'll go lie down, Clayton."

As he watched her stand up stiffly, he remembered the ointment he'd pulled from the barn just before they left. If her swollen cheek was any indication, her back was sure to be in a bad way. He stood up, too. "I better check on your back."

Vanessa swallowed hard. "There's no need."

Clayton felt her same discomfort. Now that blinding anger no longer guided his thoughts, he was far more conscious of their isolation—and of the uncomfortable new awareness he felt in her presence.

During their ride, he'd taken notice of all the things he usually tried so hard to ignore. Her purely feminine form, the smooth line of her jaw. As the hours passed, he'd found himself thinking about the calluses that were sure to be forming on her soft palms. Had they blistered? "I'm afraid there is every need. The cuts on your back need to be cleaned," he explained. "I have balm that will help with the scarring, too."

"Oh. I . . . I hadn't thought about that."

Mentally, Clayton chastised himself. He should have known better than to give her something else to worry about. He motioned to the large rock in front of the fire. "Sit down, now. This won't take long."

He stood behind her, giving her at least the illusion of privacy. Once she'd finished unbuttoning his shirt, he carefully knelt down behind her, his knees creaking with the motion. Lord, he felt old.

Luckily, the wounds hadn't festered too terribly and he was able to slip the shirt off her shoulders without causing her discomfort. But still, her back looked no better in the waning daylight. Bruised and swollen, the skin puckered around the sores, cracking as scabs attempted to form.

She held herself motionless as he washed off the day's sweat and grime, knowing the fresh air would do her injuries good.

Until that minute, he'd never wanted to be anything other than the man he was. However, as he eyed the glob of salve on his hands, he wished he had softer fingers, skin that wasn't quite so rough.

Vanessa turned her head, her eyes widening as she witnessed him eyeing her back, his right hand raised in uncertainty. "It'll be okay, Clay," she whispered. "They really don't hurt too bad."

Too bad? Slowly, he dabbed the salve along her cuts, taking care to reach each part but not hurt her in the process. Inadvertently, he rubbed the smooth silkiness of her back as well.

Vanessa had the type of skin that only years of coddled living could give a woman. Pale, creamy-soft. Covering the gentle mix of muscles and bones that made men go into battle.

Even hurt and cut, Vanessa was beautiful. And he wasn't unaware that he was the first man to spy her bare back, to caress her at all.

His hand jerked at the direction of his thoughts. Was he no better than Price?

Vanessa exhaled roughly, bringing him back to the present. "All done?"

After one more pass, he dropped his hand. "All done."

She moved to pull his shirt back up, but he stilled her. "I think it'd be best to try and sleep in just your camisole, if you can. The cuts might heal better in the air."

She winced at his tone. Once again, his efforts to remain detached had made his voice rougher than usual.

Curving her arms over her chest, she looked like she was a lost soul. "Where . . . where will we sleep? In there?" She motioned to the abandoned cabin.

"No." He rolled out two bedrolls, pulled out the blanket she'd packed as well. "We'll sleep here, by the fire. Come lie down, Vanessa."

She unlaced her boots, then stretched out on her side. Gently, he covered her, like he would a child.

Except she was far from that. Her bare shoulders glowed in the moonlight, reminding Clayton that Vanessa had become a beautiful woman before his eyes. He needed to be man enough to acknowledge the fact as well as the fact that she was off-limits to him. He'd promised her father to watch over her, not dream of things that could never be possible.

As the fire crackled, illuminating their area and casting a warm glow over their sorry circumstances, Clayton stretched out his legs and sipped his coffee. He'd sleep in a little while. For now, all he wanted was a few minutes' silence.

But Vanessa had other ideas.

"Clay?"

"Hmm?"

"Remember when I went to that barn dance two years ago?"

"I do." Vanessa had worn a mossy-colored satin that had brought out the green in her eyes.

"Remember how I'd had such a crush on Teddy?"

The question elicited a chuckle. "No one could forget your crush, sweetheart." Teddy West had worked for Circle Z for one interminable season. Clayton had breathed a sigh of relief when they'd made it through those five months without having to dismiss the randy cowboy, he'd flirted so outrageously with Vanessa.

"I never told you this, but Teddy kissed me that night."

Maybe he should have done some damage. "I never knew that."

"I'd been so excited. We danced, and then Teddy suggested we go out where it was cooler. It was warm in that barn. Remember?"

She was far too trusting. "Vanessa, honey, it wasn't all that warm. It was March."

"Don't fuss. This was years ago. Anyway, there we were, dancing and twirling, when all of the sudden, he dipped me, then held me close."

Clayton gritted his teeth. "And then?"

"He kissed me." Vanessa said it dreamily.

She was waiting for a response. He couldn't think of one that wouldn't betray his feelings.

"I thought that night was just about the most exciting moment of my life, Clayton. A dance, a kiss . . . "

He couldn't help but interrupt. "It was only one kiss?"

"Oh my goodness, yes." She turned her head to face him. "What did you think I did?"

"I didn't think anything." Suddenly, he was extremely glad for the darkness surrounding them. He was afraid he was blushing.

"Well, after that first one, we danced some more, and then Teddy wanted another kiss."

He really should have sent that boy out on his ear like he'd wanted to. "You should have called for me. I would have made sure he didn't try for more." Ever.

"Oh, Clayton. I couldn't do that. You were dancing with Charlotte Fleet—and she'd been dying to dance with you forever." Propping herself on her elbows, she stared at him, eyes all sparkling and full of mirth. "Did you kiss her?"

"I did not. Not that it's any of your business. So . . . what did you do to Teddy, since you foolishly decided that you didn't need me?"

"I gave him a good hard push and told him no, thank you, then hightailed it back inside."

No, thank you? She should have kneed him hard enough to making walking difficult. For a month. "I'm glad he listened."

"Clayton? Right this minute I feel the same way."

Only Vanessa could say so much and still not make a lick of sense. "How so?"

"That night I felt like I'd crossed a line. A cowboy thought of me as a woman. I stood up to him, all by myself. I went to bed that night feeling a whole year older."

She turned to her side to catch his eye, a sweet, sad smile flickering in the fading sparks of their campfire. "I feel older tonight, too."

Her words shamed him. She should have never felt like that. He should have known to keep an eye on Price. He should have heard her cries, gotten there sooner. Noticed that things were getting dangerous for her. "Van—"

"Let me finish, Clayton. If someone had told me two days ago that I was going to have to leave my home in the middle of the night, ride with you all day, then go sleep next to a fire, I would have told them I wasn't strong enough. But maybe I am, after all."

Clayton swallowed hard. "Yes, you are. The Lord provides. *'For now we live, if ye stand fast in the Lord,'*" he quoted.

After another moment, she murmured sleepily, "I think . . . I think I'm gonna be all right."

Only hours later, when the blazing fire had turned to glowing embers and the winds had died down enough to hear even a twig break in the distance, did Clayton dare answer. "You will be all right, sweetheart. I promise on my life."

3

Shame weighed deep on a man's soul when there was no hope of forgiveness, Miles Grant decided while wandering through Clayton's empty suite of rooms. During the last few days, the Circle Z had been in an uproar, and all of it was his stepfather's fault.

First came Price's ugly cursing when he awoke the next morning to find both Vanessa and Clayton gone. After eating his usual hearty breakfast, he'd tromped over to the barn where Miles had been hanging out.

"You know where they went off to?"

"No sir, I sure don't."

With dismay, Price had believed him. After deciding to wait a few days to see if they'd return, an evil gleam flew into his gaze. "She'll have to get off her high horse now, don't you think?"

Before Miles could answer, Price continued. "When Vanessa returns, she'll be no better than the women at Camp Hope. She's used goods now, boy. You mark my words."

Miles had been afraid to say a word.

When he was alone again, a few of the cowhands appeared. "Where's Clayton?" one asked. Miles had never learned everyone's names.

"Gone."

"You in charge now?"

Miles puffed up a bit. It was about time he got the respect he deserved. "Maybe."

But only snickers greeted his reply. Slim George took charge instead. "Looks like it'll be up to me to hold things down for a while." In quick-fire manner, he assigned chores, directing hands to various pastures and jobs.

Within minutes, they had abandoned Miles. And that was how he had ended up in Clayton's rooms.

After tentatively testing out Clayton's mattress, he sat on the edge and dared to let himself remember the night his sister had been attacked.

Price had been drinking all evening—slurring his words at dinner. Miles's mother hadn't said a word, just looked eager to escape to the kitchen. Vanessa merely ran up to her room.

"Boy, you old enough for a shot of whiskey?"

Miles had taken a glass and swung back the amber liquid. The whiskey had burned and scalded the back of his throat, but it had given him hope as well. Perhaps this was the way to gain acceptance.

It hadn't been.

Miles couldn't recall what he'd done wrong, but it had earned him a fierce slap and shove. Hours later, he heard Vanessa being dealt far worse.

Her room butted up to his. He heard her cries through the thin walls.

Standing in the hallway hadn't helped. Neither had the knowledge that though he'd worried for her, he had been too weak to help. Too weak to do much except be glad it wasn't him.

Miles had accepted Clayton's anger—a part of him knew he deserved it. But just as big a part of him desired something even more than the will to do the right thing. He wanted acceptance and respect.

He wanted what Clayton had gotten so easily. What other men gave him without so much as a raised voice or a cross word.

Even Price had never dared to cross their formidable foreman's directives.

Why was that?

But as he scanned the room, Miles saw nothing there to give him a hint of how to become the man Clayton was. All that was there was old furniture, mismatched plates, a quilt constructed of old clothes, and a cross whittled out of birch.

No, there was nothing of worth there at all.

The lack of clues gave him pause.

Vanessa was fairly sure her body remained the same under her skirts, but she wouldn't have been surprised to find certain vital parts missing. Sometime during the last twenty-four hours, her backside had become numb.

They'd ridden hard over the last two days. Clayton had been anxious to make it to Lubbock, then just beyond it. He had a friend who owned some property on the outskirts, and wanted to spend the night there so they could relax in relative privacy.

Even though they'd been on the trail for three days, in some ways it felt like forever. Everything in her life had changed, and because the outward changes were so drastic, she'd been holding onto what was inside of her like it was in danger of lifting up and taking flight.

Her sense of self was as hard to keep hold of as her seat on Coco. Everything between her and Clay was now drastically different, their roles in each other's lives gone as topsy-turvy as the flight of a chicken hawk on patrol.

No longer was she the ranch owner's daughter, he the trusted employee. Now, he was in charge. He guided her and provided for her. She was in his hands because he had saved her. Because she was so grateful to be away from Price. Because she had no control over what was about to come.

Saying they were now friends didn't quite describe things, either. They'd always been close, but now there was a tension between them, an invisible wall that kept them aware of propriety at all times. While he still called her sweet names, it wasn't nearly as often, and never quite as lighthearted.

He didn't look at her the way he used to, either. His gaze was more guarded; the muscles around his mouth looked more tense.

Vanessa felt immeasurably guilty. She was completely, totally dependent on him, draining him dry. Taking, yet giving nothing in return. He must surely be resentful.

And, though their relationship might not have been so equal when he was working for her father, and then for Price, she'd felt as if she could cheer him up on some days, sit with him quietly on others.

Then, Clayton hadn't been responsible for every part of her being.

Indeed, Clayton had given up everything for her. He'd made her life better, and she would be forever grateful to him, but she wanted to be able to give him something in return, anything to make what they had more equal, anything to help her feel a little more pride.

But all she had was herself and what was left of her dignity.

Abruptly, Clayton stopped. Vanessa reined in Coco and shifted her legs a bit, hoping to regain some sort of feeling in her thighs.

"See that ridge?" he asked, pointing to a pale structure in the distance. "Ken's place is beyond it. We should be there in no time."

A warm sense of expectation shined through in his tone, sounding welcome and familiar. Pleased—and anxious to end the stilted silence—she asked, "How do you know him, again?"

"Ken was one of my men in the war."

Clayton's voice was full of pride. Knowing the little bit about his past that she did, Vanessa said, "Is he older or younger than you?"

"Older, but not by much."

Recalling stories she'd overheard, Vanessa said, "Strange, isn't it, that you were an officer so young?"

Eyes trained on the desolate horizon, he shrugged. "Not really. By the end of the war, men joked that you could be an officer if you survived the next battle." Somewhat bitterly, he murmured, "I somehow managed to survive them all."

The things he went through broke her heart. "Oh, Clayton."

"It's true." As if he was in no hurry to go, he leaned back in his saddle. "Ken is the best tracker I know. He saved us a time or two from starvation. More times than that, he rescued us from being killed outright. I owe him."

"I'll look forward to meeting him." Vanessa loved to hear Clay speak of the war. Oh, not the pain, or how hungry and cold he'd been, or how dangerous the battles were. What she liked was hearing the stories of him and his men. Each one gave her insight into another facet of Clayton—one that didn't seem as tightly wound, as tightly contained, as wary and reserved.

"You'll like Ken's wife Mary. She's quiet, but not when she's ordering him around. When she gets on her high horse, you'd better look out!"

She grinned. "She sounds like a formidable woman. Do they have children?"

"I know they have one. I'd be surprised if they didn't have a houseful by now."

"I love children."

Brown eyes blinked in surprise. "Do you? I didn't know that."

"How could you? It's not like we had a chance to see many children at the Circle Z." Or if they would've spoken of such things if they had.

They'd had a cordial relationship, but over the years their roles had become more sharply defined. Most recently, Clayton had always taken care to treat her with the utmost respect, and Vanessa had tried her best not to let on how fascinated she was with the foreman of their spread.

The air stilled as her words sank in. Clayton seemed to notice the difference, too. "I reckon we've tarried long enough. Let's head on up," he said simply.

Vanessa took care to let Clayton lead, learning by now that he liked a good distance to separate them, just in case he needed to stop or change directions quickly. He and Lee moved as if in one motion. Vanessa, while an able horse-woman, had no claim to ride so well.

As they rode up toward the homestead, Coco nickered. Vanessa rubbed her neck. "Almost there, girl. Then we'll stop for a day or two."

Coco swung her head around, like she was nodding in agreement. Vanessa felt the same way. A day without dust blowing in her eyes and nose would be a welcome change. Finally, they neared the homestead, a sturdy stone and wooden house that looked as if it could withstand an Indian raid or a violent windstorm with ease.

All that mattered at the moment was that there would be a bed or cot for her, and for that she would be eternally grateful. Vanessa had never been so tired as she was at that very minute.

Every muscle ached, and though she hadn't dared let on, her back burned like the blazes. She'd purposely asked Clayton to leave it be until they got to the Willoughbys, knowing that even if things were as bad as she feared, there was little he could do to make things better on the trail.

A man with a military bearing and coal black hair looked up when they approached. His welcoming smile told Vanessa that he could only be Clayton's tracker, Ken Willoughby. "Clayton Proffitt? As I live and breathe."

Clayton tipped his hat. "Ken. I was hoping I'd find you home. Is Mary here, too?"

"She's in town with the children, getting supplies." Ken stood still, but it was obvious he was waiting for some introductions and an explanation.

After a moment, Clayton did the honors. "Ken, this here's Vanessa Grant. May we impose on you for a day or two?"

"You know you don't need to ask." Tipping his hat, Ken smiled, though Vanessa saw his golden eyes weren't missing a single detail. "Ma'am."

"I'm pleased to meet you, Mr. Willoughby."

"Likewise. And, it's Ken, ma'am. Please."

They walked Coco and Lee to the barn. Vanessa was too tired to do more than wait patiently until Clayton helped her down. Not caring what his friend thought, she held onto him for dear life until feeling rushed back to her toes.

Ken eyed the two of them for a good long moment before clearing his throat. "Well, now. Vanessa, I'm sure you'd like to wash up. Go on up to the house, if you'd please. In the back room, there's a pump and somesuch. Captain, I'll help you with the horses."

"Thank you, and it's Clayton now. The war's long gone." Turning to Vanessa, his voice gentled. "You need some help, Van?"

Vanessa knew he was referring to her back and her stiff muscles. But Ken didn't even attempt to hide his surprise at the question, though he wisely held his tongue.

"I'll be fine," she said more brightly than she intended, then bit her lip as she sought to walk with a little jaunt to the house.

She'd gone three yards when she heard Ken chuckle. "Proffitt, what in the world is going on?"

Clayton watched Vanessa enter the house, then waited a full minute after the door closed, just in case she needed something, before turning to his friend.

Still as impatient as ever, Ken folded his arms across his chest. "Talk."

Clayton did. Ken had been his lieutenant at the end of the war, and he trusted the man's judgment more than just about anyone else's. Haltingly, he told Ken about his job at the Circle Z, about Price, and finally about what had happened with Vanessa, though he didn't dare mention Price's name or exactly what he'd attempted, choosing instead to describe the beating.

The knowing look in Ken's golden eyes didn't disappoint. Even after all these years, Willoughby understood more in a look than in a mess of sentences. "She's a pretty girl, Captain. Lovely."

Ken was also a master of using few words to convey a wealth of meaning. "She's just that—a girl. She needs my protection. You don't need to imagine that there's anything more between us, because there isn't."

"While I'd bet money that she does, indeed, need your protection, I don't think that's all there is between you. I got eyes, Captain."

"I promised her father I'd look after her. That's all I plan to do. All I ever plan to do."

"Ever's a long time. Why are you talking like this?" His eyes widened. "Are you married already?"

"Of course not. I wouldn't be traipsing across the country with her if I was."

"Then?"

"She was almost . . . violated," he murmured. "The last thing she needs is another man pawing at her."

"Now that is a right shame." Bitterness and compassion crossed the lines of Ken's face, making Clayton remember, too, the terrible things they witnessed during the war. "'Course, with you, things would be different. You wouldn't harm her. I reckon she knows it."

Clayton couldn't ever imagine touching her in anger. He'd never dare paw at her, either. No, with Vanessa he'd be so much more. He'd cherish her, hold her close, teach her to trust, to love.

But that dream had come and gone. What's more, that hadn't been what he'd promised her father. Vanessa's father had never envisioned a man like Clayton for his daughter. He'd seen too much in the war. Clayton knew that.

No, instead of thinking of dreams and marriage, he'd promised to protect her, to keep her safe. He had a feeling that had been the Lord's purpose, too. "Ken—"

"Things are just as rough as they ever were on the range, Clayton. Men outnumber women ten to one. No lady is safe on her own. She needs a man's protection." Ken coughed, though whether it was to clear his throat or to illustrate a point, Clayton wasn't sure. "I thought you knew that."

Trapping Vanessa into a marriage she didn't ask for or want would be worse. At the moment, he was out of a job, with little money in his pocket save for the wad of bills Miles had pressed into his palm and his own meager savings.

Vanessa was hurting, too. A little bit of her innocence had been shattered by all that had occurred. The last thing she needed was to worry about sharing the marriage bed. "I can't marry her, Ken."

"You need to. If not for her future, then for her past. That stepfather is going to come after her; it's his right. Any judge in the land will side with him and string you up by your toenails for abducting an innocent young thing."

Straightening to his full six-foot height, Ken continued. "We know if she even does survive life with this man, her options for marriage are over. Word will be out that she's traveled with you. You know what I'm saying, Clay? Men will hear that she's been alone with you."

"It hasn't been like that."

"It don't matter what has happened, sometimes it only matters what people think has. But . . . no judge will take a man's wife."

"It's not fair to her. She deserves someone better."

"You're as good a man as I've ever known, Clayton. Seems to me she'd be a lucky woman to have a man like you."

"But—"

Ken cut him off. "Maybe you deserve what I'm suggesting. Maybe you deserve what that little lady does . . . someone to make the darkness of your past almost bearable." Brightening, he said, "Looky there. Here comes Mary."

Clayton followed his friend to the wagon, where Mary sat beside a young boy about six who looked like Ken's spittin' image. Two other children sat in the back, surrounded by bags of flour and grain.

"Mary, honey, this is Clayton," Ken said as he helped her from the wagon. "He and his friend Vanessa are passing through. I told them we'd appreciate their company."

"We would indeed," Mary said, all graciousness. After introductions were made to Petey, Lanie, and Boone, she kissed Ken. "Lanie and I will go visit with Vanessa."

"She's likely to be tired," Clayton warned. "We've been traveling nonstop for well on three days."

Mary winced. "I certainly know what that's like. I suspect she could use a nice cup of tea and a dose of female company."

After directing Petey and Boone to help unload the wagon, Ken motioned for Clayton to follow him to the house. There they found Vanessa sound asleep on the rug in front of a low fire, Mary and Lanie sitting on a chair and watching her with worried expressions.

"Poor thing," Mary said when the men joined her. "She hasn't moved an inch since we walked in."

Clayton felt a rush of tenderness as he looked at Vanessa. Sprawled on her stomach, her head rested on her folded elbows. Just like when she'd been fourteen and he'd found her asleep in her mother's garden, Vanessa slept with her mouth slightly open. Obviously, some things never changed.

"We've been going hard. She's exhausted." Clayton knelt next to Vanessa. "If you tell me where I can take her, I'll pick Van up and get her settled."

Ken raised a brow and had the gall to look shocked. "Where? Why, I don't rightly know. After all, we only have one extra bed—and that's in the loft in the barn."

Unable to help himself, Clayton brushed back a lock of Vanessa's hair, supposedly to check her forehead, but actually just to be able to touch her. "Just give us the children's rooms for now. I'll sleep on the floor next to her."

"I'm afraid that won't do."

Now he was getting irritated. They'd come too far, and had been through too much, to deal with the silly excuses from a man who used to take orders from him. "Like I need this."

"We have children in the house," Mary blurted. "Impressionable ones."

Clayton eyed Mary. Had she changed Ken so much? There'd been a time when his former lieutenant hadn't cared one whit about propriety. During the war, he'd witnessed Ken making his way to sporting houses more than a time or two.

Unwilling to bring up such activities in mixed company, he shrugged. "Fine. I suppose she can sleep right here for now. Tonight, I'll sleep in the barn." But oh, how he hated to even think of being so far from her. What if she woke and needed him? What if she woke and was afraid?

Ken shook his head. "Think, Clayton. Think and listen for once. You need to marry her."

Impatiently, Clayton shook his head. "This isn't the right time. Besides, even if Vanessa would marry me, who are we going to find to perform the duties? A traveling preacher might not show up for months."

Mary's eyes sparkled. "Actually, my husband could perform the ceremony."

"What?"

Ken puffed up a bit. "I neglected to tell you that I took up the Lord when I threw down my rifle."

"Well, that is news."

"The best kind, don't you think?" murmured Mary.

Clayton eyed Vanessa again. Lying there by his side, she looked more at peace than she had at any other time during the last three days.

She was precious to him; he'd do anything to keep her free from harm.

He'd already taken her from the only home she'd ever known. He'd made her ride for hours in the hot sun, barely giving her time to see to her needs. He knew she was hungry and exhausted and frightened of her future.

He knew she cried out in her sleep when she dreamed about her past.

But bind her to him in marriage? Did he dare do such a thing?

"Ever give thought that things are happening for a reason, Clayton? That we're all part of the Lord's divine plan?" Ken murmured. "There's a reason you're here for Vanessa. There's a reason I became a minister. It's no coincidence that I'm here for you. Just as the Lord brought you to the Circle Z Ranch, He brought you both to me. It's fate, pure and simple."

Almost whispering, Ken gripped his shoulder, just like he used to do when reporting to Clayton in the war. "Listen and think, man. Listen to me and to your heart."

Clayton closed his eyes. A sense of peace washed over him as memories surfaced. Memories of him and Ken. Of Vanessa at thirteen, all gumption and sass. The way she used to follow him around, holding that puppy of hers like it was her new best friend.

Of the feel of her in his arms when she'd cried about Price's beating.

The way she'd looked at him that morning. Depending on him. Trusting him.

The way he'd always felt about her. That she was too precious for him, but that he needed her like he needed water and air. He loved her.

Slowly, he stood up. Turning to Ken, he swallowed hard and stood to attention. "Ken . . . I'd be much obliged if you would marry us, if she'll have me."

Ken smiled sweetly. Looking toward the ceiling, he whispered, "Thy will be done."

4

*V*anessa woke to find two small faces peering at her under thick ebony mops of hair.

When she raised herself on her elbows, they both grinned like it was the Fourth of July. "Hi."

"You're up!" one of them—the boy—exclaimed.

"I am. Who might you be?"

The girl spoke. "I'm Lanie and this here's Pete."

"I'm Vanessa."

The bigger one, Pete, giggled. "We know that."

Feeling a bit self-conscious—she couldn't even remember crawling into her bed—she sat up and brushed her hair back away from her face. "Do you two happen to know where Clayton is?"

"Captain Proffitt?"

The military title sounded unfamiliar yet just right. There was something about Clayton's bearing that still seemed mighty military-like. "Yes."

"He's washing up outside." Lanie gasped. "Oh! We were supposed to go find him the minute you woke up."

"The very minute," Pete added with a knowing nod. "I'll go fetch him."

As Pete darted out, Vanessa wished she hadn't been in such a rush to ask about him. She must look a sight! Her head felt foggy and her limbs stiff. It would be far better to visit with him after she put her hair to rights and got her bearings back in order.

Seeing Lanie still eyeing her intently, Vanessa said, "Go tell Captain Proffitt that there's no need for him to rush on over, would you please? As soon as I clean up, I'll be right out."

"Yes'm," Lanie said before scampering out, barely shutting the door behind her.

Thankful to be alone, Vanessa shrugged off her blanket, stretched, then crossed the room to stand before the mirror over the washstand. What she saw made her grimace. She looked even worse than she'd imagined.

Three days on the road had taken its toll. Her face was mottled from exposure to the sun, her clothes dusty and unkempt. Only sleep, a jar of lotion, and a thorough scrubbing would set her to rights.

But since that wasn't possible, Vanessa decided to get cleaned up in a flash. Already feeling remiss for falling asleep before even giving more than a brief hello to their host, she unpinned her hair and looked in the bag that someone had left at the foot of the bed. In a second, she pulled out her silver-backed brush.

Quickly she unbraided the mass, then began the painstaking process of smoothing away the knots and trying to put it back to order.

Her hands stilled when she saw she was no longer alone.

"I'm sorry," Clayton said, standing at the doorway. "I didn't mean to startle you."

"I'm the one who's sorry," Vanessa said, pushing the mixed-up mass of hair behind one shoulder. "I didn't mean to fall asleep. Did I sleep very long?"

"Not long enough—only a couple of hours." He gazed at her hair before turning back to the spot above her head. "I know you're exhausted, sweetheart."

Finally, an endearment. Over the last few days he'd spoken far less of all those sweet words, seeming to find comfort in keeping their exchanges formal and proper.

She hadn't cared for it.

Now she wondered why he stood so hesitantly at the door. What was bothering him? They'd practically lived in each other's pockets since leaving the ranch.

Another minute passed.

She licked her lips. "So. The children said you wanted to see me?"

Almost reluctantly, he stepped closer. "I did."

Vanessa put the brush down. "Any certain reason?" She smiled, letting him know that she was teasing a little bit. They both knew he never needed a reason to see her.

Clayton's eyes raced to her hair once again. Vanessa felt his gaze as clearly as if he'd run a hand from her head to her waist.

He cleared his throat. "We, uh, need to discuss something."

She motioned to a chair. "All right. You want to sit down, maybe?"

After another awkward moment, he did just that, though Vanessa knew he was uncomfortable. Strange that for once she felt in control. "I had to take my hair down," she said when she noticed he stared at it again. "I think a bird could have nested in it, things were such a mess."

"I . . . I don't know if I've ever seen it completely loose like that, Van."

She noticed he merely made an observation, not a compliment. "I'll just—" Quickly she did her best to separate the flowing mass into two sections. "There's too much, don't you think?" she asked as she began to braid one side. "More than once I've been tempted to cut it."

"Don't." The word had come out powerful and short, like he'd pulled it from someplace deep within his body.

Confused, she chuckled. "You only say that because you haven't had to spend a whole hour combing it dry. I tell you, men must have been the ones to decide that women needed their hair long. I've never met a man who would have enough patience for this much bother." Now that one section was neatly braided and secure, she quickly attacked the second half. Finally, she twisted the ends together and secured the braids to her nape with a pair of tortoiseshell combs.

When Clayton still said nothing, only looked her over, just like she was the underbrush in the woods, she scooted to the edge of the bed, facing him. "I'm ready to listen."

He looked at her hands holding the hairbrush before speaking. "Ken Willoughby is now a pastor."

"Oh! Well, that is good news, isn't it? He seems like a nice man."

"He feels it would be a good idea if he married us."

Married? The brush slipped from her fingers, landing with a small plop on the white and baby blue wedding ring quilt. Surely she'd heard him wrong. "Married?"

Clayton looked uncomfortable. "I think he might be right."

There were a thousand reasons Pastor Willoughby was wrong. But instead of naming one, she gave into the words blaring loud inside her head. "We can't just get married!"

"We might have to."

Under no circumstances could she trap him to her for the rest of their lives. She'd never forgive herself. And, privately, she knew one other thing. She wasn't ready to be so close to any man. Whenever she closed her eyes, the first thing she ever saw was Price's beady eyes staring at her. The heat she'd spied in them scared her. His rough hands grabbing at her collar had been almost as hurtful as his belt had been. The other things he'd done—the things she didn't dare admit to Clayton, to herself—well, those images had branded her forever. She was sure she'd never be the same.

Strain formed around his eyes as she kept her silence. "I know it's not what you had planned, but the more I think on it, the more I think it's the right thing to do," he said, each word coming out stiff and plodding. "You need the protection of my name, Vanessa."

She already had his strength and his gun. "I'll be fine."

"If something happens to me, you won't be."

"Nothing's gonna happen to you." Even the thought of Clayton being injured made her feel dizzy and out of sorts.

"You never know. Plus, we can't run forever, Vanessa. If your stepfather finds you and has a mind to bring you back, we'll have no recourse."

"He's not going to find us." He couldn't. She knew she couldn't survive another episode like the one in her room. Well, she was sure she wouldn't want to.

"Sure he will." Harshly, Clayton added, "He married your mother for selfish reasons, Van. I asked around. Price spent quite some time looking for a big spread and a weak woman. I'm sorry to say that he found what he was looking for at the Circle Z. You were a bonus."

She didn't like to hear the things he was saying. "You were there. The hands looked to you for direction. I'm sure he's glad you're gone."

"It's not me I'm concerned about." Lowering his voice, he murmured, "Price is the type to hold tightly to anything that he even thinks might be his. You know I'm right."

Against her wishes, she did know. She shuddered at the memories. Never would she forget the sting of Price's belt or the harsh look of wanting in his eyes. "I can't go back to the Circle Z," she admitted. "Not while he's there."

He reached for her hand, calming her with his touch. "I know that, honey. As my wife, I'll make sure you never do. But . . . we need to make sure you'll never be forced to go."

The turn of events were startling cruel and more than a touch ironic. How many days, weeks, years had she imagined being Mrs. Clayton Proffitt? Of being curled in his arms on a porch swing? Of doing a hundred little things for him that only a wife could do?

In every instance, he'd been with her willingly. Romantically. Her childish daydreams had been filled with flowers and sweet words and happy-ever-afters. Not this. Never like this. There was only one thing to do, to admit one of her biggest fears. "I . . . don't want to trap you."

Eyes, so warm and tender, scanned every inch of her face, didn't look away. With a small smile, he said, "You wouldn't."

She didn't believe him. "How could you say such a thing?"

"I'm almost thirty years old. It's past time I married."

"To someone of your own choosing." Desperate, she said, "Send for Miles. He'll come help me. I know it."

Their hands still linked, he squeezed gently. "Miles won't come."

"You don't know that."

"I know how little he's done for you in the past, and I know how under your stepfather's thumb he is now. Even if he had the mind to help you, he couldn't. I honestly don't know if he has it in him to protect you. More likely, he'd inform Price of where you are and take him along."

"You don't know that for sure."

"I know that your brother's just aching for someone to notice him. This might be his opportunity to earn some respect—or whatever he's going to call it—from Price."

"That's a horrible thing to say. He's my brother."

"He is. He's not a child, but he acts like one. I was far younger when I was leading bands of men into battle."

"He hasn't had the opportunities—"

"He has. He hasn't chosen to take them. There's a difference. I don't want to be cruel, but I don't want to sugarcoat things. We don't have that luxury anymore." Shifting, he faced her fully and took her other hand. "Vanessa, a marriage between us would be right."

Her hands were warm in his.

A dozen images flashed before her. Images of being with Clayton, listening to him read his Bible. Praying by his side at church on Sundays. Laughing at his love for fried chicken and stewed greens. She knew him so well, had believed in him for so long. "Clayton—"

"Marry me."

This was every dream and every nightmare come true. Unable to help herself, she glanced at his lips, imagined the feeling of him kissing her, of his hands gliding across her shoulders, wrapping her in a warm hug.

Of the two of them doing so much more. Against her will, she shuddered.

With a creak of his knees, Clayton kneeled at her feet, once again showing her how much a man he was. No position could ever lower his innate dignity. Not even kneeling at her feet. "You'd do me proud if you would become my wife," he said quietly. "It would be my greatest honor to call myself your husband."

Vanessa's mind raced, just as her insides melted at the words.

Yes. She would be proud to be his wife. God surely had never produced a finer man. But she'd never forgive herself if she saw disappointment in his eyes or regret that things had turned out the way they had.

What if one day he found someone else? Someone better? Someone still innocent?

Clayton would take his vows to heart. He'd never consider leaving her for that person, but he'd feel the sting of regret, she was sure of it.

And how would it feel to know she'd trapped him? To know that she'd prevented him from loving, from following his heart? That knowledge would be just as sharp on her conscience as the sting of Price's abuse had been on her back.

And because she knew how sharp that sting went, far deeper than skin and flesh, she shook her head even though her heart was breaking. "Clayton, there's got to be another way."

"There isn't."

She knew he was right. It was just . . . did everything have to be so hard? She met his eyes again.

Still on his knees, he turned even more serious. "Vanessa, we've been alone on the trail for days now. You're a beautiful woman." He swallowed hard. "Desirable. Men will assume that I didn't leave you alone. They'll expect you to have been . . . used. Decent women won't associate with you. Honorable men won't treat you with respect."

Each word felt like a slap. Furthermore, Vanessa knew he was right. But still . . . she didn't care. "It doesn't matter."

"It does. Reputation always matters. I should have looked ahead. I should have thought about that, but all I thought about was getting you away." A shadow formed behind his eyes. "I should have thought about the consequences."

How could he? During the last three days, Clayton had seen to everything else—the horses, the trail, setting up camp. He'd even gone hunting and cooked a rabbit the night before.

His expression shuttered. "I know marriage to someone like me—a glorified ranch hand—isn't what you intended, but you don't need to worry. I'd never force myself on you. We could keep our relationship the same as it always was."

Her breath hitched. "Clay, what are you saying?"

He swallowed hard and finally looked away. "I'd keep myself—my needs—from you."

"I . . . are you sure?"

Curving one strong hand around her own, he linked his fingers through hers. "I'm very sure."

Just as she was about to rebut him again, she caught a peek of them in the mirror, Clayton kneeling, her hands in his. The sight was one she'd remember always; but their words were so far from the picture of them, with Clayton at her feet, she shook her head in wonder.

Who would have thought so much would change between them? Her heart loved him—yet a strange, scary voice in her head feared marriage. Clayton, too, looked torn between old wants and new responsibilities.

She dared to smile. "I guess neither of us knows what we want. Leastways, not anymore."

"I do. I want to care for you, Vanessa. I want to protect you with everything I am."

She wondered if there would come a time when that wouldn't be enough. For now she knew he was right. She couldn't go back and change her circumstances. She couldn't pretend that Price hadn't been in her room.

She couldn't deny the things he'd done. She never forget that he'd struck her—and that she'd be wearing those scars for a lifetime.

What they had was the present. That had to be enough. "All right. I will marry you . . . as long as we agree to rethink things when we get to your sister's."

"I won't need to do that, Van. My word is forever. You know that."

Forever was a long time. "But I might. I'll need a month, Clayton. A month to forget. And a month to pray, too."

He blinked. "All right, then."

Marriage. For a month. "After that time, if you still want me—"

"I always will. I promise you that, Van."

"Thank you."

"We'll say our vows within the hour." Clayton pulled away all too quickly and leapt to his feet. "I'll send Mary in. She said she'd bring a tub into the kitchen. I'll go change in the barn."

As Vanessa watched him walk away, she knew one thing for certain. Clayton Proffitt was the best man she knew.

She hoped she'd survive the moment when he realized that she wasn't the best woman for him.

❧

"Kind of chilly to be bathing with the horses."

Clayton figured the cold water would do him no harm, especially since he couldn't take his mind off the image of Vanessa soaking in warm water just feet away. "I'm fine."

Ken chuckled. "It's a strange position I'm finding myself in. Never thought I'd be one to ever give you advice, Captain."

Clayton knew it was pointless to remind Ken once again that he was no longer his captain. Old habits died hard from the war; they were intertwined in a way that prohibited a man from breaking those boundaries. If he did, it was like he was breaking so much of who he was. "You've done a fine job so far," he muttered sarcastically.

"I'm glad you feel that way." Ken handed over a shirt dyed blue. "Mary made this for me last month. I'd like to give it to you."

He raised an eyebrow. "For Vanessa's something blue? I never cottoned you to be so sentimental."

Ken grinned at the joke. "Doing the Lord's work has made me see a lot of things in a different light. Ain't no crime to think of sweet things every now and then."

"I'll take your word for that."

"Mary said your lady will be ready in a few minutes."

Clayton nodded as he wiped his face and slicked back his hair. "All right."

"The kids are caterwauling somethin' awful, they're so excited." He scuffed a patch of mud with the point of his boot. "I figure it's best we get started soon."

Clayton was beginning to get the feeling that there was a whole lot Ken was sidestepping around. But Ken had never been one to mince words before, so he merely nodded. "Tell Mary I'll be right in." He picked up the shirt Ken had laid on a post and shrugged into it, thankful Ken was as broad-shouldered as he was.

"Will do." Ken turned to walk away, then paused in mid-step. "Mary saw Vanessa's back."

There it was.

The red bandanna he'd just fished out of his saddlebag flew from his hands and floated to rest on his boots. Clayton bent down to retrieve it, doing his best to keep his emotions in check with effort. Not daring to look at Ken, he focused on how the red cotton was becoming more wrinkled in his hand by the second. "Are the cuts festering? She wouldn't let me look at them last night."

"They look to be healing. Well, more or less. They're fairly wide and deep, Mary said."

"I know."

Ken swallowed hard. "Just to let you know, Mary helped Vanessa clean the cuts and put some ointment on them."

"Tell her thank you. I . . . I should've tended to them better on the trail." Clayton tried to recall if he'd noticed her sitting or moving more stiffly than usual when she'd been brushing out her hair. He should've taken the time to think about that instead of wondering what those silken strands felt like.

"Don't know what you could have done, on the trail and all." Ken swallowed hard. "Anyway, Mary said she didn't know whether to hug Vanessa or act like she'd seen marks on a woman like that a dozen times before."

"I hope she hasn't."

"No, I don't reckon she has. Mary sure felt helpless, though. It's tough to see another person in pain."

"Yes, it is." Clayton knew the feeling. Quickly, he stuffed the bandana in his back pocket then concentrated on buttoning his new blue shirt, afraid to say a word. If he started, he'd likely say too much.

"Who did it, Clayton? What is his name?"

Clayton almost told Ken is was none of his business. But his earlier conversation with Vanessa stayed fresh in his mind. There was a very good chance her stepfather would try to find her. If he had a tracker, he might even locate Ken.

Ken should be prepared. "His name is Price Venture. He's a weasel of a man. Short, soft from easy living. Hard around the eyes. He's Vanessa's stepfather."

Ken's eyes turned to granite. "She all right?"

Clayton knew what he was asking. Grown men didn't whip their stepdaughters for no reason. "As well as she can be, I guess." Finally giving into his need to share the whole story, Clayton said, "She, uh, was beaten because she was fighting him. Price." Recalling her tears and her trembling brought his anger back full force. For about the hundredth time, Clayton wished it had been Price who'd stepped out into the hall instead of Miles or her mother.

Ken crossed himself.

Clayton reached for a cheroot from his saddlebag on the floor. After walking outside the barn, he hastily lit it, finding comfort in the action.

The cold, unvarnished truth was that Vanessa had almost been raped. He didn't know how he'd ever live with himself if she actually had been attacked.

Ken glanced toward the house. "Remember outside Galveston?"

Galveston! Just the name of the place made his stomach turn. "I remember." Clayton swallowed hard. About a mile outside a sporting house, he and his band of men had found a young girl, beaten and dying. She'd been abducted, used, and discarded by a gang of soldiers fresh from battle. Her shoulder had hung at a wrong angle.

She'd cried and wept when he'd knelt next to her, hardly aware of his promises that he merely wanted to help. When he'd knelt and reached for her arm, to try and help her sit up, she'd kicked and screamed like she was on fire. He'd held himself still, almost welcoming the pain she'd brought. It matched the pain in his heart at her sight.

He'd looked helplessly at Ken. At the rest of his men, who'd stood a respectful distance away. Each had instinctively known that more than one man holding her down would likely send her over the edge.

There, in the alley, in the hot muggy South Texas heat, Clayton had prayed for help, prayed for guidance, prayed for the girl who fought him so fearfully.

Clayton had been crying himself as he'd attempted to cajole her to listen. To settle so he could help set her arm. Find her help. To locate another woman to take her on home.

But it had been too late. She'd died in the struggle, died in his arms.

Her death still weighed on his conscience, and rightly so.

"This—this what you're doing . . . it's the right thing."

Clayton knew what Ken meant. But it was also far different. His feelings about Vanessa were far from pity. Instead, what he really wanted was to take her somewhere secluded and coax her with his kisses, to introduce her to a man's tender touch, to show her that words could mean as much as a hasty kiss or clumsy grope.

But those things were not what she needed, either. "I care for Vanessa."

"I know. It's obvious from the way you look at her. But— even if you didn't—"

Clayton knew. Even if he didn't, there was a girl up in heaven who'd had no one. "Even if I didn't . . . I'd marry her, Ken." Recalling he was a preacher, he turned to Ken. "Is that wrong?"

"I hope not, because I'd do the same thing."

5

$\mathcal{A}$s the Circle Z faded into the distance, Miles adjusted his weight in the saddle and tried to pretend he wasn't scared. But it did no good. He was in over his head and barely able to breathe.

"It's good of you to accompany me, boy," Price said from his own saddle on the left. "You're going to be needed when we locate your sister."

"Yes sir."

"I could wring Vanessa's neck for the trouble she's cost me. Cost our family."

Our family? That was a laugh. Price Venture might be married to his mother, he might be running the Circle Z to the ground, he might be trying to father Miles, but he'd never be part of the Grant family.

Even more importantly, Miles knew Price would never replace his real pa. His father had been a man of character, a man who'd protected his mother, cherished his sister, and had hinted that even a boy like Miles had a chance of being a man.

No, Price was nothing like his father.

"When I get my hands on that girl, I'll make sure she's sorry for her actions," Price continued. "She'll mind, then. No doubt about that."

Now that—that there was the truth. Miles knew without a doubt that if they found Vanessa, his sister would be punished severely. His stepfather would have vengeance so heavy on his mind, there'd be little way anyone would be able to reason with him.

Miles knew it was going to take everything he had to keep Price from getting anywhere near Vanessa.

From the moment his stepfather had woken with a hangover, a dark cloud had descended on the Circle Z. Insinuations about Clayton's integrity and Vanessa's character had been thrown about so harshly, Miles had been unable to stem any of the gossip.

Clayton's room had been ransacked. Price destroyed everything of Clayton's that he couldn't take, use, or sell. Vanessa's room had been next, Price being so sure that he would find a note or some kind of clue detailing their plans to run off together.

Yes, that had been the sorriest thing that Price had done. He'd acted as if he'd done nothing to warrant Vanessa's departure. And no one besides Miles and his ma knew better.

To his shame, Miles hadn't tried to correct the man's slander. He was afraid of Price, and that was a fact. Ever since the man had started eying his mother, Miles had done his best to stand aside and fade into the woodwork whenever Price was near.

And it had been possible, because Clayton had taken the brunt of Price's abusive tongue. Miles pretended to listen when Price gave orders. That habit had become almost second nature. It was far easier to do nothing, to just watch and wait to see what Price would do.

But wasn't that what he'd always done? Watched and waited and hoped things would get better? Or hoped to get noticed? Praised?

Accepted?

Yes, indeed. Oh, he'd tried to get along with Price. He'd even accompanied him to the saloons in Camp Hope. He'd even been with a woman or two because Price had praised him for it. But inside, Miles had felt empty.

After the hunt for clues had given them no answers, Price had contacted the sheriff. Sheriff Vance, being a fair man, had formed a posse and led a team of men north, in just the direction Miles had directed them to. That lie had been the first time Miles had ever gone against Price's will.

That wild goose chase ended with some old-timer mentioning he thought he'd seen Vanessa and Clayton out by Camp Hope.

Now Miles and Price were heading west. The trip was being bankrolled by Clayton's savings.

As the sun beat down on their shoulders and the horses picked their way along the rocky trail once used by gold seekers and Indians, Miles felt as if his whole life was tied to this one adventure.

He didn't know where to turn or who to turn to. All his life, he'd sought acceptance but had never achieved it. His own pa had never counted on him for anything.

For a time, Miles had hoped Clayton might give him more responsibility. After all, the Circle Z was his birthright, not Clayton's. Those dreams had faded away, too.

Now, Clayton blamed him for his stepfather's actions.

It wasn't fair, but it wasn't completely off mark, either. After all, Miles had heard the snap of Price's belt against Vanessa. And he'd hurt for her, and burned with shame that he was letting her get used.

But he'd been so terribly glad that it hadn't been him. He'd been so thankful that it wasn't his back feeling the sting of Price's belt. Again.

"Your mother's gonna worry herself sick about that good-for-nothing girl," Price called out sometime later.

"I hope not." The last image Miles had had of his mother hadn't been a good one. She'd hardly bathed or gotten dressed in days. She'd also begun to find comfort in Price's whiskey.

"Girl's nothing but a Jezebel," Price continued. "Searching for her is going to cost me more money than she's worth. But I'll make her pay."

Miles felt bile churn in his stomach as his weakness bit at him from deep inside. He didn't know what to do. He'd promised Clayton that he'd keep Price away from Vanessa—and he had. It was because of him that the posse went north in the first place. It wasn't his fault they'd gotten an experienced tracker to go along with them, was it?

He'd never thought that Price would be counting on him to help with the search. But he had. Other, deeper worries plagued him also. Life at the Circle Z was all he knew. It was his birthright; it was his home.

A spare, niggling thought pinched his conscience sorely, and that was simply the God's honest truth. Vanessa and Clayton had taken off. There was a real possibility that they might never be found. There were a lot of places to hide in the world.

What if he and Price never did locate the two of them? Miles would be left with only his relationship with Price and his life at the ranch for comfort. It went without saying that his mother wouldn't do a thing for either of them.

It scared him something awful to jeopardize everything he had. If he lost his value to Price, what would he do then? Life was hard enough without trying to go it alone. And that's how he would be—alone. There was no one else in his life to follow.

Resentment brewed in his gut. Resentment at the whole situation, and at Clayton and Vanessa. If Vanessa hadn't been so pretty, Price would never have looked twice at her. If Clayton hadn't gotten his priorities all twisted and turned, he would've remembered that his responsibilities should have been centered on the ranch, not Vanessa.

Boy, Miles could only imagine what his pa was thinking now. Most likely he was twisting and turning around in his grave. Miles knew he shouldn't have given the majority of his spending money to Clayton and Vanessa. If he hadn't, they probably would've already come back by now.

As it was, things were terrible, terrible indeed. He was stuck by Price's side in the middle of nowhere. Surely, his only hope was to delay their journey west as much as possible. Then he'd have more time to think. Then, maybe Clayton would come to his senses and return home and things could go back to the way they were.

As the faded glory of Camp Hope loomed in the distance, Price's eyes lit up. "I'm feeling a mite parched, boy. We might as well make a stop for a spell."

Camp Hope was as good as place as any to waste a few hours. "Yes sir."

Price increased the pace. "Maybe Angelina will be working. She knows how to make a man feel welcome, I'll give her that."

Miles squinted into the sun and dutifully followed, wondering what he was going to do while his stepfather visited the rooms up above the Dark Horse Saloon. His horse Jericho pranced a bit, obviously anticipating a break soon. Jericho was surely the laziest horse Miles had ever had the misfortune to meet.

Price looked back over his shoulder. "Boy? You eating dust? Get on, now. Time's a wastin'—we ain't got all day."

"No sirree, we sure don't," Miles said with a sigh, just as he realized that he'd never that the gumption to ask his stepfather call him by his name instead of "boy."

He'd never had the ability to make decisions and earn the respect of the cowhands—they'd only followed his orders when Clayton stood behind him.

Obviously, he was still too scared to fight; still too scared to try a little harder to be his own man.

It tried a man's soul to realize that he was not nearly the person he'd thought he'd be. Especially when he thought he might never become that person. Not ever.

✒

Clayton didn't know how Mary had done it, but by the time their wedding came around, the kitchen was filled with tasty treats. She'd also lent Vanessa a yellow gown with lace at the neckline and cuffs. The garment set off her honey-colored hair and brightened her cheeks.

Clayton thought Vanessa had never looked more beautiful.

Her eyes were shiny with excitement when he approached, making him realize once again that their wedding had been meant to be. "Clayton, you wore blue."

"Just for you, ma'am." Cupping her elbow, he stepped forward. "You look mighty fine."

Just like a bluebonnet after a spring storm, her cheeks bloomed. "Thank you."

"So, you ready for this?" His words were serious but he took care to make sure his tone was light and sweet.

"I am." She nodded, treating him to a tremulous smile that he felt through to his core.

Please help me, Lord, he prayed. *Please walk with me and help me. Please help me make the right decisions and not look back with doubts.*

His prayer for guidance felt uncomfortable and almost new. With some dismay, Clayton realized that while he'd often spent many a night reading the good book, he hadn't reached out to the Lord so freely and with such hope for some time. Maybe not since the war, when he'd had men in his care and had felt overwhelmed at times with the responsibility.

Perhaps the Lord had had many reasons for bringing him and Vanessa to Ken's. Obviously, he'd needed reminding of his faith, of the One who always watched over him and guided him.

"We walk by faith, not by sight," said Paul in 2 Corinthians. That would surely be something he needed to remember as he and Vanessa continued on their journey.

Ken cleared his throat from the next room. "You two about ready? Me and Mary won't be able to keep the kids settled much longer."

"I'm ready," Vanessa said.

Clayton knew he was, too. It was time, time to go forward with no regrets. It was what a man did, especially a man who walked hand in hand with the Lord. The sooner they were married, the better. Taking Vanessa's arm, he led her back into the sparsely decorated great room, where just hours ago Vanessa had been lying down on the floor. "Where do you want us, Ken?"

"Over here!" Lanie said, running to the front of the room. With little fanfare, she shoved a bouquet of daisies into Vanessa's hands. "Petey and me picked these from the field behind the barn. They're for you."

"They're beautiful," Vanessa murmured. "Thank you."

"You're welcome," Pete replied, looking pleased with himself. "We got lots right now."

"Then I'm very lucky," Vanessa replied as Ken positioned them in front of the fire.

"Dearly beloved," he began, then proceeded to lead them through the ceremony with a litany of simple and familiar language.

In spite of his earlier intentions to keep Vanessa at a distance, to marry her in name only, Clayton found himself believing the words, praying with Ken, and meaning each vow.

By Vanessa's luminescent glow, she seemed to be feeling the same way.

And though they had no rings, though love had never been spoken, when Ken pronounced them man and wife, Clayton knew he'd just stepped over the boundary of bachelorhood forever. He was married now. He belonged to Vanessa, and she was his. No matter what happened in the future, he knew he would never forsake those vows they'd made before God.

Gently, Clayton squeezed both of Vanessa's hands, feeling more uplifted and lighter in spirit than he had since days before Vanessa's attack. Ken had been right to push for this. He'd been right to plead with Vanessa to agree to matrimony. Even if Price came, even if he died tomorrow, Vanessa would now be safe, and that was all that really mattered.

After a moment of expected silence, the children giggled.

"Yes?" Vanessa asked, obviously confused.

"Um, this is where you kiss your bride, Captain," Ken said after waiting a beat or two.

Startled, Clayton looked to his wife. Her green eyes were wide. Expectant. "Oh. Yes, of course," he said, willing himself to lean closer and not think.

But unfortunately, it felt as if another man held his shoulders and wouldn't let him move.

✿

Oh. Yes, of course?

This was surely a mistake! Vanessa felt like sinking to the floor, she was so embarrassed. As the seconds passed, and Clayton looked at her, scanning her face as if searching for something, her heart just about beat out of her chest.

What was wrong? What was wrong with the idea of kissing her? What didn't Clayton see that he'd hoped to?

As the silence lengthened, Vanessa's stomach churned. Perhaps she should let Clayton know that he didn't have to kiss her, that although she'd meant every word she said, she knew that for him, the ceremony didn't mean a thing.

But no words came forth.

"Come on, Captain," Petey called out. "Kiss her!"

As if he was scared she was going to bolt, Clayton cupped her shoulders and lowered his head. He paused when his lips were just inches away.

His scent wafted closer, soap and tobacco, and all Clayton. Heat.

A little jolt came hammering out of nowhere; spurring her on, making her breathless. A little shiver of anticipation rolled through her, catching her so suddenly, she had to struggle not to shake.

But he still noticed. "It's okay, sugar," he whispered, bussing her cheek.

Lanie groaned. "Captain, don't you know anything? You're supposed to kiss her on the lips!"

Vanessa was half aware of Mary chuckling nervously as she shushed her daughter. Vaguely aware of Ken acting like forced marriages in his parlor happened all the time. There was only one thing to do. Quickly, she rose on her toes and brushed his lips with hers.

It was done.

As if to steady her, he gripped her shoulders. Snaked an arm around her waist, pulling her near. The fabric of his blue shirt brushed against the lace of her yellow satin gown.

And then Clayton lowered his lips to hers once again. When their lips touched again, his gentle pressure made her move her head to meet his better. Slowly, like he was imprinting the action in his mind. Tasting her, making her feel like they were truly united. It was the kiss of her dreams and of her hopes.

When they stepped aside, Mary had tears in her eyes. Ken looked pleased. The children launched themselves at her, though Clayton stopped one from grabbing her from behind.

Yes, they were married. For better or worse. Not until death would they part.

Later that evening, when the wedding festivities had settled down and the roast chicken had been eaten and the dishes had been washed and put away, Clayton called himself ten times a fool. Only a loon wouldn't have seen the gleam in Ken's eye during dinner when he got to talking about someplace private for the newlyweds.

Only a fool would keep his mouth shut when Ken escorted Vanessa and him to the barn and pointed up a sturdy wooden ladder that was half propped, half nailed to the walls of a loft. "This here is our gift to you, Mr. and Mrs. Proffitt. We thought y'all would surely appreciate a little bit of privacy tonight."

Vanessa visibly paled.

Clayton glared. "This isn't necessary."

"Sure it is, Clayton. Don't you worry about a thing. It's nice and warm in that loft. I've slept there a time or two myself when we were building the house." He winked. "Mary will bring y'all out some coffee in the morning, just like in one of those fancy hotels in Kansas City."

"Thank you. That's . . . that's real kind of you both. Convey my thanks to Mary."

"Will do." Ken backed out two steps. "So, I'll be going now. I'm going to close the main door, too. Don't worry about the horses down here in the stalls. Pete already fed and watered them; they won't be needing attention until morning."

Two minutes later, with a cloud of dust, the barn door shut, dimming what natural light filtered the space.

"I'm sorry, Van. I didn't plan on this."

"Of course you didn't. It is sweet though, don't you think?"

Sweet had never been a defining characteristic of Ken Willoughby. "It's something." Popping his hat back on his head, he motioned to the ladder. "I suppose we best go on up."

"Yes."

Rung by rung, Clayton helped her climb the ladder, staying securely behind her in case a foot tripped on her skirt or a hand lost its grip. Once they made it to the top, Vanessa peered over. "Oh, my!"

"What?"

A dash of humor filled her eyes as she scrambled onto the loft. "You'll see."

Suddenly, he did indeed see. Clayton felt his cheeks heat and change different colors as he spied their marriage bed—all six feet of it.

Luckily, the loft was high enough for them both to stand up straight, though Clayton did need to remove his hat for comfort. The large bed looked to be made of straw or cornhusks or both. Down-filled comforters made of white cotton flannel lay on top. In the corner, under a sloping window, was a small table with a ewer of water, a dish, and a fluffy white towel.

A rag rug circled the floor. The only place to sit was on the massive bed.

"This isn't what I'd had in mind when I asked Ken if we could have a little privacy," Clayton admitted, sitting next to her on the surprisingly firm mattress. "I just wanted some time to speak with you and make sure you were all right. Those pesky children of theirs kept following you around, asking you a hundred questions." Picking up the edge of the quilt that Mary or Ken had draped over the corner of their make-shift bed, he shook his head. "I never dreamed Ken and Mary would plan something like this."

To his surprise, Vanessa chuckled. "I hope not, Clayton. Otherwise, I'm sure I'd be really confused about your intentions toward me."

Clayton loosened the collar of his brand-new blue shirt. Already those intentions seemed like a foolhardy idea. How was he going to keep himself away from her, especially now that she was his for a lifetime? "I promise you I didn't—"

She chuckled again, silencing his words with her mirth. Reaching out, she squeezed his arm. "Hush. I know." As if she'd lain down beside him all the time, Vanessa slowly eased backward, taking care to rest on her side. Her skirts pouffed out as she did so; the feminine rustle mixing with the crunch of the cornhusks underneath brought forth a smile.

"This gown was Mary's wedding dress," she murmured. "Lainie sure does love it so. She must have told me ten times if she told me once that she couldn't wait to be a real bride."

She did look pretty. Had he thought to tell her? Clayton murmured, "Isn't wearing something lacy and frilly every girl's dream? Corrine told me that often enough." A flash of his sister on her wedding day came to mind. With some sadness, Clayton recalled that she hadn't worn anything fancy on that day. No, she'd only had on the same old, threadbare dress she'd worn the day before. 'Course, Merritt hadn't minded one bit.

"Maybe all girls dream of such things; I'm not sure." Vanessa said, bringing him back to the present. "I did feel special, though. This dress is as lovely as anything I've ever owned." A winsome smile played across her lips as she closed her eyes, effectively stopping their conversation.

But that didn't stop Clayton from wondering what she was thinking. This day had hardly been anyone's dream. A shotgun wedding in a borrowed dress to a man she didn't love, then forced to spend the night above a pair of roans in a dusty barn. No amount of quilts and pretty dresses could change things.

No amount of sweet words or heartfelt apologies could change how things were. No regrets could change the way things might have been.

As the sun sank and twilight faded the gilded glow and lengthened the shadows around them, Clayton reached for a match, struck it against the sole of his boot, then lit the kerosene lamp that was stored next to the washstand.

As the flickering glow replaced the fading shadows, he considered their situation.

This was their circumstance; it couldn't be changed. But even if their wedding wasn't one of little girls' dreams, Clayton felt that there'd had been times during the day that he'd never forget. Dinner had been hearty and filled with conversation. Ken and Mary had entertained them with stories about their engagement and marriage, delighting the children and reminding Clayton that they were both lucky to have survived the war. So many good men had not.

Vanessa had sat by his side and looked almost carefree. She'd laughed more in the last hour than in the past week.

Now, hoping to ease the tension that was almost tangible between them, he murmured, "Vanessa, honey, you do look beautiful."

Her eyes popped open, pleasure rising from their depths. "Thank you."

As if she knew the train of his thoughts, she murmured, "Mary spoke with me right before I joined you and Ken. She uh, offered to answer any questions I might have."

Surely Vanessa was practiced at torture. Why else would she even think to bring that up? "What did you say?"

"I hope you won't mind . . . I said you'd already talked to me."

She shifted uncertainly, the movement rustling her petticoats and the husks underneath them. "Are you mad? I . . . didn't have the heart to tell her that I wouldn't need to know anything for quite a while. And after Price . . . " She swallowed. "I'm afraid I couldn't think about it."

Her expectant pause forced him to speak. "I'm not mad."

Settling against the mattress again, Vanessa hugged a pillow as she balanced on her side. Looking into the shadows, she whispered, "Mama never told me much. I wish she had."

"That's okay."

"I don't know why she never did."

Marilyn never had been one for thinking ahead—or for thinking about Vanessa. "I guess she thought you had some time."

"I guess so. It is a shame that she wasn't here. I never thought she wouldn't watch me get married."

She sounded winsome. Unable to help himself, Clayton wrapped an arm around Vanessa and pulled her close so her back wouldn't be pressed against the mattress. As she sighed and situated herself, Clayton pretended he was back at the Circle Z and hugging her like he'd done when she'd gotten stung by a mess of angry hornets out in the pecan grove.

Yes, that was how he was holding her. Almost in a brotherly way.

However, he'd never felt anything less than brotherly. He'd never before been so aware of her presence. Had never had her head resting on his shoulder or her delicate palm lying flat on his heart. He'd never noticed that she smelled like spring jasmine silky powder. Fresh and clean and perfect.

All visions of doctoring hornet stings vanished in an instant.

"This feels kind of strange, doesn't it?" she murmured.

At least that, he could answer honestly. "It does."

"I thought I'd be scared, sitting like this with you, but I'm not." She shifted, moving one hand a little closer to his shoulder. Her hip brushed his side. "I'm glad I'm not scared." Eyelashes fluttered in embarrassment. "I'm sorry I'm so much trouble."

He had to touch her. Gently brushing hair from her cheek, he murmured, "Don't worry. Please don't worry about a thing. Everything's going to be all right." He forced himself to say the words though he didn't know how to make them true. How would he support her? Where would they live? How could he ever come to terms with the fact that her pa had asked him to look out for her—as her guardian. Marriage had never even been considered.

She yawned. "You sound so sure."

Knowing she needed her sleep, Clayton relaxed as much as he could with Vanessa practically lying on top of him. "I'm glad I sound sure."

What would she do weeks or months from now, when gratitude wasn't clouding her thoughts? When the danger of being hunted by her stepfather wasn't on their minds?

When the terrible, awful memories of Price's hand had faded? What would they do then? She'd have her eye on someone younger, someone more suitable, and she'd be trapped with him—a man too old who'd seen too much.

"We should probably get to sleep. Morning comes early."

She sat up and pulled away. "Yes. I best change out of Mary's gown, too. I'll ruin it otherwise."

Clayton stood up, anxious to put some space between them. Now that he really thought about it, he was thinking that there wasn't really all that much room on that mattress. In fact, it was likely that when they both lay down, mere inches would separate them. "I could sleep down below, Van."

"Below?"

"With the horses. It won't be a hardship. I've slept in worse places."

"I couldn't sleep with you down there."

He gestured to the rug. "Or this would be fine."

"Don't be silly, Clayton," Vanessa said over her shoulder as she started to unbutton her gown. "We've been together on the trail."

He supposed that was true. "I'm so tired anyway, I bet I won't move."

"Me, neither. And no more talk about going down and sleeping with the horses. I don't want to be up here alone."

"There's a slew of quilts so I guess we won't be too cold." He figured one could rest between them while they slept.

"I imagine we'll be just fine."

He could no longer delay the inevitable. "Well, then . . . I guess we best get settled." He unbuttoned his shirt, then his denims, taking care to hang each piece on the nails lining the wall. Clad only in the bottoms of his long johns, he crawled under the blankets.

After a pause, Vanessa continued to unfasten the long row of buttons down her front. Suddenly, shy, she turned her back to him as she slipped the gown off.

Unable to help himself, he glanced at her back. Though she was clad in a long white camisole and petticoat, his eyes only looked for her injury. Even in the dim candlelight he could spy the marks on her back. Sure enough, the welts were still there, angry and bright red. Purple bruises had formed around the cuts. Highlighting the trouble they'd seen. Reminding Clayton once again that while they may pretend their marriage was an easy one, there were a number of undefined aspects to their relationship.

"I have some ointment. You want more on your back?" He swallowed as he heard how his voice sounded more husky than usual. As God as his witness, he did not want to run his fingers along her skin again.

But as true as that was, he also couldn't seem to think of anything else.

"No." She slipped a nightgown over her head. "Mary slathered quite a bit on me. If you don't mind, I don't want to think of those cuts right now. Not tonight."

No, not on her wedding night.

Together, they reached the bed. After Vanessa eased down and finally rested on her side, he doused the candle and lay beside her.

Below them, the horses blew out air and shifted, causing the worn oak planks that comprised the barn to creak and moan.

A faint burst of air wafted through a chink in the mud that Ken had used to seal some of the biggest gaps in the walls.

In some ways, sleeping in a barn was harder than sleeping outside. It gave the illusion of warmth, but the reality was that it was almost as chilly as the night air outside. Plus, they had no fire to warm them up.

Vanessa shifted by his side, huddled onto the hard mattress. "It's cold."

Clayton curled his toes, hoping to warm them up. "It is. Would it be shameful to admit I miss sleeping near a fire?"

"I hope not, because I was thinking that, too. I wouldn't have minded sleeping on their parlor floor."

"They wanted to give us privacy for tonight. I had to accept, Van. Everyone needs to think that this is a real marriage."

"It is. And one day it will be." Vanessa shivered.

Clayton wondered if she shivered from the thought of a real wedding night or if she was thinking once again of Price's pain.

No matter what, he wanted to comfort her. "If we lie closer, the heat will warm us both. Come here, honey."

Gingerly, she laid her head on his shoulder again, against his heart. Little by little her heat mixed with his, offering him solace as well as the knowledge that one day, perhaps, she'd lie against him in a far different manner, her soft skin inviting his touch.

That idea, along with Vanessa's sweet form next to him, made Clayton realize that sleep was not going to come. How could it when all he could think about was their future—the marriage he'd promised himself he'd give her?

There was no way he was going to be able to sleep a wink. More to the point, there was no way he could go through another night of sharing a bed with Vanessa. Even though her eyes had drifted closed, he murmured, "Van, maybe we should leave tomorrow. This bed, being with you like this, I'm not real comfortable, if you want to know the truth."

"Oh. Of course, Clayton. Whatever you think best. I . . . I feel the same way."

Clayton pretended he didn't notice that regret tinged her words. Just as he pretended he never wished things could be different.

Price's hands were on her again. "Stop!" she cried, thrashing against his weight.

"Vanessa!"

She twisted her hips. Screamed again when rough fingers tore at her skirts. Tore at her petticoat. She knew what was to come. Flinching, she fought to escape.

"Van. Vanessa!"

In a panic, she opened her eyes. The room was dark. She was trapped.

"Vanessa, honey, wake up."

Two arms curved around her. Held her close, so close that if she tried hard enough, she knew she could pretend she was hidden.

"Shh. Shh. It's all right."

Slowly, she opened her eyes again as she breathed deep. Little by little, she recognized the scent. Clayton.

It was Clayton who held her. Not Price. She was in Clay's arms; he was holding her close. Wiping the tears from her cheeks.

She'd been dreaming. Struggling for control, she pulled away.

He let her go, but never looked away. "Are you all right? You're shaking like a leaf."

She wasn't all right. She felt nauseous and sick. Everything she'd tried so hard to push away was scaring her, preventing her from catching her breath. "I . . . I was dreaming about Price."

"Oh, honey." Ever so slowly, he opened his arms to her again. He offered security and comfort. And, like last night, he offered warm memories of him making everything better. Wrapping an arm around her, he held her close. Pressing his lips to her brow, he rocked her like a child. She let him.

"It's over, remember? He can't hurt you again. I promise you, sugar, he'll never touch you again."

"It felt so real."

"It was just a dream."

But it had been more than that. For a brief time, it had been her only reality.

Little by little, she became more aware of her surroundings. Of Clayton's bay rum and tobacco scent. Of how fresh and clean the quilts felt around them. Of the coolness of the night.

As the air cleared a bit and she became more aware of the faint sound of the horses below, of the howling wind outside, she relaxed a bit. She was with Clayton. He would protect her. Just as he always had.

"I wonder what brought this on?" he murmured after a few moments. "Have you been having these dreams all the time and I've been sleeping through them?"

"No." Some memories had clawed at her while riding, but she'd firmly pushed them away. But this was the first time that she'd dreamed of Price, dreamed of what had really happened, and hadn't been able to push those thoughts away.

After a moment or two, he pressed his lips to her brow again. "Sometimes talking about things can make them better, Van," he said quietly. "You know, you didn't tell me much that night. Maybe it would be better if you talked about what happened."

"No."

He shifted so they faced each other. "I've had my share of bad nightmares, Van. During the war, I saw things. . . . I did things for which I'm not proud. Nothing you could say would shock me."

Vanessa knew better. If Clayton knew what had really happened, he would be far worse than shocked. He'd never look at her the same.

And she couldn't face that. To see that knowledge in his eyes every time they came in contact with each other would be more than she could bear.

Almost worse than reliving Price's attack again. The pain. The horrible, horrible feeling of helplessness under his weight.

She'd almost been glad for his belt.

"I can't talk about it, Clayton. I'm sorry."

After a moment's pause, he nodded, then climbed out of bed. "I understand." With methodical movements, he slipped on his boots and denims. "Dawn's about to break. I'm going to go check on the horses. You go back to sleep, sweetheart."

Panic rushed forth. "Clay—"

"I'll just be down the ladder. I promise. Close your eyes and try to get some sleep, sugar. We'll leave in a few hours."

To her shame, when she was finally alone, the tears came again. Silently, she cried. Muffling her sobs with her fist. Little by little, exhaustion overtook her. As long as Clayton never knew the truth, they would be all right.

As long as they never talked about things, she could pretend they didn't happen. Almost.

Their hasty departure was met with confusion from Mary and a too knowledgeable look from Ken.

"Why don't you stay longer, Clayton?" Mary asked while they were finishing up their breakfast of biscuits and eggs. "The trail to Colorado will still be there in a week or two. Besides, Vanessa and I've hardly gotten to know each other."

After a pause, Clayton replied. "Thank you, Mary, but we were thinking it might be best if we moved on."

Everyone glanced at Vanessa, and she could feel her cheeks heat. Mary had brought out a carafe of coffee to the barn early that morning. After placing it and two thick mugs on a small table, she called up to them that she was leaving it, then hurried back to the house. She hadn't known that Clayton was in one of the back stalls organizing their gear.

Moments later, just as Vanessa had been sitting up, he'd carried her up a mug of coffee. She'd accepted it gratefully but had been afraid to meet his gaze. Yet again, their relationship had turned again. Her dream had reminded them both just how extreme their situation was.

They weren't together because they'd fallen in love. They were married and on the run because she'd been attacked. The last thing they needed was to pretend everything was just fine in front of the Willoughbys.

But, oh, how she was going to miss their snug house and the soft feather comforters. She was certainly going to miss being clean and off of her horse.

Just as importantly, Vanessa knew she would have also enjoyed getting to know Mary. She'd had precious few women friends over the years, ranch life being what it was. Vanessa would have enjoyed the companionship as well as the many things she was sure Mary could teach her about running a home and raising a family.

"We do thank you for your hospitality," Clayton added. "And, of course, for the wedding ceremony."

Ken picked up a formal-looking slip of paper that he'd placed on a sideboard. "I almost forgot. Here's your marriage certificate."

Without unfolding it, Clayton slipped it in his broadcloth's pocket. They finished the rest of their meal in almost silence. An hour later, their saddlebags were packed and Coco and Lee were ready.

"I hope we'll meet again," Vanessa said to Mary after she'd hugged Sam, Lanie, and Pete good-bye.

"I hope the same. And I'll pray for you, dear, and hope your trip continues safely. I'll pray for you and Clayton, too." Mary whispered in her ear, "I have a feeling you two are going to do just fine together."

"I hope so," Vanessa said before saying good-bye to Ken.

Then, just as the sun gleamed a broad morning glow across the prairie, Clayton helped Vanessa mount Coco, then led the way back to the trail. Coco pranced a bit, looking refreshed and eager to be on her way.

As they meandered to the valley, then proceeded west, miles passed until the Willoughby's impressive home faded into the distance. As a hawk flew overhead, the cool breeze turned heated, and the man next to her became ever more vigilant, Vanessa only knew one thing for certain. A certificate in his pocket tied them together. So had their vows. For better or worse, they were man and wife.

But inside, she felt as alone and confused as ever.

6

*T*en days later they arrived in Santa Fe. The town's streets were parched and dusty. Tall, two-armed cacti dotted the outskirts, their brilliant green silhouettes standing vigilantly like soldiers. In the distance, snow covered the mountains.

"I thought we'd stay in a hotel tonight," Clayton said as he nodded to a band of vaqueros keeping watch near the worn faded wood fronting an old boarding house. "Sleeping in a room with four walls instead of the open air will be a welcome change."

"Sleeping in a bed sounds like heaven," Vanessa admitted, eyeing other stucco-covered buildings with interest, fascinated with how their colors mingled with the hues of the earth and how their interiors looked cozy and comfortable.

Almost every day they'd ridden for hours, rising at sunrise, dismounting at sunset. With the exception of two of the days, when they'd only ridden three or four hours in order for the horses to rest, she and Clayton had stopped only to rest and water the horses.

Their pace was so hard, Vanessa sometimes wondered if Clayton was rushing to his sister or running from her stepfather.

Vanessa wasn't sure what guided their pace. Now that the searing memories of Price's attack were fading, she felt more confused than ever. Had the Lord brought her and Clayton together for love and marriage, or for her protection, as he seemed to think?

She began to have small, quiet doubts about everything they'd left behind, too. Maybe things wouldn't have been all that bad if she'd stayed. Maybe her mother and Miles would've eventually helped her stand up to Price.

Maybe things would've just been better if everything had stayed the same. Of course, there was no use wishing for what could have been. Nothing in their lives would ever be like it used to be. They were on a journey—one that circumstances had foisted on them. More than anything, they needed to see it through to the end. They needed to trust in God and pray that they'd understand His will.

As they made their way through the streets of Santa Fe, Vanessa hoped to see those signs from God, letting her know that everything was happening just as it should. She'd feel better if she was reassured that He was leading them in the right direction.

She looked around the bustling town expectantly, hoping for something, anything, to signal reassurance. But all she saw were men and women going about their business.

"We'll stop right here, at this general store," Clayton murmured, just moments before pulling on Lee's reins. "We need some supplies."

Vanessa hurried to halt Coco as well.

Two boys about fourteen years old hurried to greet them at the livery. "Ma'am. Sir," the shortest one said, tipping his floppy straw hat.

Clayton threw them both a coin. "Rub down the horses, then take our bags to the hotel."

"Yes sir."

After Vanessa rearranged her skirts, she clasped Clayton's forearms as he swung her out of the saddle. "Yes, I sure will enjoy a bath tonight," she declared brightly, hoping he wouldn't see the hurt she felt when he stepped away from her the moment her boots touched ground. What had happened to the tangles of awareness that had been strung between them the night in the Willoughby's barn? "And to wash my hair."

"I'm ready to shave with warm water," he admitted, leading her inside the mercantile. "My cheeks will thank me, I believe."

The front face of the store was made of reddish clay bricks. Its architecture was intriguing, though it was hardly bigger than a line shack at the Circle Z.

After a moment, they were greeted immediately by a man dressed in black from head to toe.

"Clayton Proffitt," the somewhat rotund proprietor said, flashing a grin. "Never thought I'd set eyes on you again."

Clayton laughed. "I was thinking just the opposite about you, Hank. I'd hoped you'd still be here." For the first time in two days, he curved a hand around Vanessa's waist, bringing her closer to him. "Please meet Vanessa, my wife."

"Mrs. Proffitt," Hank nodded, his gaze full of frank appreciation.

"How do you do?" Vanessa asked, hardly aware of anything except for Clayton's touch—and his introduction. This was the first time she'd heard herself referred to as Mrs. Proffitt. The title felt right.

When he ran his hand down her arm, finally linking her fingers with his own, Vanessa once again felt a pull toward him that had nothing to do with friendship and everything to do with the memories of his kiss on their wedding day.

"I do fine, real fine," Hank replied before turning to Clayton. "Didn't know you got yerself hitched, Captain. It's a big country, but I still manage to hear things from time to time."

"Our marriage, it was a recent thing."

"Well, ain't that something? That's even better! Congratulations."

"Thank you," Vanessa replied, though she couldn't help but notice that Clayton looked uncomfortable.

After clearing his throat, he released her hand. "Honey, you want to look around for a spell?"

"Of course," she said with a smile. Though the store was small, it looked to be packed with treasures, and it was toasty warm. After miles and miles of staring at vast open spaces, the cramped mercantile was a welcome change.

※

Clayton forced himself to turn away from his wife when he noticed Hank regarding him with a bemused expression. "So. Did you ever marry again, Hank?"

"Nope. After Penny, no woman seemed like a right fit." He shrugged. "Besides, women are hard to come by here in New Mexico Territory." He winked. "At least the good ones, anyway. Mrs. Proffitt is a real lady, Captain. You must be proud."

"I am, thank you." Looking at his old friend, he shook his head. During the war, Hank had always been on the skinny side. Now, his girth seemed to have grown with the size of his store. "By the looks of things, I'd say you're doing fine for yourself."

"Good enough. We get lots of travelers pressing through to California here. Business is good. So good I'll likely never leave Santa Fe. Where you headed?"

"Colorado."

Hank whistled low. "It's gonna get colder."

"That's a fact." Clayton looked at Vanessa again. Remembering just how little he'd stuffed in that pillowcase, he said, "We're going to need a few things. My wife needs a coat and thick gloves. Do you know anyone who could help her out?"

"Me, for one. I've got some ready-made things out back. A girl named Callie sews them up real fine. You staying at the Las Brisas Hotel?"

"We are."

"I'll send her over to the hotel with a couple of things later on. Mrs. Proffitt can pick and choose there."

"Sounds good."

Clayton watched Vanessa, fingering the bolts of fabric with a rapt expression. Her purely feminine interest brought forth a pull of possessiveness. Though their circumstances were rocky at best, Vanessa had somehow become his wife. His, for the world to see. He felt a surge of pride.

Lowering his voice, he said, "Hank, we got married a few days back, but I didn't have a ring. You got any?"

"Always." Hank chuckled. "I'd hardly be worth my weight if I didn't have some on hand. We get our share of shotgun weddings out here." After unlocking a safe, he pulled out a thin gold band. "Will this do?"

Fingering the band, Clayton felt the metal heat up under his touch. Though there was no fancy scroll work, nothing to signify it as different from any other wedding band, Clayton knew it was the right choice. It represented the vows he'd said, the companionship he felt with Vanessa, and everything he'd hoped their marriage could one day be.

A long-forgotten quotation from 2 Corinthians came to mind. "*I will gladly spend for you everything I have and expend myself as well.*" How true those words felt right at that moment!

When he realized Hank was still waiting for a reply, Clayton nodded. "It'll be fine." Reaching into his pocket, he asked, "How much do I owe you?"

"Not a thing. This is my treat."

Surprised, Clayton tore his gaze from the ring. "Hank, that's not how I do things."

"Good, 'cause this here's my store. It's how I want to do things that counts."

Clayton felt shamed. Was it that obvious he didn't have a lot of extra money? Pulling out his roll of cash, he prepared to salvage his pride. "I don't want charity."

"I'm not offering you charity." Hank stopped the gesture with a hand to his arm. "It's for payment due," he muttered, his voice turning serious. "I owe you, Captain."

Memories of patrolling East Texas hit him hard. In an instant, Clayton could feel the hot, sticky humidity, remember the feel of chiggers on his skin and the terrible gnawing of ever-present hunger settling in the pit of his stomach. They'd been desperate, indeed. His boots had worn out, his uniform was long gone, and only a handful of bullets resided in his pockets. The only thing any of them had had in abundance was respect for one another. "We're both lucky to have survived. You don't owe me a thing."

"I know you don't want to speak of it, but we both know better. Those days when you read the Bible to me, talked to me about your faith and Jesus . . . it got me through more than you'll ever know. Your words pulled me along and carried my weight, Captain. I'll never forget."

Since Vanessa was approaching, Clayton slipped the ring in his pocket. "Then I'm much obliged."

"What was that all about?" Vanessa asked as they walked toward the hotel.

Still stung by the memories, Clayton pushed them away. "Nothing. Just talk from the war."

"Hank rode with you, too?"

That surprised a chuckle from him. "No. He was a farmer." Images of them both, far younger and greener, floated back. Hank had been married to Penny, the sweetest girl this side of the Mississippi. To hear him tell it, Hank's life had been idyllic until the war. Soon after his family left to go fight, the Yankees had come and taken all their livestock.

Clayton had brought his unit there just days later, billeting in Hank's home for the night. The man had been dead-set against it, fearful for the safety of his wife. "There's nothing left," he'd said, though Clayton and Merritt and Ken and Will and the others knew Hank wasn't speaking of his things. He was guarding his woman, and they'd respected that.

The atrocity of Galveston was still fresh in their minds.

It had been raining for a week. Clayton hadn't slept in three days. Mud had seeped into what was left of his boots, had embedded itself into every inch of his blistered feet.

One of his men had been shot and was most likely going to lose his arm to gangrene, if they got him to a surgeon at all. There had been no way he was going to make his men stand in the rain for one more minute. "We don't want anything except a dry place to lie down," he'd said. "I promise."

To most men, Clayton's iron will and no-nonsense tone would have instilled fear—or at least a healthy respect.

But instead of cowing, Hank simply crossed his arms over his chest. One skinny frame defending everything he had against a band of seasoned soldiers. "Promises don't mean nothing. Not anymore, they don't."

"They do to me. I'm a man of my word."

Hank had stared hard at him. "If you're a liar, I'll hunt you down."

"If I was a liar, I'd expect you to," Clayton had replied with a level look.

They'd ended up staying five days. Hank's wife Penny doctored Billy's arm, cleaning his wound and placing a poultice on it to draw out the infection. Hank and Clayton had forged a bond over chicory coffee, the Word, and a bushel of wormy apples.

He and his men had left hungry but dry—and with filled souls, which still counted for a lot. As a gift, he left Hank with an extra rifle so he could protect his wife.

Later on, someone had heard that Penny had died of the influenza.

He was surprised Hank remembered him so well. Surely there'd been a hundred more strangers who had passed through his farm before the war ended.

Clayton took Vanessa's elbow and guided her into the hotel. It was beautiful, and a far sight grander than many he'd seen in some time.

Vanessa looked around wide-eyed, a soft smile playing at the corners of her lips.

Which, of course, seemed to bring every randy man running. He needed to get that ring on her finger as soon as possible.

"You need some help?" a short, pudgy man said from the counter.

"We need two rooms."

"We ain't got two. You want one?"

From the way the clerk was eyeing Vanessa, Clayton decided it was probably best she stayed near his side. "One room will do," he replied, intentionally making his voice clipped.

The clerk examined him with a new awareness. "Yes, sir," he said, a little more respectfully, before pushing the register in front of him. "Just sign here, if you please."

Clayton signed *Captain and Mrs. Clayton Proffitt*, then held out a hand for the key. After receiving it, he said, "My wife will need a bath. Have someone take care of that."

The clerk looked over Vanessa with interest. "Most folks use the tub in the back or go to the bathhouse. It's down the way."

There were too many men in this part of the world who'd commit murder for a woman, let alone a beautiful woman like Vanessa. "That won't do. She'll need a hip bath and someone to bring up hot water."

"Sir—"

"Captain," Clayton corrected sharply.

The clerk sighed in resignation. "We'll have it right up. You're in room five."

Grasping her elbow, Clayton glared at the men lounging against old sofas, inspecting his wife a little too closely for his comfort. One or two of the men wore pieces and parts of faded uniforms, whether by necessity or because they couldn't bear to leave memories of the war behind, Clayton didn't know.

However, he did recognize their type: men down on their luck with nothing to lose. Desperate.

Yes, the war had taken its toll on everyone, had taken a chunk out of the shine of the most God-fearing man, and had turned upright morals to their sides. A woman like Vanessa represented all that they'd lost: home and goodness and beauty in lives that had seen far too little of it. Clayton recognized the feeling, but he also knew that craving could make a man do things he'd never thought he would, just to have a single moment's salvation.

With some discomfort, he realized he wasn't going to be able to give Vanessa the privacy she needed in their room. But it was too late to cancel the bath he'd ordered. Vanessa's eyes had lit up at the mention of that tub, and there was no way he wanted to disappoint her.

"What was that about?" she whispered curiously once they entered their room and he'd locked it. "I've never heard you use your military rank with strangers."

"In truth, it's useless now. Most could care less about the past of any Confederate soldier. But there was something about that clerk that made me think it might make a difference to him. I also hoped it might make a few of the men down there think twice about crossing me." Hating to disillusion her, but knowing he had no choice, he said, "There's men here who would like nothing more than to do you harm, Vanessa. Women are still a scarce commodity in these parts."

She didn't look surprised, only dismayed, then scared. Once again Clayton wished he had confronted Price Venture when there'd been only a thin wall separating the two of them.

Hoping to tease a smile on her lips once more, he said, "Are you eager for a bath?"

"Of course."

A knock on the door alerted them to the boys who brought up their bags. After allowing them entrance, three women entered. Two were holding a sizable metal tub between them. The third carried a load of surprisingly thick towels.

The tallest woman looked over Vanessa before sidling up to Clayton with a knowing glance. "You must be quite a man, Captain. Our man Beck hasn't looked so nervous in days."

"I know what I want."

She winked. "I do, too."

"Just set the tub down."

The two other women placed the tub in the middle of the room, right in front of the fireplace.

"The water's coming, Captain," the chatty one said before opening the door and leading the way out.

Clayton kneeled in front of the fireplace and got to work. In no time a roaring fire flickered before them, warming the room and casting a pleasing glow. Vanessa was untying her boot when a knock announced four men, each holding steaming pails of water. One after the other, they poured them in the tub. Steam rose, just as two more men arrived, bringing up a pail of cool water and yet another hot.

Clayton asked them to place them in front of the tub. After they left, he securely locked the door, propping a sturdy ladder-back chair under the handle for added protection.

Vanessa hadn't moved from the chair in the back corner, her hands clasped in her lap. "Well, my goodness. That bath looks like heaven."

Clayton skimmed his fingers across the top of the water. "It feels that way, too." Straightening, he made sure to ease his voice into casualness. "Why don't we switch places? I'll sit there while you bathe. I'll make sure I keep my back turned."

She froze. "You're not going to leave?"

"I have to stay here, Van. There's no choice." When she looked to interrupt, he talked a little faster. "I'd wager just about every man in the vicinity now knows a real fine woman is in here. Everyone also knows I ordered you a tub. If I left you alone, it would be too much temptation for some. The door wouldn't last a heartbeat when faced with a strong shoulder or a well-placed kick."

"Come now, Clayton."

Because he, too, felt awkward, and would have loved nothing better than to leave her in peace, he lowered his voice, hating that his pride was coming into play as well. "If I sat outside your door, I'm afraid it might cause talk. No one would understand why a husband would take off during his wife's bath. And that's one of the reasons we married, isn't it? To keep you safe?"

"I suppose so." Her gaze strayed to the water once more. She softened with anticipation as steam rose from the buckets.

He used it to his advantage. "It's gonna get cold if you wait much longer, Van."

"Well. All right, then." Standing up, she unfastened two buttons at her neck. "We've slept side by side. You've doctored my back. We're married. . . . I guess it would be silly to be so shy about this."

No, she wasn't being silly at all. Their relationship was so filled with twists and turns, he could hardly navigate his way through what was true and what was better left unsaid. But, no matter what, he was the one man she'd never fear would break his word. He still took his vows to heart. He'd promised both himself and her that he'd give her time. Time to forget old hurts.

"I don't mean to embarrass you." Against his will, he glanced her way again.

Her fingers traipsing down the row of buttons of her dress slowed. "I trust you." She lifted a shoulder. "Truthfully, that water looks too enticing for anything but wild horses to keep me away."

He crossed to the covered window as she stepped out of her dress. He swallowed hard as he heard the rest of her garments slip away, then the telltale splash of water as she stepped in. "Oh, Clayton, it is like heaven."

He imagined it was. Wearily, he rested his forehead on the linen covering the simple glass pane. Behind him, the sounds of the water splashing sounded amplified, till he was aware of nothing except each imagined movement in that tub.

Of her bare skin, wet. Glowing.

His thoughts shamed him.

Not long after, they switched places—Clayton staying put until Vanessa had gotten covered. Then, she took his place at the window while he bathed in the cooling water.

As quickly as possible, he shaved and soaped up. Then stepped out, too. After he donned his britches and slipped his arms through a broadcloth, Clayton noticed the back of her neck was flaming red. "I'm all done, Van."

She turned, glanced at him, and almost smiled, but it didn't reach her eyes. The usual mossy green depths looked dark and unsure. Still unaccountably frightened.

Something had to be said. He wanted to keep his distance from her, but because of past promises he'd made, not through any fault of her own. But he knew her enough to see a tension about her, insecurity.

Quietly, he said, "Honey . . . you all right?"

"Maybe." Curving her arms around her waist she added, "It's just that right now, standing by the window, reminded me a lot of standing by my window at the ranch. I'd thought I'd gotten through all the memories, but I guess I haven't."

"It hasn't been that long."

"I know. It's just that, well . . . when Price grabbed me, I felt ugly, scared inside. Cold. I think parts of me still feel that way."

He was surprised she mentioned Price by name. Though she still was haunted by nightmares, Vanessa had steadfastly refused to talk about the night she'd been attacked.

After erasing the distance between them, Clayton squeezed her shoulders. Taking care not to harm her back, he brushed back her wet hair. "What Price did was ugly. Twisted. What he did has nothing to do with true love and honor. Nothing to do with a real union between man and wife."

"Maybe one day . . . " Her voice drifted off.

"One day." Clayton felt as if he was falling into a deep pit, his senses and emotions were so muddled and confused. Silently, he prayed for guidance. Prayed for patience, and to be the kind of man he wanted to be. The kind of man who put his own needs last.

Vanessa wasn't ready for more than chaste kisses and cuddles. Truth be told, neither was he.

But he would be lying to himself if he denied that another part of him was very ready for more than that.

Once again, he pushed those wants away.

They needed time. She needed to be sure that she was ready for a true marriage. To him. That everything she claimed to feel for him wasn't laced in gratitude. If he died tomorrow, he knew she had to have a future ahead of her.

And if he lived, he never wanted to see regrets cross her features. His heart would stop if she looked at him with disappointment, or worse, stoically. What would he do if he knew she wanted someone else but was beholden to him?

Or if he discovered that she'd never actually wanted him, Clayton? That all she'd really wanted were strong arms to hold her and a reason to forget the things that Price had done?

"Van, when I look at you, I see everything good in this world," he finally admitted. "Your trust in me makes me honored. Proud. It's how marriage is supposed to be, honey."

Her eyes turned luminescent. "I suppose. I'll do my best to honor you. I, uh, best comb out my hair."

Before she completely turned away, he reached for her hand. "Wait."

Quickly, he reached in a pocket and pulled out the paper-wrapped packet that had been practically burning a hole in his pants.

Her band of gold. "Van, will you wear my ring?"

Her left hand shook as she held it out for him. "I didn't expect this."

"I don't know why not." He tried to smile so she wouldn't see how nervous he was. "I know it's not much."

"Yes. Yes, it is. It's everything." Her eyes turned radiant when he slid it on her finger. The ring fit well, like a fancy jeweler in New Orleans had made it just for her. She wove her fingers together as if she was afraid he'd pull it off. "Thank you."

He wanted to kiss her, to comfort her, to show her that she was special to him, that he felt something so singular for her that it continually took his breath away.

And what's more, it had nothing to do with obligation and everything to do with deep, true feelings. With love and honor and the desire to cherish everything about her.

But of course, that wasn't right. Stepping away, he murmured, "See to your hair, Vanessa. Then we'll go down and get something to eat."

To his surprise, the light didn't dim in her eyes. Instead, she just smiled. "All right, Clayton."

Turning his back to her again, Clayton knew the worst thing in the world had just happened.

He'd fallen in love with his wife.

7

$\mathcal{M}$iles's horse turned up lame two hours south of Santa Fe. It had happened quickly. Jericho had gotten a rock embedded in his hoof. It had become irritated, then turned south.

Miles knew the problem was his—he'd forgotten to check Jericho's hooves as often as he should. Instead, he'd once again concentrated on pleasing Price, which was difficult to do because the man hardly ever acknowledged his existence. Still.

By the time Miles had started trying in earnest to help the horse, Jericho's right leg was a bit swollen and he was favoring it mightily. A man who looked to be of Mexican descent and lived on the outskirts of Santa Fe assured Miles his roan just needed some rest.

"Two days ought to do it," he drawled after Miles gave him a couple of bits for his trouble. "Then you can move on." His voice was raspy but his touch on the horse was assured and gentle. "Let this fella rest a bit and eat some oats. There's a good livery called Watson's where you can keep your horses."

Warily, Miles looked to his stepfather. Was the man going to lash out at him for his carelessness? More than once since they'd left, the older man had found the opportunity to reacquaint Miles with his fist.

But to his relief, Price didn't look too disappointed about the unexpected delay. "Anything else around?"

"A few saloons." The stranger looked Price up and down and raised a thick black eyebrow. "Few other places if you're the type interested in that kind of entertainment."

That teased a smile. "I am." To Miles's embarrassment, Price tossed a gold coin his way before turning toward town. "Go enjoy yourself too, boy."

Miles missed the catch.

The stranger saved him from the embarrassment of digging in the packed dirt for it. "Here you go," he said, reaching down, picking up the coin, then handing it over to Miles. As the dust flew behind Price and his bay, he murmured, "Guess your pa's thirsty."

"He ain't my pa. My pa's dead."

"Ah. Why you following him, then?"

That was the million-dollar question. "I don't know." Miles wasn't eager to share information about his sister. He was even less willing to contemplate why he was with a man he didn't respect, had no liking for, and who actively made his life miserable. It was becoming more and more clear that nothing was going to change between him and Price. The man only cared about his immediate wants and needs—and none of those were ever decent.

"Where you going?"

"I'm not sure."

The man chuckled, revealing a chipped front tooth. "No wonder your horse is lame, *amigo*. It's hard work, riding in circles, *si*?"

"Yes. I mean, *si*. Will Jericho be okay if I ride him to the livery?"

The man smiled at the name. "Jericho, hmm? Yes, I imagine he will become whole once again, just like the city. Take it easy and he'll be okay. And you, son, you take it easy, too. Wherever you might go."

Miles nodded and turned away, wondering about the kindness of strangers and about the extreme disappointment he'd felt with Price.

Their trip to Santa Fe had not been easy. After staying in Camp Hope for a day, they'd ridden west. The desolate, arid landscape had matched Miles's mood. The all-encompassing emptiness of the wide open spaces corresponded well with the hollow ache of past regrets he felt in his soul.

Price talked to everyone that they passed. They'd gotten lucky in Lubbock when a cowboy remembered Clayton's distinctive silver saddle. Two days later, a woman described Vanessa so closely that neither Miles nor Price had had any doubt that they were on the right track.

After rubbing down his horse and paying for water, oats, and feed, Miles wandered through town for a bit.

Finally he stopped at a restaurant and ordered the special. The place was small and clean. Red gingham curtains decorated the two windows that looked out onto the main road. Five tables filled the inside. The chairs were mismatched and the wood scarred and poorly mended.

But the smell inside was heavenly and the idea of being served anything other than beans or hare sounded good.

After Sammy, a woman old enough to be his mother, brought him a bowl of stew, she hung around and visited. "You come to town with that fella sporting a thick black mustache?"

"Yep."

"He's something, ain't he?"

"What do you mean?"

"Practically the minute he rode in, why he boarded that beautiful stallion of his and hightailed it over to the bathhouse."

"Then the saloon?" he asked around a mouthful of surprisingly tasty stew.

"Uh-huh."

She continued to talk while he bit into bread, then used the crust to sop up the remainder of his stew. Seemed Price had already made an impression. Word was, Price Venture was turning out to be a nasty drunk.

Miles already knew that.

After cleaning his bowl, Sammy brought him a thick wedge of cherry pie and some freshly brewed coffee. Both were welcome. As he blew on his coffee, he wondered how his sister was faring. Was she still afraid? Was she even all that hurt?

Maybe Vanessa was doing what Price suggested she was—using her unhappiness at the ranch as an excuse to leave. But that didn't ring true, either. If Price didn't care about her, then why were they looking so hard?

He'd heard her cries, and been treated to Clayton's explanation, but Miles didn't rightly know what was the truth. Especially since just the other night Price had sworn up and down that he hadn't laid a hand on her.

"Is that what she said?" he'd asked from the opposite side of the fire where they'd camped. "She said I beat her?"

"Well, Clayton did."

"He's a liar. I didn't touch her."

Feeling almost brave, Miles whispered. "I heard her cries from outside in the hall. I know you were in the room."

After a blank look, Price rebounded. "Just to ask her a question. That's all."

Miles knew that was a lie. But what was the truth? Why had Vanessa run? Was she running away from Price, or was she running to a life with Clayton?

Everyone knew she'd harbored a liking for Clayton Proffitt.

As he sat alone and allowed himself the luxury of letting his thoughts run wild, Miles knew he'd never forget the last encounter he'd had with Clayton, when the man had gripped his shoulders, slammed him against the barn wall, and gave him a talking to about his future. No, more to the point, he'd given him something else. A choice.

For some reason, Clayton's barely controlled anger had shaken him in a way far more profoundly than Price's knocks ever had. In all the years Clayton had served at the Circle Z, Miles had never seen him lose control.

One dark look or one succinct, abruptly spoken order got more done than the frequent out-of-control tirades Price enjoyed.

Maybe it was because Clayton was a man of honor, and Price never had been.

But Clayton had left him.

"Your pa, he fell asleep without payin'," a Hispanic woman interrupted his thoughts from the doorway. With a scowl, she said, "He's asleep back behind the Tumbleweed. Someone tossed his jacket on top of him to muffle his snores."

"He ain't my pa." It didn't escape Miles that he'd just equivocally announced that fact two times over the last hour.

"Well, whoever he is to you, you owe me money. He is yours, right? Word is that you two came in together."

For a moment, Miles considered disowning Price. If he did, he could use that coin and either take Price's horse or buy another and leave. He could go somewhere and hide. Start a new life, far away from his troubles.

Shoot, he could even decide to track Vanessa and Clayton down on his own. Maybe if he wasn't with Price, they'd even let him stay with them.

As he warmed to that idea, the very hope drew him out of his fantasies. He wasn't even brave enough to stand on his own two feet in his daydreams! That pretty much said it all.

In a crash, the harsh reality of his faults drew him to the truth and to his duty. Standing up, he fished out the change for his meal from a pocket and then walked over and placed another few bits into the woman's hand. "Here. Take it."

With a swish of her skirts, she left without another word.

He was suddenly more tired than he'd ever been in his life. Since he wasn't man enough to leave, he might as well find some solace in slumber. "Sammy, do you know where I can find a place to sleep?"

"I usually have rooms but they're plumb filled up. There's a couple of boardinghouses down the way though."

He was too tired to hunt for anywhere else. "How about the barn?"

"You sure?" She looked him up and down, eyeing his boots. Miles knew they were expensive. He'd been proud of them back when he was sure the price of his clothes meant something.

"Positive. How much for bunking in there?"

"Don't worry about that." Eyes softening, she stepped forward. "You okay? You look troubled, mister. You got problems?"

He almost laughed. His whole life was problems. "I'm fine. It's just been a long few days and I need some sleep."

Miles grabbed his knapsack and walked into the barn, finally settling down in an empty stall near the back.

It felt good to be alone, the peace a welcome change of pace. It was pure pleasure not to hear Price complaining or planning or snoring next to him. But still, sleep didn't come. Instead, old hurts and constant confusions burgeoned forth, claiming his mind and his conscience.

Was he better than Price if he wasn't actively fighting against him? Was he fulfilling his duty if he was merely slowing the pace instead of driving Price away from Vanessa? Was he less of a man because he was choosing to travel with Price instead of breaking away and making something out of his life?

He didn't know any of those answers.

Once again, Miles felt as if he was taking the easy way. The path of least resistance. It was how he'd gotten through life— by not making waves. By not offering much of himself except his presence.

And meager efforts.

Miles frowned as his eyes drifted shut. One thing was for certain. His pa would most certainly hang his head in shame if he knew what had become of him.

To Vanessa's dismay, the gold band on her finger seemed to be only driving her and Clayton farther apart. Ever since they'd left Santa Fe and had ridden hard west toward Colorado Springs, Clayton's manner had become more distant and his words more terse.

Vanessa knew the changes stemmed from their time together in that hotel room. In the space of one somewhat run-down room, their relationship had changed again. The four solid walls that surrounded them had made conversation essential. And, oh, how they'd talked. He'd shared with her more stories about the war.

She'd dared to reveal more of her feelings about her father's passing and her mother's quick remarriage. It was never more obvious that they'd both had their fair share of pain and heartbreak. Yet, still, they had continued on, choosing to move forward instead of giving up. Choosing to honor their vows to each other as well as the ones they'd shared aloud before God.

But the constant give-and-take was wearing on them. Vanessa yearned for stability once again. She yearned to feel whole and not to be afraid. To be able to forget all the bad things in her life and only concentrate on what was good.

Clayton seemed to be of the same mind. Ever vigilant, he kept a lookout whenever strangers crossed their paths. More than once he'd shied away from people who asked probing questions, not wanting anyone to be able to provide information to Price if, indeed, he had decided to follow them.

He was her protector. Her companion. His only purpose was to take her to Corrine's and to keep her safe. But sometimes in the twilight of the day, when the luminous sun was fading into the nighttime sky, Vanessa would spy something more in her guardian's eyes. She recognized it and cherished it and clung to it as well. It was hope and love and a longing so sharp she could feel its sting.

It was the same thing she was feeling.

✒

Upon arrival in Colorado Springs, Clayton asked about a reputable hotel, then got them a room. "Vanessa, I'll be back as soon as I can," Clayton murmured after settling her into a comfy winged chair.

All her enthusiasm about being in such a fine place as the Addison Hotel faded. "You're leaving? To go where?"

"To see the sheriff." He rubbed his neck. "We've kept up a good clip, but I'm feeling like that isn't enough. We need to make sure Price isn't following us."

"Don't you think we would have heard something by now?"

"Maybe. Maybe not." He looked around the lobby. "You should be just fine here. I'll order you some tea and ask someone to bring it to you." Slipping his hat back on, he prepared to go. "I'll be back as soon as I can."

She felt far too much like a child being left behind. "I'd prefer to accompany you."

"No."

She'd almost argued. She'd almost stood up and dared to make a scene, just so he couldn't ignore her feelings. But that wouldn't do. "All right then. I'll wait right here."

Brown eyes softened. "I'll go ask someone to bring you tea, sweetheart. Stay here."

That had been an hour ago.

Vanessa sipped her tea and worried. And tried not to stare at all the assorted characters loitering in and around the fancy hotel. Gold miners, silver barons, gamblers, society ladies, ranchers—she'd never seen so many people in her life.

Their unfamiliarity put her on edge. She only knew ranch hands and men from neighboring spreads. Men barely older than her, eager to go out on their own; men who sounded like Texas and respected both her and her position in the area.

These men looked like they could have cared less. She didn't know how to act among these folks, especially since Clayton wasn't there to guide her.

Years of memories floated into consciousness, making long-ago actions feel as recent and as surprisingly hurtful as a splinter in her thumb.

Yes, more than a time or two she'd snuck to the barn at the Circle Z to tell Clayton about the latest buggy ride or picnic she went on. He would stop whatever he was doing and patiently listen to her.

Now that her life was so different, Vanessa could only imagine how silly she must have sounded. But Clayton had never acted like she was childish at all. Instead, he'd always stopped what he was doing and listened, remaining stoic and serious as she prattled on about nothing.

However, she recalled one time when he'd hadn't been able to hold back his amusement.

"What's so funny?" she'd asked.

"Nothing."

"Something is."

"It's just, well, I'm surprised those boys you complain about can ever get a word in edgewise, the way you talk so much."

She'd felt her cheeks color. "I do let them talk. I promise I do."

"That's good to know."

"They just aren't very interesting. Fact is, I don't talk to anyone like I talk to you, Clayton." Just to rile him up a bit, she added, *"And for the record, most boys talk a whole lot more than you do. You're as quiet as a church mouse."*

"As a mouse? Sweetheart, don't ever compare a man to a mouse."

His endearment had made her bolder. "Quiet as a what, then?"

He leaned back in his chair, propped one dusty boot over a denim covered knee. "I don't know. It needs to be something manly. Like . . . like a bull."

She'd giggled in spite of herself. "I grew up on a ranch, Clayton. Even I know bulls aren't known for their silence."

That surprised a bark of laughter from him. "You've got a point, sugar." Tenderness had filled his gaze. "We're a pair, aren't we? I don't talk enough, and you talk too much."

She'd liked feeling that they were a pair. It made her feel like they would belong together for a very long time. "We're a good pair, Clayton. You're such a good friend. What would I have done without you?"

He'd blinked and his eyes had sobered. "You would've been just fine."

"Do you think any man will ever say he wants to marry me?"

"Maybe—if you let him get a word in edgewise."

"I promise. If a boy gets down on one knee in front of me, I'll be quiet."

Oh, how they'd laughed. Now, though, that conversation felt bittersweet. Just weeks ago, Clayton had, indeed, gotten down on one knee. And she had been quiet and let him propose to her.

But it had been nothing like her girlish dreams.

As yet another coarse-talking cowboy in a fancy shirt and brand-new denims sidled past her in the entrance of the lobby, Vanessa gripped her teacup for strength, glad for the shiny new band on her finger.

To her surprise, she'd noticed more than one man eye her band for a good long time before giving her a wide berth. In some ways that band of gold made her feel as safe as Clayton's Winchester did on the trail. As secure as his arms did when he used to hold her close. Not that it kept everyone away.

"Missus, where's your husband at?" a gaudy gent said from a couch near the door to the bar.

"Excuse me?"

He grinned, revealing a nice set of white teeth. "Me and the boys have been watching you from the other side of the room. You been alone for a while."

A slight tingling of fear snaked through her. She knew no one. And, well, the man's hands were big. Not trusting herself to speak, she turned away.

The man sidestepped so she was staring at him once again. "If you were mine, I wouldn't be giving you a moment's peace."

"He . . . he'll be right along."

"That a fact?" The man chuckled, then shared a knowing glance with two others who joined them. "I wonder when 'along' is. Are you lonely, sugar? We'd keep you company—"

A tall skinny man stepped forward, bringing with him the scent of unwashed skin. Reaching for her cup, he stuck his nose in the middle of it and breathed deep. "What is this? Tea?"

Vanessa knew she wouldn't touch the cup again. "I'm perfectly fine. Thank you."

The first man, the one in the pin-striped suit, grinned at that. "Yes, you are. Perfectly fine."

"Anson, you go on now. Leave her alone," a fancy-dressed woman in bright peacock silk called out as she descended the staircase and caused a commotion. "That there's a lady. Too good for the likes of you all."

Vanessa was transfixed. This woman seemed to draw everyone's attention just by smiling. Even the hotel clerk paused to watch her.

"Trot, set that cup down now."

Down went the cup. "Aw, Lace. I wasn't doing nothing."

Lace—or whoever she was—looked him up and down. "You were doing enough." She shooed a hand. "Y'all, go on now. I'm going to keep this chickadee company for a bit. And we don't need no male company."

Little by little, the men scattered. Heat crept up Vanessa's neck, and despite her earlier vow not to, she picked up the teacup just to have something to do.

Where in the world was Clayton?

"You okay now, honey?" Lacy asked, swishing forward with a burst of energy and expensive perfume.

"Yes. Indeed." She was obliged to the redheaded woman, but didn't know what to say. She had been sheltered, but even she knew what a sporting woman looked like. And she certainly had been taught to never speak with such women. But she owed her something. "Thank you," she murmured, catching the woman's eye. "I'm obliged."

"Anytime. I know I'm not really your type of companion, but I'm going to sit here by you for a moment, just to make sure those boys leave you alone."

Relief made her palms damp. "I appreciate that."

Tossing a loose curl over one creamy white shoulder, Lace rolled her eyes. "Some men get so used to hanging around this place, they forget that there's a whole world of respectable ladies out there. I don't think they meant you any harm, though."

"My husband will be back soon."

The woman looked her up and down and smiled. Her eyes softened with something that almost looked like envy. "I'm sure he will. That's good."

The front doors of the Addison blew open then. Vanessa turned expectantly. Surely Clayton was returning?

But it was a man all in black with a swagger in his walk. With narrowed eyes, he walked purposely toward Vanessa's savior. "You free, Lacy?"

Lacy looked at Vanessa. For a moment she seemed to pause, then looked at her hand resting on the expensive gown. With a regretful sigh, she murmured, "Sorry, sugar, but I've gotta go."

Then her transformation began. Up went her chin. "Larry, as I live and breathe. I'm always free for you—for a price."

The man in black slowly grinned. "I'm paying."

"Then I'm all yours." After winking in Vanessa's direction, she turned and pressed herself against the man who'd joined them. "I didn't know if you were going to be around today."

"Had some business with the sheriff, but I'm done now."

"Thank goodness." Within minutes, they disappeared behind the swinging doors, raucous laughter following their departure.

Vanessa leaned back against her chair's cushions and closed her eyes. That man had been with the sheriff, too. What was keeping Clayton?

She was terribly ready to get out of the lobby. If she was approached again, it was highly unlikely that Lacy was going to be available to warn other cowboys off.

She was just wondering how to get more tea when Clayton finally entered the room, drawing everyone's eye with his handsome good looks and rigid posture. She felt like running into his arms.

"I'm sorry I was gone so long," he murmured as he took the seat across from her, the same spot where Lacy had perched. "Did you have any trouble?"

She had no desire to bring up the men or the fancy woman. "None to speak of. Is everything all right?"

"It's just fine," he said, glancing at her in concern. "It took a while to find Sheriff Parker, then I had to wait a bit for another man to finish his business. It took still longer to tell him about Price."

Vanessa tamped back the feeling of mortification. "Did you tell him everything?"

His gaze scanned her features, taking in every nuance. Then, as if making a sudden decision, he reached for her hand

and pulled her across the way so that soon she was sharing the sofa with him. "That's better," he murmured. He scooted closer until their knees touched. Linked his fingers with hers again.

She appreciated the comfort she felt sitting by his side, but she wanted an answer. "Clayton, did you?"

"Enough. I had to give the lawman a reason why Price was trouble, Van. You know that."

"I know." Pressing a hand to her temple, she realized she was still terribly self-conscious. Knowing that yet another person now knew about why she was running shamed her. "Has he heard anything?" she asked nervously. "Has Price sent out a wire?"

"No, but I didn't expect him to. If Miles did as he promised, Price sent a posse up north first. By now, he's either giving up the search or making his way out west, but he's most likely a week to ten days behind us."

Rubbing his thumb along her knuckles, he said, "I showed Parker the marriage certificate Ken made up, just to be on the safe side. I don't want anyone thinking Price can pull you away from me without a fight." Shifting, he pulled off his hat. Though his long legs crept out near the small sofa like a spider's, he looked fairly comfortable. "I imagine sitting here in this fancy lobby feels mighty nice to you after our last days on the trail."

She smiled because it was expected. "Yes, indeed." She wasn't lying. Sitting in the Addison should have felt exciting—well, if those men hadn't approached her. Her history included having tea or coffee or lemonade with most every woman near the Circle Z over the last few years. That was what she had known.

But now it wasn't all she had known.

"Are you hungry?"

"No." When he looked at her funny, she made up an excuse. "I'm still full from eating hours ago."

"Oh. Well, all right. Let's go on up to the room and get some sleep. I'd like to leave before daylight. With any luck, we'll reach Corrine's place by nightfall tomorrow."

Uneager to leave just yet, because she knew as soon as they got to their room he would turn quiet, she struggled for a reason to keep them seated. "But before we go upstairs, tell me about your sister."

"Corrine? What do you want to know?"

"I don't know. I just was looking at all the many women around here, wondering about their pasts. All of them made me think about your sister. So, when was the last time you saw her?"

"Not since the war."

"Were y'all close?"

He looked surprised by the many questions. "I suppose. We were close enough, I guess. She was just always my baby sister."

"Baby sister? Clayton, I thought she was married."

He chuckled, smoothing the lines of fatigue around his eyes. "She is. I guess no matter how old she is, I can't help but think of her in any way except in pigtails, bothering me."

The image of Clayton fending off a pesky sister made Vanessa smile. "How much younger is she?"

"Five years. Another four separate her and our brother Scout."

Vanessa tried to piece together his past. "Your mother died birthing Scout, right?"

"Yes. It hit our pa hard, though I have to say that he was a man of honor. Some men can't handle life without a woman, but not my pa. Not Arthur Proffitt. He just made Corrine and me pitch in even more."

"Especially you, I imagine."

"I was the oldest. But Corrine did a lot with Scout. She practically raised him in a lot of ways, especially when Pa and I went off to fight."

Their pasts could always be traced back to the war. The battles had changed everything, transforming their lives as completely as Sherman's march through Georgia. "What happened to Corrine and Scout when y'all left?"

"She and Scout went to live with an aunt close to Austin, near where I was stationed. One day I brought my commanding officer by, promising him my Aunt Marge's biscuits." Clayton shook his head in memory. "John Merritt took one look at Corrine and didn't care a lick about anything else."

She sighed, caught up in the story in spite of herself. "That's terribly romantic."

Clayton's lips curved. "It was, I suppose. Corrine says she and Merritt fell in love from just about the moment they set eyes on each other, and I believe it to be true."

Her discomfort long forgotten, Vanessa touched his hand. "Clayton Proffitt, listen to you! I'd never imagined you'd talk so flowery."

He chuckled. "It's the truth. Corrine was all of seventeen and pretty as a summer's day. Merritt could hardly speak, he was so struck by her. Before I knew it, my captain had washed his face, slicked back his hair, and was by her side morning till night."

Vanessa tried to imagine it. "What did you do?"

"Not much for me to do—my Aunt Marge was low on food, so I took myself out and found them some chickens." He smiled at the memory. "Though the idea of a man thinking of my sister like that made me uncomfortable, I couldn't say I disapproved. Merritt's an upstanding man; Corrine could do no better." Catching Vanessa's eye, he smiled. "They started writing each other as soon as we left Marge's house, then when Merritt was injured, he recuperated at her place. Before I knew it, they were getting married."

It all sounded terribly exciting to Vanessa. "My goodness."

Clayton's voice turned soft. "Soon after, we got word that our pa died. Scout was thirteen and a handful, ready to do his part for the Confederacy. But Merritt refused to let Scout enlist." Something in Clayton's eyes dimmed.

"What happened with Scout?"

"He took off and never looked back." All trace of happiness left his voice. "Last I heard, my brother was off finding his own way. Pa's death hit him hard, as did my leaving. Merritt was a good influence, but Scout's life has been so different, you know? The war shaped Merritt and me, made us who we are today. We know how to kill. We've seen the things that matter most get ripped and damaged and torn and broken. And because of that, we kept it from Scout." His eyes turned bleak. "Who knows . . . maybe we sheltered him too much."

"I was sheltered, too. Until recently, I didn't even realize how much. Did Scout, uh, not appreciate your efforts?"

"Not so much, I'm thinking. Corrine said he left about three years ago. Scout said he was going to head to Texas, go back to where we lived before our world got split in two. I'm kind of surprised he didn't turn up at the Circle Z, though I'm glad he didn't. I wouldn't have liked him to see how things were with Price."

Vanessa squeezed his hand. "He'll come back. Miles is struggling too, I think."

"I sincerely hope Scout is turning into a better man than your brother."

Stung, she pulled away. "That's hardly fair."

Visibly controlling his temper, Clayton nodded. "You're right. It's hardly fair that he stood by the door and listened to

Price whip you." He shook his head. "I can't forgive him for that."

"I have," she admitted, thinking that she couldn't bear not to forgive her brother. "You should, too. The Lord asks us to forgive; you know that."

"I know I should, and I know He does. But still, Vanessa, I'm not ready."

"What Price did wasn't my brother's fault. Miles, he's been hurt too," she whispered.

"Not like you. He wasn't hurt like you were." With a sigh, he shook his head. "What am I saying? What happened to you is as much my fault as any. I failed to protect you." Lowering his voice, he murmured, "I'm just glad nothing worse happened."

"I know." Yet again, Vanessa was so glad she hadn't told him everything. There was only so much a man could take.

And, well, nothing that had happened was his fault. He certainly had done as much as he could to protect her. Standing up, she murmured, "I guess I'm ready to go upstairs after all."

"All right." He gently cupped her elbow as they passed the hodgepodge assortment of characters lounging in the lobby. They'd almost made their way through the marble foyer and to the first flight of stairs when a voice called out. "Clayton Proffitt?"

Vanessa watched as he reached into his jacket for his Colt, just as he stepped in front to shield her from who knew what. His stance relaxed as the woman in vibrant peacock approached, though Vanessa noticed that he didn't step to the side. "Lacy. My stars. Look at you."

Lacy guffawed. "Do you like what you see?" She winked. "Look hard, Clayton Proffitt. Why, I'm almost a lady now." Without giving him a chance to speak, she said, "What are you doing out this way? Last I heard you were in Texas."

"I was there. I'm headed to see my sister for a spell."

Lacy's eyes dimmed. "Corrine. Give her my best." She peeked around Clayton's solid frame, meeting Vanessa's eyes with a friendly grin.

Vanessa was about to introduce herself, was about to explain to Clayton that the two of them had already met, when Clayton shifted again, effectively blocking her view. "Excuse us, will you?"

Lacy stepped back, her expression shuttered. "Oh. Sure, Clayton."

After briefly tipping his hat, he motioned Vanessa forward again, still taking care to place her in front of him.

Up they went. Two steps, three. Laughter flew out in the distance, and just as they turned the corner, Vanessa heard the echo of Lacy's voice as she flirted with yet another man. Beside her, Clayton stiffened.

"I met her, earlier," Vanessa blurted. "She was in the lobby. She . . . seemed nice." Vanessa was just about to talk a bit more, to explain about the many men who were being less than mannerly, when Clayton gripped her elbow and they continued up the staircase. "She should never have approached you. You're a lady. Everyone in the place knows it."

The moment he shut the door, she blurted, "She seemed to know you. Do you know her?"

"Yes."

"How?"

"It doesn't matter."

"I think it does." Vanessa didn't understand why he was acting so mysterious and guarded. Almost like the sight of Lacy hurt him. "Who is she? Who is she to you?"

After a brief pause, he said, "Lacy was Corrine's best friend back when we were growing up."

There was something in the way that Clayton was avoiding her eyes that made Vanessa think that there was more than just his sister's connection that made him reluctant to discuss Lacy. "Is she special to you?"

"Not anymore."

Feeling possessive, she asked the question burning her insides. "Did you have a relationship with her?"

"Not at all." He looked at her curiously. "Why do you ask?"

"It doesn't matter, I guess. It's just, well, she acted like she knew you well. . . . " Vanessa's voice trailed off as she tried to analyze why she did care so much. Then, she knew. She was jealous.

Jealous that another woman knew Clayton in a way that she had not. The knowing look she'd spied in Lacy's eyes had brought to the forefront everything she was thinking about, all their promises—and all the things she'd once hoped for but was now so afraid to do. So she pushed. "Did you love her, Clayton? Did you . . . did you bed her?"

His expression hardened while he reached out and gripped her arms. She knew he was holding her at bay, but what she also knew was that he was keeping her close. Once again, their scents collided, making her feel connected; making her aware of each breath he inhaled, the pressure of each finger on her arms. "No, I did not. You shouldn't ask such things."

"Why not?"

"I'm trying to keep you safe. I'm trying to keep you out of harm's way."

"I've already been in harm's way," she whispered.

His expression turned strained. "The Lord brought me to you to guide you. To protect you."

She wasn't sure what the Lord had in mind for her anymore. If He had plans, how had he let Price attack her? How had he let Miles simply stand by? Why did she love Clayton but fear truly becoming his wife? "Maybe that's not what He wants," she said softly. "Maybe we don't really know His will."

As the silence stretched, the tension escalated. Clayton's calloused hands slid from her arms to around her waist, kneading, pulling her closer. His gaze paused on her lips. "Don't say that," he warned.

"I'm only speaking the truth." His chest was warm; his skin smelled so clean. Brown eyes scanned her face, halted at her lips, reminding her of just how much she loved him.

How much she used to yearn for him. How much she still did.

Without stopping to think, she linked her hands around his neck. He hadn't shaved in two days; through the thin fabric of her sleeves, the stubble grazed her arms, shooting bolts of attraction through her. His stance widened. His tug brought her closer.

And then there was nothing to think at all. Because he claimed her lips. Vanessa reached up and threaded her fingers through his hair, felt the soft strands spike up, loved the feeling of being in his arms. This was how she'd always imagined a kiss could be. Explosive, all-encompassing.

Before she'd been hurt.

When she'd only ever thought about one man. When it had only been Clayton.

As quick as it happened, the kiss ended. Scanning her face, his expression hardened. "Did I hurt you? Did I scare you?"

"No." To her surprise, she wasn't afraid of Clayton. Of how she'd felt in his arms. No, the only regret she had was that they were now standing apart again.

He ran his fingers through his hair before turning away. "Seeing Lacy . . . it brought back too many memories."

"Like what, Clayton? What happened to her?"

"Shortly after her pa left to fight, she and her mother were attacked by renegades. Her mother soon died, and Lacy was ruined. Pretty much her whole home was broken. So was she. Eventually, Corrine told me Lacy went to work in a town in West Texas. In a place like Camp Hope."

His expression pained, he continued. "A couple of months after all that happened, my regiment stopped there. Some of the men in our unit went to a . . . to a sporting house." His voice hollow, he whispered, "The next morning, I heard two men talking about her. They'd paid her to be with them." To her surprise, he voice cracked. "I heard the stories—men talk. But I didn't know what to say. I didn't know how to defend her."

His expression turned distant, full of regret. He edged to the door. "I need to get out of here. When we're together, alone, I forget things. I almost forget the things I've promised." His hand snaked out and gripped the handle hard. "Lock the door behind me. I have a key."

A knot lodged in her throat as she fought back tears. "Please don't leave."

"I've been as strong as I can possibly be for both of us. But Vanessa, right this minute, I don't feel strong at all. I feel weak and worn out. I . . . I can't stay here a moment longer." He edged to the door, breaking contact with her, leaving her alone with her thoughts and ghosts once again.

Vanessa's heart broke as she breathed in deep. If she closed her eyes really tight, she could almost pretend he was still in the room, by her side.

8

*Y*ou back already, Clayton?"

Clayton turned to see Lacy leaning against the doorway of the saloon, her shoulders back and proud, looking for all the world like an invitation for dark appetites. "I am," he muttered before taking a table near the back. "I, uh, needed a drink."

"So I see. Mind if I join you?"

"No."

"Thank you." Humor filled her eyes as she walked over and sat beside him, the stiff teal skirts rustling against his legs when she took her chair. "It's too bad you ain't got any whiskey in front of you. Want me to get you two fingers worth?"

"No. Not yet."

His insides were as twisted as the branches of the mesquite he'd gotten to know so well in Texas. Unfortunately, he felt as sorrowful as the squat, ugly trees had always looked to him. Across the bar, the piano was playing. In and around, men and women from all walks of life congregated, their voices mixing and floating over the tune of "Dixie."

Times had certainly changed. The vestiges of the war created a blurring of society lines, at least for the time being.

No longer was it only women of questionable character who frequented places like this. Now a true mixture of people were seated together, their common need to deaden hurts overlying most all social boundaries.

After watching him for a minute, Lacy spoke. "So, there's a Mrs. Proffitt in the world now. That is news. When did y'all get hitched?"

"A few days ago."

She blinked. "My. Well, that is interesting." She swung her leg up and down, the movement rustling her dress. "So, at this very moment, your bride's upstairs all alone?"

Her question wasn't worth answering.

At his silence, Lacy chuckled raucously. "Guess you're finding married life a little taxing. Don't worry, Clay. She'll come around. They all do."

Remembering how Lacy used to be, back when she'd played dolls with Corrine, he said, "Is that what happened to you, Lacy? Did you come 'round, Lace?" The question was harsh, the implication rude.

He was almost ashamed.

All humor fled from her eyes. "Come now, Clayton. We both know I was never a bride."

"I apologize. I shouldn't have spoken so."

She waved a hand. "No apology necessary. You said the truth a whole lot kinder than most." Lowering her voice, she whispered, "Shoot, we both know there's been plenty I shouldn't have done."

He felt the same way. "How long have you been in Colorado Springs?"

"Just over a year now. I was a real gentleman's ladybird for a spell." Fingering her skirts, she murmured, "Randolph Porter hailed from Boston. We found each other in Kansas City. He brought me here before he got gold fever and headed out to

California." She frowned slightly. "By mutual agreement, I decided to stay here when he moved on."

"Are you glad you stayed?"

"Maybe." With a shrug, she amended herself. "Naturally. Randolph left me enough money so that I can go my own way. No more cathouses for me." Quietly, she scanned the bar, her gaze constantly appraising. "Now I decide who I want to be with, not anyone else. I'll take that, I'll tell you what."

The piano player started playing "Little Brown Jug." The song was familiar enough that a couple of patrons joined in.

Clayton figured it was enough of a distraction to ask Lacy something he just thought of. "You ever hear of a man by the name of Price Venture?"

"No. Should I have?"

"I hope not. He lives out near Lubbock. Near Camp Hope."

"I ain't been that way in years, Clayton."

"I know. But he gets around. He's my wife's stepfather. Took over the Circle Z."

Concern lit her features. "*Circle Z.* That was your outfit, right? I met a few cowboys a year or so ago who mentioned your name."

"Yes. It was where I worked. Price, he might come looking for her."

Interest and humor and something like disbelief entered her expression. "Am I hearin' this right? You, Clayton Proffitt, took your bride right out from under another man's nose?"

After weighing his options, Clayton lowered his voice. "There's a story there."

"Do tell."

He wasn't eager to replay Vanessa's troubles. Especially not when they'd just argued and he'd left her upstairs. "Now's not the time."

Whether it was from his terse reply or her expansive knowledge, Lacy turned serious. "She okay?"

He didn't know. Instead of answering, he said, "For the next few months, I'll be at Corrine's spread, south of here. The Bar M. If you hear anything about Venture sniffing around, would you send word?"

"For old time's sake?"

Clayton watched as she tossed back the drink, the liquor subduing her own ghosts. "Yes, for old time's sake," he said quietly. "If what we had could be called that."

"I'll do it, but in return I have a favor to ask of you."

"Name it."

"Tell Corrine I asked about her." Blue eyes shimmered. "If you don't mind."

"I don't mind."

"If you do, uh, get the chance, please don't tell her what I've become," she said softly. "I'd like there to be one person in this world who still remembers what I could have been."

Thinking of the war, of the things he'd done, the things he'd seen, he blinked. "Are any of us like that?"

"Your wife, maybe."

"Maybe." With some hope, he added, "Maybe Scout."

Lacy shook her head, regret in her eyes. "Scout's not that kind of person, honey. I saw him six months ago."

The shock of it took him by surprise. "Here?"

"Indeed."

"How was he looking?" He could hardly believe his luck; he was so eager to hear about his baby brother.

"The truth isn't always what we hope for." She hesitated. "Do you really want to know the truth about Scout?"

Clayton nodded.

"He was dressed all in black, like a vulture. Like a cussed gunfighter, if you want to know the truth. Because, Clayton, a gunfighter is what he is."

"Are you sure? Maybe you misunderstood—"

"I'm positive. He kills for money, Clayton."

The news hit him hard, though it shouldn't have. Hadn't he heard that his younger brother knew how to shoot well? Yet, last he'd heard, Scout had never experienced the repercussions of hitting a human target.

Once again, Clayton wondered if he should have taken him into battle. If nothing else, Scout could have helped at the camps, could have leaned on him when he understood the price a man paid when he took a life.

He shouldered Scout's disgrace. "Corrine and I hoped to shelter him," he muttered by way of explanation, though the good Lord knew Lacy wasn't asking for any. "I don't know what happened. I guess we did too much for him."

"It wasn't you, it was Scout, Clay. He went wrong."

"I'm not sure about that."

"I am. There comes a time for both man and woman to realize that life isn't full of dreams and sunshine. Sometimes it ain't what you thought it'd be at all. That's when it's time to stand on two feet—even if one of them is blown off," she finished with a sideways look at a man lurking in the darkness of the bar, half his face scarred.

Her eyes hardening, she said softly, "That's when you realize that you might as well make the best of what it is—of what is real. There ain't nothing else."

Maybe Lacy was right; he didn't know. All Clayton did know was that his brother knew he'd been working at the Circle Z and hadn't sought him out. Instead, he'd decided to adopt a way of life that would've shamed Arthur Proffitt. "Thanks for the news."

"I'm sorry it wasn't better." She looked to add more, but then her roving eyes caught sight of a newcomer and stilled.

Clayton watched as her expression lit up like a firecracker as a city slicker walked toward the bar, his expensive wool suit tailored, his skin lax and pale under a neatly trimmed beard. A gold watch chain peeked out of his vest pocket.

Lacy smiled. "Now looky there, Clay. That there is a man who needs me."

The man looked as green as the hills of Georgia. "He looks like he's waiting to be robbed," Clayton said with a smile.

"He will be if he's not careful. What he needs, honey, is someone to show him the ropes."

Rubbing a pinky under her eyes to mop up some smudged kohl, Lacy shimmied her dress down a good inch, then stood up. "Thanks for the conversation, Clay. Time for me to go make my future."

"Bye, Lace."

She pointed to the grand staircase barely visible from their position at the bar. "Go on up and see to your wife," she said, her expression surprisingly gentle. "Knowing you're down here, she's probably tossing and turning, imagining the worst. Don't let her think that. Remember—we've all got to have someone who still believes in good."

And with that, she plastered a smile on her face and sauntered over to the gent. "I'm so parched I swear I'm about to expire!" she said gaily, plopping down on the greenhorn's lap before he even had time to look her way. As the man eyed her in wonder, she sidled close. "Tell me that you'll assuage my needs."

The bartender grunted as he slammed a shot glass in front of her. Obviously he'd seen the act before.

The poor greenhorn's eyes bugged and his hands drifted in the air, obviously not having a clue as to where to place them on Lacy's voluptuous body.

Clayton tossed a bill on the bar as he left, Lacy's voice carrying across the room. "Look at you, sugar. There's so much of you. And it's all so . . . sweet."

A gunslinger in the back coughed. The scarred war veteran shook his head at Lacy's slick line but leaned forward to listen closer.

And Clayton fought back a smile. He hoped Lacy's latest target had a stash of cash, otherwise she'd take it all and leave him and his weak physique floundering in the mountains.

Once more, there wasn't a man in the room who'd fault Lacy nor pity the greenhorn, neither. Like Lacy said, everyone had to make their way as best they could. If a man was too dumb to see he was an easy mark or in over his head, he got what he deserved.

To his relief, Vanessa was asleep when he entered. Quickly, he undressed, splashed water on his face, then crawled into the massive bed next to her.

Vanessa shifted, causing another strand of her hair to escape its braided confines and flow brightly against her pillow. Clayton lay on his back and tried to ignore his yearning for her, but it was no use. Her sweet, clean scent—so different from Lacy's cloying perfume—called to him as sharply as if she'd spoken his name.

Vanessa shifted again. Opened one eye. "Clay? You're back?"

"Yeah."

She tried to sit back on her elbows. "About earlier—I'm sorry—"

"There's no need, honey. Go back to sleep."

Moments passed. When her breathing turned deep, he eyed her back, completely covered in a long white gown. She was slim. Really, such a tiny thing.

Too slight to have been through the things that she had. Unable to stop himself, he ran a finger along her back. Two long ridges met his touch—reminders of their pasts.

Her scars were hidden from most, but perhaps not as deep as Lacy's.

And God help him, but he was glad she wasn't Lacy. He was glad nothing worse than stiff leather had hurt her. He was glad that she didn't have to depend on crafty wiles and men's ignorance to get what she wanted.

The world needed Vanessa's sweetness, her virtue. There had to be someone in the world who could survive the war and remain unsullied.

Most people hadn't. Not him, not Ken, not the men in the saloon downstairs. Not Lacy or the girl in Galveston.

Not even his baby brother. Not Scout.

Clayton fell asleep worrying about things that should have been. And things that never were.

9

"By tomorrow, we should be at the Bar M," Clayton said around noon.

"That's hard to believe," Vanessa replied, trying to imagine how things were going to be once they stopped traveling. Far different, she supposed.

To her surprise, Vanessa felt almost melancholy that their trip was about to end. She and Clayton had covered a lot of ground since Texas, both in distance and in their hearts.

Time and again, they'd crossed paths with people Clayton had known from the war. Each had carried wounds both inside and out. Vanessa had found each person's perspective offered a hazy picture into her husband's past. Those pictures were as clear as any photograph she'd seen in art galleries, but far more heart-wrenching. The descriptions of Clayton were full of lost battles and fierce hunger and men lost. Of empty dreams and determination and regret and pride.

She'd always wondered why Clayton had never told her stories about the war and the variety of people he'd befriended during that time. Couldn't help but wonder why he never said more about his family, about the men in his regiment, during his years at the Circle Z.

Now she wondered why she'd never really asked.

She'd fooled herself into thinking of the War between the States as something sanitized and clean. Even a year ago, she would've been too shocked to think about a man like Hank, doing everything in his power to survive soldiers' occupation of all he knew and loved.

She certainly would've been too shocked to ever imagine that a woman like Lacy would have any good qualities at all. With some surprise, Vanessa realized that when she lost her innocence at Price's hand, she had also unexpectedly gained new insight toward others. Now, she could recognize depth of character, and respected the sheer determination to live and prosper.

Clayton's path and hers had been meant to cross; she knew it as certainly as she knew the stars would come out at night. God was with them, always. Unbidden, one of Clayton's favorite psalms rang through her mind. *"I will guide you along the best pathway for your life. I will advise you and watch over you."*

Surely no experience could be a better illustration of His guidance.

Outside of Denver, the land became ragged again, the terrain mountainous, the earth as hard as the rocks jutting out of the ground in the distance. Bits of shrubs poked out from rocks every now and then, seeming to grow in spite of the harsh environment. Vanessa did her best to help Coco navigate her way on the trail, though she had a feeling her efforts were superfluous. Coco was a smart mare, and determined to keep up with Lee.

The hours passed, bringing with them the waning sun and a slight breeze. And as Coco took her time following Lee, taking care to avoid rocks and thorny bushes in the way, Vanessa once again settled into a complacent daze.

Her hands loosened on the reins, and she yawned as they crossed yet another long patch of desolate prairie. Coco's head slowly bent forward, her soft nose nipping at stray weeds.

The sharp, shrill cry to the south was enough to scare her out of her skin. Vanessa gripped the reins sharply, tugging at Coco, making the mare neigh in protest.

The sound came again, harsh and strong and fearless. Coco's hooves faltered and fear boiled up. Vanessa looked to her husband in alarm. "Clayton?"

"Come closer." He'd slowed his pace considerably, his back rigid. In fact, the only one not looking skittish was Lee. The warhorse merely pricked his ears intelligently, as he picked his way through the long grass. "Stay by my side."

Vanessa hastened to nudge Coco closer still. "What's going on?"

His mouth thinned into a line. "Indians. Cherokee, most likely."

With some dismay, Vanessa turned to where he was looking, her heart stopping in her throat as she saw two figures in the distance. Fear, tangible and true, attacked her, grabbing her hard, not daring to let go.

Not taking his gaze away from the pair of riders in the distance, Clayton reached for her. "Don't leave my side," he ordered again.

It didn't escape her notice that he neglected to allay her nerves, to confidently proclaim they were going to be all right. After squeezing her fingers, his hand dropped, and Coco fussed.

Searching for strength, Vanessa valiantly tried to keep her composure and calm her mount. The last thing either of them needed was for Coco to bolt.

The Indians were close enough for Vanessa to see they were clothed in buckskin. Slick black hair grazed one of men's shoulders. The other's hair looked to be braided and tied with a strip of leather. No markings or paint decorated their faces; in contrast, their smooth skin looked impassive, their expressions solemn and proud.

Determined.

Vanessa started to shake. What if they came closer? What if they abducted her?

Everyone had heard stories of Indians scalping innocent people. Everyone knew they could be ruthless.

Remembering the way Price's fingers had felt on her skin when he'd torn her dress, she squeezed her eyes tight. She didn't want to hurt again. Didn't want to be another man's victim. She felt as if her heart had lodged in her throat, she was so aware of every beat.

Eager to stay with Lee, Coco plodded forward.

She opened her eyes to see Clayton looking at her with worry. Though he reached out and patted her shoulder, the words he murmured came out toneless and firm. "Don't say a word, Van."

She didn't think her lips could form a word, even if she could think of something to say at the moment. Terror filled her, and against her will, the terrible memory of the sting of Price's belt rushed forth. The feel of his fingers along her neck as he pulled at her dress. The strong odor of his breath as he'd leaned close.

The Indians looked just as violent. All sorts of frightening stories flew through her head. Stories of hatchets and tomahawks. Scalps and war cries. Women captives and their men who didn't want them when they were freed.

What if they shot Clayton and took her hostage? What would they want? What would she allow?

Sparing her a quick glance, Clayton murmured, "Don't fret so, honey. If they had wanted to attack, they would've already. I don't believe they'll do us harm."

Just as she was wondering how he knew that, she saw Clayton suddenly shift in his saddle, just enough to be within lightning-quick reach of his Colt. Perversely, his confidence only alarmed her. She had no idea how she would react if she found herself in the middle of a gun battle.

She gripped her saddle horn with shaking hands and trusted herself to do the best she could, which at this moment was to sit still and keep Coco calm.

Almost fifty paces away, the Indians stopped.

"Stay here," Clayton murmured, never turning his gaze away from the fierce-looking warriors.

But wasn't she going to stay by his side? "But what if—"

He didn't answer, merely coaxed Lee forward. As if in slow motion, his palomino approached the Indians. Both braves sat motionless as he approached, their expressions blank.

After ten paces, Clayton held up a hand in peace.

A long moment passed. Then, finally, one of the Indians did the same. Then he spoke, his words guttural and deep, making no sense from Vanessa's distance.

But Clayton must have understood because he pointed toward the west, where they'd been headed.

Vanessa shivered as she waited. She was certain they were being watched. Who knew how many other men were hiding in the rocks, waiting and watching? Too afraid to look anywhere but at Clayton, she sat still, wishing she knew what the men were saying.

Then he met her eyes and motioned her forward. She swallowed hard, then nudged her horse to follow Lee.

"My wife," Clayton said when she was close enough to see the scar on one of the brave's left arm.

The Indians fastened black eyes on hers. Warily, she stared back at them and tried not to flinch at their appraising stares. To her relief, they didn't look aggressive, only curious.

Perhaps Clayton had been right. Maybe everything was going to work out fine after all.

"Clayton?" she whispered. "What do they want?"

"Supplies." With easy movements, Clayton unbuckled one of the thick blankets, rolled it out to show its use, then proffered it.

One of the braves shook his head. He pointed to Vanessa's saddlebag.

"Hand that to me," Clayton whispered.

Quickly, she did as he asked, then watched in shock as he rummaged through her things. After a moment's pause, he pulled out her silver-backed brush and mirror.

Though her first instinct was to cringe at the thought of some renegade Indian taking one of the few items she had from home, she said nothing as Clayton showed the men both the brush and the fine mirror.

"It's worth a fair price," Clayton said. "A fair trader would offer ten or twelve dollars for a set like this."

The Indians' eyes widened. Even Vanessa could tell they were thinking just how much money like that would mean to a poor tribe.

After another moment's consideration, the brave held out his hand. Clayton passed both the mirror and brush to him.

"What you?" the Indian asked after pocketing the items in a leather sack tied near his hips.

"Safe passage. My wife and I want to sleep in peace tonight. We mean you no harm, we're headed to Larkspur."

After conversing with his friend in what to Vanessa sounded like a series of grunts and hand movements, the taller of the two men motioned his paint horse forward. "I take you."

Without hesitating, Clayton nodded. "Much obliged." As he motioned Lee forward, he turned back to look at Vanessa. "Darlin', keep up."

He needn't have worried. She was determined to stick to his side like glue. When they'd ridden about twenty feet, the other brave let out another shrill whistle.

As she'd feared, several other Indians appeared out of the dips in the terrain, a few from positions behind boulders. The fact that she'd been so unaware of their presence was startling.

Yet, they didn't approach. Instead, after listening to one of them speak, they turned in the opposite direction and rode out of sight.

Clayton did nothing to acknowledge his surprise, if he was surprised at all. He simply followed their guide, his posture curiously at ease, though his jaw looked rigid and his eyes very aware.

Vanessa didn't dare look anywhere but at Clayton's back as they continued to ride, though she was aware that they were leaving the broad plains and entering a hillier terrain, filled with far more bushes, grasses, and evergreen trees. Little by little, the air felt fresher, lighter. Crisp.

Were they riding into more danger? It seemed likely.

After guiding them for more than an hour, the Indian stopped. "Stay," he ordered.

Clayton reined in Lee and dismounted. "Thank you."

The land was pretty. A large boulder, as big as some of the line shacks on her ranch, jutted out of the ground, effectively blocking the wind and offering privacy.

Of course, it also prevented them from spotting any would-be attackers. She shivered, then noticed on the other side of them was a fast-moving stream.

Vanessa smiled in spite of the severity of their situation. She'd learned to welcome any opportunity to camp near water. It provided a much-needed place to wash up and could be boiled for coffee or tea.

Clayton pointed to himself. "Proffitt."

"Proffitt," the Indian said. Tapping his own buckskin-covered chest, he said, "Red Cloud."

"Red Cloud. Until we meet again."

Red Cloud dismounted. At first, Vanessa worried that he was going to approach her, but he passed her and Coco without a spare glance and went to the creek. Clayton motioned for her to stay where she was.

From her perch on her horse, she watched Red Cloud wade into the creek, eye the rippling current for a moment or two, then reach in and deftly pull out a fish.

She was so surprised, she yelped. "Oh!"

Red Cloud almost smiled as he carried the fish back up the banks. "Take," he said to Clayton.

Clayton did smile and took the flopping fish with a gesture of thanks.

And then before anyone said another word, the Indian mounted the paint and rode off, not looking back once.

When he disappeared from sight, Vanessa exhaled a deep breath. "Oh, my."

Clayton put the fish on a pile of leaves, then walked to her and wrapped his hands around her waist. She'd just slipped her own palms on his shoulders in preparation to dismount, when he rested his head on her thigh.

"Lord have mercy," he breathed.

She held his head close, ran her fingers through his dark hair. "I've never been so scared in my life," she admitted.

"Neither have I." Raising his head, he searched her face. "What would I have done if they'd harmed you, Vanessa?"

He swung her out of the saddle, but instead of immediately releasing her like he'd been wont to do lately, he folded her into his arms.

She responded by stepping into his embrace. Closing her eyes, she rested her head on his chest and sighed with relief. Felt his body, so strong, so reassuring against hers. Then she realized his shirt was damp.

The weather was cool, too cool for an experienced horseman like Clayton to break a sweat. The perspiration had been brought on by fear. Resting her cheek against the hard planes of his chest, Vanessa felt the staccato beats. She was so thankful he wasn't harmed, that neither of them were littering the ground with blood.

When they parted, he brushed back a stray hair from her cheek. With a look of sympathy, he murmured, "I'm sorry about the mirror and brush. I'll find a way to make it up to you."

"It meant nothing."

"You sure?"

She understood his skepticism. There'd been a time when her vanity had meant so much more to her. But that was before Price's attack, before she'd left everything she'd known.

Before Clayton had done the same, completely selflessly.

"Everything that matters is right here," she said, clutching his arms. "I promise."

He eyed her lips, almost leaned forward to kiss her, then stepped back suddenly. "I'll deal with the horses if you can gather up wood."

She looked around. "Do you think we're safe?"

"I do. In fact, I'd be surprised if right now we're not the safest we've been in some time. I imagine Red Cloud and his counterparts are keeping watch."

The thought of that made her mouth go dry. "Will they come back?"

"I don't know." Gently, he squeezed her arm. "It's okay, honey. It's going to be all right."

Hastily, she gathered wood for their fire, then set to work scaling and gutting the fish Red Cloud had brought them. She was thankful that she'd never been particularly squeamish about preparing food. After filleting the meat from the bones, she placed it in an iron skillet. Only when the fish was ready did she wade into the creek to wash.

Silently, Clayton took care of the horses, then set to work on the fire. Finally, he laid the pan on the wood, letting the fish crackle and pop as it browned. After they ate, he made coffee.

By this time, the sun had set and only the bright red and orange glow of the fire illuminated the land. She felt exposed and aware of everything around them, sure that Red cloud was watching their every move.

"Come here, honey," Clayton murmured, opening his arm to her from his spot, leaning against a tall spruce.

Little by little, she relaxed against him. Tantalizing smells wafted up from the smoke. The pungent aroma of cedar made their campsite smell inviting, relaxing her nerves.

"How did they know we wouldn't shoot?" she asked.

"I don't know."

"Were you tempted to fire on them?"

"No." He paused, as if choosing his words carefully. "Back in the war, I got used to judging people quickly, even the enemy. After a while—in those last few weeks—we all got tired of killing. I'm thinking that was what Red cloud was feeling, too."

"Tired of killing."

The muscles of his arm around her shoulders tensed. "The violence—it takes your breath away. Little by little, death and pain seems to sink into every part of you. Almost becoming part of who you are—part of your soul." He shifted. "Sometimes I think I'll do just about anything to never feel that way again."

Vanessa knew Clayton would be forever scarred by his past—just as she knew she'd have no true idea of what he'd actually been through or how bad the things he'd seen really had been.

All she could do was echo a bit of his advice and hope it would catch. "Never's a long time."

Her words seemed to startle a chuckle. "You're right, sugar. Never is definitely a long time." After a moment, Clayton said, "One day we'll need to talk about us, about what is between us."

Vanessa knew he was right. Unfortunately, she had a feeling he wasn't going to want to listen to a single word she said.

So instead of agreeing, she closed her eyes and pretended to sleep. If she did that, maybe he'd want to keep her in his arms just a little bit longer.

10

Miles started at a brash knock on his door. No one knew him at the Addison Hotel, so there was no reason anyone should have sought him out.

The knock came again.

"Yes?" He hurried out of his bed and pulled open his saddlebag. His pistol lay at the bottom.

The pounding was harder. "Hello? Anybody in there? Hello?"

"Yes. Just a minute." His palms started to sweat as he grasped the deceptively cool handle of his pistol. Had he loaded it? Did he even know where the bullets were?

The voice floating through grew loud. "Can you walk any slower? My word, but you are taking your time. Do you think I have all day to stand here in the hall?"

Was that a question? "Um . . . well." What should he do? Point the gun as soon as he opened the door?

"Anytime, now. Sir, are you Miles Grant?" Now she was practically yelling.

That's when it hit him. *She*. There was a woman outside his door looking for him. He sat down.

What's more, that voice was deliciously feminine and amazingly forceful.

Most important, it was completely unfamiliar. His hands started to perspire. "I am," he said, still not budging from his seat on the hard chair near the window.

"Well, I don't speak to doors none. Open up, sugar. I've got a message for you and time's a wastin'."

As he realized that most likely the woman would tell him what she came to say whether face-to-face or through the door, Miles crossed the room. With a sense of trepidation, he turned the handle slowly. From the moment the door swayed backward, the woman on the other side took control.

Miles could only step back in awe as a sight like nothing he'd ever seen greeted him with a saucy smile.

"Oh!" she murmured. "Hmm."

A real belle was staring at him, long and hard. Her eyes were lined with kohl, her lips rouged. She wore a tight-fitting orange-colored dress, all decked out with enough lace and ruffles to make his eyes zip from one point to the next just to see what they could see. And, boy howdy, it was a lot.

When he hastily closed his mouth after one full jaw-dropping moment, her blue eyes sparkled. "Now you, Mr. Miles Grant, are nothing how I imagined."

Miles didn't invite her to step inside, but she pranced in anyway. In a flash, she shut the door behind her and faced him full on, just like there was nothing scandalous about her being alone in a room with a man who had his boots off.

Or perhaps she was used to that.

As he glanced at his feet, Miles felt his cheeks heat something awful. He could not believe he'd forgotten to slip on his boots in his haste to locate a gun.

That embarrassment led him to recite the obvious. "I don't know you."

"Oh, honey. Believe me, I know that."

Miles felt his palms getting sweaty. She looked like a sporting woman. Had someone mistakenly informed her that he was wanting a service?

Just as he started wondering how he was going to correct her of that assumption, she placed one hand on her hip and regarded him frankly. "See, it sure don't matter that you don't know me, because I sure as cotton know you. You belong to Price Venture, don't you?"

He didn't know if he "belonged" to anyone. "Price is my stepfather."

"Well he just tried to pay for my time, but I told him to move along." Narrowing her eyes, she murmured, "Now, I'm also wondering if maybe you know a different man. A man I happen to know real well."

Miles just wanted her out of his room. "I doubt we know any of the same people." He walked to the door, gripped the handle to hold himself steady. "Now, if you'll just leave, I—"

"I'm speaking of Clayton Proffitt," she interrupted.

Miles noticed that all traces of guile and flirtation had left her painted face. Instead, he was staring at a woman who knew all the answers and wanted to know if he knew any.

A fear swept through him unlike anything he'd ever known. *What did she want? Why had she sought him out? What's more, how would she have known about Clayton?*

If he failed at this point, he'd not only lose his self-respect, he'd know he had finally let his sister down. Fear guided him forward. "I . . . I don't know what you're talking about."

She rolled her eyes. "Now you're just being silly. Look. My name's Lacy. Believe it or not, I've known Clayton for years. Since childhood, since when neither of us could barely tie our shoes. Clayton Proffitt has eyes as dark as hot coffee in the morning, matching hair, square jaw, and stands like he's at attention. Always." She batted her eyelashes. "Ring a bell?"

Miles was beginning to think he'd have had an easier time with a bandit. He could've just shot the guy and shut the door. This woman was making him panicky. Her blue-eyed stare got to him, forced him to speak. "Yes."

"All righty, then." Placing one slim hand on her hip, she got to business. "Clayton was here a few days ago, along with his wife—who's your sister, I presume." She looked him over. "You two have the same eyes."

Miles doubted Clayton and Vanessa had actually wed—their relationship had never seemed especially romantic—but he could see Clayton passing off Vanessa as his wife in order to protect her. "Yes?"

"Clayton told me a Price Venture might come around, looking for them." Looking him up and down, she murmured, "I can only assume that's why you're here."

A dozen thoughts were running through his head. He and his stepfather were close behind Vanessa and Clayton. The two of them were traveling as man and wife. And, just as important, he'd done very little to get Price off their track. Despite his promise to Clayton.

Fear rose inside him like bile. Swallowing hard, Miles said, "When you saw my stepfather—did he . . . did Price ask you about Vanessa?"

"No."

Relief poured through him. He hadn't failed. Not yet.

"But I have a feeling once he gets a good amount of liquor in him, he might." Lacy shifted, forcing the other hip out, directing his attention back to her generous figure. After a pause, she raised a brow. "What I'm wondering is . . . what's going on?"

"Nothing you need to know about."

Her voice hardened. "That's where *you* are wrong, Miles Grant. Clayton Proffitt is about the only person in my life who can still make me think that I'm worth more than the dress I'm wearing. Who still can make me feel like I count for something, even now."

"Even now," Miles echoed. Miles felt so lost, he wished he had anyone on his side who made him feel that way. But there was no one.

"His regard means a lot to me, you know?"

Miles felt his neck flush. "I do know." Well, he could guess.

Seemingly satisfied, Lacy nodded. "Tell me something, Miles. Why are y'all after them?" She held up a hand before he could fumble for a lie. "Now, honey, I don't need to know the whole truth. A part of the truth will do."

She had him there. "Our stepfather . . . Price . . . abused my sister." Funny how he no longer was even trying to pretend it hadn't happened. Was it Lacy's direct look or his growing and changing that had brought that on? "Price wants her back."

"Ah. I see."

Miles noticed she didn't look particularly surprised. Had she known the violence of men once before?

As he eyed Lacy and wondered how much more of Vanessa's circumstances he should relay, Miles thought about the abuse he'd become accustomed to receiving from Price. Now he hardly flinched when Price backhanded him or rudely embarrassed him in public. "The truth is, Vanessa would be better off without ever seeing him again."

"Amen to that."

Knowing Price was volatile too, from whatever sickness ailed him, Miles warned, "Be careful of him, Lacy. He's a desperate man. There's money involved, too. He won't stop at hardly nothing right now. Don't tell him a thing about you or Clayton or Vanessa. He'll not forget."

Seeing where his eyes were focused, Lacy leaned against the door. "Don't you worry none about Price. We've seen his like here before, and we'll see his like again. Janey's got him real occupied for now, anyway. But what I'm thinkin' is we need to do something instead of just evading. Don't you agree that would be the proper course of action?"

For most of his life, Miles had only wanted to be safe. Then, as the years passed, he'd only hoped to blend in. After his pa died, when he realized that no one was still going to look at him like a man, he'd tried to drift along, not offering to push himself, never volunteering to lead.

But after Vanessa's attack everything changed.

Now responsibility had slapped him on the back, and he was going through some of the most difficult days of his life. He didn't know who to trust, or who to count on.

Even worse, he wasn't sure who would be with him after all was said and done. Would his efforts make him any closer to Price? Would he, by chance, ever grow any higher in Clayton's estimation?

Would any of it even help Vanessa?

It seemed doubtful.

At that moment, he had no notion of what to do, how to seek help, or if he was even capable anymore of standing on his own two feet.

Finally, he spoke. "I'd be obliged if you would help me."

Folding her arms across her chest, Lacy looked pleased. "Good. Here's what I've been thinking. If Price never says a word about Clayton, we're not going to, either. Nothing good will come out of bringing up trouble."

"I agree."

"But if he does, why Janey and me are gonna to tell him that we're sure we saw Clayton and his palomino riding south, toward Mexico." Holding out her hand, she slipped a brass button in his hand. "Look familiar?"

It did, indeed. It looked like the brass buttons Clayton had attached to his most recent wool coat. He'd once confided that he kept the buttons to remind him of other days and people who he'd lost. "That's Clayton's. It was on his jacket. How did you get it?"

She waved a hand. "A man named Jeremiah at the general store happened to have some on hand. He just happens to know which insignia was on Clayton's coat." After depositing the button back into a fold of her dress, she continued. "If Price asks me, I'll put him off a bit but then I'm going to very reluctantly let him know that a certain man of Clayton's description tried to trade it for some dry goods. That I'd heard the owner had gone south. What do you think?"

Miles doubted such a story would be believed. Price was certain they were close to finding Vanessa. Obviously, that was the case. But it was worth a try, he supposed. "I don't think Mexico is a good location."

"Why's that?"

"Clayton would never take Vanessa there; there's too much uncertainty and too many bands of renegades. If I was betting, I would think he'd go to Colorado Territory, to see his sister Corrine." He paused when he noticed that Lacy stilled—showing that his guess was correct. "But maybe we can say some place like Kansas? A place like Dodge City might be believed. Especially if you were to say that you heard Clayton and Vanessa were hoping to start anew."

"Start anew." Lacy almost smiled. "Wouldn't that be something?" she said wistfully. "Wouldn't it be something to really be able to start over, shiny and new?"

Miles felt so tainted, he knew he'd never feel shiny or worthwhile again. But the idea did have merit. "It could happen. Maybe."

"Maybe is good enough. I'll pass that on to Janey." And before Miles could ask her anything else, she turned the knob and cracked open the door. "I best get on out of here. Janey can only do so much, you know?"

"I'll take your word for it."

After peeking out into the hall, she poked her head back his way once more. "Thank you, Miles." And then she disappeared down the hallway with a rustle of orange skirts, leaving only a whisper of flowery perfume in her wake.

Within seconds, Miles felt her loss. When was the last time someone had asked his opinion and actually listened?

To his shame, he couldn't remember.

✑

"I'm a little nervous to meet your sister," Vanessa admitted as they made their way from their campsite and toward the Bar M.

"Why?"

Vanessa chuckled at the question. Honestly, sometimes it seemed as if she was the more experienced of their pair. "Clayton, I've heard about her for years."

Clayton grunted. Lee blew out an impatient breath as well.

Like cowboy, like horse. Vanessa struggled to explain. "I've heard so much about Corrine, I feel like I know her inside and out. I tell you, if she'd shown up at our hotel, I would've recognized her, I'm sure."

"Maybe." After a pause, he whispered, "People change."

"I know."

Clayton grunted again.

Motioning Coco to keep up, Vanessa added, "From the way you've described her, she sounds remarkable."

"She's a special woman." After a moment, he added, "But you are special too, Van."

Vanessa rolled her eyes. "Didn't you tell me she married her husband after he visited her only twice? After she doctored several soldiers in your unit?"

"You're making it sound like more than it was. During the war all women nursed the wounded. There wasn't an alternative."

"And didn't she practically raise your brother?"

"Our mama died giving birth to Scout. Corrine didn't have much choice." He shook his head. "Don't worry so much. Corrine is just *Corrine*. She's whiny and bossy and loud and caring. You're going to like her and she'll like you. I promise, sugar. That's really all that matters, don't you think?"

"I suppose." Vanessa wasn't really worried about how she'd get along with Corrine. She'd never had a problem getting along with other women in the past, and Vanessa didn't sense things would change in that regard now that she was a married woman.

In addition, the thought of being around such an experienced woman gave her comfort in a surprising way. Her mother had been a wonderful role model until her marriage to Price, but she'd also led a rather sheltered existence. Even during the war Vanessa's father had tried to keep her as safe from harm as possible.

He'd done such a good job that she'd witnessed far fewer painful scenes than most women in her company. Consequently, when Vanessa was a child, she'd rarely viewed the ravages of war as anything other than sad stories.

Vanessa had watched her mother's eyes open wide in the first days of Clayton's arrival to the Circle Z, back when her pa had encouraged Clayton to open up about where he'd been during the war. She, too, had been shocked by the tales he dared to share.

And then she'd been so infatuated with Clayton, little else ever seemed to matter.

Back then, her dreams had been those of a girl, full of tender glances and sweet hugs. She hadn't imagined that love could ever have the full give-and-take of maturity, where there was no black and white, only shades of gray, each melting into the next color so a person wouldn't notice the difference right away.

Now, she knew Clayton for the man he was; not who she'd imagined him to be. And he was still wonderful. And, as sure as the stars laced the sky, she wished things were different. She wished she felt different, like she used to.

Not so scared and jumpy. Not so haunted by another man's hurtful hands. By the memory of another man's anger and pain.

Coco nickered, making Vanessa's thoughts return to the present. And the future. "You never said what we're going to do after we get to Corrine's."

"She and Merritt are going to take care of you."

Take care of her? "Clayton, what are you talking about? What are you going to do?"

"I'll talk to Merritt and see if he needs me. If not, I'm going to have to find a job."

Vanessa's heart sank as she realized that she'd been so focused on getting to his sister's spread that she'd had little opportunity to think about much other than getting away from Price. "What kind of job?"

"Not sure. Maybe something in the law. That's good money."

That sounded dangerous. "Really?"

"I know how to fire a pistol, and I'm not afraid to kill," Clayton said, though his eyes looked haunted and dark at the possibility. "In some places, that comes in handy."

If money was what they needed, she knew of a better way to get it. Her momma hadn't shared much with her, but she had said enough for Vanessa to know that her daddy had put money aside for Vanessa's future, just in case she needed it. It lay in a bank in town, just waiting for her to claim it.

It would make her feel good to do something for her husband. "Clayton, I could wire Miles."

He glanced at her in surprise. "Why on earth would you want to do that?"

"My pa left money for me. Miles could get it transferred." Her voice faded as he glared at her.

"No." The force of his word startled Coco, who danced underfoot for a moment, kicking up dirt and gravel.

Hoping to get Clayton to listen, she prodded Coco forward so they were side by side. "But it could help you, help us—"

"No. Don't contact him, Vanessa. Ever." The dark eyes she knew so well narrowed under the brim of his worn Stetson. "If you contact the bank, Price could come find you."

"I doubt he would go to so much trouble. No doubt he's probably forgotten all about me."

"It hasn't been that long. I doubt Price has even begun to give up on you."

"But that money is mine. Ours. He can't touch it. . . . It's just sitting in the bank. Waiting."

"No. Forget that it even exists. It's part of your past."

His words stung. Part of her wasn't ready to forget about everything before she'd run away. "But—"

His voice hardened. "I won't compromise on this. Don't contact the bank. Ever. You understand?"

Stung, she backed away. "Clearly."

After a moment his voice gentled. "Don't worry about money, sugar. You're my wife. I'll take care of you."

Vanessa patted Coco for comfort, to keep from saying anything, from pointing out the obvious once again. Yes, she knew he could take care of her.

But what he didn't seem to understand was that she wanted to take care of him, too.

✍

Five hours later, they came upon a large log house, its girth spanning an area wide enough to hold two of Circle Z's barns. A small pond sat off to its side, a thicket of thick green pines and starry-leafed aspens hiding it. Within minutes of coming into site, a rider on a shiny black stallion rode forward.

"There's only one palomino that trots like that!" the rider called out. "And that's General Robert E. Lee."

Clayton laughed, all traces of worry erased from his features in a split second. "Merritt, look at you, all spry and eagerness. Coming out to greet us?"

"Your sister wouldn't have it any other way," he said, riding closer.

Vanessa sucked in her breath as she got a closer look at Clayton's brother-in-law. He was a bear of a man. Wide and strong, sitting upon his sturdy horse he looked like a stone wall. A thick black mustache as dark as his stallion graced a face that was scarred from the pox. The most mesmerizing thing about him was a pair of blue eyes that were as bright as the Colorado sky.

Unabashedly, he sidled up to Clayton and smiled. "You are a sight for sore eyes," he murmured, clasping Clayton's arm. "You're sister's going to soak my shirt, she's going to be so pleased to see you."

Clayton grinned. "I've missed Corrine. I've missed you both."

"You've been gone far too long, Clay."

"I didn't mean to; things just happened."

Merritt turned to Vanessa then, his sparkling eyes seeming to take in every part of her. "Who might you be?"

The question was direct. Before she knew it, she'd replied in kind. "Vanessa."

"She's my wife, Merritt."

Merritt cocked an eyebrow. "I hadn't heard you'd taken a wife."

"We're recently married." Clayton shifted. "I'll tell you the whole story if you'll let me get off my poor horse. Lee's ready for a rest, and I know Vanessa is."

"Come on then," Merritt said, kicking his horse into a trot. "Let's get you settled."

"You all right?" Clayton asked as they followed at a far slower pace. "I should have probably warned you that Merritt has never had a problem with speaking his mind."

"I don't mind. I like him."

They said nothing more as they approached the barn, then became involved with the painstaking work of dismounting, sorting saddlebags, and caring for the horses.

Vanessa did as much as she could, though Merritt and one of his hands took over without much fanfare, easily showing that they could do twice the work in half the time.

Merritt had just asked another hand to take Clayton's and her saddlebags into the main house when Corrine, all five feet of her, came racing in.

"Corry, you should have waited inside. It's chilly out here."

"I couldn't wait another minute, John. Clayton!" she gasped before launching into his arms. "Clayton, I told John I was sure that was you."

A lump formed in Vanessa's throat as she witnessed the tearful reunion. Clayton gently wrapped his arms around Corrine and rested his head on top of hers. He closed his eyes, obviously memorizing the moment.

Corrine was laughing and crying and talking all at the same time. Clayton murmured something quietly, too softly for Vanessa to discern the words.

After another minute, Merritt winked at Vanessa before stepping a little more closely to his wife. "Easy now," Merritt said. "And you be careful with her, Clay."

After a couple of hiccups, Clay set Corrine at arms' length and fought a smile. "What, now that you're a fancy married lady you've become a china doll?"

"No. I'm in the family way, Clayton."

"Again?" He felt his face flush as his sister chuckled.

Merritt rolled his eyes as he pulled Corrine into the comfort of his arms. "A baby. My guess is another girl, Corrine's carrying on so."

All teasing faded away like the flick of a switch. Clayton thought she still had a baby. "Is that right, Corrine? So soon?"

She nodded. "We're thinking I'll be due in a few weeks or so." Quietly, she added, "It's a blessing. After Melissa, I didn't think I could have any more."

Merritt scowled. "She probably shouldn't."

Just as Clayton looked to be saying something about that, Corrine turned to Vanessa, capturing her with brown eyes just like Clayton's. "I'm so sorry; what must you think of me, ignoring you like that? How do you do? I'm Corrine Merritt."

"Pleased to meet you. I'm Vanessa."

"My wife," Clayton added simply.

But at that moment, Corrine hugged her hard before flying back into Clayton's arms. "Married? Oh my word, this is news! Clayton, when did this happen? I can't believe it! I've always hoped he'd find someone special," she rushed on, tears filling her eyes once again.

Merritt sighed.

Clayton hugged his sister while reserving a wink for Vanessa. "I'm glad you're happy."

Unabashedly, the tears flew faster. "Happy? I'm more than that. I'm just so thankful." Stepping away, Corrine wiped at her cheeks with a fist. "Oh, Clay. After everything you've been through, it's such a blessing to know you've found peace in your life."

"Settle now, Corry," Merritt said, curving an arm around her. "Everything's good."

Peeking out from her husband's hug, Corrine gazed Clayton's way. "You sure?"

"Positive," Clayton said with a nod.

A lump settled in Vanessa's throat. Oh, how she wanted to believe that! She wanted her marriage to be something to celebrate, something to embrace, instead of feeling the harsh grip of doubt and apology that gripped her every time she looked at Clayton.

He caught her gaze and smiled softly. "I think you and Vanessa are going to like each other very much."

"I'm sure you'd like us to get you out of this barn! Are you thirsty? Hungry? I bet you're starved!" she finished before anyone else could get a word in edgewise. "And you'll have to meet the girls! They're with Rosa right now. Rosa loves to sit with them while they play with their dolls, and I love Rosa for doing it."

Vanessa picked up her skirts and gave up even thinking about answering as Corrine prattled on. Then, as Clayton gently curved his fingers along her elbow, she felt warm and happy.

Almost like being home at last.

Almost.

11

Clayton lit his cigar and inhaled deeply as the match burned low, finally snuffing out in a burst of bright orange next to his fingertips. He certainly did enjoy the comforting feel of his sister's homestead. It had been a long time since he'd been anyplace where he felt truly relaxed, and the sense of belonging was almost as welcome as the chicken and dumplings Corrine had served.

"Dinner was very fine," he said to his brother-in-law.

"You got lucky," Merritt said with a laugh. "Your sister is bar none the worst cook I've ever had the misfortune of knowing. Chicken and dumplings is the only thing she can make, and she's managed to ruin that a time or two as well."

Recalling how their father had insisted she keep trying to bake decent biscuits instead of river rocks, and how their Aunt Marge had schooled Corrine more than once on the proper way to season a pan, Clayton frowned. "She's still no better, even after all this time?"

"Not even a little. Usually José cooks for us, but he's visiting his wife tonight."

"She doesn't live here with him?"

"Nope. She works for another family down the road."

"That sounds like a story."

"It is one at that," Merritt stated in between puffs. "I guess they took to living apart right around the time his mother moved closer, to keep an eye on them."

Clayton grinned. "Uh oh."

"Yep. From what I hear, José's mama gave her what-for one too many times, so Pearl took herself off to another job. Took me some time to get the idea straight in my brain, but now I have to admit, I can't fault them. José and Pearl fight like cats and dogs. She has no patience for the man. And, well, José is a lot of things, but a saint ain't one of them. He cusses and chews and spits as well as any man under my command. Pearl's femininity hasn't dimmed his habits in the slightest."

"They visit each other frequently?"

"And infrequently. About once a week José gets a look in his eye and takes off in Pearl's direction. After twenty-four hours together, José returns, working like a madman and full of stories about the many problems with his wife. It truly is not one of the more peaceful relationships I've ever witnessed."

"Unlike yours."

Merritt raised an eyebrow in wry acceptance. "Indeed. Unlike mine."

Clayton struck a match against a plank underfoot and avoided commenting on that. They both knew he was in no position to say a word about the sanctities of marriage.

Merritt rocked back and forth, pointing out the misshapen form of a horn toad before resting his boots flat on the planks below him. "Now that we've gossiped about my cook, you want to tell me what's really going on?"

Clayton watched his cigar's smoke dissipate in the cool night air. "Not especially."

"I think it might be a fine idea."

"But not a good one."

His chair stopped. "A man would have to be blind not to see that Vanessa is a fetching woman."

"I'm not blind."

Merritt prodded a little more. "She seems very sweet."

"She is that. But tougher than you might imagine," Clayton added, thinking once more about her fortitude on the trail to Colorado. "She's got grit."

"That's good to hear. So. Care to finally tell me why you showed up here in Colorado?"

"I didn't know I needed a reason to visit my sister."

"Don't play that game, Lieutenant. Last I heard you had a job at the Circle Z. Don't see how you can take off from it."

"It's Captain, Major," Clayton retorted just as sharply. "At least, it was. And Vanessa and I just decided to come out this way."

Snuffing the rest of the cigar out from under his boot, Merritt stared hard at Clayton. "Settle now. All I'm saying is that it would be a good idea to tell me the truth. You need to level with someone. Might as well be family."

Family.

The air stilled between them, becoming thicker with expectation and unspoken words. Merritt was as close to him as Scout had ever been, and even more so since Clayton had had little contact with Scout after the war began. Merritt loved him like a brother, and more than once had saved his hide.

Perhaps that was why Merritt had not been reluctant to speak to him so bluntly and forcefully. Not since his father was alive had anyone dared to speak to him in such a way. Not the men on the trail who he used to command, not Vanessa, not the boys at the Circle Z.

Merritt waved his cigar and kept right on talking. "Take tonight, for example. Here, you've been married a few days, a few weeks at the most. You have a beautiful wife who looks at you like the sun rises and shines on your shoulders. Most men of my acquaintance would be in their bride's arms at a time like this, enjoying every minute of the marriage bed. Enjoying some privacy after nights of sleeping outside. But you, Clayton Proffitt, are paying social calls."

Clayton didn't like his old friend's tone or implication that he somehow was a groom in need. "There's not a thing you need to be worrying about."

"I was once a newlywed, too, you know."

With his sister. "I'm well aware of that."

"There's something going on between you two; I just don't know what. But I do know that it isn't all candy and roses." Leaning forward, Merritt met his gaze and looked as lethal as a rattler. "Talk."

"I worked for Vanessa's father," Clayton finally said. "They have a spread out in West Texas."

"Circle Z. I remember."

"It was a good place for me. Then, Bill Grant died."

"And?"

"After a time, her mother remarried. Marilyn Grant, she wasn't the kind of woman who could imagine handling things on her own. When Price Venture came around, offering protection and a future, she took it. They were married within weeks of Bill's passing."

"And let me guess, Venture is no good?"

"No."

Merritt whistled low.

Clayton nodded. "In some ways, I can't blame her. The Circle Z is a big place, and neither Vanessa nor Miles were fit to manage the property."

"But you could have."

"I could have, and I managed a lot of it. But I wasn't family." Recalling the chain of events that led him and Vanessa to this place, Clayton cleared his throat. "Mere weeks after the ink on their license was dry, Venture showed his true colors. He degraded his wife and mismanaged the ranch. To put it lightly, the transition was difficult. Price kept me on as foreman and went on to put as much of Bill Grant's money to use in the cathouses over at Camp Hope as he could. He made no secret of the fact—everyone knew. As time passed, Marilyn retreated even more to her rooms."

"You ever going to tell me about Vanessa?"

"Van . . . Van took it all fairly hard. She was close to her daddy, and he doted on her." Clayton closed his eyes, remembering her dressed in head-to-toe black, standing by her lonesome next to her daddy's grave. "I started giving her special attention—she needed it."

"And got smitten?"

Perhaps that had been when it happened. Or—had it been earlier?

Maybe he'd been smitten from the first moment he'd laid eyes on her. When she'd worn braids and had freckles and had looked at him with such trust that he'd thought his heart would break.

"I respected her," he corrected. "I tried to look out for her, tried to be her friend." He paused, seeking control. "Back in September, I found her out in the barn, crying. Price had whipped her with his belt."

Merritt's eyes hardened. "I can guess the reason."

"I took her out of there that night. Ken Willoughby married us outside of Lubbock. He's become a pastor," Clayton added.

"And now you're here."

"And now we're here. I should let you know that I've offered her your protection."

"Not yours? She's your wife."

"I truly don't know if I'm the best man for her. She's young. Raised to have the kind of things I can't get for her." Looking down, Clayton said, "I've been praying about her, and praying about what we should do."

"What has the Lord been telling you?"

"I don't know." Looking out across the wintery grasslands of the Bar M, Clayton said, "I feel like He placed me near Vanessa to keep her safe."

"Perhaps He did."

"If that's the case, then I shouldn't be in love with her too, should I?"

"Why not? It all makes sense to me. Husbands should look out for their wives. Protect and honor them." Lowering his voice, he murmured, "And love them."

"I do love Vanessa. But she needs time."

"Ah." They sat in silence a moment longer, listening to the sounds of the night. In the distance, a lone coyote cried out. The stars above them burned brightly, illuminating their presence with a spectacular glow. Finally, Merritt spoke again. "You remember how I found Corrine?"

"I do."

"Your sister was washing Scout's clothes in lye soap. Her hands were raw and burning. And she still offered to cook me supper."

"Thank goodness you said no."

Merritt laughed. "She did more on her own than you might believe, Clayton. After the Yankees came through, your Aunt Marge retreated into her own world. It was up to Corrine to find food, to take care of Scout. She shouldered a lot of burdens. I prayed a lot about my feelings for her, Clayton. It was no easy task to accept her gift of love in those days. There was a strong possibility I'd love her and then leave her a widow."

Clayton knew his situation with Vanessa wasn't any easier. But the difference was that he didn't feel at peace with either leaving Vanessa's side or giving into the temptation of being her husband for the next twenty years.

Merritt broke the silence again. "What are you going to do now?"

"I'm not sure. I need to find a job."

"There's plenty of work here. Why don't you stay on at the Bar M for a bit?"

"If Price comes—"

"If Price comes, I'll greet him with everything he deserves."

"That might solve Vanessa's worries, but not all of my problems. I need to earn my way."

"You can do that here."

"I depended on you during the war, Merritt. You can't ask a man to do that twice in a lifetime."

"What if I told you I don't see it that way? What if I said I need you as much as you need me?"

"I'd say thank you." Maybe Merritt was right. Maybe it was time to settle down and stop looking behind his shoulder. Time to move on.

They rocked a little more in silence. Sat together the way men can when no words are necessary between them. After a while, Merritt spoke. "Maybe what Vanessa really needs is to know you care."

"She knows I care." After all, he'd guided her across the country!

"I suppose that's enough, then." After snuffing out his cigar in a box of sand on the edge of the porch, Merritt turned to the door. "Now, I best go take care of your sister. She's the worst pregnant woman I've ever seen. She whines and complains like no other."

After Merritt went inside, he gazed at the stars, all of them looking to be within a hand's reach.

Clayton wished he could very well pull one down and make a wish. That fanciful thought almost made him smile.

❧

To his surprise, Corrine was standing outside his bedroom door when he came upstairs an hour later, her hand hovering over the knob. "Oh, Clay, thank the good Lord you're here."

Panic rose in his chest as he strode forward. "What's wrong?"

"It's Vanessa. She's having a night terror, Clayton. For the last few minutes she's been crying something awful, thrashing, too, by the sounds of things. I was going to go get you, but was afraid to leave her . . . and I was going to go in, but was afraid that might just make things worse."

Vanessa's cry pierced the air again.

"Go on back to bed. I'll take care of her," Clayton murmured as he slipped into his room.

Across the way, atop a pile of down comforters, Vanessa was crying. Her hands were clenched in fists, gripping an unseen enemy. Pale ankles and calves peeked out under her wrinkled nightgown. A moan escaped her, high-pitched and frightened.

As her head moved side to side, Clayton sat next to her. "Sweetheart? Vanessa, honey, hush now," he whispered, yanking off each boot and letting them fall to the floor. "Van?" he whispered, reaching for her shoulders.

His touch spurred her on. With a cry, she swatted at him like a woman fighting for her life. Clayton stayed still, trying his best to curve his arms around her. "Vanessa, darling, shh. Shh, now. It's all right."

When she quieted for a time, Clayton pulled off his sweat-stained chambray. Though he had a feeling his white under-shirt didn't smell much better, at least the dust and dirt from riding Lee wouldn't soil her skin. Then he gathered her in his arms and slowly rubbed her back. The raised scar tissue felt almost familiar by now. "Van? Vanessa?"

She opened her eyes, screamed, and cowered again.

This was worse than usual.

Something terrible was locked in her mind. Something she'd obviously done her best to push aside. He'd done much of the same thing with memories from the war.

Feeling helpless. Scared, he did the only thing he knew that could help.

He prayed. "Lord, please help," he whispered. "Please be with us. Please help her." Silently he added his own selfish appeal. *Please help me help her.*

As she cried out again, he rubbed his wife's back as gently as possible. "Vanessa, honey. Wake up."

Her only reply was a torrent of tears.

He felt his eyes tearing up, too. "Sweetheart, you're all right," he coaxed. "You're okay."

Slowly her eyes opened. He smiled encouragingly. "Vanessa, honey? Wake up now. You with me? No one's going to hurt you. I'm here. I'm here, honey."

She blinked twice before speaking, her voice groggy with wonder. "Clay."

"I'm here."

Tremors coursed through her, so he shifted, pulling her onto his lap. "I'm here," he repeated, almost as much for his sake as for her own.

To his relief, she laid her head on his chest and sighed. "I had another dream. A bad one."

"I know."

After another minute, she leaned a little bit away and caught his gaze. "It felt so real."

"It was just a dream." Because she was shaking so, because he couldn't bear to let her go, Clayton cuddled her even closer, wrapping his arms around her securely, doing his best to accept all of her pain. Doing his best not to notice just how right she felt, sidled up against his chest.

Smoothing a hand along her back, wincing as he felt the ridges of her scars, he murmured, "Do you want to tell me what it was about?"

"Price was in here. Attacking me."

Clayton leaned back, caught her gaze until she stilled. "He'll never lay a hand on you again. I promise."

"I smelled the whiskey." Wonder crossed her face. "I smelled it as strongly as if he were on this bed. How could it have felt so real?"

"I don't know."

Slowly, she pulled away, frowning at a lock of hair that had become tangled in the lace collar of her gown. "What a mess I am." She tugged at her nightgown, damp with sweat. "And what a sight."

Only Vanessa would think he cared. "You look fine, sugar. Perfect."

"I'm far from that."

"Never say that."

"Clay . . . I'm still so afraid."

"I know. But you're all right now. Remember? You're okay. Your mother got there in time. He hurt you, but we got you out before anything worse happened. Remember?"

Something shattered in her eyes.

Foreboding filled his soul. "Van?"

She looked down.

"Van? Did something else take place in that room?" His heart raced. All this time—all this time he'd thought that she'd only been beaten. That even though she'd always be scarred from Price's belt, he'd gotten her away before she'd been abused far worse. Mouth dry, he moved away from her. "Vanessa? Van, what else did that man do?"

She bit her lip.

"Tell me," he ordered, his voice low but full of force.

"My mother, she didn't get there as quickly as I led you to believe."

His hands shook. Violence and anger burst forth, feelings of helplessness, so fresh and new, rushed through him. He could hardly speak. "Did Price . . . did Price violate you?"

Her eyes clouded, and with that, something snapped inside of him. He needed to know the truth. The truth without vague words or veiled suggestions. Even though his voice was harsh —even though he knew his temper was only making things worse—he asked the question. "Vanessa, did Price rape you?"

Slowly, she nodded, just as tears ran down her cheeks. "I'm sorry."

"But you said I got you out." Words stumbled one over the next as he tried to make things right. "You told me that he hadn't done more than whip you."

The tears kept coming. "I know. I know what I told you."

"Why? Why didn't you tell me everything?" He knew his voice was becoming harder, clipped. "Vanessa, why didn't you tell me the truth?"

This time Vanessa didn't look away. Staring at him, her green eyes almost luminescent, she shrugged. "Clay, I didn't tell you because I was afraid." Her voice lowered. "I was afraid if you knew everything, things would never be the same."

She was right. They weren't. Unable to look at her, Clayton turned away. After all his promises, after all his efforts, he knew the plain truth.

He hadn't protected her at all. He hadn't saved her in time.

He'd completely failed her after all.

12

*F*rom the moment Clayton stood up and turned away, Vanessa knew that she'd lost him. She'd been afraid of such a thing happening. Had been afraid of him looking at her the way he had.

"Why did you never say what really happened?" His intonation was husky, deep. The words sounded rough from across the room. "Vanessa, why didn't you tell me the truth?"

It was hard to know how to voice all the words spilling over themselves inside of her. Too much time had passed, she supposed. Too much time and too many lies.

Finally, she spoke, though she doubted she'd make any sense at all. "I was ashamed." Oh, she'd been more than that. She'd been so scared.. And mortified. And worried that if she'd confessed everything to Clayton that he would think differently about her.

He turned to face her. "I would have killed him if I'd known. I would have walked into his bedroom and wrung his neck—" He stopped abruptly as they both looked at his clenched fists.

"I know." There was bitterness about him—a coldness she'd never spied there before. He looked different. Distant. More like the soldier he'd been. She didn't doubt that he could kill.

To her shame, she most likely would have been glad if he'd killed her stepfather. Price Venture had ruined her, had changed her life. Taken away her dreams and left scars on her back as a constant reminder.

But of course, if he'd murdered Price, he, too, would have been ruined.

Hesitantly she added, "I'm glad you didn't."

"I still don't understand. *I asked you*, Vanessa. I asked you that night. You told me he hadn't—"

She cut him off. "I just wanted to forget. I didn't want you to know."

"Vanessa, you should have told me. I could have helped you." He flinched. "You were hurt. We rode for hours." Pure pain entered his eyes as he combed his fingers through his hair. "I should have done something. I should have helped you more. Carried you. . . ."

"You did, Clay." Emotions billowed through her, frustrating her attempts to speak clearly. "Clayton, don't you see? I didn't want to remember. I didn't want to think about it. I was too ashamed. I'm *still* ashamed. I never wanted you to look at me this way." She reached out to him. To her mortification, he pulled away. "Please don't be mad."

"I'm not mad, Van. But I surely wish you would have trusted me."

She reached for his hand again. "Please hold me. Hold me like you used to, back before everything happened."

Almost gingerly, he returned to the bed. Leaned his head against the wall. She scrambled to his side and pressed her cheek to his chest, as always reassured by his beating heart.

Oh, he felt so warm and wonderful. Safe. She shifted closer. She was relieved when he curved an arm around her back. Maybe everything would be all right one day after all.

And because she knew he wouldn't speak of it, she did. At least a little. "All I wanted after we left was to be free of him. I didn't want to remember. Didn't want to talk about that night. About the things we did. But those dreams, they just kept coming, didn't they? Maybe I had to face the truth after all."

"Maybe." He swallowed. "Maybe so."

"Clay, do you think my bad dreams will go away now?"

"I don't know." After a bit, he spoke some more. "Mine did, after a time. One day you'll have other memories to take their place."

Turning on her side, Vanessa faced him. "Is that what happened for you after the war? You got new memories?"

"I did. Six years ago, I stepped foot on the Circle Z and found a thirteen-year-old girl with long brown hair and pretty green eyes and the sweetest smile on earth. She made me laugh. Because of her, I started to heal."

"I'll never forget the day you arrived," she said, thankful for the memory. "You were an answer to a prayer."

"I was a mess inside. So empty. But you gave me so much, Vanessa."

Had she? "I probably only gave you a headache. I never left you alone."

Almost reluctantly, his lips curved. "You did, indeed, follow me everywhere."

Remembering how pesky she'd been, Vanessa said, "I was always after you to go riding with me."

"Oh, Van, but you could ride. Like the wind. Yet, you were so foolish, too. Remember when Miles put that snake in your room?"

"I screamed like it was a rattler."

Clayton chuckled. "I'd never seen anything like your carrying on. That poor little garter snake, you probably scared it half to death."

She smiled at the memory. Clayton had picked up the snake with one hand and had marched out of her room like he was the most put-upon man on earth.

And then stood by her side when they watched the little snake slither off. "Maybe . . . maybe I already do have some good things to replace the bad ones with, Clay."

"One day, you'll feel better. One day you won't hurt. I promise."

Sharing her secret had made her feel like a dam had burst inside of her. She felt freer. Holding the horrible memories close to her had been eating her up inside. "I feel better for having told you what happened."

It was some time before Clayton spoke. "I'm glad." But she didn't hear any gladness in his voice. It simply sounded broken and harsh. Brittle and tired.

Edging away, she turned to her side, closed her eyes, and prayed. Prayed for healing and trust and forgiveness. Just as sleep washed over her, she recalled a favorite verse from Psalms. *"The Lord helps the fallen and lifts those bent beneath their loads."*

God would help her. Perhaps, by giving her Clayton, He already had.

❧

"I've half a mind to give up and go on home," Price told Miles in front of the campfire. "The Circle Z is sure to be suffering by our absence."

Miles was afraid to hope for something so good. "We've been gone a while."

"Twenty-three days. Twenty-three days too long, by my estimation."

Every day had been a matter of trial and tribulation to get through. Miles felt as if his insides had been torn up and spit out over and over again—he'd been in such a state of worry and guilt.

But he could never share any such weaknesses. He settled on stating the obvious. "It's been a tough month."

"It's been worse than tough. It's been an eternity." Tentatively, Price rubbed at his foot, which was propped up on a nearby rock. "I hadn't counted on everything being so difficult or the terrain being so unforgiving. This blasted ankle hurts like the devil."

Miles suspected it did. Price had twisted it something awful when they were crossing a shallow creek practically filled with ice. Most everyone had warned against the crossing, saying a misstep could do irrevocable damage to the horses. They, of course, had ignored the advice. Good thing only Price had been the injured party.

As the flames crackled from the sap in the pine they were burning, a slow, expectant silence filled the air. The two of them were almost talking like true family members. Almost like Price didn't think nothing of his stepson.

Yes, indeed, they'd come a long way. Miles didn't know whether to sigh in relief or frustration. Their days had been filled with tension and worry. As Miles had feared, Price hadn't listened to Lacy or Janey's insinuations about Clayton's brass button.

"Like I'd ever listen to anything a whore says," he'd muttered.

With a last parting glance at the Addison Hotel, they'd turned north instead of west, and fought the rocky terrain and cooler weather. Days were spent looking for people to interview. Nights were far longer, since Price almost always chose to find lodging, whiskey, and comfort.

For days on end, they'd traveled and talked to everyone and no one. All that time, they heard no word at all about Clayton or Vanessa. If the wilderness wasn't so vast, Miles would have guessed his sister had disappeared forever.

In the daylight, everything seemed to be going all right. Miles felt proud that he'd done his best to divert Price's mission. That Vanessa was safe from harm.

But in the evening, when the stars were out, doubts set in and he reverted back to selfish ways. In the dark, still evenings, Miles thought about his future and realized it held no promise. All he had to look forward to was a lifetime of being under Price's thumb and being thought a thoroughly poor caretaker of his father's legacy by the ranch hands and townspeople. He'd made a poor decision in Santa Fe. He should've just gone ahead and left and tried to make out on his own.

And that, of course, made him wonder who was guiding his life and principles. His stepfather? His own self-centered weaknesses? Or was it the Lord?

Even thinking about religion made him uneasy. But he couldn't discount Clayton's insistence that a greater power guided him. Miles had never claimed to be especially smart, but even he could recognize that he'd yet to place God's practices into the everyday routine of his life.

"What do you think, boy?"

"I think we should head on back," he said, hoping he didn't sound too eager. "Vanessa's bound to return home sooner or later. She can't run forever, can she? Plus, the Circle Z is her birthright. She'll want to be home."

"Do you think she really did marry Proffitt?"

"Maybe. Clayton promised my pa he'd look out for Vanessa. He swore that vow on a Bible—well, so I heard. I reckon he took that seriously."

Price turned from his study of the fire and looked at Miles with serious regard. "You might be right about that."

Miles blinked in surprise from that unexpected compliment. Feeling a little more certain, he added, "There's another reason she's going to come back, even if she did marry Clayton Proffitt. That's money. Vanessa is going to want the money Pa left her. Clayton doesn't have much."

"He sure doesn't, since I've spent what I could get my hands on."

As the night pressed on, a shadowy fluttering appeared in the distance. Dark shapes darted and flew up and down, bobbing in a wild formation. Sharp squeaks floated through the air.

Price scowled. "Bats. I hate bats."

Miles grabbed a stick and stoked the fire. With a crackle, flames grew. He hoped the smoke would encourage the creatures to head somewhere else. He wasn't fond of bats, either.

As Price looked warily above him, obviously ready to duck in case a bat swooped close, he growled, "If we get on home, I can make sure we get the cattle to market on time."

"And check the land. The telegrams we've been receiving haven't said much. No telling what the boys have been doing without you supervising."

"Those wires haven't given us a bit of information. Most likely the help has been bleeding me dry and hardly doing a lick of work." After another moment, Price laughed. "The smoke did the trick; those nasty little varmints have moved along. I think we might as well do that, too." With a new appreciation in his voice, he said, "Boy, you might not be completely worthless after all."

Miles closed his eyes and wondered how low his life had come, because for a split second, he'd felt pleased to receive such a compliment.

Someone help me, he silently prayed. *Someone please help me find some kind of light in the dark recesses of my life.*

But of course all he heard was the faint fluttering of the bats as they flew overhead.

❧

"I'm glad you can cook because I can hardly boil water," Corrine said as they sipped coffee after a delicious breakfast of eggs and bacon. "José does a fine job, but when he's not around it's a toss-up between Merritt and me who will make the worst meal."

Vanessa smiled at the quip as her sister-in-law continued. "I'm so glad Clayton brought you here. The days get long when it's just me and the girls. But even more important, it does my heart good to see the two of you together, to see the way Clayton is with you. My brother looks happy for the first time in years. I can't tell you how I've worried about him."

Vanessa looked toward the door. He'd left their bed before daylight and she hadn't seen him since. Merritt told her at breakfast that Clayton had saddled up Lee and was riding the property. Though she couldn't fault his willingness to work, there was something about his continued need to be busy— away from her—that didn't sit well.

Their conversation the night before had opened raw wounds. She knew she'd hurt him deeply by withholding the whole truth about Price's attack.

But though he might never believe it, she hadn't kept her secret only because of how she feared his reaction might be. No, she'd kept it also because it had been too much to deal with. She didn't want to think about those minutes when Price had pulled up her dress.

Didn't ever want to think again about being pinned down beneath him.

Still halfheartedly fussing around the kitchen, Corrine said, "It sure is something how life works out, I'll tell you that. I was terribly opposed to Clayton staying in Texas. I wanted him to come out here with Merritt and me so we could all be together. Clayton wouldn't have anything to do with that." Corrine frowned at the memory. "He said he needed space and time to get over the war."

Vanessa remembered the first time she'd talked to Clayton. She'd caught sight of her pa near the barn and had come running to show off the crown of daisies she'd just strung together only to be brought up short by the very tall man with the sad, solemn eyes.

She'd skidded to a stop, ready to be ignored or yelled at. But instead of doing either, Clayton had bent down and praised that daisy chain like it was the prettiest thing he'd seen in some time.

Now, so many years later, Vanessa realized that it most likely had been.

"He was an amazingly good foreman," she said.

The two girls toddled in, Rosa behind them. After handing them each some bread and butter, Corrine turned to Vanessa again. "I can't imagine Clayton being anything other than talented at whatever he does. He's always been the type to shoulder responsibility with ease. At least, that's what I remember. John feels the same."

"All the men on the Circle Z respected him, my pa the most." Remembering another lifetime, Vanessa said, "A few months after Clayton arrived, a dust storm flew up over our area. The red dust was so thick and grainy; my mother had to pack all the windows and doors with damp towels so the furniture wouldn't get covered. Livestock died—a lot of cattle died. Clayton was the first one out, taking care of their carcasses." She shook her head. "He took the worst job without a word. Never expected thanks; never expected to even be recognized. We were all in awe of him."

Standing up to pour a glass of buttermilk, Corrine cocked her head, looking as endearing as one of her little girls. "Tell me how the two of you fell in love. Was it at first sight?"

The question made her uncomfortable. It was so much easier to talk about Clayton in general terms than as her beau. "I can't rightly say."

"Come now, take pity on me," Corrine said as she sat down and wearily propped her feet up on a ladder-back chair across from her. "How did you two get so close?"

Remembering the times she'd visit his rooms for company or advice, her voice turned wistful. "Clayton, he was always there for me. So strong, stalwart. No boy who came courting could hold a candle to Clayton's quiet ways, his integrity. He made me feel special inside." Vanessa looked to Corrine. "One day I knew I loved him."

Corrine sighed. "Your story sounds how love should happen, gradually, like a good dream. With me and Merritt, it was like an ax practically severed my heart. I didn't think I would last until I'd get a letter from him . . . or he'd visit again."

Vanessa sputtered, taken off guard by the boldness of the tale. "My goodness."

Corrine nodded sagely. "Um hum. It's always been like that, too. Strong and intense. John Merritt is everything to me. I first saw him when I was washing clothes, looking like everything I was—poor and hungry and tired. But then he tipped his hat and almost smiled, and I felt like all of a sudden I had a reason to get out of bed another day. Times were so bad, I needed any reason at all."

"And the next time?"

Corrine's face sobered. "The next time I saw him, he was recovering from a bullet wound. He'd left the hospital tent and joined his unit, but wasn't doing too well. By then, Clayton wasn't around to talk sense into him—he'd been given command of his own company. Anyway, John's unit happened to be near our farm and when they realized what bad of shape he was in, they brought him to me."

Sorrow etched Corrine's expression as she continued the story. "See, he refused to go back to one of the field hospitals. Said he couldn't take any more of the dying and the pain and the smell. So, his men brought him here for a time. I cleaned his wound and nursed him. After a time, we knew we were meant to be together. We married not long after."

Vanessa had heard bits and pieces of the story. "Didn't Clayton arrive in time to see the wedding?"

"He did, and he wasn't too happy about it, neither. That silly brother of mine kept trying to tell me how I should want another man. Someone younger. Less scarred. Someone less cranky."

Corrine shook her head with a sad smile. "Even if I did have a younger man in mind, Clayton had seemed to forget that we'd been at war for years. All the young men were gone—and the half that survived were all scarred."

"But you wanted Merritt anyway? No matter what?"

"I did." Lowering her voice, Corrine said slowly, "See Clayton thought of me as his younger, sweet sister. Still fresh and new. But I hadn't been that way for a long, long time. See, the war damaged me, too."

Corrine sipped thoughtfully on her drink, then looked directly at Vanessa. "It didn't matter what was wrong with either of us. No matter what, I knew John Merritt was the man for me. I knew God had heard my prayers and answered them. Why else would such a good man fall in love with a skinny girl like me? John took the time to see me, the person I was inside. I loved him for that."

"I guess so."

Corrine shook her head in wonder. "Imagine . . . both Merritt and Clayton living in the same place! I still have to pinch myself, I feel so blessed. Now all I have to do is convince Scout to come home."

Remembering that Clayton had said Scout was riding in Texas, she said, "Do you ever hear from him?"

"Last time was a letter at Christmas." Looking sad, Corrine confided, "Years ago, when he was a little boy, I pretty much raised him. I thought we'd be close forever. But ever since I married and Clayton and John both forbid Scout to enlist, things between us all changed. I should have tried harder to keep in touch. To at least have tried to help him more. I've failed him somehow."

"I'm sure that's not the case," Vanessa said slowly. "I used to think I failed Miles. But now I'm not so sure he didn't make his own decisions. For good or bad, we must each make our own way in the world."

"I suppose, but I thought Scout might be eager to make his way nearby."

After a few minutes of contemplation, Corrine went to lie down. Vanessa stood up and cleared the table, then chatted with Melissa and Kate while José stirred what looked to be a massive pot of pintos and peppers.

Next, she walked outside, surveying the majestic views of the Rocky Mountains rising proudly in the distance. A herd of black and white cattle grazed just a few yards away. Their lowing and chomping echoed through the thin mountain air, making it seem like they were closer than they were.

But then Vanessa became aware of a different sound—the choppy rise and fall of men arguing. She winced as she realized the noise was coming from Clayton and Merritt. Eyeing the altercation with some alarm, Vanessa stepped a bit closer. Their voices rose. Merritt scowled. Clayton glared and bit out a reply.

Finally, Merritt threw up his hands and walked into the barn, while Clayton stepped toward the house. After a few steps, he spied her. His pace faltered, then he continued on, his expression grim.

"Clayton?" she called out. "Is everything all right?"

She was almost thankful that he didn't answer.

✑

"Hold on. We're not done," Merritt called out as he followed Clayton around the barn.

After watching Vanessa fade from view, Clayton glanced over his shoulder at his best friend and former commander. "Still issuing orders?"

"Oh, settle down," Merritt said as they turned the corner to the spigot. "I'm not ordering you around; I'm sharing my opinion."

"Sharing? That's what you call what you're doing?"

"Sharing, stating, whatever. Fact is, I think you're making a mistake. You can't leave. You've got a wife right here who needs you."

"She needs *protection*. She can get that from you."

"A woman needs more than that."

Clayton knew. He knew that Vanessa needed tenderness and care. She needed someone to stay by her side and make her remember that there were still men in the world who held fast to their promises.

Perhaps one day he could be that man. But right now, all he could think about was that he'd failed her. He hadn't even guessed that she'd been holding back from him. He'd thought he'd loved her. If he'd loved her so much, how could he not have guessed that so much more had happened between her and Price?

She'd said she trusted him. What kind of trust held back something so important?

He needed some time. They both did. And they weren't going to find it by living together day after day. "There's some other circumstances that are factoring into my decision," he told Merritt slowly. "Circumstances I feel strongly about."

"Such as?"

"Nothing that concerns you."

"You're running away, Clayton." Pausing two beats, Merritt added, "I never figured you for that kind of man."

The words slapped at him, good and hard. But in a way, it was no different or worse than the things he'd been feeling about himself.

Merritt splashed water on his face. He shook his hair like a dog to rid it of extra water. "You got nothing to say to that?"

"She had no choice but to leave her family, and you all are hardly strangers." After pausing, Clayton added, "If I stay I won't be able to keep my promise to give her time to get adjusted and think things through."

Plus, he knew it was time to search for Price instead of running from him. Now, more than ever, he needed to make things right.

"Your wife has had time. Lots of time, don't you think?"

Her nightmares last night had proved that their time together hadn't been long enough. Not yet. "Vanessa married me out of necessity. Ken Willoughby was sure she'd need my name on the trail—in case something happened."

"He was right."

"He may have been right, but it doesn't make doing the right thing any easier. Vanessa's had so few choices lately, I'm giving her time to reconsider."

After another moment. "I see. When were you figuring on leaving?"

"Soon. Tomorrow."

"Not wasting much time, are you?"

"I've waited long enough."

Merritt poured out their water onto the ground and stood silently as they both watched the rivulets snake their way over the parched ground, hardly soaking in a bit.

Finally, he said, "I've got some contacts in Denver. You could sign on with one of their outfits."

"Thanks, but I should be hearing from an outfit in Wyoming. I'll contact them when I get on my way." He'd contact them while he was searching for Price.

"Well, if that don't work out, I heard folks are needing some help maintaining order up in Nebraska, in Benson."

"A lawman?"

"Why not? You'd be good at it, and you're a better than decent shot."

Killing again felt wrong. Getting paid for it felt worse. Though killing to protect the innocent might be just what he needed. And, well, if he came across Price Venture, Clayton wasn't sure that he'd be able to stop himself from seeking justice. "I'll think about it."

Merritt nodded. "All of us have to find our way. Maybe it's time you found yours."

As images filtered back of the Circle Z, of the constant work, the hands, his day-to-day routine on horseback, he frowned. "Funny, I thought I had." Clayton scraped a match against the side of the barn. "'Course, running another man's spread was one thing. Running it for a man who'd done nothing to earn the right to have so much felt worse. Now, as I think about how everything was going, I wonder why I stayed so long at the Circle Z."

"That should be obvious. Clayton, you stayed because Vanessa was there."

"You think I knew deep down that she wasn't safe?" The thought was disturbing. Had he known deep down that she'd been in danger?

"I think you knew, deep down that you loved her. What's more, I think you know that now," Merritt added softly, not mincing his words. "I think you stayed there because that's where you wanted to be. Where the Lord wanted you to be . . . where Vanessa needed you. That's what I think."

That idea was even scarier. "I'll talk to Corrine later tonight and ask her to watch out for Vanessa."

"Best be ready for some tears. She's been pining for you. One brother is practically lost to her right now. She won't take kindly to her other one leaving so quickly."

Clayton admired the way Merritt knew Corrine's feelings, and championed them time and again. "You're good for her. Did you know right away?"

"When I first saw your sister, I was hungry, hurting, and freezing. What's more, I was itchy from a dozen varmints that had taken home on my skin. I looked worse than a dog on its last day. She smiled at me like I was everything she ever wanted."

Knowing how his sister felt, Clayton said, "You *were* everything she wanted."

"I never admitted to you how poorly I did in the hospital tent. When the surgeon started talking about saws, I burst into tears like a baby. The war and the fighting had taken everything from me—even my dignity."

Clayton knew he would've fought tears, too. "You're lucky you got to keep that limb."

Merritt glanced at his arm, covered in flannel. "It still has a ragtag maze of markings marching across it. When I arrived there, Corrine pulled off the bandages and almost swooned."

Clayton felt he should defend her. "You had to know—"

"I knew that my arm was infected and smelled to high heaven. What you might not know is that she squared her shoulders, brought in water so hot it nearly blistered her skin, and bathed me." He shivered. "And like a fool, I cried again. But this time not because I felt despair, but because I'd found salvation. Her hands became my lifeline, her voice the reason I stayed sane. Her soothing whispers were the only way I could go to sleep. God brought me to Corrine Proffitt. She, in turn, saved me."

Clayton felt humbled. "I never knew. I just remember what I witnessed when I saw you two together."

"Love and lust?"

"Something to that effect. I recall that when she entered the room, you could hardly speak."

"She took my breath away."

"I'd found it hard to believe—you were one of the toughest soldiers I'd ever known."

"I had tried. But war and killing wasn't all there was for me. I desired something softer, prettier, more fine."

"Corrine."

"That's a fact. I liked her gumption, liked her laugh. I needed her. I needed her tender touch. I needed sweetness and something beautiful in my life."

Clayton grinned at that, though he knew what Merritt meant. He'd stood transfixed the afternoon he'd spied Vanessa stringing daisies—the vision was so peaceful and innocent.

They walked farther, the biting cold making itself known, jarring both of them, reminding each man how harsh life was, how full of promises and regrets it was. Merritt spoke. "Land sakes, Clayton. I sure hope you know what you're doing. A good woman is hard to find, harder to keep hold of. When you find one who's willing to be yours, it's a crying shame to throw her away."

"I'm not throwing her away, not at all. I'm just doing what I promised." Lowering his voice, he said. "I need to be the type of man who pushes aside his wants in favor of what is right."

"You already are that kind of man."

"Your worst memories are of hospital tents and scares and fears. Mine are of dropped promises. Of promises to my pa to take care of my brother and sister. Of promises to the Lord to put myself behind others, to be the type of man I can be proud of." After a pause, he added, "I remember fighting and being happy that I still lived while men—boys—in my charge needed to be buried."

"You weren't alone in that. We all said prayers of thanksgiving after battles. And we've all felt guilty for being glad we were the ones digging graves instead of being placed in them."

Clayton couldn't dispute that. He couldn't dispute anything his good friend said. So, instead, he begged. "Help me keep a vow. Help me give Vanessa time."

Merritt snuffed the end of cigar in the hard dirt. "All right. Come with me, then, and we'll tell your sister together."

13

$\mathcal{V}$anessa waited for the tears to come as she watched the red dust fly up from Lee's hooves. But as her man guided his horse into a trot down the entrance of the ranch, all she noticed was that he never looked back.

So instead of crying, she felt numb.

Fact was, she'd felt dead from the moment Clayton had brought her to Corrine's fancy back parlor, the one the girls weren't supposed to step into except on special days. It was the same place where she'd entered with Clayton when they'd first arrived. Then, she'd been full of nervous excitement, anxious to get acquainted with Corrine and Merritt.

During their latest conversation, the room had felt small and stifling—filled with too many things, too many people, and not enough air. Especially since she and Clayton weren't alone.

In no-nonsense terms, Clayton had informed her that he was going away for the next two months and that she needed to stay. She'd felt abandoned.

Oh, Clayton had tried to pretty it up. Kind of. Sort of. After saying he'd admired her grit and determination, he'd gotten down to business, and spoke plain and succinctly.

And lied.

"I need to earn some money, Vanessa. I need to make sure Price isn't still after you—after us. I can't do all that from the Bar M."

She'd known there was far more to it. He was guilt-ridden about her news. He was upset with her for not being completely honest with him from the start. Because of both of those things, he wanted time and space.

Vanessa didn't know which hurt worse—Clayton's abandonment or the fact that he couldn't tell her privately that he was leaving. No, he'd had to bring in reinforcements. As if they were no more than a casual courting couple getting to know each other.

She'd been so all-fired mad that she'd glared at him, at his nerve. After everything they'd been through—riding for hours, eating fish and jackrabbit and beans for days—he was moving on.

She sat rigid and shocked as Clayton talked more about nothing than he had in the entire six years she'd known him. For a man who'd always been opposed to idle chitchat, he could sure do it well. She bit her lip, doing her best to keep her composure, to remain calm and serene. Not daring to argue with Merritt's harsh expression. Holding desperately onto what little control she still had left so she wouldn't dissolve into a fit of tears.

She'd shaken her head when Clayton asked if she had any questions. After all, what else did they have left to say? What else did she need to know?

Her husband was leaving, and once again she was going to be alone.

As the last echoes of Clayton's departure faded, Vanessa straightened her shoulders and walked back into the house. The pity party had to be over. It was time to hold her head up high and do what she could to help for the next few weeks. At least then she would feel useful.

Both Corrine and Merritt turned when she entered the dining room. "Is he gone?" Corrine asked, her eyes red-rimmed and puffy.

"Just left." After a pause, Vanessa added, "He said he'd write."

Corrine rolled her eyes. "That'll be the day."

Corrine looked so bitter, Vanessa couldn't help but apologize. "I'm sorry. I feel so responsible. If it wasn't for me still being here, why I'm sure—"

"If it hadn't been for you, Clayton wouldn't have come at all," Merritt interrupted.

"His leaving isn't your fault," Corrine added.

"I'm afraid it is. I know he's leaving because of me."

"He's leaving because of vows he made to your father. But more important, he's leaving because of some promises he made to himself."

Merritt wiped a tired hand across his face. "Don't get me wrong. I'm not saying he made the right decision. In my opinion, he picked the wrong vow to keep. But, I do have to admire a man who sticks to his principles, even when they're difficult to adhere to."

"When do you think he'll change his mind? When enough time has passed?"

Merritt looked toward Corrine who shrugged her shoulders. "Maybe. Or maybe when he's finally at peace with himself. I fought by his side. I'd trust him with my life. Matter of fact, I have trusted him with it on more than one occasion. But he's not infallible. None of us are."

"Those war years changed all of us, don't you see?" Corrine added softly. "In a lot of ways, we all grew up so quickly; we've forgotten that we're all works in progress. In the midst of that tumultuous time, it was too hard to say that we didn't know what to do. So we learned to pretend we did. Maybe he's still doing that."

"Maybe Clayton doesn't know all the right words yet," Merritt said.

"Or actions," Vanessa replied. Thinking of the lengths he'd taken to avoid her.

"Or actions. But we don't either." He clapped his hands lightly and looked over the top of his fingers. "In the meantime, don't give up. Remember the book of Matthew when you get blue, Vanessa. *"With God all things are possible."* Keep praying, and those prayers will be answered."

Merritt's words gave her hope. How many times had she watched Clayton read from his Bible when he was alone? More than she could count. She hoped he would read the Word and realize that he alone couldn't solve all their problems.

Jesus could help him—and so could Vanessa. "Those are fine words, I think. Good and meaningful."

Merritt scuffed his foot. "I hope you know that we're glad Clayton married you and we're certainly happy to have your company now."

"We mean it," Corrine said earnestly. "It's terribly lonely out here. The spread's so big, during roundup and market I don't see Merritt for weeks at a time. Added to that, there's not too many other women about, especially since José and Pearl like to keep their distance and Rosa speaks little English. I'd love to have the opportunity to chat with another woman. I'll appreciate your company, and your help, too." She patted her stomach. "This new baby is going to take some getting used to."

"I'll be honored to help with the baby and anything else you might need." Vanessa meant every word. But, well, she knew she had to make the best of things at the Bar M, too. Truthfully, there was nowhere else to go. She couldn't go home nor could she follow Clayton around. She had no money. She was completely dependent on the couple in front of her. Vanessa knew it as clearly as she knew the sun would rise again.

Merritt's chair scraped back as he rose to his feet. "Don't worry about Clayton. He'll come around in time. He's always been stubborn."

"Stubborn? Is that what his demeanor is called?" Corrine asked after the girls grabbed their dolls and went into the main room. "I was thinking more along the lines of bullheaded. Obstinate."

Vanessa knew Corrine was exasperated with her brother. She was maddened by his actions, too. But in her heart, Vanessa knew something more than mere stubbornness guided him. Tentatively, she whispered, "I think it's honor that guides him, not sheer mulishness. Clayton Proffitt is the most honorable man I know."

"Well, you've pretty much just described him in a nutshell, Vanessa," Corrine said as Merritt kissed her cheek and left them. "My brother is once again trying to do his best without realizing that there's an easier way—a better way—to do things. Without fail, he always seems to take the road less traveled." When they were alone, she looked straight at Vanessa. "So, do you love him?"

"I do."

"Have you told him?"

"Not in so many words," Vanessa admitted. "Every time I try to talk to him, things get clouded and confused. I end up losing my nerve."

"One day you're going to need to find your gumption. The only thing harder than telling someone your thoughts is living with the guilt of keeping your silence."

That would be a horrible situation, indeed, Vanessa reflected. It would be awful if something happened to Clayton before she'd found a way to truly let him know how much she cared for him. "I hope he comes back soon so I can tell him how much I care. In the meantime, I guess all we can do is pray for his safety."

Corrine smiled softly. "Hey, I like that idea." Holding out her hand, she reached for Vanessa's and closed her eyes. "Dear Lord, please be with Clayton on his journey. Please help him work through everything he needs to, but be aware at all times that we are with him, for always. Please be with everyone who loves Clayton, too. Loving someone takes patience and strength. Please help us find both over these next few weeks. In Your name we pray, Amen."

Already Vanessa felt lighter. "Thank you, Corrine. Sometimes I forget just how much I need the Lord's help right now."

"I'll pray with you as often as you'd like." After a moment she added, "But maybe you should think about writing to Clayton as well. John knows of a couple of stops he's going to make. We could post the letters to arrive at those places."

"I'm not quite sure what a written letter could accomplish."

"I found that sometimes the written word works better than hours of conversation."

As she remembered all the things she wished she'd said to Clayton but never had the nerve, Vanessa nodded. "Maybe I will write to him."

"Merritt used to say my letters were almost like being home."

Vanessa didn't quite understand. "Even though your home wasn't his?"

Something soft and melancholy lit Corrine's eyes. "Oh, Van. Don't you know? Home is where your mind goes when

A Texan's Promise

the night is black and your heart is hurting. Home is where you go when things are happening that you can't control but you wish you could. Home is where the person you love is waiting for you." Reaching for Vanessa's hand, she continued. "That's what letters are, really. They're your heart, your feelings . . . your love."

Vanessa felt stunned. Corrine's words had reached inside of her and pulled tight. They'd given her a new purpose—and a new way of looking at Clayton's leaving.

Perhaps their separation was all part of God's plan, after all. Maybe they needed space apart in order to become closer.

Time to heal and to be honest.

It was time to go back home, to her heart, even if she was likely never to go back to the place where she used to live.

It was time to share her love with Clayton. At least then, she'd have no regrets.

205

14

Dear Clayton,

Well, I've decided to write you. Merritt
seems to have an idea where you're heading to,
so I'm going to send you letters in the hopes
that they will fall into your hands sooner than
later.

But even if they don't, Clayton, even if they
don't, I think that I need to write, just so I will
know that I've shared my thoughts with you
somehow. Just so I will finally tell you what's in
my heart. I love you Clayton.

Not because you're my protector. Not because
we've exchanged vows. No, it has more to do
with everything else. Something with the way
I feel inside when I say your name. Something
with the way I feel when I catch sight of the
smooth band of gold wrapped around my finger. I feel . . . secure.

Even though we are apart, and so much is
separating us, I'm going to keep sending you
letters, Clayton. Letters from your sister's

home. Letters from me. From what is now your
home, too.

Yours,

Vanessa

When she was done, she folded the letter and slipped it in
an envelope. That evening, when she heard José was going
into town, she asked him to mail the letter.

When it was out of her hands, she breathed deep. She had
begun. What she was doing was little enough. But it definitely
helped.

Who knew what he would think when he saw her decla-
ration of love! But as she recalled how she'd felt when she'd
prayed with Corrine, Vanessa realized she at least did know
that answer. The Lord knew. He always knew.

The following day, after giving Corrine a cooking lesson
and helping sort baby clothes and polishing and shining the
crib, Vanessa sat down, picked up her quill and ink, and wrote
again.

> Dear Clayton,
>
> The rain came last night. I watched the
> storm roll in from Corrine's front porch. Dark
> clouds raced across the sky like a herd of stal-
> lions running from capture.
>
> All at once, the sky burst open, the wind
> picked up, and the temperature dropped. My
> hair was soaked in seconds. Corrine called me
> inside, but I stayed out as long as I could. In
> truth, I couldn't leave. In many ways, I felt
> like I was part of that storm—powerful, strong,
> wanting to shout and scream—and to pray.

I've grown up so much since that night when we left the Circle Z, Clayton. I feel stronger, less afraid of what the future might hold. Less shamed about what brought me here.

Later, after the storm passed, I was once again in bed by myself. When I closed my eyes, I wondered when I was ever going to feel you again. And if I would ever have the chance to tell you how I feel while looking into your eyes.

Vanessa

Two days later, she wrote again.

Dear Clayton,

I managed to get burned yesterday. The griddle slipped and like a fool I grabbed for it. Of course I yelped and the griddle clattered to the ground with enough clanging to wake the dead. The noise brought everyone running.

Corrine slathered my hand in butter, and the girls drew me pictures. Merritt said you'd be right proud of the way I hardly complained, but truth be told, if you'd been here, I'm sure I'd have cried like a baby.

I know it's a sin to be so vain . . . but I'm afraid I'm gonna have a sizeable scar on my arm now. Between my back and this new one, people are going to say I'm a "marked" woman.

Vanessa

"Do you feel better, Vanessa?" Corrine asked late one evening. "You seem more content."

"I feel more at ease with how things are, I suppose. I've stopped trying to guess what Clayton is thinking, and stopped wishing the past was different. I can only deal with what is in front of me. That does give me comfort."

Corrine wrapped her arms around her middle. "I imagine you're right. Now if I could just get comfortable, things would be a whole lot better." Then her eyes widened. "Oh, Vanessa, I just realized why my back's been hurting me so much today."

Vanessa hopped to her feet. "Yes?"

"It's the baby. It's on the way."

"You sure?"

"Oh, yes. This is baby number three. I'm sure." With a grimace, she wrapped her arms around her middle again. "I think this baby isn't going to wait long. Go find Merritt, will you?"

Vanessa reached for her sister-in-law, snatched her hand back, then reached out again. "Do you need help?" Maybe Corrine needed help getting to bed? Some towels? Water?

In between gritted teeth, Corrine unwrapped one arm from her middle and pointed to the door. "Get. Merritt. Now."

Vanessa tore out of the room like it was on fire.

Two hours later, she was wiping Corrine's brow as Aaron Jackson Merritt made his way into the world.

Though they were on their way back to Texas, things were slow going. Now that revenge wasn't fueling his blood, Price was finding that he was in no special hurry to return to the ranch.

He'd denied Miles's request to travel on his own, saying any lone man traveling in Indian country was no better than a fool, and Price was most certainly not that.

Therefore, they stopped often, at almost every town they could. Price seemed to draw fallen women, gamblers, and drinkers like flies to molasses. When he'd disappear, Miles would either sleep as much as he could or take to sketching in the notebook he'd bought on a whim at the general store back in Santa Fe.

Just after crossing the Texas border, Price left for longer than usual. He'd found a handful of renegade men from the Confederacy and had somehow convinced them that he'd fought, too.

When Price didn't return by nightfall on the second day, Miles was left to cool his heels in a makeshift camp nearby. He drew and planned and almost left a time or two. It was only the very real warning about traveling alone that made him wait. Couples and families came and went. Some still carried the dewy glow of optimism; others just looked plain tired.

Some were foreigners. The thick accents, the struggle with English words, the exotic languages the men and women resorted to when speaking among themselves caught Miles's attention. Most everyone got cheated fairly and squarely by the depot operator.

That should have given Miles a bit of satisfaction. In actuality, he was far better off than most of the poor people who had dreams of farming in Nebraska or of seeking gold in the mountains of Colorado. Miles, at least, had land to go back to.

But still, he felt worse than usual. Dissatisfied and annoyed with himself. A better, stronger man would have managed Price better. A better man would have a woman by his side to share his burdens. Instead, he had no one.

Pulling out his notebook and charcoal pencil, he settled next to a dried-up creek and sketched the outlying area. In the distance, a snake sunned itself, blending in with the elements so well that it took Miles a moment after spotting him to realize what it was—a rattler.

That's where Jacob Power found him. "You look like you could use some sustenance," he said as he climbed the butte. "I saw you here, looking into the distance, and you caught my interest."

"No reason I should have. I'm just sketching."

After clambering over a pile of rocks, the man walked right over and peered over Miles's shoulder. "Ah. Snakes. Never cared for them much myself, though I suspect I should. They're God's creatures after all. Not their fault they go through life on their stomach." Before Miles could say a word about that, the bearded man unrolled some dried beef from a rectangular red bandana, crouched by his side, and offered Miles a chunk. "Care for some? I'm Jacob Powers, by the by."

"Miles Grant." Because the beef jerky looked good and he had no reason to say no, Miles pulled off a portion. "Much obliged."

"You're right welcome." As Miles picked up his pencil and shaded in some of the background, Jacob watched and chewed. After the silence stretched on, he said, "So, have you been on the trail long?"

"Long enough."

"Me, too, I'll tell you that." His eyes crinkled. "'Course, I guess just about anyone around here would say that. I've always found West Texas to be smack dab in the middle of nowhere."

In spite of himself, Miles smiled. That was the truth. Noticing that the rattler still hadn't moved, he filled in a bit of the outline.

Jacob chewed some more. "So, where you headed?"

"Home."

"Lucky you." Jacob tore off another piece of jerky and bit into it hard. "The plains, they're my home now," he said, chewing something fierce. "These open spaces are all I need, to tell the truth. Well, space and a bit of food and water now and then." He cackled. "And a bit of conversation."

Miles looked around. All he saw was miles of rough terrain and the promise of renegade attacks if a man wasn't careful. "You don't miss civilization?"

The other man raised a bushy gray eyebrow. "Is that what town is to you? I'm not too sure about that myself. I've found all kinds of problems in the best of places, and much of it far from civilized. You ever been up east?"

"I can't say I have."

"Lots of those immigrants arrive in New York City all prepared to see openness and space. Instead, they get put in homes hardly big enough for a single man, let alone a whole family. The rooms have no windows. No water. The owners charge too much. People look down on 'em 'cause they're different. It's a terrible situation."

Miles swallowed. He'd been so focused on his own troubles, he'd never thought about others' situations. "I never thought about those places," he admitted. "I never gave much thought about where those foreigners have been."

Instead of judging, Jacob just shrugged. "No reason you should have, I suppose. It just made me think, though. How we're all stuck in one place and trying to get somewhere else."

Miles set his sketchbook aside. Pictures of the landscape weren't as interesting as the man beside him. "Except you."

"That's right. Except me. Me, I'll take wandering every time. That way I don't have to worry about where I'm trying to get to or where I've come from." He gestured around him, a look of wonder on his face. "These plains are plenty civilized for me. Nature has a way of doing things that cut through jealousies and hate. If that rattler eats a field mouse, it's just his way. I mean, even a snake's gotta eat."

"I suppose there's truth to that," Miles said. When Jacob offered more jerky, he pulled off another chunk. Their conversation was starting to feel almost comfortable.

"One of the things that helps me never feel alone is my mission," Jacob said after a while.

"What is that?"

"I feel mission-sent to preach the Gospel. That's what got me started, you know. I had a dream one night, a clear, perfect dream. In it the Lord told me that he knew I was a True Believer. And because of that, He asked me to share what I know with others."

"How did you know that was the Lord talking?"

"I just did," Jacob said. Giving Miles a sideways look, he whispered, "You ever felt like that? Have you ever heard the Lord speaking to you, like he'd just come for a chat? Just like the way you and I are sitting here?"

Miles wanted to disbelieve him. He wanted to feel uncomfortable and shake his head and tell Jacob Power that he'd never heard so much nonsense spouted in his life. But something in the man's earnest tone of voice got to him.

Or, maybe it was the situation. If they'd been surrounded by other people, Miles would have felt self-conscious. Maybe he would have been reminded of too many other things to worry about such proclamations.

"Have you, Miles?" Jacob asked, his voice low and earnest. "Have you ever felt so close with the Lord our God that you developed a friendship with him?"

"I have not."

Jacob stretched out his legs in front of him. "The land's awful vast when not another soul is around to talk to. Who do you talk to if not Jesus?"

Miles couldn't even bear to lie and say his stepfather. "I don't know," he admitted softly.

"That's a right shame." After another pause, the man spoke again. "Son, are you a Christian?"

Miles had been wondering that very thing himself. "I don't know."

"Do you believe in a higher power?"

"Maybe." Then, when the man kept looking at him, Miles thought about his trip. About how he'd somehow managed to keep them from finding Vanessa. He thought about his conversation with Sammy, that waitress who'd let him sleep in her barn. About Lacy, who should've been bent and broken but instead looked as if she was at the top of the world.

He'd thought about those immigrants he saw, and about how he had someplace to go home to even though he'd never done anything to deserve the honor.

He realized then that everything hadn't been a series of accidents.

"I mean, I think I do."

"Good!" Jacob's smile was full of encouragement. "Good for you."

"Are you a preacher?"

"Not officially, no."

That made Miles feel better. If the man really had been a man of the cloth, Miles was afraid he'd shock him. "Actually, I want to be a believer, but I don't know if God wants me."

"God wants everybody."

"There's things I've done that I don't think would be thought of as Christlike."

That earned him a smile. "In my faith, I've found it to be true that Jesus will always forgive, as long as you are truly repentant. After all, we are all sinners. Do you feel sorry for things you've done?"

"Yes, but—"

"Don't need no buts. It's done. You're forgiven."

That sounded too easy. "It might be too late for me."

"It's never too late to accept God's mercy. What is bothering you? Can you share some of your burdens? I've got two good ears, well equipped for listening."

Maybe it was because Jacob acted like he really cared. Maybe it was because the closer they got to the Circle Z, the more disturbed Miles got, thinking about his future—or more likely, his lack of a future—at the Circle Z.

Maybe it was because he'd been alone for thirty-six hours.

But most likely, it was because he was too weak to keep his pain to himself. Yes, that flaw shamed him. But Jacob's words gave him hope, a hope he desperately craved.

But no matter the reason, Miles started talking. "It all started when my stepfather was beating my sister and I stood outside the door," he admitted, waiting for Jacob to get up in disgust and walk away.

He didn't. Instead, Jacob's eyes softened, just like he really cared and wanted to listen and understand. "What happened after that?"

"My mother saved her. And then Clayton took my sister Vanessa away."

"Who's Clayton?"

"He's . . . he was the foreman at our ranch. He used to be an officer in the war."

"Ah. He a good man?"

That, Miles could answer without reservation. "He is. He's a very good man. The best man I know."

"So how did you get all out here?"

"I made a promise to Clayton that I'd do my best to keep my stepfather off their trail."

"How did you do?"

To his surprise, Miles said, "Actually, I've been doing okay."

"Faith."

"Excuse me?"

"Clayton's faith in you must feel nice."

"I don't think he had faith in me. He couldn't understand why I didn't run in and protect Vanessa."

"Why didn't you?"

No one had ever asked him that. Not even his mother. Actually, pretty much no one had ever expected him to do much; they just found fault because he didn't. "I was afraid," he said.

"Afraid he'd beat you, too?"

Hesitantly, Miles shook his head. "No. I've . . . I mean, he's hit me before. I was afraid I wouldn't be able to stop him. That's what I was afraid of. That's why I didn't go in. I was afraid I'd fail, which felt worse than never trying at all."

"Tell me what happened next, son."

With broken words, Miles continued. "I first told the posse the wrong directions, and then Price and I decided to head out."

"The both of you?"

"No. Price wanted to go and I had no choice but to accompany him. That's how things really were." Slowly, Miles continued the story, telling the stranger about the days on horseback and the evenings spent in shantytowns.

Jacob Power asked questions, made Miles rethink his words, rephrase things, and reevaluate his descriptions.

Little by little, he admitted his faults and revealed his sins. Admitted his worries and shortcomings and hopes and dreams.

And after a while, Jacob Power didn't even talk anymore. No, he just sat by his side and listened. The experience was the most freeing moment of Miles's life. Admitting his sins and placing them up to another person who didn't judge, didn't preach.

A sense of love and peace surrounded him. Entered his heart. Gave him hope.

The experience was so earth-shattering, Miles found himself crying. Tears welled up in his eyes, then slid down his cheeks. He felt his body cleansing itself, and cleansing his soul. Because, in the midst of all of it, Miles Grant suddenly realized that he was not the bad, weak-natured man he'd supposed himself to be.

As the sun moved toward the west, as the rattler sought the earth, as a pair of prairie dogs popped out of the earth, looked around, then went back to their homes, Miles realized that he was a man of God, and was worthy in His eyes.

He'd been given Grace.

Finally, as the sun faded to a memory, when the night air was quiet and still and Miles was worn out, Jacob stood up. "Something just happened. I've been wandering these plains for years, Miles. I thought I'd experienced most everything. I thought nothing could touch me anymore. Not deep in my heart. You changed that."

Miles could only stare at him, too worn out to say much.

With a ragged sigh, Jacob bent down and grabbed hold of his duffle. "I don't think I'll ever forget this evening," he said, looking oddly humbled. "Not for as long as I live."

After scrounging around in his knapsack, he pulled out a worn Bible. "My uncle carried this with him during the war." He glanced at it fondly, fingering the frayed edges. "See, the thing is, Bibles are a personal thing. Sooner or later, you come in contact with one that suits your needs. Then you don't need another." After rummaging around for a moment, Jacob pulled out another book. This one was a little bigger, a little newer, but just as well used. "This one's mine. I've always had my own; just kept the other as a kind of spare. . . . But I think this old book has found a new owner." Without any more fanfare, Jacob pressed the Bible in his hands. "Here you go."

As soon as Jacob laid the book in his hands, Miles curved his fingers around the spine. "Are you sure? Maybe it should go to another soldier."

"I'm sure. Miles, don't you see? All of us fight our battles. Some men are just given uniforms to do so."

Miles examined the worn book in his hands. Indeed, it was certainly far from new. Markings and folded pages and notations littered the margins. Obviously, it had gotten Jacob's uncle through harder times than the ones Miles was finding himself in.

And that gave him comfort. "Thank you," he said. "I'll take care of it. I promise."

Jacob's eyes lit up. "Oh, son, don't you worry 'bout that. If you read those words and believe, it'll take care of you. All you need is faith."

And with that, he patted Miles on the shoulder and then moved on. Moments later he was gone, absorbed into the night air like a memory.

Miles built a fire and thought about Jacob's parting words long into the night. Long after Price arrived and fell asleep on the other side of the fire. Hours after the coyotes trotted by in the distance, their mournful howls bringing chills along Miles's spine. For the first time in his life, Miles knew he was a Christian. Knew he'd found himself.

Knew he'd finally become a man.

15

*C*layton folded Vanessa's latest letter and tried not to admit how much he liked receiving them. But he did; oh how he missed her.

Though only a few weeks had passed since he'd left Vanessa and sought work and an easier peace of mind, it might have been two years. After forwarding his whereabouts in case he was urgently needed, he visited a few local sheriffs and asked if they'd heard of Price Venture.

Whenever Clayton shared his reasons why he was looking for the man, the lawmen always turned grim-faced and promised to assist in any way they could.

Then Clayton focused on his other goal—earning money.

He joined an outfit up in Wyoming to help with a roundup. There, he buckled down and got to work.

Convincing cows to go where they didn't want to had never been his favorite part of ranching. He liked the companionship of the other men, finding it strangely like managing soldiers in the war. He also was at ease with only Lee for company. He, his Bible, and his horse had been through many a night with only one another. He found their companionship to be more than sufficient.

Well, almost. More often than not, he found himself thinking about a pretty young thing with green eyes who looked at him so closely he was sure she could read his mind. Who'd cried when she'd admitted to being ravished and had clung to him while she dreamed.

Little by little, the pain of her secret didn't feel so raw.

Soon after he arrived at the ranch, he received two letters from Vanessa. A week later, the foreman passed on a third note, written so painstakingly that Clayton felt guilty all over again. That didn't stop him from reading her correspondence over and over until he'd memorized every word. Finally, he gave in. After waking up in the middle of one night missing her, Clayton broke down and wrote her back.

> Dear Vanessa,
>
> I spent the day extricating a pair of bogged calves from the thickest patch of black mud I'd ever seen. One of their mamas roamed nearby, bellowing her displeasure over the whole situation. We were sure her carrying on was going to lead her right into the mud, too. Long after sundown, the boys and I limped back to the barn covered in mud and manure. Charlie, the youngest in our crew, swears he'll never get his boots to fit right again. I didn't have the heart to tell him they probably won't.
> Clayton

Another week passed. He did well enough that the foreman and owner had asked him to stay, but Clayton wasn't eager to spend any more time with ornery cows. He'd clipped enough ears and branded enough backsides to practically do the job in his sleep.

There was another reason as well. Hours alone in the saddle had meant hours with nothing to do but think about his trip west with Vanessa and think about how eager he was to see her again.

Before his time was over, he realized he'd written her another four notes.

At that rate, Clayton knew he'd never make it apart from her for long. That wouldn't do, because he knew she was still hurting.

Yet sometimes, when the night was long, he'd read her letters and forget about everything that had happened. He'd forget about Price and her attack and her scars and his weaknesses.

And when that happened, she'd take him back to another time. A time of sweet longing. Innocent memories would come rushing forth, bringing to mind years ago, when she used to sit with him in the barn and they'd trade stories about their days. Back then, he'd treasured her simple problems and his ability to easily solve them. It hadn't taken more than a reassuring word or a quick hug to make her smile again.

And each one of those smiles would make all the memories of the war fade just a little bit more.

Yes, he missed her. He longed to see her again. And, short of going back on his word, there was nothing he could do.

Instead, he pocketed his wages, sent half to Merritt with a request to set up an account for him in the nearby bank, and told them he'd be returning to the Addison in Colorado Springs before heading to Denver. On the way, a farmer had asked him to help clear a section of woods for spring planting. Clayton took the job without hesitation. Days passed like lightning as he strained his muscles and sweated, chopping down pine trees and half-freezing to death.

Clayton did his best to not think about what he was missing. Tried not to think about his sister's home or a warm fire with Vanessa sitting near it, her skin glowing and soft, her eyes beckoning him closer.

Three days later, he left the farm with another pocketful of cash and a blister on his right hand the size of a silver dollar and headed into Colorado Springs.

Upon arriving at the Addison, he'd been greeted with six letters from Vanessa, each one a breath of fresh air to his burdened heart. One had been especially sweet.

Because no one else was around, he pulled it out of his coat pocket and read it again.

> Dear Clayton,
>
> It's been a full month since you left me. I hope and pray you find what you are looking for. I hope and pray you are not too cold from working outside.
>
> The night is clear here. As I sit, staring at the north star, I think of the many nights I used to sit with you and stare at the night sky. You'd try to teach me about constellations, and I'd pretend to listen. Looking up at the night sky seems to bring me closer to you, Clay. I'm hoping that some nights we're looking at the same stars together.
>
> And maybe even remembering the same things, too.
>
> I hope so.
>
> Yours, Vanessa

He, too, had looked at the stars and remembered sitting on the ground outside her house with their heads tilted back. Once again, he thanked Vanessa for writing the letters and thanked the Lord for leading him to a woman who could make him remember how to feel again.

He loved how open she was with her feelings, enjoyed her stories about life with Corrine and their children. He smiled at her silly prattle about cooking and sewing baby garments and how she yearned to see the bulbs she'd planted outside flower in the spring.

He worried over her burn, wished he'd been there to doctor her. And because he couldn't deny her a thing, he wrote her back and tried not think about what their correspondence meant. Was the Lord guiding them both? Helping them find their way through words instead of just actions? It sure seemed like it.

He'd thought long and hard before deciding not to say anymore about his feelings. After all, wasn't that why he'd decided to leave—so they could have some time to reflect on what had happened between them? Just in case her feelings changed? And Vanessa, being Vanessa, wouldn't turn him away if she felt he'd be hurting.

But as he lay awake that night, listening to the banjo player in the bar and raucous laughter from the lobby, Clayton knew he was fooling no one. Not himself, not Merritt and Corrine. Not Vanessa. He'd fallen in love with his wife. He wanted her, and he wanted a real marriage. If he let himself, Clayton knew he could start counting the days until they would be together again just as much as she was, though he'd feel embarrassed for admitting such a thing.

Wearily, he pulled out his Bible and fingered the soft worn leather cover. Needing an old friend, he opened the pages to the book of Luke and found himself reading the verses aloud, just as he used to do by his mother's side. Like a gift, the words leapt out to him, calling to him, giving him comfort and easing his loneliness.

"So I say to you . . . Ask and it will be given to you. Seek and you will find; Knock and the door will be opened to you."

Clayton pondered the words and their deeper meaning. "Have I done everything completely wrong, Lord?" he said aloud, staring at the blurred words on the page in front of him. "I tried my best to save her. Yet I didn't save her at all. I tried to heal her and help her needs. But I had no knowledge of the places she hurt the most. When she asked for time, I gave it to her. But now that she wants me, I find I am the one who needs time."

Closing his eyes, he spoke again from his heart. "Years ago, during the war, all my plans seemed so clear. I felt Your presence beside me, helping me, guiding me. But now, sitting here in Colorado, waiting for each day to slip by, I feel confused and unworthy. I should have asked You for guidance. I'm asking now. Please, Lord, help me find the way. Help me follow Your will."

With that, Clayton closed the book and rested his eyes, glad for the sense of peace that washed over him. Glad for the gentle reminder that he was never truly alone.

And then, before he lost his nerve, he finally picked up a quill, and wrote Vanessa back.

> Vanessa,
>
> You shouldn't feel the need to do so much. Merritt and Corrine are happy to take care of you. As I'm sure my sister's said, she's grateful for the company.
>
> I just recently received your letters. I spent the last month rounding up cattle for a ranch in southern Wyoming, then clearing brush west of Denver. I'm not quite sure where I'll head from here, but I believe I'll be going up north shortly. I'll write you when I get there.

I hope your burn is healed. You be careful of yourself, you hear me?

And Vanessa, no scars will ever dim your beauty in my eyes.

Clayton

Was it too tender? Too sweet? Did he sound weak?

He wasn't sure. But as he imagined how Vanessa would feel if he never wrote her back, he bundled up his nerve, folded the letter into thirds, then took it to the front lobby where they postmarked it and mailed it off.

He felt better already.

☙

The following morning, he spied Lacy across the fancy dining room eating breakfast. She came over just as he was finishing his second cup of coffee.

"How's your greenhorn?" he asked, recalling the naive cowboy she'd flirted with the evening they'd sat together.

It took her a moment to catch who he spoke of. "Oh. Him?" She waved a hand. "Oh, Clay. He was worthless. Didn't make it out here in the Rockies a week. Last I heard he boarded a train back to St. Louis. And good riddance, too, I say. I found out he was all show and no go. He hardly had a plug nickel to his name."

"That's a shame. Well, I guess he got what he came for, huh? Tales to tell about the wild west?"

"Mercy me, he did get that." Lacy laughed. "He was a sweet thing, by the by. I do hope he one day finds what he's looking for."

Clayton studied her a little more closely, taking note of what he saw. Lacy had on less paint, and her dress was a plain calico, its neckline cut modestly. She looked like any rancher's wife he might see in town. He was just figuring out how to ask about her transformation when she grinned at his expression.

"Your sister wrote me," she said by way of explanation. "I do believe, Clayton Proffitt, you lied to me."

He coughed. "Pardon?"

"You know what I'm talkin' about. You told your sister the truth about how I've been living, even though I asked you not to."

"You're right, I did," he said, remembering how interested Corrine had been in Lacy. She'd genuinely missed her friend and wanted to stay in touch with her. "She cares about you, Lacy. Besides, no good comes from living lies."

She rolled her eyes. "You're a fine one to talk. You're lying to everyone and anyone who will listen about your lot in life."

It was so uncomfortably true, he felt his cheeks heat up. "Hold on, there."

"You hold on, I'm telling you my news. Anyway . . . Corrine wrote me right back and spoke of many, many things. The war, her man Merritt. The girls . . . and about Jesus' birth and the many blessings of the season." Softly, she said, "Corrine's words encouraged me do some thinking about myself."

"What did you decide to do?"

She swallowed hard. "Move on."

Without judgment, he said gently, "Lacy, are you done being a ladybird?"

She smiled at his descriptor. "Maybe. This life I've chosen, it's been a hard one. For a while I didn't think I had a choice, but now I'm thinking maybe it's not too late to start over again. I want to be done, though." Looking at her hands, Lacy added, "Corrine spoke about forgiveness. Not finding it from others, but of finding it from myself. I reckon she's right. All these years, I've been hurting myself and my memories, hoping if I did bad things to myself, I wouldn't have to remember the past. I wouldn't have to fear others treating me bad."

He knew what she spoke of. Remembered hearing about the deserters who'd broken into her home and had ruined both her life and her mother's. "The past always comes back, doesn't it?"

"It does." With a shrug, she said, "I tried to be a different person. I tried to pretend all that mattered to me was money in my pocket, a pretty dress and a line of kohl around my eyes, but that weren't the truth. I'd still lie awake at four in the morning, wishing I could sleep."

Clayton knew exactly what she meant. Nights were hard when the days were filled with regrets.

"Yeah, well . . . it occurred to me that maybe I don't need to work so hard being someone my parents never intended me to be." Sitting up a little straighter, she brightened. "Guess what? There's a couple of men who've offered me marriage."

Truly pleased for her, he smiled. "Congratulations."

Her eyes widened. "Don't get out the champagne yet, Clayton. These men aren't the love and cherish kind, not even a little bit. But they do seem decent."

"Decent's good."

Lacy nodded. "Decent men have been few and far between in my life. Clayton, I don't need excitement. I don't even need romance. I just want security and companionship," she said softly. "Anyway. One or two of 'em are looking for a partner. They've got kids and cows and goats to take care of and they need help."

The image of Lacy on a milking stool in a dusty barn made him smile. "I never fancied you milking a cow or wiping noses."

Lacy shrugged. "I know how to do those things; I've just chosen not to do them. But now I'm thinking caring for cows and kids is a small price to pay for the chance to walk into a shop and not feel a dozen hard stares at my back. Or worse, being asked to leave the premises. I'm thinking it's time I became respectable."

Longing entered her eyes, longing so strong and deep that Clayton felt as if he was peering into the deepest recesses of her soul. "I know God will forgive my sins," she whispered. "I just want to be able to walk in a church and know that the pastor will, too."

"If the pastor is the man of God he says he is, he will."

"Maybe."

"I'm right." Reaching out, Clayton squeezed her hand. "Good luck to you, Lace. I mean that."

"Thank you." A look of panic filled her gaze as she clapped her hands. "Oh my goodness, I almost forgot. I saw Price Venture, Clayton."

The news made him feel like the whole world had just turned on its side. "When?"

She bit her lip. "About three weeks ago. Not long after you and your wife left."

"What happened?"

She shook her head. "That Price Venture, he was a piece of work, I'll tell you that. He chased skirts and tried to drink the whole city out of whiskey."

"Did he ask about Vanessa?"

"I'm getting to that." She motioned for Clayton to sit down, and did the same. "I went and knocked on Miles's door."

"Miles?"

"Yep." She cast him a sideways look. "He's not so bad, Clayton."

"He was never real good. What did you tell him?"

"We devised a plan. . . . I had an old Confederate brass button, much like the one you had on your dress uniform. I told him to pass on to his stepfather that it was yours and that you and his sister were headed toward Kansas."

"I doubt he bought that."

"I figured it didn't really matter if he did or not. Thought it might buy you some time." She shrugged. "Maybe it did. That boy—Miles—I think he was doing his best."

Just remembering Miles's weakness the night that he and Vanessa left made Clayton's skin crawl. "His best isn't worth much."

"This time, I think it might of been," she said softly. Fingering her demure dress, she whispered. "Sometimes we all need second chances, Clayton."

Her words, so true, caught him off guard. "I suppose you're right. Perhaps I've been too harsh where he's concerned."

"I know I'm right." Standing up again, she patted his arm. "So, Captain Proffitt, what about you? Why are you here in the Springs? I thought you and that sweet wife of yours were going to be staying with Corrine."

"I've got some things I need to do first. There's a job out in Nebraska I think I'm going to take. The town of Benson needs a sheriff."

"You thinking about handling a gun again?"

"This time it's for the right reasons," he said, wondering for the first time if he'd been a fool to fight so long and hard for a lost cause.

Though Lacy's eyes filled with concern, she merely shrugged. "Perhaps," she murmured. "Mrs. Proffitt's not up in a room, is she?"

"No. She's with Corrine."

"Ah."

"Lace, can I ask you something? Something hard?"

"Of course."

"Can a woman who's been hurt . . . " He swallowed and diverted his eyes from her own. He couldn't bear to see the same haunted expression that had filled Vanessa's eyes. Especially since he didn't know how to make things better.

She prodded him, her voice curiously gentle. "Yes, Clay?"

He started again. "Can a woman who's been hurt badly, by a man . . . can she ever recover?"

Because she deserved to be looked at, he turned back to her. She met his gaze steadily, though the skin around her lips turned white. Obviously his questions still hit her terribly hard. "I don't know."

"I see."

"Clay, when those men left, I had no one." A pleading look brightened her blue eyes. "There was no one left. However, I have a feeling a woman under different circumstances might do better than I have."

"Thank you for saying that."

"Give her time, Clayton. And give yourself time, too. Ain't no shame in that."

Her knowing gaze made him feel like he'd felt too much, said too little. Shifting uncomfortably, he said, "You're not the only one with regrets, Lace."

"I won't try to stop you from your travels. Just let me say that if you've got a mind to keep the peace, please do your best not to get shot. The world's a better place with you in it, Clayton Proffitt."

He stood up when she did. "Some might say the same thing about you."

Her eyes softened. Impulsively, she kissed his cheek. "Thanks for saying that."

And with that, she left, just as a telegram from Nebraska arrived. The town of Benson was, indeed, still in need of a sheriff. A sizeable salary would accompany room and board. After reading what they were offering, Clayton knew he couldn't refuse.

At the moment, dealing with people in need of peace and order sounded like a welcome change. Lord knew he was in dire need of some himself.

16

My Dearest Vanessa,

Enclosed please find twelve dollars, half my wages from my time at the Diamond G Ranch. Please use the monies as you see fit, or ask Merritt to help you open an account at the bank in town.

We rounded up nearly eight hundred head of cattle, and I would be lying if I said I was anxious to see another cow anytime soon.

Lee and I are on our way to Nebraska. Benson, to be exact. I have an old friend who is a banker there. He tells me the folks are in need of a man who can keep his cool under pressure and can fire a gun with ease. God has seen to bless me with both qualities. Therefore, I've accepted the position. The pay is good, and the work is honest.

Pray for me, just as I pray for you. I think of you often, and while I know our separation is for the best, I'll look forward to the day when we are reunited again.

Please tell me how you are doing and if you've met another man who has taken your fancy.
Clayton

"You still writing my brother?" Corrine asked Vanessa as she joined her on the front steps of the porch. "Our life is so quiet, sometimes I wonder how you fill the pages."

"That hasn't been the problem; it's the waiting for the time to pass that is."

"I can understand that, though time is indeed passing." Looking out at the budding flowers in the field across from them, Corrine said, "It's been several weeks now."

"Yes." Vanessa knew quite a bit of time had passed since that terrible day when Clayton had ridden off without a backward glance. Slipping her quill and ink to one side, she shrugged. "I enjoy writing to him. I hope Clayton enjoys receiving my notes, even if they are a little plain and full of ordinary days."

"I'm sure he enjoys them; how could he not? Clayton told me that my letters were a true gift during the war. Anything reminding him of home was. Merritt's said the same thing a time or two."

The thought of Clayton actively anticipating her letters warmed her through and through—though she wasn't completely sure that that was the case. "I guess one day I'll be able to ask him in person."

"At least he's been writing you back. Most men don't think of such things. How many letters has he sent you?"

Three. She'd received three cherished notes from him, the pages worn and wrinkled both from him writing to her on the trail and her constant rereading of them. "I've gotten a fair amount."

"I see that look of worry you're wearing," Corrine admonished. "Try not to, now. I imagine it's a mite harder for

Clayton to have the time to write, given the jobs he's doing and such."

"He's a busy man," Vanessa said slowly. And he was. She had been brought up on a ranch and had no illusions about the ease of mailing letters from the back of a horse! In addition, he'd been branding, nursing calves, and clearing farmland. She imagined that there was many a day when all he wanted to do was sit in front of a campfire and nurse his coffee.

She'd sure witnessed that pleasure of his often enough on their way to Colorado.

But she certainly did cherish each letter he wrote. Full of descriptions of the northern plains, she felt sometimes as if she was traveling through the brush and across rocky terrain by his side, or at least in his heart.

Seeking to alleviate the strained silence, Vanessa said, "Where's Aaron?"

"Sleeping, thank the good Lord," Corrine replied with a smile. "He's a dear, but a handful since he hasn't gotten the notion that nighttime is for sleeping. Pearl's watching him for a couple of minutes so I can take a break."

Aaron, though a challenge to any sort of regular schedule, was in every other way a complete angel. Already it was impossible to remember life without the giggling baby boy. His smile and manner were infectious, earning him admirers right and left, especially his two older sisters. Melissa and Kate were sure he was their new toy. "I think Aaron has helped José and Pearl overcome their differences."

Corrine smiled at that. "I'd like to think my sweet baby had a role to play in their reuniting, but I'm not sure that happened. Maybe it was finally their time to mend ways and step over their problems. *For everything there is a season.*"

"Maybe it was," Vanessa murmured. And, of course, the inevitable crossed her mind. When was it going to be her and Clayton's time? Their separation seemed like an eternity.

"Maybe," Corrine agreed. With a heartfelt sigh, she pointed to the west. "My, now look at that. Isn't that a beautiful sunset?"

Together, they watched the sun make its slow descent along the horizon, casting the mountains in the distance an orange, then pink, then purplish glow. Soon, the first star of the evening appeared, signaling the end of the show.

"That was a good one," Corrine said with a smile and a little clap. "I never get tired of looking at the sun setting over the mountains."

"It's so different from Texas," Vanessa said, then wished she'd said something less inane. Of course the scenery was different. "I mean, here, we seem so much closer to the stars at night. Being outside here feels different, somehow."

Corrine nodded. "I feel that way, too. Strange as it may seem, sometimes I miss the hot, humid air and the smell of rain. It hardly ever rains here."

"I miss the fields of bluebonnets and Indian paintbrushes."

"Mesquite trees and flat ground."

"Red dust and parched lips," Vanessa added with a laugh. "I take back what I said. There are some things about Texas I don't miss at all."

"We could say the same about here, I suppose."

Vanessa turned to Corrine. "No matter what my reasons for being here, I do want you to know that I've enjoyed my stay. I hope I've thanked you enough."

"You've thanked us too much. We're family, Vanessa. Families look out for one another."

"I'd forgotten that, I'm afraid."

"You've had your reasons to. But, no matter what, I must say that we've enjoyed your company and your help." Smiling slyly, Corrine added, "I don't think Merritt's going to let you leave—you certainly make some wonderful biscuits."

"I'll teach you how to make them. It's really all in how you roll them out." Remembering their many disastrous lessons in the kitchen, Vanessa amended her words. "I mean, I'll try and teach you again."

"We both know that would be a futile proposition. Flour and me go about as well together as you and gardening!"

Vanessa laughed, taking no insult from the jibe. "You're right. It was certainly harder than it sounded."

"Most things are." Corrine snapped her fingers. "Goodness, now I remember why I came out here. It was to ask about Clayton's latest letter. José told me he brought you one from town. What did it say?"

"Clayton's settled into Benson, Nebraska, as a sheriff. They've given him a sizable room above the jail."

Corrine wrinkled her nose. "Clayton working as a lawman. Can't say that's good news. I can't picture it, can you?"

Honestly, Vanessa could not. "He's an upstanding man, but I never figured he would enjoy doing that sort of job."

"That's very sweetly put. I'll just say what I'm thinking. He's no good regulating bad guys."

The honesty made Vanessa feel better. "I believe that to be true. It's hard to think of him living in town, not mak-ing his living on the back of Lee. Clayton always seems most at home in the saddle." Had she ever wanted anything more than to have him back? Giving into weakness, she admitted, "I miss him, Corrine. I miss him so badly I ache. The feel-ings have nothing to do with you or Merritt, or your beautiful homestead."

"I understand completely. You feel like you're missing your heart."

"That's it, exactly," Vanessa answered, glad that Corrine understood her feelings so well. As the quiet of twilight surrounded them, she whispered. "I want to go to Benson and be with him."

"You can't," Corrine said, pressing her hand on Vanessa's arm. "Just because Price hasn't shown up on our doorstep doesn't mean he hasn't gone out searching for you."

"If he's still searching, it's been a long time."

"He may not be putting as much stock into a calendar as you are, Vanessa. He may just be thinking that he'll see you sooner or later."

"I hope not." Sometimes, if Vanessa held her eyes closed long enough, she could fool herself into thinking that her stepfather's attack had taken place during another lifetime.

She certainly felt like another person. The innocent girl who worried about the correct term for *periwinkle* was long gone.

"Merritt did some checking during the last roundup. Folks in Santa Fe were offered money to bring news of you. Price hasn't given up yet."

That rattled her. "Did anyone talk?"

"Not that Merritt heard. Seems the mercantile operator is just as loyal to Merritt as he is to Clayton. He said he'd never heard of a man named Clayton Proffitt, and he'd certainly never seen the woman he described."

Remembering Hank, and the story Clayton had told about him and his farm, Vanessa smiled. "The mercantile owner is a man named Hank. Clayton knew him from the war. He certainly seemed like a good man. Did you ever meet him?"

"No, Merritt didn't either. I guess Clayton met him before he went to Merritt's unit. But Merritt did recall Clayton's story of Hank taking in Clayton's unit while one of his soldiers recovered."

"He's still taking care of Clayton, I guess," Vanessa mused. "I'm thankful Hank didn't tell the whole story to whoever was asking about me. See, I was indeed there at the mercantile, but as Clayton's wife. Clayton bought my wedding band there." Fingering the warm band of gold, she recalled their bath in the hotel room. Her shyness around him—the sweet way he'd given her the ring.

That day, too, felt like a lifetime ago.

"I think he kept your secret safe, but somebody else didn't. From what Merritt gathered, Hank thinks someone in your hotel talked."

"That may be true. There was a lot of riffraff there."

"That's why you can't leave our property, Vanessa. What would Clayton do if he found out that something happened to you after he's gone to such great lengths to keep you safe?"

He'd be devastated. Vanessa knew that as well as she knew that she'd keep writing to Clayton—just in case he looked forward to her letters as much as she wanted him to.

Suddenly her aching loneliness made her feel petty. "I know I'm being selfish, but still . . . I think he needs me. For all my faults, I can be strong, too."

Corrine said nothing for a moment, just stared at the ball of bright orange as it hid behind the mountains at last. Through the cracked doorway they could hear Aaron fuss and just as quickly be shushed by Pearl.

When it was quiet again, Corrine said, "Merritt told me about your agreement with Clayton. The one y'all made at the Willoughby's."

Vanessa was sure her face glowed with embarrassment. "I didn't know it was common knowledge."

"Not so common, only among people who care." Leaning back on her hands, she said, "I'm sorry if I'm going to shock you, but here it is. When Merritt came back to my house, all injured, I'm the one who talked about marriage."

"Really?" Corrine's story didn't help in the slightest. In fact, all it served to do was make it more obvious that Clayton had little desire to see her as anything but a pretend bride—and she was too timid and shy to take matters into her own hands.

"Yep. From the moment I saw him, I knew we were meant to be together. He was everything I wanted, everything I didn't even know I wanted. One night, when we were sitting together, I proposed."

In spite of herself, Vanessa forgot her own troubles and focused on Corrine's story. "Then what happened?"

"He stared at me in shock. Said yes to my proposal, and then finally kissed me."

Vanessa laughed, completely charmed and amused. "I don't know whether to be scandalized by your behavior or amused at Merritt's reaction."

"Be both!" Corrine smiled. "Vanessa, I think you're going to have to take some forward steps toward Clayton if you want to see him anytime soon."

Vanessa feared her sister-in-law was right. Clayton's letters were sweet but distant. Almost like he was holding himself away, letting more than miles separate them.

Bravely, she admitted the awful truth. "Sometimes, I think he's not intending to return at all. Sometimes, I think Clayton has moved on." She swallowed. "The idea of being forgotten scares me."

Corrine looked pained. "Oh, Van. Give him more time. If you don't hear anything promising, and we don't hear any news about Price, perhaps you should go to him after all."

"I'd rather do that than just wait here, wondering what he's doing and hoping Price doesn't find out where I am."

Corrine agreed. "There's a time for patience and a time for action. If you decide to go in a month, I'll even help you pack. Sometimes a woman has to do what she can to make her marriage successful."

Just then Aaron started crying in earnest and Pearl called for Corrine. As Vanessa watched Corrine run back inside, she finally felt more at peace.

As the sky turned dark, Vanessa knew, deep in her heart, that her time of being patient had almost reached its conclusion. She hadn't run from Price and followed Clayton across the country merely to wait for him and write. She'd gone to follow her dreams.

And her dream was to be his partner, his helpmate. His wife. As she recalled Corrine's proposal, Vanessa knew the time had come for her to brave the uncertainties of life and begin taking her future in her own hands.

❧

It was truly amazing how God worked, Vanessa thought one week later as she held the hastily scrawled message from the telegraph office. Merritt had just delivered the note to her with a shaky hand. "The news . . . it's bad," he said, his voice thick with worry. "I'm sorry, Vanessa."

Tears swam in her eyes, and she was unable to do anything but grip the paper and hold the folded ends shut.

"We'll get through this together," Corrine said with a tremulous smile. "I promise, you won't ever be alone."

Vanessa knew that to be true. So far, God had blessed her with Merritt and Corrine and their children. He'd blessed her when she read the Bible every night, reminding her of so many men and women who had gone through far harder things than she was going through and had come out of their circumstances better people.

Blinking away tears, Vanessa let Merritt guide her to a chair and tried to remember to breathe as she read and reread the short missive.

Sheriff Proffitt shot. Recuperating at Tall Oaks Inn. Situation dire. Your assistance needed. Doctor Tom Bodey. Benson, Nebraska.

"Situation dire?" Corrine gripped her hand. "Oh, Clayton."

Vanessa felt pain pierce her heart as shock and tears came tumbling forward. But still, she felt hope. Turning to Merritt, she asked, "What does this mean?"

"I'm not sure."

She had to ask—and she had to trust her brother-in-law to give her the truth. "Is he dead? Do you think he already could he be dead?"

"Not . . . yet. They would have said so if he was."

"I knew he shouldn't have taken that job," Corrine said angrily. "I knew it didn't suit him. I knew he'd get hurt and then hurt the rest of us, too. Why couldn't he have just stayed here?"

Merritt ignored the question, focusing on Vanessa instead. "What do you want to do?"

How could he even ask? "Go."

He held out a steadying hand. "There's a chance Clayton will already be dead."

"If . . . if that's the case, then I'll be with his body. Someone needs to be with him, Merritt."

Corrine clasped her hand. "Traveling can be difficult for a woman. Merritt will need to go with you." She looked to her husband for agreement.

Merritt nodded. "That's a fine idea."

"No," Vanessa said. "You've got a new baby, plus two other children who need you. I can travel on my own." Standing up quickly, she added, "I'll go pack my carpetbag right now." She stood up only to be pushed back into the chair as the room spun and bright dots flashed before her eyes. "Oh!"

Corrine pushed her head to her knees. "Breathe."

Though the position helped her dizziness, it made it even more difficult to catch her breath. Slowly, she sat up. "I'm sorry; I don't know what came over me."

"Worry, that's what did," Corrine said.

Worry wouldn't solve anything. She shook her head to clear it. "I'm better now."

"Not so fast. Rest easy, Van," Merritt murmured. "We don't want you falling down now."

Vanessa inhaled and exhaled, consciously feeling the air flow into her body and back out. Once, twice, three times. A sense of calm washed over her. "When is the next stage leaving?"

"I'm not sure, but I'm coming with you."

"I need to do this on my own."

Even Corrine shook her head. "You can't. You need to remember about Price."

For the last few months, all she had done was worry about Price. Worry about what he'd done to her, worry about him catching her again.

Worry about whether she and Clayton were right for each other, worry about if they should have married at all. It was time for that to end. "I'm not going to live in fear anymore. I'm not."

"Vanessa, I promised Clayton I'd keep you safe."

Oh, men and their promises. Did they really think that they were the only ones who took things seriously? "I made some promises too, you know. I took vows and meant every word. Before God, I promised I'd be with Clayton for better or worse. Through sickness and in health," she countered. "It's time I honored those vows."

"Good for you," Corrine murmured.

A trace of a smile played at the corners of Merritt's lips as he assisted her to her feet. With a wink in his wife's direction, he said, "Maybe you aren't so different from Corrine after all. All right then, we best get this show on the road. You go get packed."

"I'll organize some things for Clayton, Vanessa. I'll roll some bandages and pull out a few fresh shirts."

Merritt strode to the door. "And I'll go ask José to pack some provisions for your drive to the stage. If you're certain you want to go soon, I'm not going to stand in your way."

"Good. I would've hated to have had to step over you. Thank you, Merritt." Walking to her room, she smiled, feeling curiously empowered although the very center of her world was in terrible trouble. For the first time since her pa's passing, she felt as if she was going to be of use.

And she would help Clayton. She'd nurse him back to health and mend his loneliness. She'd convince him that their time apart had been nothing and no one could tear their vows asunder.

But before she pulled out the carpetbag that had once hung on a hook in Clayton's room in a musty old barn, she knelt at the side of her bed. "Thank you, God," she whispered. *"Thank you for bringing us back together. I need Clayton so desperately. Just . . . just please help him hang on until I get there, would you?*

I'm willing to help heal him as best I can, but I'll need your help. In your name, I pray," she finished.

Yes, *"weeping may linger for the night, but joy comes with the morning."* She was ready for a new morning to come.

Finally, as she quickly placed her belongings in the carpetbag, she recalled a verse from Psalm 145 that she loved so much. *"The Lord is gracious and compassionate. Slow to anger and rich in love."*

She was finally going to see Clayton again.

Praise God. Praise God in the highest.

And just to make sure he knew she was serious, she wrote him one last letter.

> Dear Clayton, I'm on my way. Hold on and
> be strong. I'm praying. You pray too. Nothing
> can happen to you. Not Now. Not Ever.
> Always yours, Vanessa.

As soon as she got to town, she was going to do two things. She would post the telegram to Benson and she was going to contact her father's banker in Texas and ask for her money to be transferred to her.

Clayton had already done more than enough to provide for her. She didn't want him to worry anymore. All they were going to do, once they were finally together, was concentrate on healing his body and planning their future.

No, Clayton might not approve, but she was not the young naive girl she used to be. It was time she took control of at least some of the things in her life. And it was beyond time that she do her part.

Feeling more at peace than she had in a very long time, Vanessa closed the carpetbag and walked out her door. It was time to move forward and stop looking back.

17

*C*layton neatly folded the telegram before lying back in his bed, grimacing when the sweat-soaked sheets chilled his back.

He was alone in a small upstairs bedroom of a run-down boardinghouse with a bullet wound in his thigh that burned like blazes. Another man was filling in for him as sheriff, and from what the doctor had told him, the majority of the towns-people were displeased that he'd been so reckless as to have gotten himself shot barely ten days after taking office.

He wasn't too pleased with the latest chain of events.

He was sore and lonely and feverish. He was full of regrets, not for what had happened to him—that had been an acci-dent—but for the choices he'd recently made. He should have stayed near Vanessa. He should have been more aware of how different a job upholding the law was from soldiering. He should have known his strength lay in leading loyal men into dangerous situations, not keeping order in a cow town.

Clayton winced as he attempted to shift positions. Outside his room, he heard a door slam, followed by a hint of male laughter. As the rough echo of footsteps traipsing up the stairs and down the hall matched the pounding of his head, he tried to think of other things.

But all he could think about was Vanessa. Vanessa—who he'd sworn to take care of but hadn't. Who he'd tried to keep sheltered but failed. Vanessa was now traveling to his rescue. The irony of it all felt cruel.

Merritt should have done more to keep her at his ranch.

Corrine should've warned her against traveling at all.

He should have been better to her. He'd failed again. He'd failed to keep her safe, and he'd failed his vow to her father—and to himself.

This is what it had come to, and it probably was no more than he deserved. Three days ago an upstart cowhand had gotten too rowdy at a bar. While Clayton had done his best to keep the peace, a shot had been fired right into his thigh. It had burned like the devil.

Doc Bodey had gotten the bullet out and cleaned the wound good enough, but now he was bedridden for at least a week, maybe longer. Each day seemed to take an eternity.

His body hadn't taken kindly to having a hole shot into it. He'd run a fever, bled like a stuck pig, and had enough discomfort burning through his leg to be more than a bit worried about an infection setting in.

No, he hadn't the need for stark reminders from Doc Bodey. Clayton figured he had enough memories of men losing limbs on the battlefield for a lifetime. The biting, sour odor of the hospital tents had taught him a worthy respect for infection.

He'd just resigned himself to be patient and let the healing take its course when he'd received Vanessa's note.

As he lay there wounded, staring at the faded wallpaper, Clayton wondered who had contacted Vanessa. He hadn't planned on telling her about the injury until it was a distant memory. Vanessa had enough to worry about; she didn't need something like this to fret over, too.

But somebody had written her by way of the telegraph wire and now Vanessa was attempting to be his rescuer. From the brief message in the telegram, she sounded ready to stake her claim on him as handily as if she was a miner on her way to California.

Obviously, he'd managed everything between them all wrong. Wearily, he glanced around the room again, finally taking refuge in his Bible.

Once again, he'd taken to reading it, especially finding comfort in the Psalms. Flipping pages, he scanned the fine print until he came across the words he most needed to hear.

"I bless the Lord, who gives me counsel; In the night also my heart instructs me. I keep the Lord always before me; because he is at my right hand, I shall not be moved."

Yes, Psalm 16 reminded him once again that God walked by his side. He always had. He always would. He wasn't alone, and he needed to remember that.

His misguided patience and dogged determination to uphold a vow to a dead man had twisted everything and tied up his life in a mess of knots. There was a very real possibility that he might be sitting in bed when Vanessa arrived, and that was the last place he wanted her to see him. He could hardly stay away from her when he was healthy and whole.

How was he going to keep his distance when there was no way for him to run?

He'd just taken to stewing on that one when the owner of the Tall Oaks Inn came in without knocking.

"Ah, I see you're up again," Rhianna Cambridge said matter-of-factly the moment she peeked in and caught his eye with her own bright blue ones. "Good. Now I won't need to be worrying about waking you up to change your sheets."

"Don't worry about them. They're fine."

"They're not, though you probably can't tell." Smiling easily, she shook her head, the movement dislodging an auburn curl from under her lace cap. "How you ever managed on your own, Clayton Proffitt, I'll never know. You're as helpless as a newborn calf."

He fought in a war during his teens, had managed a thousand-acre cattle ranch in his twenties, and had taken responsibility for a girl who'd needed it before he was thirty. "I've managed just fine."

"That's not what Mrs. Jenkins said."

Clayton grimaced. Mrs. Jenkins was the elderly woman who the town paid to fix his dinner four nights a week and to clean his rooms on Saturdays. She didn't excel at either endeavor.

Unfortunately, the only thing she did do very well was gossip about everyone and everything. Still, even her haphazard efforts were preferable to where he was stationed at the moment, in a small, rather bare room on the second floor of the Tall Oaks Inn.

Doc Bodey had insisted Clayton transfer lodging while he healed, saying it would be a mite easier for everyone if Clayton wasn't trying to rest in the same place the drunks and vagrants were cooling their heels. Though Clayton appreciated the fact, he found he didn't appreciate the lack of privacy. Rhianna and her daughter had taken to checking up on him with astonishing regularity, and always at inopportune times.

Rhianna set her hands on her hips. "Come now, Sheriff. You had a fever through the night. I'm betting those sheets are soaked through."

They were, and twice as uncomfortable, but that didn't mean he was in a hurry to get out of bed with her in the room. "They're fine."

Rhianna shook her head. "You're the most private man I've ever met. Settle down and let me do my job, would you? No way am I going to tell Doc Bodey that I can't look after the sheriff."

Because he knew she'd continue until he gave in, he finally agreed. "Fine."

Rhianna grinned. "Good. I'll be done in a pinch."

Clayton watched as she scurried around, setting down sheets, picking up clothes, and easily straightening chairs. She wasn't quite old enough to be his mother, but Clayton figured she sure acted like it. Now and again she fussed and fumed and told him just what she thought about him.

It had felt strange to have a woman coddle him. He'd grown up without a mother from the age of ten, and Corrine had never dared to be so bossy. Vanessa had always been warm and friendly, but had let him take care of her, not the other way around. He'd had no problem doctoring her back or making sure she was moderately comfortable.

But this woman—this Rhianna—didn't respect his boundaries. Nope, she did what she wanted and didn't care what other people thought about it either.

Waving her hands, she motioned him to twist to the side of the bed. "Let me help you tend to business, then you can sit in the chair while I get you settled."

Just yesterday, Clayton had found out that meant using the chamber pot. When he'd protested, Rhianna had practically tore him up one side and down the other. Turned out, the landlady had two sons in their early twenties, and she knew a thing or two about bossing helpless men.

Because his leg was burning like the devil, he'd finally allowed her to help him walk to a small curtained area and walk back again.

Today, they went through the motions again, though Clayton didn't even think of arguing with her. After she helped him to an ancient rocker, he sat down on the old frame with more care than he would have liked and watched her fix his bed.

With quick, efficient motions, Rhianna pulled off his soiled sheets and unfolded fresh ones on the feather bed. Finally, she helped him back on, and without a moment's embarrassment, helped him bare his thigh to her so she could change the bandage.

He examined the wound as she cleansed it with salt water. Hot needles of pain pierced the skin, making him cringe and his eyes tear up. He bit his lip to keep from crying out.

To his shame, Rhianna noticed. "Don't hold back now, sugar," she murmured, not unkindly. "There's nothing you can say or do that I haven't seen or heard another time before."

"That's a crying shame," he said. "No man should be acting so in front of you."

Rhianna tilted her head and smiled for a moment. "You, Sheriff, are a man of sweet words."

He'd never been that. As she cleaned and wiped, and the needles turned to giant pitchforks, sweat dotted Clayton's forehead.

"We're almost done. Hold on, now."

He gripped the arm of the rocker just a little bit harder. "Now, why do I get the feeling you've seen more bullet holes than this one?"

"Because I have. I nursed in the war. I've seen more pain and suffering than I hope you'll ever see, Sheriff." Almost tenderly, Rhianna patted the skin around the injury, causing him to wince. She paid him no mind. "Doc did a good job sewing you up. The skin's warm but healing."

"It still hurts to kingdom come."

Rhianna met his eyes with a small smile. "I wouldn't say it looks good, but it looks a fair sight better than I thought it might. And, well . . . you've still got your leg, right?"

"Yes, ma'am." When all was said and done, that was really all that mattered. Better men than he had lost legs and their livelihood from stray bullets. "I know it's healing because of your efforts, Rhianna."

"I think you're right." At the knock on the door, they both turned to see Rhianna's daughter Etta peeking in, a plate of food in her hands.

"Lord have mercy, you're going to let me eat?" Clayton asked, only half teasing. For the last two days, Rhianna had only allowed him porridge and soup.

"I'm going to let you eat a little," she clarified. "It's about time you got some meat back on your bones." She motioned to Etta. "Come on in, girl. Food's gonna get cold if you don't get a move on."

Etta did as her mother bid, casting a furtive glance his way.

Clayton hastily made sure he was covered, though his chest lay bare to her roving eyes. Her hungry glance embarrassed him. Its stark contrast to Vanessa's tentative glances and so-sweet stares made him wish he wore a band on his finger—anything to say without speaking that his heart had already been claimed.

Rhianna clucked impatiently. "Pull over that table and help the sheriff here get settled."

After Etta scooted the table over, she placed the plate on it and with a flourish pulled off the handkerchief covering it. Eggs, bacon, and thick slices of bread, lightly toasted, greeted him. It surely was a meal for a king.

"This looks mighty nice, Etta; thank you."

Cornflower blue eyes batted twice. "You're welcome."

Clayton looked away. Promise lay in Etta's eyes, and that was one thing he didn't need. He'd been in Benson long enough to know that Rhianna ran a respectable boardinghouse; but the woman's past had been hard, and her daughter Etta had never met her father. The very fact that Etta wasn't looking for love and marriage, but something far less, made him wary.

Scooping up the soiled sheets, Rhianna handed them to Etta. "Take these down to the laundry, and be quick about it."

"Yes, Mama." After another moment, Etta left, her step hesitant, letting Clayton know that she would willingly turn around with just a kind word. Slowly, Clayton moved back to the bed and let Rhianna help him with the sheets and quilts. He had to admit the fresh-smelling sheets were a welcome change.

So was the heady aroma of the fresh breakfast.

"Eat up, Sheriff," Rhianna encouraged from the chair he'd vacated.

Clayton closed his eyes at the taste of her cooking. "You certainly have a way in the kitchen."

Lines crisscrossed the area around her eyes. "Etta made it all, and you know it." After a pause, she added, "My daughter might be a tad forward, but she's got a good heart, Sheriff."

"I believe that."

"She's a girl who would do just about anything for some encouragement from you." After a pause, she added, "Haven't you noticed the way she follows your every move? She's done that since the moment you arrived in town. She'd be good for you."

"I'm married."

"I've heard that, but haven't seen the evidence." Fiddling with a crease in the skirt of her dress, she whispered, "I was thinking that marriage bit was a ruse on your part."

"It's no ruse. We just happen to be living apart for a time."

"Sounds like no marriage I've ever heard of." Narrowing her eyes, she said, "I wonder what your missus would do if she knew you were laid up in bed."

"As a matter of fact, she'd due here soon." Picking up the telegram from the bedside table, Clayton asked, "I take it that you aren't the one who sent for my wife?"

"No." Her eyes widened before she hid her emotions. "You say she's coming?"

"Doc brought me the telegram," he said in between mouthfuls of eggs. "Read it if you'd like."

Rhianna skimmed over the words unabashedly. "Well, now. You managed to surprise me, and I didn't think that was possible."

Rhianna looked disappointed. After biting into another piece of bacon, Clayton said, "I didn't mean to keep my marriage a secret, but I guess I did. It's been hard, being apart."

"I imagine so. I just can't believe you really do have a wife and she really is coming to Benson."

"I can't fault your surprise. I've never mentioned Vanessa." Clayton turned his attention back to his food. Just saying her name brought back memories that were almost too hard to recall.

But Rhianna had no such qualms. "*Vanessa*, huh? That name sounds pretty fancy. Where's this wife of yours been?"

"Staying with my sister near Denver."

"In Colorado. Well, my-oh-my. Why did she decide to stay there—if you're here? If you don't mind my asking, that is."

Her forwardness grated on him, yet Clayton didn't shy away from answering. He owed Rhianna, and it seemed she was going to meet Vanessa soon, in any case. "It's safer there. Safer for her."

"Safer how?" she asked, spitting out questions in a rapid fire. "What's wrong with her? She some kind of hothouse flower? Too delicate? She couldn't handle life by your side?"

He shook his head. "It wasn't that." He pointed to his saddlebag, which someone had deposited on the floor underneath the washbasin. In that satchel was every letter she'd written. "She's written to me faithfully for weeks. I asked her not to come with me."

"Why?"

There were some things he still wasn't ready to share, and a great many things that weren't any of her business. "It's complicated." He bit into the toast, hoping the woman would take the hint and let him eat in peace. Lord knew he needed the peace at the moment. His mixed emotions were churning his insides something awful, threatening to coax him into confiding things that were better left unsaid and unshared. "Vanessa and my pasts have painted our future," he added, liking the images the metaphor created, like they were part of something permanent and special.

"I imagine so." Eyeing the letter, she nodded to his leg. "So, if you didn't send for her, someone else did. Sheriff, were you planning to tell her about getting shot?"

"No. She has enough to worry about."

Rhianna's eyebrows rose. "More to think of than a husband? Do tell. Back when I was married, I did my best by my man. Gerald would've gotten a mouthful if he'd even thought about leaving me somewhere." After a snort of humor, she added, "More than that if he neglected to tell me 'bout his injuries."

Clayton knew there was no sense in replying. Everything between he and Vanessa was complicated. "Thank you for the breakfast, ma'am."

Her blue eyes dimmed. "Well, now. I guess I went and offended you."

Clayton couldn't tell if she cared or not. "You didn't. There's just some things I don't care to share."

"I understand."

Rustling and a sharp bell clanged outside his window. Rhianna stood up and looked out. After a bit, she whistled low and pressed a little closer to the pane.

Finally, Rhianna turned to him and smiled. "I do believe you have a visitor, Sheriff. And I'd bet my last dollar it's your wayward wife."

It was all Clayton could do not to stand up and look out, too. After what felt like an eternity he was alone no more.

18

*R*hianna just kept talking. "Yep, there's a woman out there in a blue dress, a straw bonnet, and a spray of freckles across her nose." Her voice grew louder and slightly garbled when her forehead pressed against the pane. "Why, now. Look at that, she's speaking to Henry, and Henry's pointing to my place."

After a moment, she submitted another report. "Oh my goodness, now that gorgeous gal is picking up her skirts and walking this way. She has brown hair all braided up fancy and walks like she's on a mission all her own." Casting a sideways glance his way, Rhianna raised an eyebrow. "Clayton . . . do you reckon that there's your wife?"

He'd know that walk anywhere. "Probably." Clayton fought to hide his panic and keep his voice steady. Though he'd spent almost every night since they'd parted thinking of her, at the moment, he'd have been happy for just a little more time. Time to gather his thoughts and formulate a plan.

After all, this was not how he'd wanted to see Vanessa again. Certainly never while he was in bed, half-clothed, and still in pain.

Certainly not with a rackety woman in his room who had no qualms about speaking her mind and no doubts about her narrow views on the world.

Raking his hand across his cheek, he scowled. When had he shaved last?

Voices echoed outside the front of the boardinghouse, snippets of conversation floating up and teasing him. As Rhianna moved away from the window and had the audacity to step in front of the room's tiny mirror and check her hair, Clayton swallowed hard. Prayed for control.

But that control was not to be. In its place was a passel of mixed-up emotions, each individual and unique. Together they churned up his dismay and caused him to exhale deeply.

And then he heard Vanessa's laugh, bright and vivid, causing him to smile in spite of himself, bringing forth a burst of feelings that overpowered all other negative influences. No matter what, he was eager to see Vanessa. He loved her. He'd ached for her smile. More important, they were married. She was his, and their waiting period was over.

At long last, a faint sense of peace flowed through him.

The Lord was in charge, not Clayton, and the Lord had decided it was time to see his wife again. The least Clayton could do was accept the invitation gracefully. "Hand me my shirt, Rhianna."

Surprisingly, she did as he asked, handing him a loose-fitting chambray shirt. He'd just shrugged into it when they heard an impatient knock at the front door echo through the entryway and on up the stairs.

And then they heard Vanessa's beautiful voice. "Mrs. Clayton Proffitt."

"I do believe we're about to meet the elusive Mrs. Proffitt," Rhianna murmured before raising an eyebrow his way. "You sure look panicked. What's she like?"

She was perfect. "You'll see."

Rhianna cackled again. "Now that's sparked my curiosity, Sheriff." Rushing to the door, she popped out and called down to her daughter. "Bring the woman on up and be quick about it, Etta."

Clayton felt as if a thousand hammers were pounding into his heart as he heard a soft, sweet voice. Heard ladylike footsteps on the hardwood floor.

Vanessa.

Rhianna strode to his side and picked up his plate. "Something tells me you won't be needin' breakfast now."

Finding his voice, he murmured, "Thank you."

"It's been a long time since my man died . . . but I do remember some things like sweet reunions," she murmured, a faraway look filling her eyes. "I think I'll just sneak on out before she shows up. You two might like some privacy for your meeting."

Clayton nodded, unable to do a thing besides watch the door. What was taking Vanessa so long?

"I doubt your woman appreciates you enough, Clayton Proffitt," Rhianna said, slowly opening the door and stepping out into the hallway. "And all I have to say for certain is that that's a crying shame."

And with that, Rhianna closed the door and left far more quietly than she ever had before.

⚘

"This way, ma'am," a girl—a woman—of about Vanessa's age said as she slowly led the way down the hall. Vanessa's eyes widened as she tried to figure out what was going on. The telegram had said Clayton was injured. She'd imagined him in the back of the doctor's rooms or in his own place near the jail. Not a room on the second floor of a run-down boarding-house. She'd imagined Doc Bodey or the deputy greeting her the moment her stage arrived and escorting her to Clayton's side. Never the complete emptiness that had greeted her.

And she'd never imagined Clayton would be spending time with a woman like the one she was following. Oh, this lady was attractive, in a hard sort of way—polite but not friendly.

An unaccustomed stab of jealousy flared—igniting all the doubts and worries that had plagued her during their time of separation.

Why was Clayton here? "This is where Sheriff Proffitt is? Sheriff Clayton Proffitt?" Vanessa asked, just to make sure.

"Uh-huh."

The vacant, half-attentive reply was anything but reassuring. So was the run-down building. The heat was stifling, and more than one fly buzzed its displeasure as they walked on threadbare carpet down the hallway, then up the stairs.

As an older lady with bright red hair and an easy smile chuckled as she passed them, Vanessa swallowed hard.

Doubts ran rampant in her head. Was there a reason he'd chosen to live here? He'd been full of reasons for them not to make their marriage real. Noble reasons about her youth and his responsibilities. What if they'd been all lies?

Was Clayton living here by choice? Had he not wanted her in Nebraska for private reasons, known only to him? Not because he was looking out for her interests but because he'd replaced her?

One walk down a hall had never felt so long. Vanessa squared her shoulders as she followed the girl. They turned left and went through a pair of double doors. Finally they stopped.

"Well, this here's his room," the gal said, scrutinizing Vanessa up and down, making her feel dirty and almost ashamed. Obviously, even in this northern town, women didn't call on men in their rooms.

She decided to rectify that misconception immediately. "Thank you for taking me to my husband."

The girl looked skeptical. "So he really is yours?"

Vanessa didn't have the inclination to discuss the girl's bold question. All that mattered was that she was going to see Clayton for the first time after a long separation.

Now all that separated them was a wooden door. When she opened that door, would everything be all right? Or would Clayton blame her for not obeying his wishes?

Would he be as happy as she was to see her? Or would he only want her to go away? Confusion reared its ugly head, giving her doubts, making her pulse race.

"You going in?"

With some dismay, Vanessa realized the other woman was still beside her and was eyeing her with a look of half pity and half impudence. And no wonder! Who else would travel so far just to wait so long to make her presence known?

It was time. With a shaky hand, Vanessa steeled herself and knocked on the door. "Clayton?"

He answered in a heartbeat. "Yes."

"It's me, Vanessa."

A smile floated through the doorway with his words. "I know that, honey. Come on in."

Honey. The endearment brought forth a torrent of welled-up emotion and long-dried-up dreams. Without another thought for the girl standing next to her, Vanessa quickly turned the knob and almost tumbled into Clayton's room, hardly aware of anything but his brown eyes, drinking in her every move. Clayton.

For just a moment, time seemed to stop. She closed her eyes, taking in his scent. Thanking God that they were together again. Finally, *finally* feeling at peace.

"Close the door, sweetheart," Clay whispered, his voice sounding like an echo through a train tunnel, hoarse and almost whisperlike.

Feeling the worn wood behind her, she pushed the door closed.

It connected into the frame with a sharp click.

Confusion and relief and embarrassment for her doubts soared through her as she approached the large four-poster. He really was hurt. He really did need her. Tears pricked her eyes as relief and worry and, well, everything rushed to her full force.

They'd been apart for such a very long time.

His eyes drew her close. Deep chocolate brown eyes that said so much. Always had. They beckoned her without a word. She answered their call, unafraid.

Clayton needed her. *Needed her.* He needed not just anyone to care for him; he needed someone who loved him. His wife.

"Oh, Clayton."

He tried to smile, but didn't quite make it. Instead, his eyes lit on her, drinking in the sight, just like she was doing for him. Held out a hand. "Vanessa, honey. Why did you come?"

"How could I not?" she replied, examining him again, clinging to his hand like a lifeline.

The bandages on his leg looked freshly changed, yet his skin looked pale. His cheeks, always so shaved and neat, had days' worth of stubble, making him look almost like an outlaw.

His chest was loosely covered with a chambray shirt not quite buttoned. When he shifted, she could make out a thick, jagged scar below his ribcage. It looked just as it did when she'd first spied it years ago when she'd seen him changing shirts.

Vanessa tried to smile, though it was difficult. All she wanted to do was rage at him for getting hurt and not letting her know. For taking a job as a sheriff.

For being in Nebraska in the first place. For allowing another woman to nurse him.

For letting his cursed pride take control of their relationship, preventing them from becoming man and wife because of some vow she'd never believed in.

But she did none of that.

Perhaps it was because she'd grown up?

"I couldn't stay away another minute," she said, breaking contact for a moment while she placed her carpetbag and kid gloves on the floor. "I missed you."

A mixture of emotions lit his eyes. Happiness. Relief. Longing, plain and simple. "I've missed you, too."

His words, and the way he hungrily followed her every move, propelled her forward to sit next to him, gave her strength to be strong instead of dissolving into tears and confiding all of her troubles and fears.

This is why she'd come. This was what she'd hoped would happen. A connection. The realization that there was still a love between them. Gingerly, Vanessa scooted a little closer. Close enough so that her hip grazed his thigh, close enough to feel him, to touch him, even though he hadn't held out his arms.

Now, neither seemed to have anymore words to say.

But perhaps that wasn't necessary. Immediately, her senses were captivated by all things Clayton. His scent, his warmth. The way he looked at her like she was everything to him.

She couldn't wait another moment to touch him. Reaching out, she cupped his cheek, ran her fingers along his jaw, enjoying the jump of muscles as her fingers played. After a moment's hesitation, he claimed her hand and pressed her knuckles against his lips, sending ribbons of longing through her.

He swallowed.

Her mind went blank.

She couldn't remember a thing—not what she'd planned to say, not what she'd planned to do.

All of a sudden, her doubts about their relationship meant nothing. Nothing mattered but Clayton. After what seemed like forever they were together, and she made a vow that never again would they be apart.

What they had was too important. Worth claiming. Worth fighting for.

The strong bonds she'd witnessed between Corrine and Merritt cemented her will. She trembled when he bent his head to kiss the delicate inside of her wrist. "Tell me what happened. Clayton, are you okay?"

He dropped her hand. "I'm fine. There's not much to tell— not really," he said with a small smile. "I was shot."

"Oh, Clay."

He rubbed his thigh absently. "It's unfortunate, but not a surprise. In one of the saloons, a boy got hold of a gun and made a mistake. I paid the price."

Hating his pain, supremely aware that the bullet could have done more damage, that she could have lost him, Vanessa clasped his hand again.

With some disquiet, Vanessa realized that now she had an inkling of what Clayton must had felt when he'd seen her back for the first time. She felt rage, helplessness, and strength all wrapped up together. She wanted to shake Clayton for being so brave and go give whoever had fired that gun a piece of her mind, after she slapped him silly.

"Oh, Clay," she said again.

"Shh, now honey. Don't fret."

Like always, his endearment made her smile. "I got here as soon as I received the telegraph."

"Doc Bodey must have taken care of that. I didn't know he sent you a wire."

"I wish you had asked him to."

Brown eyes met hers. "Right now, right this minute, I wish I had, too. I'm glad you're here, Van."

"Are you in pain?"

"No."

Vanessa knew he was lying but didn't have the heart to correct him as she scanned his face. Slowly, she watched his eyes dart to her lips. She felt his imprint just as surely as if he'd had his arms around her and they were kissing for all they were worth—just like the evening before he'd left.

Without a word, their palms shifted and their fingers linked. Amazingly, she felt more calluses. Vanessa wondered if he felt the difference in her palm as well. She'd done her best to be useful while staying with Corrine, chipping in when she could. Vanessa was proud of her accomplishments, but now, feeling her skin rubbing against his, she wondered if he thought she was lacking in some way. If her rough hands made him long for the cosseted girl she used to be.

But then he eased her mind. "You're so lovely, Vanessa. Perfect." He paused. "Perfect for me." He blinked and tried to smile. "I just can't believe you're here in front of me in Nebraska. Not a dream."

A lump formed in her throat as tears pricked her eyes. "I couldn't stay away. With you is where I belong," she said, wishing the tears that were now falling could disappear. "I hate the thought of you sitting here suffering by yourself."

His expression softened. One hand snaked up and caressed her cheeks, wiping away moisture, sending a thrill through her body from just that simple touch. "Don't cry," he murmured. "Honey, you know I never could stand your tears."

"I never could stand to see you hurt."

Humor lit his eyes. "Since when have you seen me hurt?"

"Since today." She blinked harder and tried to find some sauciness in her voice. "Since right this minute. And that's enough, Clayton."

He squeezed her hand. "So, you traveled all the way here alone?"

"I did." She lifted her chin. "I took the train from Denver to Cheyenne, then the stage from Cheyenne to here."

"It's a hard journey."

As she recalled the bumpy terrain and stifling heat, she nodded. "I will admit that I've been rattled enough to be a rattlesnake."

He chuckled, looked to say more. Instead, he said nothing.

Instead, he lifted his arms, captured her shoulders, pulled her down to him. Finally.

And kissed her. Brushing his lips against hers. Slowly, each touch full of tenderness and wanting. Exquisitely gentle, full of care. With each brush, she felt his love, his care. She felt treasured and valued and special.

And because it was everything she ever dreamed of, she fell apart and did start crying, right then and there. Months of built-up tears sprang forth, and she no longer had the will-power or the need to stop them.

He rubbed her back. "It's all right Van," he murmured. "Everything's all right. Cry it out."

The tears kept flowing. "I missed you so much. I've been so worried," she blurted with a hiccup, right before she began crying even harder.

Clayton pushed back a wayward strand of hair from her face. "Hush now, sugar. It's going to be all right."

"I know," she sobbed. "I know it will be now."

She'd dreamed of this moment. Dreamed of being in the same room, of being in his arms, of feeling secure. Feeling wanted.

Yet her dreams didn't compare to the reality. Clayton brushed fleeting kisses across her brow, along her cheeks. Held her close and murmured sweet words. Those hands she knew so well caressed her face and massaged her back as if he was memorizing every touch.

*

As he held his wife in his arms, Clayton finally gave up fighting. Finally he allowed himself to realize that God's will had been done. Providence had guided her to him just when he was sure he couldn't take another moment alone.

A phrase from Deuteronomy flashed into his mind. And when she calmed, he wiped her eyes with two fingers and murmured, "He led you through the vast and dreadful desert, that thirsty and waterless land, with its venomous snakes and scorpions."

Vanessa nodded in understanding. "Yes. He did lead me here to you. He did lead us to finally be together. Oh, Clayton, I know God has been guiding us from the moment you arrived at the Circle Z. He's been with us all along."

Understanding dawned. "He's been there with us, even when we didn't know what we wanted. Even when we didn't know how to achieve our dreams."

"I think so."

Clayton took a moment to close his eyes, to just enjoy the feel of her in his arms. And because it couldn't wait anymore, he asked her the question that had been plaguing him for the last few weeks. "Are you doing better? Really?"

"I am."

"The dreams?"

"The dreams are better." She pressed a hand to the center of her chest, over her heart. "And inside, I finally feel healed."

Vanessa's lips were glistening from their kisses. Her hair was mussed from his fingertips. She looked beautiful as she scrambled off the bed, obviously unsure of how to react, of what to do next.

Clayton let her set the pace, knowing it was important to give them both time, though at the moment all he wanted to do was ask her to enter his arms once again.

With two quick strokes, she shook out her skirts, setting herself to rights. "I guess we should speak about other things. Is this where you live?"

Clayton sat up and tried to clear his muddled thoughts. "No. Rhianna offered me a room to recuperate in. I sleep above the jail. The old wooden stairs in the building are narrow and rickety. They would've been a mite difficult to navigate."

"I imagine so." Looking worriedly at the door, Clayton was sure Vanessa was going to ask about the woman, or offer to feed him, or rush to the basin of water and wash her tear-stained cheeks. But she did none of that. "I love you, Clayton. I really do."

He needed her love more than he could say. Her letters to him had been a soothing balm in his life of chaos. No longer could he pretend they hadn't meant the world to him. No longer could he pretend that he didn't need her, that a vow to her father was more binding than their marriage vows. Truth be told, he needed her. He needed her in every way, by his side, both night and day.

"I love you, too."

"Oh!" Her eyes softened, and his heart melted with her.

Tenderly, he brushed back a stray hair from her temple. "Van, there's so many things we need to discuss."

"I know."

"So many things have happened. So many things I couldn't write in a letter."

"We have time for that now. I want to hear everything that's happened to you, Clayton."

He started talking. An hour passed, then two, as they sat together and tried to get caught up. It was nearly impossible, though, since long moments passed when all they could do was stare at each other and smile.

Later that afternoon, reality came back.

"Knock, knock," Rhianna said just a scant minute before opening the door. "Clayton, it's time to check your dressing again."

Vanessa stood up. "I'll tend to him now."

Rhianna chuckled. "Honey, I know you mean well, but I doubt you even know what to look for. Infection can set in a matter of hours. And then what would you do? Call me and hope and pray?"

Instead of backing down, Vanessa stepped forward, looking as outraged as a bantam rooster. "I would never underestimate the power of prayer." Turning to Clayton, she asked quietly, "Do you know how to check for infection?"

"I do." Unfortunately, he'd mended and tended to a fair share of men during the war. If he was familiar with anything after the years of fighting, it was cuts, sores, and their everlasting effects.

Vanessa turned to Rhianna. "Ma'am, if you would be so kind as to direct your help to bring up some warm water, I'd appreciate it."

Clayton didn't know whether to be proud or dumbfounded by his wife's cool tone and matter-of-fact ways. Where was the girl he'd nursed on the road to Lubbock? Where was the woman who had waited for him to do everything for her?

Rhianna, too, glanced at Vanessa with a new respect. "I'll have someone bring some warm water up right away."

"Thank you."

Rhianna looked to Clayton, but he didn't dare do a thing except dart a glance at his wife. He was right proud of her, and proud of her forbearance.

"Expect Joe to arrive in a few," Rhianna muttered before sashaying out the door.

Vanessa breathed deeply when she left. "Let me help you with your pillows. They look like they need to get fluffed."

"Yes, ma'am," Clayton said as he slowly leaned forward. Evidently, Vanessa wasn't in the mood to argue.

19

"She up and did it," Price called out triumphantly. "Vanessa telegraphed the bank. Burl rode out and gave me the news this morning."

Miles's hand shook as he tethered Jericho to the hitching post, taking his time with the slipknot so he didn't have to meet his stepfather's gaze. But oh, how he wanted to show every emotion he was feeling at the moment! Surprise. Dismay.

Bone-crunching terror for his sister.

How could Vanessa have done something so foolhardy? Though months had passed, surely she didn't imagine that Price was just going to forget about her?

More to the point, even if he had, there was one thing everyone knew counted the most to Price Venture, and that was money. There was no way on God's green earth that Price was going to let her retrieve her funds without him putting up a fight.

As Miles turned his thoughts over again, a band of worry tightened in his chest. Something must have happened to Clayton. The man Miles knew was too responsible, too care-ful to have let Vanessa contact the bank. No one would have needed to spell it out for him that Burl Iverson would notify Price the moment they received word from his stepdaughter. Not only would Burl think that Price would be overjoyed to hear about her whereabouts, but Burl would be too afraid not to inform Price about that money.

Anyone who'd been on Price's bad side thought twice before being on it again. It just wasn't worth the pain and destruction the man was capable of.

What had happened to Clayton? Miles could only imagine the very worst. Clay was either dead or seriously injured. Those were the only explanations that made sense.

As the silence dragged on, Price got impatient. "Boy, you hear me?"

Taking pains to keep his expression impassive, Miles turned away from Jericho's line. "I heard you, sir. What do you want to do?"

"Go get her, of course."

"Where is she? Does Burl know?"

"She sent the wire from Denver. Even was good enough to send a contact by the name of John Merritt. Seems Merritt has a sizable piece of land just south of Denver. Does that name ring a bell?"

"That's Clayton's old commanding officer. His sister Corrine married him, I believe."

"We'll need to go within the hour. We can make it past Camp Hope by nightfall if we push the horses hard enough." With a grin, Price added, "What a stroke of luck. It's a good thing we decided to cool our heels for a bit back here. Now both we and horses will be ready." Over his shoulder, Price lifted a finger. "One hour, boy. Be ready."

Miles was almost tempted to step aside and say he didn't want to go. He actually even thought that Price would let him stay behind. After all, their last bit of traveling had proved that neither found the other to be a particularly good traveling companion.

But Miles had grown up a lot in the last month. And, his Bible studies had made him be a better man.

He needed to accompany Price, if for no other reason than to help Vanessa when they all met. This time, instead of merely riding by his side and hoping to delay their trip, Miles planned to accompany his stepfather for one reason only, with the intent to protect Vanessa from harm.

He walked into the house, still taken aback about how vacant it seemed without either his mother or Vanessa.

Yes, the last month had been hard, indeed. Though Price made it sound as if he'd been reluctant to halt the search, Miles recalled just how long it had taken them to get home. Just east of the Texas border, Price had befriended a cattle rancher from Missouri and struck a friendship. The two of them had taken to gambling for high stakes late into the night more often than not.

When Miles had asked if he could go on back to the ranch, Price had refused the request, saying he would be needed if they ever did find Clayton and Vanessa. Since he'd had no choice, Miles used the extra hours to get better acquainted with the Bible, taking comfort time and a gain in the Scriptures and in Jesus' calls for patience time and again.

Once they arrived home, more bad news had awaited them. The Circle Z was in a sorry state. Fences needed mending; fields needed to be rotated. Even the house needed some repairs done, since a fierce dust storm had broken a variety of shutters and damaged the back porch.

The ranch hands had done their best, but with no one used to making decisions—and each having a healthy fear of being blamed for mistakes by Price—very little had gotten done.

Price had just ordered Miles to go to tell his mother they'd returned when Samuel, one of their long-time vaqueros, approached them the moment they rode to the barn and dismounted. "I am sorry, Mr. Miles, but your mother died last week."

He felt as if he'd been struck with a poleax. "What? What happened?"

Samuel looked at the ground, completely ignoring Price. "She took her own life, I'm afraid."

"Are you sure? How?" His voice broke off, unable to comprehend the news. With some surprise, Miles realized he felt ashamed as well. For quite some time, he'd taken his mother for granted. It had been easier to lay all the blame for his problems on her shoulders than to take responsibility for his own actions. "When?"

"It happened last Tuesday, Mr. Miles. Maria found her."

Price had gone livid. "What did she do to herself?"

As if he had trouble talking over his words, Samuel said, "It was a gunshot. She shot herself in the head. The doctor said she died instantly."

"You bury her yet?" Again, the question was coldly spoken, with no emotion behind the words, no feelings of loss evident.

For a brief instant, the true extent of Samuel's dislike for Price showed in his eyes, then he covered it. "Yes. In the family plot, next to Mr. Grant."

"She was my wife," Price said. "You shouldn't have buried her there. Besides, suicide is a sin."

Yes it was, but Miles knew in his heart that Price was guilty of so many others. "Samuel, you did fine. Thank you for burying her for me."

Samuel nodded his head in recognition. "You are most welcome, Mr. Miles. She, your mother, she was a good woman. We said a prayer for her as well."

"I appreciate that. She was a good woman," Miles said quietly.

Just as Samuel turned away, Price ordered him to stop. "She didn't leave a big mess, did she?"

"No, sir." With an apologetic look toward Miles, he added, "The men cleaned the house."

"Good."

Miles felt the biting sting of tears as he watched his stepfather walk away. Price's reaction to his mother's death was heartbreaking and expected. After all, he'd ruined his mother. He'd never been a husband to her. No, he'd only used what he could and bled her dry, taking her dignity, her money, and her land, and driving her daughter away. Never had he even pretended to love her.

Only while courting had he pretended to care about her at all.

Now, in the house once again, Miles walked the halls and remembered the good things about Marilyn Grant. How she'd giggle like a schoolgirl when his father would tell jokes. The way she'd always had time for each of them.

How she used to stand outside and look into the distance, waiting and hoping when their pa would be off on a cattle drive.

In her heart, she was a good woman. Though the act of praying was still new and made him feel unsure, Miles took the opportunity in his room to bend his head.

"Lord, please be with my mother. Please let her be with my father and with You. Let her feel Your love and forgiveness. Please let her know that I am going to miss her but that I understand why she did what she did. Some things are awfully hard to overcome. I hope she is at peace now. Amen."

❧

Almost a month later, Miles rummaged in his room once again. This time, however, he knew in his heart he wasn't just leaving for a bit. No, this time he was leaving for good. After making sure Vanessa was fine, Miles was going to leave the memories of the Circle Z forever. He wanted no more bad experiences to taint the good memories he had of the large, once prosperous ranch.

It was time to shake off his childhood and step forward into his own path. He was finally ready to become his own man.

He packed clothes and handkerchiefs in his saddlebags, then took care to slide Jacob's Bible in there too. Only a few other items were stored. Looking around, Miles realized that there was nothing else in his room—in his life—that couldn't be replaced.

With slow steps, he walked down the stairs. Price was at the back door. "I'm just about ready."

"Me too. Remind me when we get back to visit with Burl again over at the bank. I need to see if there are any documents regarding the ranch. Since Marilyn's gone, the place is fair and square mine now."

There was a time when Miles probably would have fought that. Now it didn't matter. No, the Circle Z was not Price's. It was Miles and Vanessa's by birthright. But Miles wasn't willing to fight.

He'd rather be long gone and free than have the most luxurious lifestyle and be beholden to Price. "I'll remind you," he murmured.

Price nodded, grabbing some chewing tobacco and stuffed it into his own saddlebag. "I can't wait to get my hands on that girl. It's gonna take years for her to make up what she's put me through."

"I imagine so."

"And more important, no way in the world is she going to get one red cent of her family's money. Not one."

Miles didn't even try to point out that he too deserved the inheritance.

A gleam entered his stepfather's eye. "I'll find a way to get that money, boy, one way or another. Now, go saddle up the horses."

It was an order, and Miles had no inclination to disobey. It was time to find Vanessa and to take care of their future once and for all. With a surety he used to only imagine having, Miles knew two things. One, Price was going to get to Vanessa one way or another, so all Miles could do was accompany him.

The other was just as important to him. No matter what, Price would never touch Vanessa again. If Clayton couldn't protect her, he would.

"Miles, you coming?"

"I am," he said, pausing when he spied Samuel in the tack room. "Good-bye," he whispered. "I doubt I'll ever be back."

Just as quietly, Samuel murmured, "You going to take care of your stepfather?"

"No. I'm going to take care of Vanessa. And then I'm going to take care of myself."

With a look of understanding, Samuel nodded. "Then good-bye. And may God be with you, Mr. Grant." When

Miles stared at him in confusion and surprise, a funny half smile formed at the corners of Samuel's lips. "You earned the title now, *si?*"

"Yes. Thank you for your prayers."

Quickly, he checked Jericho, making sure his cinch was not too tight and the saddle was fastened correctly. After laying the bags down in front of him, Miles slid a boot in a stirrup and easily got in the saddle. "You ready, Jericho?"

The horse shifted impatiently.

Guiding his horse out to Price, Miles felt both excited and proud. And just a little bit nervous. Things were about to change. *Help me, Lord,* Miles prayed. *I will follow you.*

For the first time, peace settled on his shoulders, comforting him like a warm blanket.

"I'm ready," Miles said.

"About time," Price fired back; but for the first time, there was little rancor in his voice. Then, they motioned the horses forward and left the ranch.

As Miles finally left everything behind him, he took comfort in a verse from Mark 10 that had spoken to him more than once when he was confused or frightened. *"Amen, I say to you. Whoever does not accept the kingdom of God like a child will not enter it."*

Miles prayed with all his might. He had accepted God's presence in his life. Had become a child of the Lord.

And because of that, he knew he was following the right way. Miles would follow Price to Vanessa's side because that's where he needed to be. And after that, he would trust Jesus to lead the way.

20

The wound where the bullet had entered was far bigger than any injury Vanessa had seen before. Jagged, red, and almost as a wide as a silver dollar, it looked angry and swollen.

"Doc said he had quite a time fishing the bullet out," Clayton said by way of explanation. "It'll heal up in no time."

"You almost sound proud of it."

He dared to smile. "I'm proud I survived it, I suppose."

Vanessa fought to keep her bearings. No woman ever wanted to see such injury to her husband. "I see."

As carefully as possible, she washed the area thoroughly, then wrapped it neatly with the clean bandages Corrine had rolled for her.

Through all her administrations, Clayton had sat rigid, hardly moving. When she noticed that he looked a little gray, she hurried a bit more, fastening a strip of linen too tightly. Clayton grunted.

Immediately, she loosened the binding. "I'm sorry I'm causing you more pain. I don't mean to."

"I know. You're not. Stop fussing, Vanessa."

Fussing? "Clayton, I'm trying to help you."

"Then leave the bandages alone and keep me company. That's what I need more than anything else."

That was all she needed to hear.

Once she made sure he was comfortable, Vanessa sat in the chair next to him.

"Come lie by my side. I've missed you, Van."

She didn't need to be asked again. She, too, felt like they could never be close enough. After carefully smoothing the sheets around him, Vanessa lay by his side on top of the quilt. He shifted, and in no time Vanessa was curled up next to him, her palm resting on the soft cotton of his shirt.

Within minutes, he moved closer, shifted so he spooned her in his arms, her back touching his chest and stomach. Little by little, they both relaxed.

"This is where I've wanted to be," she said. "By your side, keeping you company."

"I've wanted you here in my arms, sweet and so perfect."

She knew how much his admittance had cost him. Clayton hated to sound dependent on anyone else. "You should have let me come to you earlier."

"I wouldn't have wanted you to see me in such a condition. Besides, our time apart fulfilled our promises. And, I made some money."

"Let's not talk about money now."

"All right, honey. We won't. We don't need to talk about much now, do we?"

Her eyes drifted shut. It was true, she was exhausted. Everything she'd been through in the last week—the hurried packing, the hasty good-byes, the interminable rides on the stage and in the train cars—it all had taken its toll.

But now, all she needed was time to sleep. Finally, just like she'd never slept before, she closed her eyes and succumbed to oblivion.

Finally, they were together again.

Over the next week, Vanessa and Clayton settled into a routine. Vanessa slept in a room next to his, but otherwise spent the day by his side.

She visited with a cantankerous Doc Bodey, changed Clayton's dressings, and helped Rhianna and Etta as much as she could with Clayton's meals.

She helped him walk and exercise his leg, first just up and down the long halls that were in need of a good washing. Later, they tackled the scarred and stained staircase.

But more than anything else she and Clayton talked. They spent hours recalling old friendships and telling each other about things that happened during their time apart.

They talked of Miles and Corrine, of Lacy and the Willoughbys. Of Red Cloud, of her mother, and of his tremendous worries regarding Scout and the mistakes he'd made regarding his brother.

Finally, ten days after she arrived, Vanessa accompanied Clayton out the boardinghouse and down the boardwalk to the mayor's office.

Mayor Stuart looked up in surprise when Clayton led her through the door. "Sheriff? I didn't expect you to be up so quickly."

"I'm not the type to stay in bed," Clayton said. "Please meet my wife, Vanessa."

Mayor Stuart stood up. "A pleasure to meet you, Mrs. Proffitt." With a grin, he said, "Looks like we're going to need to find you a better place to live than above the jail, son. That ain't no place to house a wife."

Clayton shifted. "That's why I'm here. I'm resigning my position, Mayor. I'm afraid this job and I aren't a good match."

After motioning them both to sit in the rickety wooden chairs across from him, Stuart sighed. "You sure?"

"I'm afraid so." Staring intently at the mayor, Clayton said, "It's not just getting shot, sir. I . . . I realized I'm not well suited to keep the peace. My strengths lie on the back of a horse, rounding up cattle, working the land."

"You did fine."

"I'm afraid the decision is made."

"I see." Leaning back, Mayor Stuart looked Clayton directly in the eye. "I wish I could say this was a surprise, but quite honestly, I figured you would be resigning. No man who has something to live for is going to remain happy at a job as dangerous as this one."

Looking at Vanessa, Clayton reached for her hand. "I've found that to be true."

"Well, I'm glad of that. You two look very happy. I'm guessing the separation was difficult?"

"Very much so," Vanessa said.

"Well, I hope you keep him in line from now on, ma'am. No more jobs with guns, all right?" With a touch of humor, he said, "Getting shot should be avoided, don't you think?"

"I believe so," Clayton replied dryly. Then, after a quick look at Vanessa, he held out his hand. "Sir, I've appreciated the opportunity; it's just time I went back to my family."

Mayor Stuart smiled at Vanessa. "I can see your point. Godspeed, Clayton." Standing up, he crossed to a massive safe in the back. After opening it up, he pulled out a thick envelope. "I've been saving this for you. Take it; it's your wages. You've earned them."

After a few more parting words, they left the office. As they walked down the boardwalk again, Clayton smiled. "I feel as if a giant weight has just been lifted from my shoulders."

"I feel the same way. I didn't like you being a sheriff," Vanessa said. "I worried too much about you."

"I can't say I'm going to miss upholding the law. Every night I worried I'd have to shoot some poor soul . . . and I promised myself after the war that I wouldn't take up a gun again if I didn't have to."

Taking her arm, they slowly headed back to the Tall Oaks Inn. "My leg's almost completely healed. Doc Bodey said in two more days I'll be ready to ride. I'd say it's just about time to leave."

Vanessa was ready for their new beginning, for them to go back to Colorado—or to wherever Clayton wanted to take them. "I'll be ready when you are."

<hr>

They left Benson two days later, Clayton on Lee, Vanessa on a pretty chestnut-colored mare named Buttercup. Clayton figured they could sell the horse without a problem back in Denver.

As the broad, desolate plains of Nebraska spilled out before them, Vanessa turned to him. "Are we headed to Cheyenne?"

"Not yet. I thought we might take a few days to ourselves. I wrote a friend soon after you arrived in Benson. I heard back from him yesterday. He's got a cabin about twenty miles from here that he said we were welcome to use." He paused. "Vanessa, if it's all right with you, I thought we could stay there for a few days. No reason for us to be rushing around again. I feel like that's all I've been doing. All we've been doing since we left the Circle Z."

"I'd love to take our time traveling. And the cabin sounds charming."

He chuckled. "I'm not sure it's that, but I'm hoping we'll find it comfortable. At least we won't have a dozen boarders traipsing up and down the halls."

"It will be very fine, I'm sure," Vanessa answered, not needing to say much more. She knew why they were going to the cabin. Finally, they were going to make their marriage true. Instead of being nervous about the idea, a feeling of peace washed over her. Now, everything was going to be just fine. They were together and they had a future. Clayton was healing. They'd moved on, both literally and in their hearts. Finally, she was living her dream.

⟊

They'd gone almost a dozen miles when a loud crack exploded not three feet from Lee's front hooves. Both horses whinnied in surprise. Vanessa held tight as she tried to keep her seat on Buttercup.

Clayton turned to his left and scanned the area. The area was flat and so vacant that its edges seemed to disappear in the horizon. Tall golden brush blew in the breeze, creating a faint rustling in the distance. But just in the shadows of the plains, three figures appeared.

"Hold!" Clayton called out.

In reply, the grasses rustled again, followed by a sharp whistling sound. With a start, Vanessa realized they were getting shot at. Buttercup pranced a bit and shuddered.

Panic engulfed Vanessa as she fought to calm her horse. What had just happened? Had Indians found them again?

With a staying hand, Clayton motioned her to be aware for anything. Slowly, he pulled out his peacemaker.

Just the thought of being in the company of another band of Indians made Vanessa's stomach churn. Carefully, she scanned the horizon once more, following Clayton's direction. The shadowy forms were clearer now, and riding toward them without a bit of hesitancy.

Four men were approaching. All wore black hats and long tan dusters. Though their gait was easy, there also seemed to be something sinister about them. Each held a Winchester loosely in his hands.

Now, it seemed she had even more to fear.

"Stay by my side," Clayton commanded, never taking his eyes off of the approaching men. "And, whatever you do, keep your seat and don't say a word."

Vanessa patted Buttercup and hoped the horse wouldn't bolt. Minutes passed. The men's horses slowed. But as she heard them laughing to one another, each telling ribald jokes, Vanessa's terror intensified. Inside her leather gloves, her palms dampened.

She could feel Clayton's tension next to her, sensed his anger as he glared at the men. Ever so slightly, his hand shifted as he positioned his Colt.

One rode forward, his shoulders covered in a thick buffalo coat. "Who are you?" he called out. Even from that distance, Vanessa could tell he was a real mountain man.

Clayton answered easily. "Sheriff Proffitt. My wife and I are just passing through. Who are you?"

The man smiled, showing a definite lack of teeth. "We're no one you've ever heard of."

Clayton let that pass. "Why did you shoot?"

"This here's private land. You're trespassing. We take that seriously round here."

Clayton looked as if he didn't believe a word of it. "I saw no fence."

"Don't need one."

The other riders approached, their frank gazes sliding along her form with enough boldness to make Vanessa's skin crawl. Amazing how since she'd started this journey, she'd met a wide assortment of folks, some more dangerous than they looked, others the opposite. Yet none had made her feel as dirty or afraid as her own stepfather had.

No one had until these men. And, if Clayton's motion of bringing his Colt more out in the open was any indication, he felt the same way. Vanessa knew her husband would not hesitate to shoot any of them if he suspected they would try to do her harm. That said a lot. Vanessa knew Clayton was tired of guns and violence.

But he would do anything to protect his own.

However, the tone of his voice didn't betray any of that. No, he sounded slow and steady, like he had all the time in the day. Almost bored. "We don't mean any trouble. You can put your firearms away. As I said, we're just passing through."

The toothless man just grinned and pulled out a pistol.

The men split up, two on each side. Buttercup nickered and restlessly paced. Vanessa patted the mare's neck, and leaning forward, quietly tried to settle her, though it was little use. She was frightened, and her horse, Clayton, and the four men surrounding them all knew it.

While two had beards—one red, the other black as night— the man talking to Clayton was clean-shaven, making him look even younger. The last had a mustache. All stared at her and Clayton like they were minutes from doing them harm.

Vanessa kept her gaze trained on Clayton, afraid to catch any of the other men's eyes.

But Clayton didn't show a hint of fear. If anything, he looked eager for the confrontation. Lee, underneath him, stood motionless, his stance ready for battle. Vanessa realized she was seeing Clayton Proffitt as he once was, a leader and a soldier.

"Pretty woman you got here," the clean–shaven blond said.

Clayton's cheek twitched, but he said nothing.

Encouraged, the two to her left edged closer, close enough now for Vanessa to inhale their scents. The smell of dirt and sweat and grease emanated from them. Just the thought of any of them touching her made her petrified.

But there was only Clayton and herself. They were outnumbered.

Slowly, Vanessa wrapped Buttercup's reins around her right hand, desperate for a plan. There was a very good chance she was going to have to fight them off. What if they shot Clayton? What would she do?

She was a fair horsewoman, but not an expert in any sense, especially not on an unfamiliar mount like Buttercup. The horse did seem agreeable and smart, but was she fast? Would she be able to outrun them?

She was going to have to try.

Unfortunately, Vanessa now knew what men could do. She'd felt violence, she knew the feel of a man's hand slapping her cheek, tearing her dress—and doing so much more. She would wear scars for the rest of her life from the slap of a leather belt. Yes, she could survive whatever these men did, but she knew that the cost would be painful, indeed.

She bit her lip and prayed with all her might that the Lord would be with them. *Please God*, she silently prayed. *I'm so scared. Please help Clayton. Please help guide us.*

Then she remembered the last verses of Psalm 91: "*I will protect those who know my name. When they call to me, I will answer them.*"

Yes, the Lord had already promised He'd be there for her. She just had to believe.

A twig broke.

The wind rose up. A coyote howled in the distance right at the same time the man with the red beard reached out to touch her.

Clayton cocked his gun. "You lay one hand on my wife, I'm gonna have to kill you."

The men only snickered.

Raising his Colt, he straightened his right arm. Not a single inch of him looked the least nervous. "She's mine. Back away."

"You're the law. You ain't gonna do nothing."

"Try me."

"You shoot me, you'll be dead," the man retorted.

To everyone's surprise, Clayton grinned. "Is that what you want? To die, right here? Right now?" He turned to the others, who—by Vanessa's estimation—didn't look nearly as full of themselves as they had just minutes ago. "What about the rest of you? Do you all really want to have the body of a sheriff on your conscience? On your plate? Because that's what is going to happen. You murder me and harm my wife, the law from miles around will hunt you down."

The clean-shaven man's eyes narrowed.

Vanessa shifted in her saddle, prepared to ride as hard as she could. There was no way she was going to just sit there when Clayton got hurt. There was no way she was going to be attacked by these men without doing everything she could to help herself.

Then, a single arrow sailed through the sky, startling everyone to silence as it landed in the redheaded man's shoulder. He yowled in pain.

Vanessa leaned down and hugged Buttercup's neck. Any moment, she was sure she was going to lose her seat or slip off in a faint.

The others were just as frightened. "Injuns!" the smallest of the band of men screamed. With a fierce kick to his horse's side, he rode east. When a lone Indian came into view in a fierce battle cry, the others followed quickly.

Once satisfied the others were leaving, Clayton shifted Lee and faced the Indian head-on.

Vanessa didn't even attempt to control her shaking. "Clayton, what's happening?"

"I'm not sure. Be still Vanessa."

Tears fell down her cheeks as she did her best to remain calm while looking out toward the horizon. Were there others? She never heard of an Indian riding alone.

Warily, Clayton looked to the south as well, then just as Vanessa was sure he saw more danger, his shoulders relaxed. "That's Red Cloud."

Gathering her strength, Vanessa made herself look directly at the lone rider again. To her amazement, he'd neither shot another arrow nor approached. Instead, he seemed content to stand still and watch the ragtag band of men continue to scurry away. "You sure?"

"I am. That's his paint. See the chocolate markings? No two horses could look like that."

"I wonder why's he's so far north."

"I don't know, but I'm glad he is." Raising a hand in the air, Clayton saluted Red Cloud. "He just saved us, Vanessa. I'll be forever in his debt."

As Red Cloud returned the salute, then slowly meandered back out of sight, Vanessa recalled her prayers. Hoping that the Lord was still listening, she silently added her thanks.

Twilight fell as they approached a cabin in the distance. "This is it," Clayton murmured, dismounting. Next, he swung her out of the saddle and took care of the horses. Vanessa was still so spooked from the confrontation that she stood quietly, watching as he watered the animals.

Clayton's eyes were gentle when he finally turned to her. "Vanessa. You all right now, sugar?"

"I'm better than that." His answering smile was all the coaxing she needed to propel herself into his arms.

Clayton didn't disappoint. The moment they touched, he gripped her to him, letting his solid physique give her a feeling of safety.

She reached up and kissed him. After a moment's pause, he took control and kissed her back. His lips were tender and gentle. Eager and loving.

Clayton swung her into his arms and carried her through the threshold.

There wasn't much inside. Vanessa was aware of darkness and sparse furniture. Thick quilts were folded on a bed. Dried apples lay in a basket, filling the room with a tantalizing scent. A stack of firewood stood ready by the door.

Then Clayton shut the door and all Vanessa was aware of was him.

They were alone. Alone in ways that they'd never been before. Finally, they were free to explore their attraction. Free to share their love.

He closed the door behind him before pulling her into his arms. His mouth met hers, and he said all the words that meant so much. "I love you. I'll love you forever."

And as she looked at him with shining eyes, Vanessa knew the truth just as she knew the depths of her soul. "I love you, too."

"Are you afraid?"

She shook her head. Now when Clayton held her, she wasn't plagued by memories of Price's rough hands. She wasn't haunted by memories of coarse touches and abusive words.

Now when Clayton touched her, she wasn't fearful of a man's hand. Time and maturity and patience had vanquished her fears, and Clayton's love and respect for her had brought new meaning to their relationship.

All she saw was Clayton. All she recognized was her husband. Right as he claimed her lips, she knew the truth. Finally, after so very long, she was home.

21

The following morning, life went on just as it always had, just as it would always once again. They were a team now, and would be for the rest of their lives.

At daybreak, Clayton hurriedly got dressed, stoked the fire in the cabin, then went outside to bring in Lee and Buttercup after letting them graze for the night.

Vanessa took care of the inside chores, pumping water and brewing coffee. She'd just hastily pulled her hair back with a pink ribbon when Clayton returned, his cheeks red from the brisk morning air.

"Good morning," she said, handing him a tin mug filled to the brim with steaming hot brew. "I hope the coffee is to your liking. I had a bit of a time heating the coffee in the pan that was near the fire."

He sipped, never taking his eyes from her. "It's fine. Good morning, Van."

And because she felt giddy and happy and brand-new, she couldn't refrain from saying the obvious. "We're married."

His gaze softened. "We are." Tenderly, he pulled her into his arms once again. Holding her close, gifting her with warm words and sweet kisses, he said the words she loved so much to hear. "I love you, darling."

"I love you, too."

A half smile played across his lips. "I feel like I just ran ten miles and came out the winner." His gaze softened as he leaned back and brushed a kiss across the nape of her neck. "I was a fool to stay so far from you for so long. I need you, Vanessa. I guess I always have."

Tentatively, she said, "Sometimes I wonder if maybe my pa knew we belonged together. Maybe he'd hoped something would come of us one day. Maybe that's why he encouraged you to make the Circle Z your own."

"Perhaps." He nodded, thinking of the many conversations he'd shared with Bill Grant. The man had been knowledge-able and patient. Never like a second father, but more than just a friend or a boss. "I seem to recall telling him more than once how much you made me smile."

"I'm glad for that, though I imagine I made you silly with irritation a time or two. I was not my best at fourteen."

"You were fine. I wasn't my best a time or two, either."

"You just had a lot on your mind, I think. When you first came to the Circle Z, you were so somber and quiet. I remem-ber my mother and daddy were so worried about you."

"I felt dead inside—the war did that to me." Looking into an unseen picture, Clayton's eyes clouded. "I saw so much death and destruction. I witnessed so many good men die. I wondered often why I was living when so many other men weren't."

Vanessa didn't know the answer to that. Only the Lord did. "I'm glad you survived."

"I am, too. It was a scary time, though, I'll tell you that. Two months before Lee surrendered, things seemed bleak indeed.

Some days the only way I'd be able to get through each hour was to numb myself to the pain and just subsist."

"But then you came to us."

"That I did."

"Many a night, you'd just sit by yourself, staring off into the distance."

"I cherished the quiet. It was never quiet during the war. Either gunfire haunted the air or the cries of men floated through the night breeze. Daytime brought complaints and bitterness and rowdy tempers. My soul felt bruised and battered, incomplete. I'd even become lax in reading the Bible. It was as if I didn't feel worthy of love. Not even God's greatest gift."

"But you always had God's love," she pointed out. "He never left you."

Pressing his lips to the top of her head, he murmured, "I know that now. I know God was always there, guiding me, leading me forward. I always had His love . . . and His grace."

"He's been with us through so much, Clayton," Vanessa said. "Around every corner, He's guided us toward this moment. To our future." Laying a hand on his sleeve, she quoted from Isaiah, *"Before they call, I will answer. When they are speaking, I will hear."*

"And he did." Sharing a smile over how far they'd come, Clayton clasped her hand. "Now we just need to make plans."

"I don't care what we do or where we go, as long as we're together." Amazingly, she found that to be true. They'd been through so much, she'd worried that things would never be okay between them—it seemed incomprehensible that they were going to make it through things all right.

He pressed his lips to her brow. "That makes me happy. But are you sure you don't have a preference?"

She thought a bit more, then reflected on the healthy amount of money her pa had put aside for them. It was as much his as hers—she knew that Clayton would never see a single plug nickel of his wages that were still owed to him. Slowly, she said, "Maybe we should think about getting the money my pa left me. It could help us get settled."

"We don't need it."

"I know, but it could help you buy some land or purchase cattle. It's quite a bit, Clayton. And it would be ours, never just mine. At the very least, we could live on that until we decided where you wanted to work."

"If we go to Merritt's spread, I won't need the money. And I have some money now that I worked all those odd jobs over the last two months."

"It could help with building materials," she said slowly. "You might find that money comes in handy." She knew she should feel regret that she'd already contacted the bank without his permission, but since nothing was likely to come of that admission but a long argument, she kept that information to herself.

Especially since she was only trying to help him so he wouldn't worry so much. Oh, she so wanted to be helpful! She wanted to be able to hold her head high and know that she hadn't just taken from Clayton. That she'd given him something tangible. Something beyond just her love.

"No." The word came out harsh and abrupt, startling her out of her daydreams of helping him achieve his aspirations. "Don't ever contact anyone about that money, Vanessa. I don't want it."

Stung, she stepped away. "Oh. I see." Perhaps he really didn't want anything from her after all.

"No, you don't." Tilting her chin up, he whispered, "Listen, Van, I know you mean well, and I certainly do appreciate your intentions. But we can't risk the chance of Price finding you. We've been through too much."

Guilt slammed her hard. She knew she should tell the truth. But for some reason, she wasn't quite ready to tell him what she'd done. "I know Price and Miles have been looking for us. Merritt told me about the reports y'all have gotten. But that was some time ago. I bet they've given up." Surely Price, like she and Clayton, had moved on.

"They might have," Clayton allowed. "Miles might have put him off our path, or Price might have just lost interest."

"See, I knew it. I bet either of those things could have happened."

"We don't know anything. Not really. I've been listening for news, and while I haven't heard much of anything, that doesn't mean we're safe. I don't want to take any chances with your safety, Van. I think Price is just crazy enough to come running after you. I feel it. Don't contact the bank."

"But I'm only thinking of helping you—"

"You'll help me by being by my side. That's all I need, Vanessa. If and when Price does find you, we'll deal with that. But I'm not going to give him an invitation."

He wasn't listening to what she was trying to tell him. With her money, they could start out fresh, with no worries. That had to be worth some risk, right? *Especially since she'd already contacted the bank.* "Clay—"

"No, Vanessa. I mean it." After taking a deep breath, he said, "Promise me you won't contact anyone about your money. It's just not worth it. It's not worth the risk."

She knew what she had to do. She had to tell him the truth. Clayton had saved her. He'd removed her from Price's hands, had guided her across the country, had married her when he didn't want to in order to save her reputation. He'd put himself between her and Indians, gamblers, renegades, and dangerous elements.

Now, he'd given her his love and his vow of faithfulness. The least she could do was be open and honest with him.

But what would happen then? It would ruin everything they'd been working so hard to have. Clayton would most likely want to race back to the ranch and contact Merritt. Everything that they'd forged between them would suddenly be gone.

Against her better judgment, against what she knew to be right and acceptable, Vanessa lied. "I promise," she replied.

He nodded, pleased and relieved. "Thank you."

Looking around the cabin, she saw peace and security. It certainly wasn't much inside, but it was cozy enough, and the fire countered the wind blowing every so often through the cracks in the mud that mortared the planks. "When do you want to head back to Colorado?"

"Not today." Smiling softly, he reached for her hands. "How about we stay here for a few days? It's been a long time since we've been together. It's been even longer than that since I've stayed anywhere long enough to rest my legs, never mind Lee." Leaning closer, he kissed her cheek, his scratchy beard brushing against her cheek as he did so. "Besides," he whispered, "Truth be told, I'm in no hurry to share your company with anyone just yet."

That made her smile. "Good." After their long journey on the trail, then their long separation, a time of being together without the rush of insecurities sounded heavenly.

Clayton whispered. "In a day or two, you can let me know when you're ready."

Grasping his hand, she nodded. She wasn't eager to go back to their real world, either. Time had shown her that private, lazy moments were few and far between. In addition, they had months of catching up to do. Months of getting to know each other again.

She'd grown up in his absence.

He'd become tougher, more assured.

It was time to remember who they were and what they were to each other. "I'll let you know when I'm ready," she said.

A gentle expression warmed his eyes, making the chocolate color more pronounced. "Yes, ma'am."

"It's Mrs. Proffitt to you," she teased.

"Come here, Mrs. Proffitt," he whispered. "Let me get to know you again."

✑

For five days they did little but set up house in the cabin. After being on the trail for so long, neither had much of a desire to hike or fish, hunt or explore.

Instead, they used the time to talk and do domestic things. Clayton fixed the mantle over the fireplace. Vanessa repaired a rip in the checkered curtains that hung on the one window.

Vanessa also took care of Clayton, making him rest his leg often and sit with his foot propped up. She knew he only agreed to the situation because she offered to read to him from her Bible. Both slept more than they had in years.

In one of the cabinets, they found an old deck of cards. On a whim, Clayton taught Vanessa how to play poker, which she thought was great fun and quite scandalous. "I can't believe you even know how to play five-card draw."

He raised a terribly handsome eyebrow, looking rakish and mysterious. "I was a soldier for a number of years, Van. What did you think we did when we were waiting to go to battle?"

"I don't guess I ever thought about it. What all did you do?"

"You . . . sure you want to know?"

"Of course. I love you, Clayton. I don't want you to be perfect; I just want you to be mine. Tell me more stories. Please?"

He shuffled the cards again as a smile played across his lips. "All right then, I'll tell you a few more tales."

In between hands dealt, Clayton did just that. In fact, they talked about more than they had in months. Clayton opened up about his experiences during the war. Vanessa asked questions about Scout. They planned their futures and pushed the past behind them.

It was too bad that the last thing Vanessa thought of every night was the fact that a new, bald-faced lie now lay between them. And it was all her doing.

✍❧

"You came back," Merritt said by way of greeting when they arrived back at the Bar M late the following week. As was his custom, he rode out and greeted them the moment they descended down the ridge toward the home. "I was wondering if you two were ever going to pass this way again." Looking over Clayton, Merritt said, "It's good to see you survived that bullet. Corrine will be pleased, I'll tell you that."

"You and me both," Clayton replied.

As the three of them slowly walked toward the barn, Vanessa thought about Corrine and the girls and their new little one. "I can't wait to see Aaron," said Vanessa after greeting Merritt with a sunny smile. "How is he?"

"About what you'd expect," Merritt said with a wink. "Demanding and noisy, but as cute as all get-out." After clasping Clayton's hand, he motioned them toward the house. "Too bad he won't sleep through the night."

"Do they ever?"

"No." Merritt chuckled as they continued to ride, filling them in on the antics of José and Pearl and the girls.

Clayton didn't speak too much. Vanessa knew the long ride had finally begun to pain him. The last part of their trip had taken longer than either anticipated. Both the horses and Clayton seemed to tire easily and needed more rest stops.

Vanessa tried to look after him as much as he would allow. She'd become adept at making a campfire and rubbing down horses. Clayton let her do a lot of the chores, teasing her so she wouldn't ask too many questions.

They both knew his thigh had healed, but it was a long way from its former condition. Only time, rest, and exercise would help that.

After they dismounted and passed off the horses to two of Merritt's stableboys, John took hold of both their saddlebags and looked Clayton over carefully. "Well, you're limping and you look like you've lost quite a bit of weight, but other than that you seem to be in good shape."

"I am in good shape. Well, more or less," he answered, his limp pronounced.

Although it had been a few weeks, Vanessa examined the pens and grassy areas between the barn and the main house. There were several changes. Spring was finally on its way, warming the air. Corrine's precious rose bush was blooming. Bright red petals shone brightly against the stucco walls of their home. "Everything looks wonderful, Merritt."

"Spring is a glorious time of year, it's true." He picked up his pace. "Let's get you two inside so you can finally relax. That is, as much as you'll be able to, what with Melissa, Kate, and Aaron making the usual racket."

Next to her, Clayton stilled. "Before we see Corrine, Merritt, I'd like to ask if you still have a place for me here. Is your offer still good? See, we'd like to stay, if it's all right."

"*If it's all right?*" Merritt shook his head in disgust. "I don't get you, Proffitt. After years of living in Texas while your sister misses you something awful, you show up. Then, living here hardly a week, you leave your poor wife and take off to work odd jobs. Now, almost a month has passed, you've gotten yourself shot, we've all been worried sick . . . and you have the nerve to ask if we want to see you? You make it awfully hard to hold my tongue."

Vanessa gasped.

Clayton, however, knew he was getting his just reward. Merritt had just delivered as thorough a dressing down as he'd ever received, and Clayton figured he deserved every word. From Merritt's perspective, Clayton certainly had made a number of mistakes. His only excuse was that he'd been doing his best to do the right thing.

However, he certainly wasn't in the mood to get chewed out after hours of sitting on the backside of a horse. He didn't care to have his wife witness it, either. "I had hoped to get this over with, but obviously I mistook everything that needed to be said. So, why don't we talk about this in a bit?"

"I think I've already waited long enough."

He turned to Vanessa, who looked strained to her limit. If their weeks apart had taught him anything, it was that time was too short to be wasted on prideful concerns. With all that in mind, he bit out, "John, I'm deeply sorry if I've caused you worry."

Immediately, Merritt turned contrite. "I'm sorry too. I know you've been through a lot. I'm just trying to help you. And your sister. Listen. You've put your sister through a mess of tears, and I've had to wipe up so much water I'm practically soaked through. I don't want you to hurt her again."

"I'm not planning on it." They stared at each other again, each man weighing his words, wondering how to move on, when Vanessa spoke.

"Clayton, is there any way we could finish this up in a little bit? I'm sure Corrine is wondering why we're all standing here, and I'd love to go see Aaron."

He'd almost forgotten she was there.

As Clayton turned to his wife, he noticed Merritt did the same, and he was wearing the same look of shocked embarrassment Clayton felt.

"Sorry, Vanessa. Let's go on in."

With a wink in Merritt's direction, she said, "Mrs. Proffitt to you."

Clayton felt every muscle in his back relax. Their playful banter was a new and extremely appealing dimension to their relationship. "Yes ma'am, Mrs. Proffitt."

It took only seconds to open the back door. Seconds after that, they were surrounded by the exuberant hugs of Melissa and Kate and the happy cries of Corrine.

Vanessa and Corrine started crying, little Aaron did too, and then, in the wild cacophony of the welcome reception, Merritt pulled Clayton into a hug.

"God Almighty, we thought we lost you," he said, his voice husky.

"For a while there, I was afraid you had," Clayton admitted. The other man's arms felt good around him. It was a reassuring hug, an embrace between brothers. And in Scout's absence, it was most welcome. Clayton hugged him back, thankful for the stubbornness of people who cared about him.

He needed John Merritt's friendship and love as much as he needed his sister's and Vanessa's.

No longer was he willing to just work and exist, like he had at the Circle Z. Now he wanted to live and to plan and to feel. The months of enforced isolation had proved costly; he'd been more lonely than he'd ever thought possible.

When he stepped back, Clayton saw that Vanessa was visibly moved as well. Those clear green eyes that he loved so much were glistening with unshed emotion, telling him silently that she was on his side, and always had been.

But still, something needed to be said. "I went away because I had kept a vow to Bill Grant," Clayton told Merritt and Corrine slowly. "I'd told him I'd keep Vanessa safe. When I didn't do that, when Price attacked her, I felt like I'd failed. I felt like I was less than the man I thought I was."

Merritt shook his head. "Price's faults weren't your doing. I tried to tell you that before you left."

"And I tried to listen, but I wasn't ready." Reaching out to his sister, he clutched her hand, just like he used to do back when they were small.

"Corrine, I never meant to cause you pain. I was simply trying to do what I thought was right. Months ago, I was sure the Lord had placed me at the Circle Z to simply watch over Vanessa. When I realized I'd fallen in love with her, I worried that I was doing things wrong yet again."

"But now?" she prompted.

"Now I realize God had another plan for me. I needed to spend some time on my own, to remember all the people in my past."

"Did you come to terms with it?"

"Now I have; but for a time, it was almost too difficult. At first, I felt that everything was out of my control. I was running from Price and Miles. Then, Ken Willoughby forced me to wed Vanessa." He glanced apologetically toward his wife.

"It wasn't that I didn't want to marry you, Van. It was that I wanted it to be the right time."

"I understand," she said softly. "Like I told you before, I needed the right time too."

"Will you try to understand too, Merritt?" Turning to his best friend in the world, Clayton said, "I did listen, and I wanted to believe everything you said, but I didn't feel worthy. I felt I didn't deserve Vanessa. I'd seen too much, had felt too much. I didn't know if I could be the type of man her father had dreamed for her."

Vanessa shook her head in mock exasperation. "He also conveniently forgot that I was old enough and had been through enough to know my mind. And who I wanted."

Merritt grinned. "She's right."

"When we got here, I wanted to make things work, but all I felt was that if I stayed, it would be charity on your part."

Merritt shook his head. "I never felt that way."

"Neither did I," said Corrine.

"I realize that now. When I was alone up in Nebraska, I came to the realization that I would gladly work with any of the men under my command. Not because of our former ranks, but because we trusted one another. They were men I admired." Remembering some of the men coming through Bensen, Clayton shook his head. "I can't say the same of everyone."

"I can't either," Corrine said softly.

Clayton turned to her in a heartbeat. "Corry? Are we going to be all right?"

"Always." She ran into his arms and held on tight. He hugged her back.

Corrine said, "Tell me about getting shot, Clayton."

Briefly he told them about the gunfight over stupid liquor and how he'd been fool enough to get caught in the crossfire.

Vanessa then spoke. "I'm so glad Doc Bodey sent me that telegraph. Clayton was recuperating in a boardinghouse. Two women were doing their best to take care of him, but it was a mediocre job at best."

"Vanessa came and healed me . . . and now we're here. At long last."

Corrine crossed her arms over her chest. "Does this mean you'll stay here forever, finally?"

"We'd like that," Clayton said. "That is, if that's what you want."

"I want that," Corrine replied. "I want that very much."

❧

Dinner was a wild affair. The baby was crying, and Corrine burst into tears a time or two herself whenever she looked at Clayton.

Vanessa helped José and Pearl and chatted with the girls, while Merritt forced Clayton to let him doctor his leg for a bit and set it up on a chair to rest.

The whole mealtime was noisy and chaotic, warm and funny. It felt like home; it felt like family. And to Vanessa's surprise, she supposed it was. After the past two years of living with Price and dealing with her mother's distance and her brother's sullen attitude, Vanessa felt at peace.

"One day I really am going to learn to cook," Corrine declared after the kitchen was clean and they were walking into the great room to join their husbands.

Vanessa peeked over her shoulder at José, who was leaning against the back doorway. When he caught her eye, he shook his head slowly.

She chuckled in return. No one in their right mind would ever want Corrine in the kitchen. "I hope you don't start cooking," she said pertly. "Your kitchen may never survive it."

Corrine shook her head in disbelief. "It just makes me so mad. How come I can't make even eggs palatable?"

"God must have other plans for you."

"I suppose." Seeing the baby asleep in a quilt in a wooden cradle that Merritt and carved himself, she sighed. "Maybe I should stick to taking care of the children."

"They are all turning out mighty nice. I think that sounds like a fine idea."

"You're not talking about cooking again, are you, pet?" Merritt called out.

"Only in passing."

Clayton grimaced. "You never could cook. You managed to make cabbage taste like shoe leather during the war."

"You were grateful for my efforts."

"I'm grateful now . . . but maybe we don't have to be so grateful that you're cooking?"

"Ha, ha," Corrine retorted, sitting on the large sofa near the fireplace.

Vanessa took a spot near Clayton, preferring to be near him. He rubbed her shoulder when they got settled.

Merritt followed that with a knowing look. "It's good to see you two getting along so well."

"I feel the same way. It's been a hard, long road, but the end was worth it all."

"It always is," Corrine said, tears once again filling her eyes. "It always is."

22

$\mathscr{A}$s the sun rose over the Rocky Mountains in all its fiery glory, Clayton and Merritt forged a new bond as they walked along the timeworn planks of the front porch. "So, you're sure you don't mind me working here? It would only be for a while," Clayton said slowly. "Until I get my feet settled."

"Until you get your feet settled?" Merritt scowled. "Nope, that's not good enough. Honestly, Captain, you minded me a whole lot better when we were in the military."

"We're both different now," Clayton pointed out. Now that he and Vanessa had found happiness and a promise of a future together, the days of fighting seemed another lifetime ago.

"Me, yes. You, however, are just as stubborn as ever." Slapping a hand across his good friend's shoulder, Merritt said, "Listen to me, Clayton, and listen well. I need your help. I need your expertise and your way with men. Helping me run the Bar M is needed and would be greatly appreciated."

"I hear you."

"Do you?" Squinting in the sunlight, Merritt continued. "I believe in charity, but this isn't it. I've got eight hundred acres stretching out across this hilly, arid, beautiful, difficult part of God's kingdom. My cows know the terrain better than I do." He looked sideways at Clayton, his scarred cheek showing every mark in the waning light as he did so. "Even a man like me can't handle all this on my own."

Clayton's lips twitched as he fought the laugh rising forth.

As Merritt chuckled too, he added, "Truth is, I can hardly handle your sister."

As if to point that out, Corrine let out a shriek from the back of the house loud enough to make a weaker man go running. To give Clayton and Merritt their due, each hardly moved a muscle.

Except for Clayton, who finally gave into temptation and let out a roar of laughter. "Maybe we need to go recruit more men; you might never get away from the house."

"Shoot, maybe I need to recruit more married men to keep an eye on my wife." He shook his head. "How did she do it, raising Scout on her own with just your Aunt Marge for company?"

"I don't know." Pondering the thought, Clayton said slowly, "Maybe she didn't have anyone to complain to back then. Maybe now that she does, she lets loose."

"Again and again." As Corrine's shriek turned into peals of laughter, he chuckled as well. "I wouldn't have it any other way."

"I'm glad."

Merritt rested his hands on his lap. "So, we set? You'll work with me for the price we set?"

"It still seems high."

"It's the going rate."

"It's more than I made as a foreman."

"You've got a wife now. No boss pays the same to single men as married. Not fitting."

Clayton supposed that was true. "Thank you, then. I appreciate it."

Merritt stood up. "Let's not talk about this again. No need."

❧

"I do love to come to town," Corrine said. "It always feels good to see things other than a cluster of cows."

"Cedar Springs is a darling place," Vanessa agreed.

"I don't know if *darling* is the right descriptor, but I do like the shopping and seeing the ladies who are visiting to take the waters."

Vanessa had heard about Cedar Springs's famous bathhouse. One day she imagined she and Clayton there for a holiday, just enjoying being together.

After another few minutes of talking and looking in windows, Corrine gasped at a fetching bonnet in the window of Mabel's Millinery. "I'm going to stop in here and try on that hat. Do you mind?"

"Not at all. I'll just be in one of these other stores. How about we meet in a half hour or so?"

"Sounds good," Corrine said before entering Miss Mable's.

Vanessa watched Corrine gesture to the peacock blue bonnet, and remembered a time when such a thing would have caught her notice. But those days seemed like a lifetime ago. Now, instead, she had other things on her mind.

She couldn't shake the argument she and Clayton had had about her money. There wasn't a great amount, but it would surely help buy some necessities, and to her way of thinking, she owed Clayton so much.

She'd seen his saddle, saw how worn it was from years and years of use, and knew that a new one would be extremely appreciated. She also knew Clayton well enough to realize that he'd buy a dozen peacock blue hats to make her happy before spending any money on himself.

That money would help pay for supplies for the house, too.

Besides, it had been months since she had left the Circle Z. Time and again, Clayton had checked with people to see if they'd heard her name being bandied about. No one had. It was time to move on.

Obviously, Price had. She felt certain that no matter what Clayton believed, no one was coming after her.

With that in mind, she strode into the telegraph office again. After visiting with Mr. Humphrey, she learned that the bank had been contacted, but no reply had been heard yet.

Since so much time had gone past and nothing had happened, Vanessa gave Mr. Humphrey permission to contact the bank again. She gave him the information he requested.

"It would be my pleasure to assist you in any way I can, Mrs. Proffitt. Shall I let Mr. Proffitt know when I hear a response?"

A tiny tingling of doubt edged closer at just the thought of Clayton finding out about the transfer of money before she did. "That's not necessary. I should be accompanying Mrs. Merritt back here in a month. I'll visit with you then." Leaning forward, she confided, "It's a surprise for Clayton."

"And a very good one it will be, I'm sure," the banker said jovially.

Vanessa left the bank and had just turned the corner when she spied Corrine exiting, a gray hatbox in her hand. "Did you buy a hat?"

"Two!" Corrine said happily. "I can't wait for Merritt to see me in them."

"Does he like hats?"

"He likes me to be happy."

Vanessa chuckled. "I know the feeling."

"Where did you go? Did you see anything special?"

"I've just been window shopping," she said, brightly. "It's a good day to do that."

Corrine linked her arm through Vanessa's. "This has been fun. Let's come back next month."

"I'll count on it."

23

Six weeks later, Clayton shook her gently awake. "Vanessa? Are you all right? You went back to sleep after I woke you up."

She struggled to open her eyes. "I'm sorry. I'll be up and dressed in a minute."

"No hurry." Concern clouding those brown eyes she knew and loved so much, he said, "Are you sure you're all right? You seem a mite sluggish this morning."

There was no way Vanessa was going to tell Clayton that her sluggishness wasn't a one-time occurrence. Unfortunately, it was happening with more and more regularity—and severity!

From conversations with Corrine, she had a feeling she knew what was happening to her body, but wasn't quite ready to share the news yet. For the moment, she wanted to hold the secret close to her heart and wait for the perfect opportunity to tell Clayton that they were soon to begin a family of their own.

"I'm fine," she ended up saying after he looked at her suspiciously again. "Just a little tired, I guess."

A frown appeared between his eyes. "You're doing too much, sugar." Gesturing toward the pretty calico curtains she'd made with Corrine's help and the feather bed she'd just completed after much hard work with Pearl, he said, "We don't need to be settled right away. We've got time."

"I know; I just like to keep busy."

Engulfing her in a hug, he pressed his lips to her brow. "I know you do. You're a wonderful wife."

The words soothed her as well as the ointment had soothed the marks on her back. For what seemed like forever, she'd wanted to be his wife. Sometimes she felt like pinching herself when she realized that her dreams had become her reality. "You're a good husband, too."

Pretend outrage entered his eyes. "Not wonderful?"

"Well, now. Wonderful is a pretty strong description, Clayton."

As she'd hoped, he tossed his hat to the floor and crawled next to her. Next came the kisses and tickles. She laughed, not just because of his fingers to her ribcage, but from the heady feeling that their togetherness brought.

They'd had so much drama in their lives, it was a new experience to just relax and play with him. After everything they'd been through, Vanessa didn't think they could ever relax enough.

Lee's neighing outside their cabin's door brought their playing to a halt.

Clayton pulled himself up and grabbed his hat. "Looks like I just got my reminder call."

Vanessa scrambled up as well, folding her arms over her chest as she watched him grab his worn leather gloves. "Robert E. Lee is the hardest working horse I know."

A smile played at the corners of his mouth. "He's a good horse." As he loosened the latch to their home, he said, "I'll be in the far pasture today, counting head and checking calves. I probably won't be back till sundown."

Vanessa fetched him the tin pail that she'd filled with slices of beef and a half a dried apple pie. "I'll be at the main house until you get home. I told Corrine I'd help with the children today."

"I'll look for you then."

He bent to kiss her again. "I'm not anxious to leave. Maybe I can stay a little longer."

Lee neighed again, causing Vanessa to laugh. "Go on now, Clayton, before Lee barges in here. I wouldn't put it past that horse."

"Yes, ma'am," he said, tipping his hat before finally leaving her.

Alone once more, Vanessa sank to one of their table's chairs. If her suspicion was right, one day in their future, Clayton wouldn't be leaving her alone at all. She'd have their baby to care for.

How could things be any better?

*Merritt met him near Bent Creek, looking as dusty and weary as Clayton felt himself. Merritt's red handkerchief was a wadded mess around his neck—looking ragged and worn after hours of shielding his mouth and nose from dust and grime. Yet still he had a smile for Clayton. "It is days like this when the memories of tracking Yankees doesn't seem so bad," he said by way of greeting.

"I'd agree, except that all I remember of the war is being scared, hungry, and cold."

Merritt grinned slowly. "I had more holes in my boots than a weevil could drill in hardtack."

Clayton laughed. "I'll take this over fighting Yankees, though I have to admit, it's days like today when I miss Texas. Back on the Circle Z there's most likely a bumper crop of pecans. Me and the boys would grab handfuls while we rode for hours."

"I'd enjoy a handful of pecans right about now," Merritt said. "Supper came and went hours ago."

They dismounted and led the horses to Bent Creek, a shallow ravine that ran along the edge of the property. There, they drank their fill and watered the horses. Clayton dipped his bandana in the cool stream for what he hoped was the last time that day and swiped his face with the cool fabric. The instant relief revived his parched skin and invigorated his senses.

Beside him, Merritt cupped his hands and splashed a good amount across his face. "Much better," he exclaimed as thick rivulets slid down his cheeks and jaw. "Now I think I can finally breathe."

"I counted forty head in the front field," Clayton said as soon as they sat down on the banks. "Three new calves born since last week."

"How're they doing?"

"Fine, as near I can tell. Their mommas look to be doing their job."

"Good. I found one dead calf; looked like it didn't survive the birthing."

Clayton nodded. On a spread the size of Merritt's, life and death were natural occurrences. "Tomorrow, I'll go east. I haven't been out in that direction in a spell."

"I might go with you. Bob Thatcher told me on Sunday he's going to be riding his perimeter this week. I'd like to check in with him. I like to keep in touch with him."

Everything Clayton knew about Merritt's neighbor was positive. "Sounds good."

They spoke for a bit more, then mounted the horses and headed back to the homestead. They rode companionably, so well together that Clayton realized he'd been a fool to even contemplate ignoring his friend's offer of employment. Merritt obviously appreciated his help, and Clayton found he enjoyed working with someone who saw him as an equal.

No matter how well he and Bill Grant had gotten along, there'd always been a fine line between boss and employee. It had been expected and had felt comfortable, especially during those first few months after the war, when sharp noises would spook him. Back then, Clayton had been glad to let someone else bear the brunt of responsibility.

Now, however, he sought a different type of relationship. He appreciated the relaxed give-and-take he and Merritt shared. Instead of maintaining their former chain of command from the days in the war, Merritt respected his ideas and often asked him for advice.

When they were almost back to the homestead, Merritt halted Red, his sorrel gelding. "Riders approaching."

Clayton squinted as he looked to the west. There, across the horizon, right where the sun was setting against the rocky terrain, two puffs of dust flew up. Lee perked his ears in awareness. Under his thighs, the muscles in the horse's powerful frame tensed, ready to charge or flee.

Clayton patted him on the neck. "Be patient, Lee," he murmured. "Let's see what these men want."

The beat of hooves echoed on the rocky soil. Anticipation burned brightly as it became more and more apparent trouble was approaching. Riders didn't approach anyone without first calling out a warning.

Never did they approach at such breakneck speeds.

"Looks like trouble."

"Yep."

Clayton pursed his lips that had suddenly become dry. In contrast, his palms sweated inside his gloves, and his posture, like Lee's beneath him, tightened. "I guess we haven't forgotten everything from the war, have we?"

Merritt pushed his hat back and solemnly watched the two riders come closer. "Nope. I guess we brought back more with us than just memories. I'd know this prickling in the back of my neck anywhere."

Hoping against hope, Clayton glanced his way. "By any chance you expecting anyone, Merritt?"

"Nope. You?"

"No."

Still, the trespassers neared. Soon it became apparent that both riders were experienced, their ease in their saddles relaxed and assured.

"One's a paint," Merritt said.

For a moment, Clayton wondered if Red Cloud had found him, but disregarded that idea as soon as it occurred. For one thing, Red Cloud wouldn't be riding out in the open, especially not if he was with a companion. Secondly, the Indian would have ridden bareback. Finally, Clayton couldn't discern a bit of the distinctive brown markings of the Indian's horse.

These men had saddles, one inlayed with pieces of silver, if the reflection glinting off the leather was what he thought it was.

"The other must be a quarter," Clayton said, as a touch of foreboding trickled through him. "It's got four socks."

"Yep," Merritt said. Red and Lee shifted uneasily. "You armed?"

"I've got my Colt."

Merritt laid his Winchester over his lap. "I've got this, but only a couple of shells." He shook his head in frustration. "It's been a long time since I've had any trouble to speak of on my property. Guess I've gotten lax."

"Let's see what they want. We could be wishing for trouble."

"Maybe. But I doubt it."

Clayton squinted. Two men rode side by side and had obviously spotted Clayton and Merritt, but didn't seem to share their unease. By Clayton's best estimate, their pace hadn't slowed one beat.

Clayton scanned the land to the riders right and left. It looked empty. "I think they're alone."

Merritt grunted. "One's young."

Merritt always did have eyes like a hawk. Clayton narrowed his own eyes and saw slender shoulders, a slight build. The other rider didn't look to be holding his seat quite so well. In fact, on further inspection, he looked to be holding on more tightly. Either he was sick or plumb worn-out.

Once again, he felt the tingling sensation run through him. "Other one's sick or old."

"Yep," Merritt said. "I'm tired of being patient. Let's go see what they want," he said, nudging Red forward.

Clayton followed, his Colt now cocked and held loosely in his right hand. To Lee's credit, the horse didn't flinch at the feel of the metal against his shoulder. Looked like they all could be battle-ready in a pinch.

They rode twenty yards, then another fifty.

Then, just as the younger man raised his hand in greeting, Clayton saw the lightning-bolt mark across the chestnut quarter horse's nose. "It's Price," he said, confirming his fears. "He found us."

Merritt looked at him quickly. "You sure?"

"Positive. I'd know his horse anywhere by that lightning mark on her face. I broke her."

"Who's the other?"

"It has to be Miles, Vanessa's brother." Clayton fought to stay intent on the situation at hand and not on the hundred questions that were burgeoning forward. How had Miles and Price found them? What did they want? Vanessa? Him? Her money? Something more?

Most important, how could he have let himself forget about Price and Miles? How had he let himself get so lax?

"So . . . what do you want to do?"

Merritt's question was asked quietly and without rancor. Without judgment. Clayton knew that his best friend would now willingly follow his directives without question, whether it was shooting to kill or to put away their weapons and greet them warmly.

Neither seemed like the right choice.

"I don't trust either of them. Let's see what they have to say before we act," Clayton said. "I have to do at least that much. At least for Vanessa."

"Most likely, it's nothing good."

"Probably not."

They'd gone another ten or so paces, when Miles's voice called out. "Clayton Proffitt?"

Clayton raised his arm in response.

Slowly, Miles walked his horse forward. A new maturity that Clayton had never spied before showed in his bearing. In the tense way he held his jaw.

Clayton wondered what was on Miles's mind. Was he about to join his side? Or had he long ago turned to Price and was now waiting to do his bidding?

No one spoke as Miles rode forward, Price a little to his back and left. The older man's his eyes looked sharp and intent. Within another minute, they all stood together, mere yards apart.

To his surprise, Price looked like death warmed over. His eyes were cold, his cheekbones rising starkly. "Proffitt," he finally muttered, his voice as chilling as Clayton had ever heard it.

"Price. Miles. What brings you to Colorado?"

Price glared. "You have something of mine."

"And what would that be?"

"We came . . . we came to see Vanessa," Miles said, his voice calm, his eyes different. Wiser, steadier. Less youthful. "Is she here?"

Merritt grunted. "You're not going to see her."

Price grunted. "You're wrong. Go bring her out. Now."

"Never." Louder, Clayton said. "Why are you so intent on seeing her, Price?"

"She was mine. She was going to be mine."

Miles's gaze hardened.

Vanessa had never been Price's. "You're mistaken."

Clayton finally looked at Miles and studied him. To his surprise, the boy no longer looked hesitant or cowed. Instead he sat straight in the saddle, his face rigid.

Actually, he looked like he was fighting an inner battle. His green eyes darted to Price uneasily while his posture looked strong and full of resolve.

"I'd like to speak with my sister," Miles said.

Merritt rolled his eyes. "I'll ask Mrs. Proffitt if she would like to see you. If she does, her husband will escort her to your hotel. You need to get off my land and head on back to Cedar Springs and await our word."

"Mrs. Proffitt?" Miles stared at him. "You really did marry her, Clayton?"

Clayton's respect for the boy rose up a notch. "I did. In front of a preacher, soon after we left the Circle Z. I married her while we were still in Texas."

Price narrowed his eyes. "I wouldn't have thought you would go to such lengths to keep her by your side."

The oily insinuation sickened Clayton. Once more he resolved to never let Price Venture anywhere near Vanessa again. "She did me the honor. I'm grateful for the privilege."

Miles visibly relaxed, while Price's cheeks flushed. "She won't be your wife for long, Proffitt. I'll make sure of that. I've searched high and low for that girl."

Because he was curious, Clayton said, "How did you find us?"

"We received a telegraph telling how Vanessa wanted that money from the bank, Clayton," Miles said. "We didn't know where she was until then." With a glare, he added, "I'm surprised you let her do something like that."

Clayton felt as if both men had just leveled blows to his stomach.

Had Vanessa truly gone against his orders and contacted the bank on her own? Without his knowledge?

"I mean to get what I came for, Proffitt," Price said in a rush. "I spent too much time on that girl to just up and leave. Besides, she owes me money."

"That money is hers, not yours, Venture."

Price narrowed his eyes. "It's mine, fair enough. I clothed and fed her after her pa died. I've got it comin'."

Swallowing hard, Clayton was just about to tell Price exactly what he had coming, when they heard a rustle behind them.

Miles's eyes widened. "Vanessa."

"Miles?" Vanessa called out. To Clayton and Merritt, she looked apologetic. "Corrine and I saw you out here and decided to ride out and see what was going on."

Clayton didn't know when he'd ever been so angry. "Go on back, Vanessa."

"Corrine, go back now too," Merritt called out, never taking his eyes from Price.

Corrine stayed where she was, but Vanessa rode forward, her eyes glistening as she looked at her brother. "Miles, I never thought I'd see you again."

"I was afraid of that too, Van. I was afraid something happened to Clayton and you were alone."

"No." She flashed a smile. "Something almost did, but he's fine now."

Miles still didn't smile. "Clayton said he married you. Is that true?"

"Yes."

Happiness shone in her eyes, though Clayton noticed that Vanessa still hadn't dared to look at her stepfather. Price, however, couldn't seem to look anywhere else.

Merritt grunted, bringing them all back to the present.

Clayton felt the muscles in his jaw ticking. Things couldn't seem to get worse. This was his most terrible nightmare come to life. He'd done everything he could to keep Vanessa safe from Price. He'd married her to keep her safe from other men—men more intent on their own personal desires instead of a young woman's feelings.

What's more, he'd left her for two months just to give her time to adjust to married life—or to change her mind about their future.

It was unbelievable that she would have undermined it all.

From behind them, Corrine spoke. "Gentlemen, please come to the house. We'll discuss this over some glasses of tea."

Merritt looked like he was ready to strangle somebody, anybody. "Go back home, Corry," Merritt called out. "Now."

"But—"

"Now, Corrine!"

"Vanessa, go on back too," Clayton murmured. To his relief, she turned Coco and headed back to the house with Corrine.

Price sneered as the other horses' hooves faded off into the distance. "That girl never could mind. Spoiled as the day is long." Looking at Miles, he said, "Once I take my strap to her, she'll remember to mind."

"No," Miles muttered. "Never again."

"What, you going to stop me, boy?"

Clayton was almost relieved. He'd yearned for an excuse to shoot Price. Wanted it like he'd wanted little else. His finger hovered over the hammer of his gun, ready to kill. Ready to do once again what he'd learned to do so well in the war.

Price spoke again. "You were a fool if you thought I was gonna just let you have that money, Clayton. I want it. I need it. The Circle Z is dying."

"I don't care about the money," Clayton said honestly. As God as his witness, he truly didn't. All that mattered was keeping Vanessa safe from harm. Keeping Vanessa close to him, where she belonged.

"You should. It's a fair amount. Though Vanessa has a lot to learn, she's turned into a right beautiful woman. Now that her mother's dead and gone, I do believe I'll take myself a new bride."

Clayton spared a look at Miles. Pain ravaged his expression and the truth came to light. Price Venture had taken everything from the boy. His mother, his sister, his rightful inheritance. But, had Miles gained something in their place?

Resolution and strength emanated from him.

Fortitude. Honor.

In the midst of losing almost everything, Miles Grant had finally turned into a man.

"You won't have my wife," Clayton said, not leaving even the slightest bit of hesitancy in his voice. "You will never have Vanessa or anything that is rightfully hers."

Price raised a tremored hand, pointing a pistol at him, straight and true. "You won't have a choice."

"Tell me," Merritt murmured to Clayton. "Tell me and I'll kill him. Then it won't weigh on your conscience."

Merritt was offering the ultimate sacrifice. He was offering to shoot Price so Clayton wouldn't have to live with the consequences.

Commandments ran through Clayton's mind. He knew right from wrong. He'd lived with the knowledge that he was a sinner. He'd lived with feeling like he was unworthy of God's love, or of Vanessa's.

But thanks to God's grace, and the knowledge that he would ultimately be forgiven, he'd survived. He'd reveled in the Lord's power.

But even knowing all of that, he knew if he had to he would face the repercussions of killing.

Price was never going to touch Vanessa again.

Never going to take another thing from Miles.

No one was ever going to hear another girl crying in a barn at night because of what Price Venture had done.

No woman was going to wake at night screaming, fearing Price's touch.

And so, the choice was easy to make. "Drop it, Venture," he called out, pointing the pistol directly at Price's heart. "Drop it or I'll shoot to kill."

A slow smile lit the older man's eyes. "Doubt it. You'd never shoot a man in cold blood."

Clayton had never been more serious. "You shouldn't doubt what I will do for Vanessa. Vanessa is my life."

And then, everything seemed to move in slow motion. Price pointed his gun, Merritt raised his Winchester, Clayton cocked his Colt, and Miles shot his stepfather.

24

*B*ack at the house, she heard Corrine call her name, but Vanessa ignored the summons. Her heart pounded as she raced ahead through the weeds and brush, over the rocky terrain, afraid to see who'd been hurt, afraid to be honest enough with herself to guess.

What if it had been Clayton? Could he survive another gunshot wound? Could she ever survive without him, now that they were finally together?

Or Miles? Could she live with herself if her brother was shot before she'd ever have the opportunity to mend things between them?

But what if it had been Merritt? If he'd been hurt because of the trouble she'd brought to their ranch, how could she bear that? How could she ever look Corrine in the eye, knowing that she'd been the cause of her sister-in-law's grief?

The tall grasses whipped across her legs as she raced forward, tripping over divots in the dirt.

When she approached, three men turned to face her. The world shifted as she scanned their grim-faced expressions. Dizziness took hold of her and caused her vision to blur.

Giving into weakness, Vanessa sank to her knees, right beside the man sprawled prostrate on the ground.

Right beside the man who'd changed her life forever: Price.

Clayton rushed to her side. Kneeling, he gently turned her from the man's dead body. "Vanessa, sweetheart, you should have stayed back at the house like I told you to. Go on back now."

"Clay, I heard the gunshot. There was no way on earth I could have just sat and waited. I most certainly cannot leave now, either." Helplessly, she glanced at Merritt and Miles, too. "I'm glad you all are all right. I was so concerned about each of you."

Gripping her elbow with one hand and her waist with another, Clayton carefully helped her to her feet. Yet firm resolve coated his voice. "Vanessa, honey—"

"I'm all right. And I'm staying. This is as much my business as anyone's, don't you think?"

Clayton slowly nodded. Vanessa moved closer, finding comfort in his warmth and realizing just how selfish and weak she'd been. She'd been so wrong to try to manage things on her own. She'd been so wrong to lie to the one man who she could trust with her life.

She'd been so foolish.

From the moment she saw Price and Miles, she'd known their presence was her fault. She'd brought them there, had brought danger to all of their lives. It was time to take responsibility. "Oh, Clayton, I have something to tell you. I'm so sorry."

Brown eyes narrowed, then softened. "For what?"

"I . . . I wired the bank to get funds when you were hurt," she admitted. "I was so upset that you'd risked your life to make money for us, I wanted to do something."

"But then later?"

"Later, I couldn't get up the nerve to tell you."

Turning to her brother, she grabbed his hand. "Is that how you found us?"

Miles turned away, as if he couldn't bear to reply.

Panic set in. What if Clayton didn't want her now? What if she'd ruined their future because she hadn't listened to Clayton?

Practically tripping over her skirts, she kept hold of his hand when he tried to shake it off. "Tell me. Is that what happened, Miles?" she asked. "Is that how you found me? How you found the Bar M?"

"It is," he said after clearing his throat. "The bank telegraphed Price the moment they heard from you." His eyes looked sad and vacant.

With some shock, she realized that he was still staring at Price with disbelief, his whole posture tense and stiff. He'd shot Price! "Oh, Miles."

Her brother's face was stark white, but his stance was firm and straight. His hands were empty; it looked like he'd dropped his gun as soon as he'd fired the bullet. "Don't fret, Vanessa. We were back at the ranch when we'd received word from the bank. Though Price often said he was going to give up his hunt for you soon, I don't think he ever would have. Price was never going to give up, no matter what. His fixation on you, on your money, on his problems—it was unhealthy."

Clayton spoke. "Why did you stay by his side?"

Miles swallowed hard. "At first, I thought I had no choice." Looking down at the body, Miles said, "All my life, I've been used to following directions. Trying not to be noticed. But then something happened and I began to take control of my destiny. That's when my priorities changed. I began to want to stay with Price in order to delay his search for Vanessa. Finally, I attempted to steer him away from your paths."

Wearily, Miles shook his head and turned to Clayton. "A day hasn't passed that I haven't remembered your proclamation, Clayton. The day you took Vanessa—" He shook his head. "No, I promised myself that I'd no longer speak in half-truths and covered-up lies. On the day Price *attacked* Vanessa . . . I grew up. But another thing happened as well. I met a missionary in the Indian Territories who passed me his Bible and listened to my confessions. I took his advice to heart, and began to study the Scriptures. From then on, I've had more strength than I ever knew was possible."

Slowly Miles walked toward his sister. Unable to stop herself, she took his other hand. With wonder, she examined them. Tried to associate the man in front of her with the boy of her memories.

Looking at how their hands were linked, she studied the differences. His hands were firm and tough now. In her mind, they were once far smaller and always trusting. All her life, she'd wanted to protect him. Now he was ready and able to protect her.

Staring at her with green eyes so like her own, he whispered, "I became a man. I found the Lord. I finally started shouldering my weight. I'm ready to go on my own way." Closing his eyes, he murmured, "I don't regret what I did, even if it was a terrible sin. Price was never going to let you go."

Vanessa knew what a transformation his admittance was. Obviously, he had found God's way and had begun a new, better way of life. "Oh, Miles."

Miles lifted his head to look at Clayton. "This probably won't mean much, but I'm beholden to you for everything you've done for my sister. Thank you for keeping her safe."

Clayton nodded, his expression solemn. "You're welcome."

"I also want you to know that the Circle Z will be glad to have you back, if that's where you'd like to be."

Clayton glanced at Vanessa. "That won't be necessary. This is our home now."

Miles smiled softly. "Then, I think I'll take charge of my family's land."

"It's your right. I'm glad you're ready."

Vanessa was still trying to understand all that had happened. "So Price came after me for my inheritance?"

"Price wanted your funds. And Ma never quite recovered from what happened with you. She began taking morphine—more and more—until she could barely leave her room." He paused, then added, "She ended up shooting herself. She's dead."

Vanessa's heart trembled. How many lives had been ruined by Price Venture?

Yet, as she looked at her brother, standing so tall and straight, as she thought of her marriage with Clayton, she reconsidered her feelings. Perhaps that wasn't the question at all.

Perhaps she should wonder, how many lives had been saved?

Miles continued. "Sometimes Price seemed mentally deranged, he was so fixated on you. He wanted you back. In his twisted mind, he was sure that if you returned, his luck would too."

"But that never happened."

"Four months ago, we set out. I did my best to slow us down and keep him from finding you."

Clayton turned to Vanessa. "If not for Miles, Price might have found you while I was still in Nebraska."

Vanessa squeezed Miles's hands. "You did good."

Miles shook his head. "I didn't do enough that night back in Texas. Clayton told me that, but I didn't see. Didn't want to see."

With efficient movements, Clayton and Merritt bent down, picked up Price Venture's body, and gently laid him over the saddle of his horse.

After pausing for a moment, Merritt sighed heavily. "Let's go on in. Corrine's probably scared to death, and I think all of us could use some time to unwind."

"We'll be right after you," Clayton said. "We just need a few minutes."

"I understand." Merritt tied the quarter horse's reins to Red's and slowly rode to the barn.

Miles saddled up and followed suit, leaving Clayton and Vanessa alone.

"Well, it's over," Clay said.

Was it? "Will you ever forgive me for not listening to you?"

"You don't need to ask. I'll always forgive you—for anything."

Though she'd always sought Jesus' forgiveness and guidance, Vanessa wasn't sure she could accept Clayton's absolution so easily. Surely he was only saying those words. Even though his arms were outstretched, she hesitated. "Please don't be mad. I don't want you mad about the money."

Slowly, he said, "I'm not mad, especially now that I understand why you sent for it. Of course you were scared and feeling alone. Everyone in your life had left you. It was understandable."

"I didn't feel I had a choice then, but I certainly did have a choice later." Closing her eyes, she said miserably, "Now it all seems so childish. It's just . . . Clayton, I didn't want you to be mad at me. I didn't want to see your disappointment. Finally, I was just plain silly. You had done so much for me, I wanted to do something for you."

"For me? Vanessa, don't you understand? You already are my everything. I need you like I need air to breathe."

"I need you, too. Of course I do! But if I'm telling the whole truth, I wanted what was mine. I had nothing else. I left my whole life, with just what you could grab. All of my things were abandoned in one night. And even more than that, I lost my mother and brother in one fell swoop too." She rushed on, well aware that her words were stumbling over one another. "I missed out on what could have been."

"I feel the same way about Scout."

"So you understand, at least a little bit? I wanted part of myself."

"I can understand that."

"And I understand that I should have confided in you more. And I should have told you what I'd done." Still so afraid that he wasn't telling her the full truth, Vanessa pleaded once again. "Please don't stay mad."

After kissing her cheek, Clayton pulled her into a comforting embrace. "Vanessa, honey. I can't stay angry. Especially not after everything we've been through."

❧

Later, much later, when Miles was sleeping on a cot by the fireplace and Vanessa and Clayton were snug in their own room, she whispered, "Are you sure you're not mad?"

Clayton rolled his eyes. "I'm sure. Honestly, Van, what is it going to take to make you believe me?"

It was time to tell him the last big secret. "One more thing."

He pretended to sound aggrieved as he wrapped his arms around her as she rested her head on his chest. Absently smoothing back her hair, he murmured, "And what might that be, sweetheart? Can't it wait until morning? It's late now; I'm tired."

"I guess it could wait until morning, but I really would feel better if you could promise me one more thing." She moved away and sat cross-legged next to him.

With a raised eyebrow, he nodded. "Promise what?"

"That you're happy about the baby."

His expression was blank. "About . . . what?" Then, joy filled his eyes. "A baby?"

She nodded happily. "We're going to have a baby, Clayton."

Tears pricked his eyes as he held her close. "Oh, Vanessa, truly?"

She nodded. "I've wanted to tell you for some time, but I wanted everything to be right. Perfect."

He smiled gently. "Is that how everything is now? Perfect?"

"Yes. Well, as perfect as anything ever needs to be. During these last few months I learned a lot. Most important; I realized that if I open my heart to Jesus and to prayer, everything will be all right. No one has to be perfect. We shouldn't expect them to be, either."

"That's a hard lesson learned."

"But a very good one." Moving closer, she pressed her palm to his chest. There, she felt his heartbeat, so reassuring, so strong. Reminding her of everything that she'd clung to during their time apart. "So, you're happy about the baby? Everything is going to be okay?"

He covered his hand over hers. "You feel my heart? Can you imagine how it would have broken?" Emotion thickened his voice as he whispered, "Vanessa, honey . . . what would I have done if Price had hurt you? Hurt both of you?"

"But he didn't."

"But—"

"God is with us, Clayton. I know that as surely as I know you are the man for me. As surely as I know that I'd follow you to Nebraska again."

"And bring me back home?"

"Yes, and bring you back home. To me."

Clasping her close, he closed his eyes. "You're my everything, Vanessa Proffitt. You're where I long to be; you're who I dream of at night. You're my future and my past. In many ways, I started living when I rode into the Circle Z and saw you for the first time. You, Vanessa, are my home."

When their lips touched, Vanessa knew his words couldn't be more true. With God's help, they'd gone on a journey to a place far more meaningful and special than she'd ever imagined. And because they believed, their faith had created a strength to their love that nothing could put asunder.

Not distance. Not time. Not doubts.

Not ever again.

Epilogue

Almost a full year had passed since Price had died and Miles had made amends with Vanessa. Since then, Vanessa and Clayton had settled into their cabin and filled their days with ranch work and family.

After a relatively easy pregnancy, Christina May was born and Vanessa spent even more time with Corrine and her children.

Miles kept in touch, taking time to write Vanessa once a month. His latest news was that he'd been squiring a young woman from a neighboring town to church and was finally at peace.

Unfortunately, Scout had not been as good at keeping in touch. Only one letter had arrived, and its contents brought quite a shock.

> Dear Clayton,
>
> I was out in Denver and saw Lacy. She said you got married to a real fine woman. Congratulations.
>
> Clayton, I know I haven't been everything you've wanted. I haven't been everything I've

wanted, either. But it's hard, trying to be the man you are. After a time, I decided to become a different sort of man. I suspect you might of heard of my new occupation.

I'm not proud of myself, but I'm not ready to leave the life I've chosen, either. All things considered, it's best if you don't try to find me. Maybe one day our paths will cross again. Until then, I promised Lacy I'd write so you wouldn't worry. I figured if you receive this, you'll pass it on to Corrine. You take care, and take care of your wife, too.
Scout

P.S. I read in the Bible that repentance is difficult at best. Pray for me, will you? My sins are many and my future will likely be filled with a great many hurdles.

Clayton read Scout's brief letter one more time over his sister's shoulder. "I don't understand," he said, feeling frustrated and helpless. "I can't believe that when Scout finally decides to write, he tells us so little."

Corrine quirked an eyebrow. "You care to tell me again why you think Scout would have written more? He's written more here than you ever did, I'll tell you that."

Clayton ignored his sister's jab, knowing that she probably did have a point—and if he let her know she was right, she'd most likely never let him forget it.

Instead, he focused on the letter again, taking it from his sister's hands and frowning. "It just doesn't make sense, Corrine."

"I don't think it's supposed to."

"If he doesn't want me to find him, why did he even write?"

"I think he just wants you to know that he hasn't forgotten us. " After a moment, she mused, "And maybe he's trying to apologize for what he's become?"

Clayton tossed the letter on Corrine's writing desk and moved to the other side of the table. It looked like their little brother had finally grown up, whether Clayton was ready for him to or not. The fact that he had no control made him irritated, and a little bit argumentative. "I wish he'd just come this way. He's got to know we'd welcome him with open arms if he came to Colorado."

"I don't think he's ready. There's a time and a place for everything," Corrine said practically.

"You seem awfully calm about all this."

She raised an eyebrow. "You forget, I've already been through this with you."

Clayton couldn't figure out if she was teasing or not. "Corry, Lacy told me he was an outlaw." Clayton didn't even want to admit how much that knowledge had disturbed him.

"I guess he is."

"I've failed him. I'd do anything to make things better."

Softly, Corrine said, "Clayton, you were once searching for peace and forgiveness. Perhaps one day he'll be ready to do the same thing. Maybe one day . . . " his voice drifted off.

"One day we'll see him again, I'm sure of it," Corrine whispered. "One day we'll all see him again."

Feeling worn out and wrung dry, Clayton walked back to his home. The night was mild, the full moon bright. He walked on.

Behind him, Corrine and Merritt and their brood were bedding down. In the bunkhouse, the lone whistle and tune of a harmonica floated out, followed by raucous laughter.

But just ahead was his place. Made of logs, it boasted four rooms, one of which had a fireplace that almost spanned a wall. As he got closer, he realized a window was open.

Floating toward him was another laugh of a very different kind. Christy was giggling and cooing. From the sound of things, Vanessa was very happy too.

Eager to be closer, Clayton picked up his pace.

Inside that cabin was his world. Inside was everything he'd dreamed his life could be. Everything he'd prayed for.

Everything he wanted.

Never again would he wait to obtain it.

Never again would he doubt he could.

Discussion Questions

1. A *Texan's Promise* revolves around a promise Clayton Proffitt made to his employer. What was that promise, and do you think he fulfilled it?

2. At first glance Vanessa is a terribly vulnerable heroine. However, she's more than just a woman in danger. What qualities does she display that make her admirable?

3. Did Vanessa and Clayton have a choice about leaving the Circle Z? How do you think things could have been resolved if they had stayed?

4. Clayton and Vanessa come in contact with many people scarred by the war. Who was your favorite person they met along the way?

5. Was Ken right in encouraging Clayton to marry Vanessa? What do you think about his reasons? Was it simply for safety?

6. Miles was as much of a victim as Vanessa. At the beginning of the novel, he hopes to make Price respect him. How was this goal doomed from the start?

7. Lacy was a character who was fairly multifaceted. Although she used people in order to survive, she also did many good deeds. What do you think will happen in her future?

8. Vanessa lies to Clayton several times. First, she lies about what really happened between her and Price. Later, she lies about contacting the bank for money. What do these lies say about her character?

9. When Clayton discovers the truth about Vanessa, he feels that he's not only let her down but also his promise to her father as well. Was he right to leave her?

10. During their separation, their letters serve to bring them closer in ways that conversations couldn't. Have you ever found letters to be useful to you in that way?

11. How does Clayton's injury help both his relationship with Vanessa and his friendship with Merritt?

12. Scout, Corrine and Clayton's brother, is never actually in the book, but he plays an important role with both Corrine and Clayton. What purpose do you suppose he serves?

13. Why do you think it had to be Miles who shoots Price? How might the story have ended differently if Clayton had killed him? What do you think would have happened if Price had lived?

14. Many of the characters feel the Lord's presence in their lives and try to live according to his will. How have you felt the Lord's guiding hand?

15. Throughout the novel, Clayton and Vanessa quote scripture from the Psalms. Was there a particular verse that spoke to you? Why?

Bonus chapter from Book 2
in the Heart of a Hero series

A Texan's Honor

1

January 1874
Kansas

The barrel of a six-shooter was cold against Jamie's temple. As the iron pressed on her skin, a chill raced through her body.

She should've kept her wool cloak on.

She thought it certainly was amazing how in the most dire circumstances, a body resorted to concentrating on the most basic of things. The gunman pressed the barrel harder against her with a shaky hand. Jamie winced and her fear crept up a notch. Closing her eyes, she waited for the inevitable. Tried her best to recite the Lord's Prayer. Surely, that's what God would want her to think about during her last moments on earth.

"Put that gun down, Kent," one of the men ordered from the other side of the train car. "There's no need to start firing on defenseless women."

Her captor wasn't in the mood for advice. "Shut up, McMillan. The boss might think you're somethin' special, but we both know you ain't none better than the rest of us." Reaching out with his free hand—the one not pressing the firearm to her temple—he took hold of Jamie's arm. Wrapped five thick leather-gloved fingers around her elbow and tugged.

Jamie bit her lip so she wouldn't cry out.

Kent noticed and grinned.

Across the aisle on the floor, one of the six men trussed like turkeys looked away.

"I'm just saying we've got no cause to start killing hostages," McMillan said as he stepped closer. His tan duster glided over the planes of his body, accentuating his chest and the pure white of his cotton shirt.

"I ain't killed no one today. Not yet, leastways."

"Don't start now. You heard what Boss said," McMillan said, stepping close enough for Jamie to see faint lines of exhaustion around his eyes.

Jamie found it almost impossible to look away. The man— McMillan— spoke so quietly. So calmly. Like he was speaking of the bitter cold temperatures outside. Or the snow covering the ground. In fact, he looked almost bored, holding his Colt in his right hand and scanning the rest of them with little curiosity.

Just like none of them counted.

Jamie blinked back tears as she tried to stay as still as possible. But it was hard, because the train was still moving.

As panic,grief, and a thousand other emotions engulfed her, Jamie wondered why the Lord had placed her on this train with a band of outlaws. Both her parents had succumbed to influenza just two months ago. After selling everything she owned, she boarded the train in Denver and planned to continue traveling east on the Kansas Pacific toward Kansas City.

Her future? To go live with her maiden aunts until she and Randall—her aunts' favorite neighbor and her very recent correspondent—decided matrimony was in their future.

However, from the time she'd boarded, the journey had been difficult. She had little extra money, so she was in the second-class coach along with everyone else who couldn't afford to travel more privately in first class. No one had needed to tell her that traveling in third class was not an option.

Only poor immigrants traveled that way—and it was certainly not safe for a lady traveling alone.

Of course, now it looked like second- class wasn't safe either.

When she'd first boarded, she'd noticed that the inside of the car smelled much like the scruffy men surrounding her. However, none of the men had been overtly disrespectful, and soon, most ignored her as they fell into brief slumbers.

But somewhere near the border of Kansas and the Colorado Territory, everything changed. When the train had slowed around a bend, a group of men on horses had approached, their guns blazing. The engineer had braked hard, creating a sick feeling of inevitabile doom. Moments later, the train screeched to a stop. Passengers in the two front cars were forced off, one by one, onto the frozen expanse of barren landscape.

Jamie had just gotten to her feet when the man who held her now had grabbed her with a gap-toothed smile. "Oh, no, sweetheart. You're not going anywhere. We're gonna need you."

With another screech, the train had rolled forward, picking up speed. Jamie had been forced to stand by his side as other bandits came in and separated six men from the others like culling calves. Now those six were tied up and pushed to the floorboards.

She was forced to stand in front of them with a gun pressed to her head, pulled into an awkward embrace by the most evil man she'd ever had the misfortune to meet.

Waiting.

The train rocked some more, and Jamie stumbled as her knees locked. Desperately, she reached out to the seat next to her—anything to keep her balance. For a split second, the iron separated from her temple, freeing her from certain death.

Then, with the next sway, her captor slid his arm higher on her taffeta covered arm, yanking her closer. As her head snapped with the motion, her tender skin tapped against the ice cold barrel. She cried out.

"Stay still and stay silent!" Kent yelled.

One of the six hostages gasped, and then fell silent as another man cocked his Colt and leveled it on him.

"Easy, now, girl," Kent said, his voice now laced with triumph as he forced her closer still. Now Jamie was completely pressed against his side, close enough to feel the other six-shooter fastened against his hip jutting into the soft fabric of her black mourning gown. Close enough to feel the heat rolling off his body and spy the unmistakable light of anticipation burning in his eyes.

Though she closed her eyes, his presence surrounded her still—his breath beat a rhythm against her neck, causing chill bumps on her skin.

The train was practically flying along the tracks now, gaining speed as they headed to Kansas City. And with it, her hope was fading fast. There was little hope of standing as still as the outlaw wanted her to, and even less of a chance that she would be able to control her fear completely.

She was going to die.

Jamie—Jamilyn Ellis—closed her eyes and tried to pray once more. But this time, the words she searched for were not filled with beautiful poetry passed down from generation to generation.

No, this time, her prayer was far more clumsy and desperate. *Please Lord, if this is what you have in mind for me, give me a quick death. Would you please? I'm trying real hard to be courageous but I'm just about out of bravery.*

With a grunt and a whoosh, the connecting door to the passenger car opened. The fragrant aroma of an expensive cigar filled the car, ultimately bringing a bit of a reprieve from her captor's rank smell. All went still as the door closed behind a well-dressed man as he surveyed the lot of them.

With his expensive turquoise silk vest, neatly trimmed ebony mustache, and slicked back hair, he had an air about him that spoke of power.

Instinctively, Jamie knew that the gang's boss had just joined them. All the gunslingers around her seemed to take a step back.

When he stood still, taking in the scene with obvious distaste, Kent's grip lost some of its strength. Moisture beaded his brow as his body began to shake. The cool barrel bobbed against her temple, reminding her in no uncertain terms that she was at his mercy.

If he had any.

Jamie forced herself to breathe as her captor's tremors increased, and the leader stared at her with the greenest eyes she'd ever seen. She blinked, thinking that the color reminded her of the meadow in early spring. When everything was fresh and new and full of hope.

Time seemed to stop.

"Kent, what are you doing?" the leader asked, his voice as smooth as velvet. "We don't treat ladies like that. Release her. Now."

Her captor's response was instantaneous. However, the moment she'd become free of the man's harsh grip, Jamie felt her knees give way.

Especially since at the same time, the train chugged around another bend. Precariously, she strived to retain her balance, but it was no use. The nearest seat was just out of her reach, and the man standing next to her was never going to be anyone she'd willingly touch.

As if in slow motion, she wobbled. Struggled, gasped. The stays on her corset were tight. She was losing precious oxygen. Dizziness engulfed her.

Suddenly, two strong arms and the scent of bay rum and mint surrounded her, the muscles like iron. The touch reassuring and surprisingly gentle. "Easy now. I've got you," the man—McMillan—murmured, so quietly she was sure she'd only imagined such kindness.

Turning her head, she met his gaze, then froze at his impassive expression. His touch might have been light and easy, but there was certainly no sympathy in his expression.

"Sit down," McMillan ordered, this time speaking more loudly.

Awkwardly, she let him guide her to the nearby bench. Didn't struggle as he helped her sit down. She clumsily adjusted her skirts as she'd been taught years ago, the action so familiar and automatic she hardly realized she was doing it.

For a split second, he glanced at her hand on the taffeta, then slowly lifted his gaze, stopping when their eyes met. His ice-blue eyes, lined with gray were as chilly and disturbing as the deep waters of Cascade Lake.

Shivers claimed her as the last of her hope dissipated into the cold confines of the icy train car.

"Everything all right, McMillan?" the leader asked.

"Everything's fine." McMillan shifted his stance, edging closer, as if he was shielding her with his body.

But surely that couldn't be?

Nerves kicked in again as her pulse raced. Shaking, Jamie attempted to inhale properly, but her body fought the action. She couldn't catch her breath, couldn't grasp any air. Panic overtook her as she tried to sit still, tried to breathe.

Immediately, the gunman turned and took hold of her arm. "Breathe," he commanded. "Settle down and breathe slowly."

But no firm directive was going to be of much assistance. Her lungs felt frozen. Almost immobile. Still panicked, she gripped his arm, attempting to get control.

But instead of a gentle touch, he closed his fingers around her wrist. "Calm yourself, or I'm going to strip you here and slice the ribbons of your corset."

His voice was little more than a thin whisper, but Jamie had no doubt that he meant every single word. Closing her eyes, she concentrated on breathing.

When she followed his directives, his lips curved slightly. "Good girl," he whispered.

But surely she'd imagined that softening?

The door opened. Another bandit entered the car, this one dressed completely in black, from his felt Stetson to his denims, to his boots and duster. Even his eyes and hair were dark.

"Everything's under control," he said, his voice gravely and deep. "The brakeman isn't going to stop until I tell him to."

"That is reassuring," the leader murmured, as formal as if he was dining at the Brown Palace. After checking his gold timepiece, he slipped it back into his vest.

The man in black motioned toward the men tied up. "You want me to deal with them?"

"No. We're going to keep this group here for the time being."

After surveying the lot of them, the man in black nodded and stepped to the side.

Leaving the rest of them to decipher the boss's meaning.

The man standing next to her tensed. "Even the woman?"

Jamie felt the leader's cold gaze settle on her. Forcing herself to keep her gaze fixed firmly on the clasped hands in her lap, she began to pray. *Oh, Lord. Please don't let this be my time. Not yet.*

"Especially the woman," the leader finally replied. "She might prove useful in the future."

As Jamie processed those words, struggled with the awful images of what the bandit meant by that cryptic remark, one of the men tied on the ground spoke. "Why are you keeping us? Why me? I haven't done a thing to you, and I sure don't have any money."

Kent laughed. Unable to help herself, Jamie glanced his way again. Though he wasn't near as muscular as the man standing guard over her, he seemed the most dangerous. There was something in his constantly moving eyes that seemed shifty.

The curly-haired hostage on the ground didn't seem to have any qualms about egging Kent on, however. "Whatever grievance you have can surely be diverted. Violence isn't the answer."

"Might be."

But instead of being cowed, the hostage gained confidence. "Sir, I demand to know what you intend to do with me."

"*Demand?* You demand?" Slowly, Kent smiled. Slowly pulling his Colt .45 out from a worn holster on his hip, he ran his thumb lovingly along the silver handle. "You demand to know? Really?"

Jamie's breath hitched as the hostage sputtered. "I'm only asking . . ." Pure fear tainted his voice now.

"Here's a hint," Kent quipped as he raised his gun and pulled the trigger.

The sound reverberated through the train car as a circle of blood formed on the man's chest.

Jamie's eyes filled with tears as she tried not to look at the man's wide, vacant expression frozen in surprise.

Beside her, McMillan cursed under his breath.

Hardly a second passed before the boss stepped forward and slugged Kent—hard. "That was unnecessary," he bit out, as Kent's gun slipped from his hand with a clatter.

Kent tripped backwards, finally ending against the wall. As he obviously did his best to remain on two feet, a dazed expression colored his face, mixing with the bead of blood forming on his lip.

Then the man in charge glared their way. "Deal with that."

Without a word, McMillan, the man who'd come to her aide, walked over and picked up the pistol from the ground. Offering the weapon to the boss, handle first, his voice was rough. "Sir?"

He waved a hand at the weapon. "Keep the gun. But dispose of the body."

As McMillan pocketed the weapon, and the leader cleared his throat as he faced the remaining five men tied on the ground. "Gentlemen, since you're so curious about your future, perhaps I had better explain your situation. You are now my hostages."

The leader's mouth twitched as similar looks of shock and fear flashed across the restrained men. "I need this train. And I need collateral." He looked around the compartment, taking in each person's features with such cold calculation that Jamie knew he probably never forgot a face.

The oldest of the hostages, an elderly gentleman who looked to be almost seventy, blinked in wonder. "What are you talking about?"

"There's something much more valuable on this train than you all. The first car is loaded with the rewards from the latest silver strike out of Cripple Creek. I mean to keep ahold of it. Unfortunately, the law won't see it that way. So I've sent out a telegram stating the rules to Mr. Sam Edison."

He paused as the name registered with the hostages. Even Jamie knew Sam Edison was the currently in charge of the U.S. Marshals. It seemed his name was always mentioned in the papers.

With another smile, the man continued. "I was fairly clear in my instructions. As long as no one tries to blow us up or interfere with our progress, you all get to live. But if the law tries to impede my goals, I'll shoot you myself and order your body to be tossed out as evidence of my displeasure." Lowering his voice, he added, "I promise, I will do this without the slightest hesitation."

The elderly man's eyes narrowed. "Who are you?" he asked quietly.

Jamie waited for him to get cuffed for his insolence. But instead, the question seemed to amuse the leader.

"I am James Walton, of course."

As the elderly man's eyes widened in recognition, Mr. Walton flashed a smile. "Please don't tell me you haven't heard of me . . . or my business partners."

There was a new awareness in the elderly man's gaze. "I've heard of you. Of course I've heard of you."

Jamie could only be grateful that she was sitting on the bench. The Walton Gang was notoriously dangerous and extremely successful. Yet, for all of their villainy, more than one news rag had painted them—especially their suave, cigar-smoking leader Mr. James Walton as heroes of a sort.

In some corners of the area, they were. Everyone knew most lawmen only took the jobs in order to keep three meals in their bellies.

In contrast, some said the Walton Gang took money from the most corrupt and spent their spoils on a whole plethora of things—from their infamous hideout to orphanages.

Word was that no one quite understood them . . . but that everyone knew one thing: They were dangerous and as cold-blooded as they wanted to be. They were as unpredictable as a blue norther.

They killed and plundered and they never, ever, looked back with regret.

It was becoming evident that they were all completely at the gang's mercy. And that Jamilyn Ellis was the only woman on the train.